A

Focus Puller

In Rome

For Geoff
Best wishes
Mike

ABOUT THIS BOOK

When London-based film technician Adam Kirby flew into Rome to work as a focus puller on one of the biggest budget films to be made at the prestigious Studio Lazio, he was not planning to be mugged at gunpoint and enter into a secretive relationship. He was also not expecting people connected with the production to die in sinister circumstances. His friendship with the film's military advisor takes an unexpected turn as their world is turned upside down by a series of events that threaten the lives of many people around them.

Creative ingenuity, a hallmark of the film community in Italy, is required in all its forms to bring back a sense of justice and to return life to normality.

ACKNOWLEDGEMENTS

To my wife for her unstinting support and her chocolate cake.

To my sons Geoffrey and Nicholas, this is for both of you.

To the late great Michael Samuelson, and all at Samuelson Film Service in the mid-sixties and seventies.

To Nick Pearson, the master of all Grips for his technical advice, humour and support.

To Anna Paterson at ADL Editorial for her patience and punctuation

To Emma Judd for the book cover, a true work of art.

DISCLAIMER

This book is a work of total fiction. All the names, characters, businesses, places, events and incidents in this book are either the product of the author's imagination or used in a fictitious manner. Any resemblance to actual persons, living or dead, or actual events is purely coincidental.

If you wish to report typos and errors then please

E mail; anthonynewber@gmail.com

Focus Puller

A Focus Puller is the number three on a normal feature film or drama camera crew. The most senior is the Director of Photography or Lighting Cameraman, the second is the Camera Operator and the fourth is the Clapper Loader. (See below for full descriptions.)

The Focus Puller is the single person responsible for looking after all of the very expensive camera equipment, including keeping it spotlessly clean and performing basic maintenance, like lubricating.

His or her main function is to make sure that every shot is in focus, as soft shots cannot be remedied in post-production. Every time the distance between an artist, or subject matter, and the camera changes, the lens focus setting has to be altered. The closer the artist is to the camera and the more telephoto the lens, the more precise this focus adjustment becomes. Some close-ups have a tolerance of just a few centimetres. So the work is very precise. The job involves the laws of optics, and though sometimes focus work can be artistic it is always totally dependent on the laws of physics.

Precise measuring with a tape and artists hitting their pre-arranged marks are the recipe for a fault-free take.

Because the Focus Puller always works totally blind and the adjusting has to be so precise, it is universally regarded as the worst job on the studio floor. Although the Camera Operator can tell during a take if the shot is grossly out of focus, but they normally avoid taking responsibility.

Director of Photography

The Director of Photography works exactly to the Director's instruction, to give a scene 'The Look', the appearance and mood that the Director demands: dark, sunny bright, shadowy, foreboding, depressing, desaturated and cold. He has total control of where the lights are placed, where the shadows fall and what colour filters are put on them and the camera. Many Directors will only work with certain Cameramen. This relationship is almost like a marriage of like minds.

The Camera Operator

The Camera Operator, like the Director of Photography, works exactly to the Director's instructions. How a shot is framed and what is in the frame at any one time are all down to the Camera Operator. A good Camera Operator can work with the Director when setting up, to make a scene seamlessly flow from one dialogue sequence to another, creating screenplay that lasts for minutes without an edit.

Once again many Directors will only work with certain operators. This working relationship is also almost like a marriage of like minds. You will often find the same camera crew following the same Director from film to film.

The Clapper Loader

Usually, though not always, the Clapper Loader is the youngest member of the crew, responsible for the loading and unloading of the camera magazines with film and keeping them clean and fluff-free, and marking up a clapper board with all of the information that the labs and the editor require. The clapping of the board at the beginning of a take coupled with the verbal announcement enables the editor to synchronise the right picture to the right soundtrack.

The Clapper Boy also writes up report sheets so that the film laboratory only prints the chosen takes. He or she is responsible for ensuring that there is enough film in the magazine to film a complete sequence; to run out of film in the middle of a take is totally unacceptable.

The Clapper Boy is also the camera crew 'gofer' and is responsible for making sure that his crew have whatever refreshments they want during the day. Most Clapper Boys are very good-humoured, which is just as well as they find themselves the target of a lot of leg-pulling!

CAST OF MAIN CHARACTERS

In order of appearance

Luigi Mussomelli	Film Producer
Peter Dublin	Production Manager
Alex Dublin	Peter's Wife
Isabella Marco	International Film Star
Sophia Mandini	Make-up Supervisor
Dino Burgio	Film Producer
Bruno	Luigi's Driver
Adam Kirby	Focus Puller
Sven Lungren	Dir. of Photography
Jan Mattias	Camera Operator
Solveig Lungren	Sven's Wife
Jose Villabianco	Head of Wardrobe
Pia	Wardrobe Assistant
Llanfranco Lucarelli	Tenor
Toni	Unit Car Driver
Gill Consalvo	Production Secretary
Nella	Housekeeper
Rino	Gardener
Duke	1st Assistant Director
Joe	Head of Art Dept.
Enzo Girosi	Chief Electrician
Carl	Sound Supervisor
Dario	Construction Manager
Lasse Norstad	Film Director
Belinda Sharp	Actress
Beatrice Mosena	3rd Assistant Director
Anatra	Camera Grip
Luca	Clapper Boy
Alessandro Mosena	Vehicle Mechanic
Petros Theophilus	Unit Interpreter
Viola Ballesi	Fishmonger

Grace De Mattais	Continuity Girl
Benito 'Ben'	2nd Assistant Director
Luciano Scordia	Business Investor
Sylvania Scordia	Luciano's Daughter
Anita	Actress
Andrea	Chief Macchinista

Saturday 12th April

The pre-production party for the forthcoming co-production of *The Script Girl* was in full swing at Studio Lazio, every word and plotline allegedly written by the influential Italian Film Producer Luigi Mussomelli.

His ancient sandstone Roman villa in the heart of the elite residential area of Parioli was now once again hosting the great and good of Roman cinema and theatre. The imposing oak-panelled lounge held a light smog of boutique perfumes that competed with the complex smell of woodsmoke and bubbling resins from the central piece of comfort. The large, stone fireplace spat and glowed, crackling its warmth and flickering red light at the hundred or so select guests, most of whom had gathered like moths under one of the two ornate crystal chandeliers hanging towards each end of the room. There was a more basic, musty smell to the room; its carpets and curtains had been beaten into submission for now but would rule again tomorrow when everyone had gone.

Small occasional tables and upright, backed chairs were spread around the sides for those guests wishing to be less gregarious. The occasionally curious could wander out to the somewhat attractive landscaped gardens lit by hanging lanterns, but few did. It was a damp and chilly April evening. Attentive, black-jacketed waiters and waitresses milled around with flutes of champagne and trays of appetisers. A string quartet added to the luxury of the evening, gently playing in the corner by the main door, their concentrated faces warmly lit by the flickering fire.

Peter Dublin, Production Manager, oiled his way around the room while his bejewelled, hawk-faced, mini-skirted wife Alex took little interest in his manoeuvres; it was what he did for a living, a very good living at that, her diamond necklace bearing testimony to the fact. He was currently attempting to interrupt a conversation between the diminutive actress Isabella Marco and her Make-up artist, Sophia. The latter, sensing that Peter was keen to interrupt, gently excused herself and backed away to join her friends at a side table, leaving them both alone.

'Isabella,' Peter said. 'I wonder if you have a minute. Dino would like to have a chat with you, if that's okay?'

'Yes, of course. I'm always happy to chat to Dino.'

Her voice was soft, velvety, with just enough trace of an Italian accent to make her appeal to any hot-blooded male. Her drastically low-cut dress amplified her more than ample, bulging cleavage, defining quite clearly her position in the film star hierarchy. She was very popular in Italy and had appeared in nine or so Italian films, receiving varying degrees of critical acclaim. More of a sex symbol, less of a serious actress.

Peter steered her towards the hall and the wide, oak, carved staircase that led to the upstairs landing. The stair carpet was opulent, thick, patterned red and blue with polished brass stair rods. He gently took her left elbow to assist her but more likely to try to increase the intimate contact between them. Her tailored, tight, Mary Quant mini dress required her to take one small step at a time, and her extremely high heels did not help the process either. Chanel perfume clashed with his eau de cologne as they reached the top of the stairs. Peter indicated to turn right on the landing and head back towards the front of the house.

Framed portraits of rigidly posing men and women from the past were tastefully spaced along the landing wall, reinforcing the luxury and history of the ancient building. The far door was ajar; they were expected.

The oak-panelled room was a bedroom at the far end with a very ornate, carved wood, four-poster bed covered in a mauve and red counterpane. A black and white cat was curled up, dozing in the middle like a furry cushion. In the centre of the room, lit by a large gold chandelier, was an area for entertaining with a well-stocked sideboard drinks cabinet to the left, and a low, carved oak table and four high-backed, winged, red leather chairs. A couple of doors led off to the right, presumably to an en suite and a dressing room.

Dino Burgio rose to meet them, putting down his near-empty, crystal-cut whisky tumbler on the glass tabletop. He was in his late fifties, stocky, medium height with a round, melon-like head, clean-shaven with dark brown eyes that darted up and down his visitor, dwelling on Isabella's voluptuous figure as she stood before him in her specially commissioned Mary Quant, light brown mini dress.

'Isabella, Peter, how nice to see you.' The voice was deep and gruff, the accent harsh, West Coast American.

'Isabella here couldn't wait to meet you. We're very lucky to have you here in Rome, putting your money into our local endeavours!'

'It's a great place to be. Rome in spring, you know, when a young man's thoughts turn to what he has been thinking about all winter!' he said, laughing.

Isabella smiled nervously, her expression denoting uncertainty.

Peter smiled. 'If you'll excuse me, Dino, I must be getting back. I'm sure you both have a lot to talk about.'

Isabella's eyelids flickered, which, to someone who was observant, would have conveyed her unease at being left alone with Dino.

Peter, seemingly oblivious, turned to the door, the hubbub of the party floating up from downstairs.

'Well, thanks, Peter, appreciated!' Turning from the retreating figure to his tightly adorned guest, Dino said, 'Please, Isabella, have a seat.'

As Peter left the room, he obsequiously closed the substantial, carved mahogany door, completely drowning out all sounds of the noisy party downstairs.

Isabella sat down on the low leather seat opposite Dino's empty glass, pulling the hem of her mini dress down as far as she could; it was more for standing and looking cool in trendy 1969 than sitting down and retaining one's modesty, she thought.

'Can I get you a drink?' Dino was at the well-stocked sideboard, gesturing at the four or so wine-filled ice buckets and the line of spirits.

His tailored, dark brown, single-breasted suit failed to hide the fact that he was pretty overweight. His bottom shirt button had come undone under the pressure, revealing a glimpse of a hairy, bloated, pink stomach.

'A champagne, if you have it, would be nice, thank you.'

'Champagne it is, my dear!' He held up a flute against the light of the central chandelier to check that it was clean, his slightly bulging eyes squinting against the light.

Peter Dublin reached the bottom of the stairs to be greeted by his wife Alex with a quizzical smile on her face. 'What have you been up to?'

'Pimping!' came the reply, as he led her back to the beautiful people, the hubbub of chatter and the droning classical music.

Dino placed the bubble-filled flute into Isabella's outstretched hand, deliberately brushing her skin as he did so. 'Lovely perfume. What is it?'

'Chanel.' She smiled a little uneasily. He was an intimidating figure, not only by reputation but also by physique; he was a powerfully built man.

'Lovely! Good perfume, very sensual, the sign of a well-dressed woman.' He paused, looking up at the chandelier. 'As you know, I am a very successful Film Producer back home in Hollywood,' he said, accenting the word 'Hollywood' to emphasise the significance of the place. 'Over the last three years, I alone have been responsible for five award-winning academy films, launching the careers of a huge number of actors and actresses. Very profitable careers too, I might add.'

One of the drivers, a tall, well-built blockhouse of a man, hurried into the building from the damp, chilly night air, his unbuttoned, full-length, black gaberdine coat flapping behind him. He had been standing by his car outside the entrance doorway, casually watching the hall and stairs. He now strode very quickly through the entrance hall and turned left into the main room, backing himself up to the string quartet. He looked around, searching for his boss.

Luigi Mussomelli noticed him almost immediately, mainly because the urgent, unexpected movement caught his eye, coupled with the fact that Bruno was over six foot, but also because his driver would never come into a party without a very good reason. Drivers are not part of the great and good; perhaps his additional responsibility as Isabella's bodyguard had caused his entrance. The two men met in the middle of the room. The figure in the coat bent down and whispered confidentially in Luigi's ear; his message clearly a cause for concern.

The impromptu conversation had not gone unnoticed and people now began to watch, waiting for further developments.

Dino walked slowly behind Isabella. He ran his fingers through the hair at the back of her neck, staring down at her bulging, lightly tanned cleavage as he did.

'You are fortunate, Isabella. God has been very kind to you. You are a very gifted actress. You film well and the public like you. Plus, you have a good following here in Italy, a perfect foundation.' He paused to let his words sink in, then slowly sipped his drink. 'But I can help you reach a much wider international audience.'

Isabella muttered, 'Thank you.' She was not happy about how this was going at all. She didn't like her hair being touched. She leant forward, put her glass down on the edge of the table and rose to turn and face him. Being seated was far too passive. She pulled down her mini dress that had risen up. Pouting her full red lips, she tilted her head and, forcing a smile, asked, 'What do you actually want?'

Dino paused for dramatic effect; in the silence you could have heard a pin drop.

'If we could come to an agreement, I am sure that would be to both our advantage.'

She paused for a couple of seconds, pondering the implication of the word 'agreement'.

'What sort of an agreement?'

'Well, I am here in Rome for the next three months or so, and it would be really nice to have some intelligent, quality female company. To help us both pass the time.'

'Pass the time how exactly?' Now she understood! She realised the purpose of having been 'delivered' to this room.

Dino smiled, gave a little arrogant smirk and gestured towards the four-poster bed – the sleeping cat hadn't moved – and then almost as an antidote, smiled wolfishly. 'Going out to the theatre, going to parties, meeting up with producers, scriptwriters, influential people.'

Isabella wanted out of this encounter, out of this room, but Dino had put himself between her and the door. As she moved to go round him, he stepped quickly forward at the same time, wrapping his arms around her. His stubby, clutching fingers pulled her towards him. Her forehead barely came level with his mouth. She was a third of his bulk; his paunch pushed into her stomach, her breasts pressed into his chest. He held her in a vice-like grip, his breath smelt of whisky.

She did not want to scream. No one would hear her anyway. It would cause too much of a stir, negative publicity. He was a very powerful man, this Dino. She just needed to persuade him to let her go and get out of the room.

Luigi Mussomelli and his driver Bruno were walking as fast they could up the stairs to where Bruno had seen Isabella being escorted, trying not to draw too much attention to themselves. But it was obvious to the guests mingling in the hallway that something was going on. Bruno led the way. He was young and fit. Luigi, in his late sixties, was much older, grey-haired, bespectacled and a little overweight. His left knee had caused him to limp since childhood, and the right knee was not as supple as it used to be, causing his body to jerk as he used his right hand to pull himself up the bannister, each ancient stair creaking in synchronicity with every step he took.

'Easy now, easy, honey! Just calm down, just calm down! You're missing the point. It could change—'

Bruno reached the door first, knocked twice very firmly, then, without waiting, opened it, and stuck his head through the gap.

Dino spun round, letting go of Isabella, throwing her away almost, causing her to fall against the chair with the suddenness of the release, her high heels contributing to her loss of balance. The cat, alarmed at the noise and sudden movement, leapt off the bed, running flat out through the door, nearly tripping up a breathless Luigi in the process. Bruno stepped to his left, slowly folding his arms, signifying that no one was leaving unless Luigi said so.

'What the hell is going on here, Dino?' Luigi asked, somewhat breathlessly.

Isabella was regaining her composure, pulling her dress down around her hips with sweaty hands. She was shaking like a leaf, near to tears. Her mind racing, she decided to take the initiative.

'It's okay! It's okay! Just a misunderstanding. We were having a chat…talk!' she said, desperately trying to control the situation and make light of it. She did not want any negative publicity; similar encounters had happened to her before, but not to this degree of intensity. 'I'm okay. There's nothing to worry about.'

Dino was about to say something, but Luigi beat him to it. 'Bruno, take Isabella to my room up here, then go get Sophia Make-up to come up and be with her.'

Dino had picked up his whisky glass from the table and moved towards the drinks. He needed one!

Luigi was breathless, his voice shaky and a little croaky. ‘I don’t know what’s going here, Dino,’ he paused to take a hurried breath, ‘but I have more than a fair idea.’

Dino spun round, whisky bottle in hand. He was red in the face, shaking. ‘You have no bloody idea what’s going on here, Luigi. We were merely having a chat. Just a little chat. Get it!’

Isabella moved to the door, tottering slightly in her high heels, towards her protector, Bruno, who looked even bigger next to her. He led the way out of the room and turned to the right towards his boss’s room at the top of the stairs.

As far as he could tell, Adam Kirby was the only Englishman apart from Peter Dublin at the party. He had managed to find himself a small empty table in a far corner, away from the musicians, back to the wall, as usual, Coca Cola in hand, the best place to sit and people-watch. He recognised a few people. Dublin, of course, Production Manager. He had met him four days ago, on the Wednesday when he first arrived. He of the permed curly hair, eau de cologne and expensive pale blue suit was casually chatting to a group of four people among the dozen or so under the nearer of the chandeliers, all bathed in its warm, red-yellow glow. Dublin’s eyes were never still, constantly flitting around the room, checking, looking to see if there was anyone more important he would be better off chatting to.

Adam was not dressed to impress: a denim jacket, white polo neck, jeans and his beloved well-worn desert boots. He had only just arrived. He was in the second shift to be collected by his unit driver from his hotel. The most important people were picked up first, then the drivers went back for the also-rans. Adam was obviously one of the latter; Camera crew usually are, particularly Focus Pullers.

Adam noticed a big guy in a gaberdine coat enter the room and approach the table next to him, where three unaccompanied women were sitting sipping champagne, chatting animatedly. His towering presence interrupted them. Adam could not hear what was being said as occasional explosions of boisterous laughter floated around the room. The dark oak side panels helped to reflect and confuse the sounds of music and people socialising. One of the women with her hair done up in a red bandana quickly got up, grabbing her oversized shoulder bag. She followed the fluttering black mac out to the hall and entranceway.

Dublin noticed the encounter, the hurried exit. He decided to get another drink, arrogantly clicking his fingers at a passing waitress with a tray of glasses, a few of them still full of champagne. He took two, one for his wife.

Adam had never been to such a posh do in all his life. He was just happy to be tucked away in a corner taking everything in. He was daydreaming and lost in a world of his own as he people-watched.

A voice interrupted his thoughts. 'Mind if we join you?'

It was his boss, Sven Lungren, Director of Photography, with Camera Operator Jan Mattias, followed by a tall, slim, fifty-ish, blonde woman in a plain blue dress. The slightly pale areas around her blue eyes accentuated her light tan. A little mascara and no trace of lipstick. Sven and Jan both moved aside to allow her to the table.

'My wife, Solveig!' exclaimed Sven. 'This is Adam, our Focus Puller.'

She extended a long-fingered hand towards him. Her beauty had faded slightly, but the laugh lines around her eyes compensated for that. Not so long ago she had been a beauty queen and model. She was a class act, no doubt about it.

'Glad to meet you, Adam.'

She had a very noticeable Scandinavian accent, which added to her appeal. The handshake was very firm, probably because she lived the outdoor life whenever time would allow. A skier, judging by the pale areas around her eyes caused by wearing a ski mask.

Luigi Mussomelli came back into the room, back to the party, clapping his hands over his head in time with the music, smiling all over. He walked over to a group of guests standing under the nearest chandelier. They were like Peter Dublin, using it to highlight their presence in the room. The party must go on; nothing has happened, keep the face!

As Jan, Sven and Solveig sat down and established themselves Adam's eyes were drawn to the door of the entranceway. New arrivals, fashionably late, Jose Villabianco, Head of Wardrobe, with a slim, elf-like girl of a woman in the most beautifully tailored, tight-fitting, white mini dress. Her dark brown hair was cut short in a bob with a long kiss curl. Adam did not recognise her immediately. Then it dawned on him: it was Pia, the young Wardrobe girl who had done his washing for him when he first arrived. She had totally changed. She had full 'war paint' on, and it was awesome; she had captured the current 'Twiggy look' and enhanced it. Bloody hell, thought Adam, what a stunner! Jose guided her towards the animated, noisy Luigi group which opened to let them in, then closed around them.

Suddenly there were blue lights flashing over the house. Two Alfa Romeo police cars being driven at very high speed through the tarmacked streets swiftly turned off the road and hurtled down the long slope towards the villa. They blipped their sirens as they braked hard outside the entranceway. Eight blue doors burst open almost as one, and seven armed, uniformed police determinedly marched in through the open front doors, turning left into the main room. They formed a blocking line across the door, parting to allow in a tall, grey-haired, leather-coated detective who walked very confidently through them into the main room.

The musicians, one after the other, stopped playing, creating an eerie silence. The detective had everyone's attention.

'I am Ispettore Superiore Lucarelli of the City of Rome Police. I have reason to believe that illegal drugs are being used on the premises.' His English was impeccable, virtually accentless. 'My officers here will search the building.' He paused to allow his words to sink in. 'I ask you all to empty the contents of your pockets and bags onto the tables, ready to be checked.'

Luigi's face was a picture. He was horrified. This was his house, his party, it was up to him to sort out whatever was going on. The glitterati moths from under the lights moved towards the side tables and added to the bric-a-brac of items that were being piled high, muttering under their disconcerted breaths. Luigi faced up to the Ispettore, demanding to know what was going on.

Adam obeyed the last order given, placing his bulging wallet, a half-empty pack of Wrigley's chewing gum and a rather grubby, folded hankie on the table. Solveig unzipped her small red handbag, inverting its contents onto the table: a small, engraved make-up compact case, a small brass Buddha, a couple of folded tissues and a mascara wand. Like Adam, Jan and Sven added nothing of interest: a couple of wallets and some visiting cards. Sven pulled from his inner pocket a small notepad, with a pen attached.

Everyone looked uncertainly at each other, relieved to see there was nothing on their table that could be considered a cause for concern. They all turned to look back into the room. By now, the great and good were all standing around the side tables, not wanting to let their possessions out of their sight. There was a hubbub of discontent. The centre of the room was empty apart from Luigi and the Ispettore under the far chandelier still locked in a heated argument, a lot of arm-waving and protesting going on.

The music quartet were frozen like statues in their seats, absolutely terrified. Three policemen were going round the tables, checking the stacked piles of items. They moved slowly from table to table, like wind blowing leaves, causing people to part to allow them to poke leather-gloved into their private possessions. One of the shorter officers was working his way round to Adam's corner table. Arriving with a grunt, he stared at Solveig for a second. His eyes flicked down to her cleavage. She gave him a really warm smile, which caused him to let out another primaeval grunt in acknowledgement. He brushed against Adam's shoulder. He had extreme BO, but he also had a holster with a Beretta pistol. Adam leant as far as he could to his right to allow the black-gloved hand to finger the few spread-out items lightly. Not finding anything of interest, he again grunted and moved on. The four of them let out a slight exhalation of breath, followed by an eye flick of reassurance to each other. No one spoke.

The Luigi-Ispettore confrontation was still heatedly going on in the middle of the room under the chandelier when the four remaining policemen came in from the hallway flanking Dino Burgio in handcuffs. The taller officer on the right held up two small polythene bags of white powder in his left hand. The whole room fell silent.

Dino burst out, 'WHAT THE HELL'S GOING ON HERE? THIS IS ALL SHIT! THAT STUFF IS NOTHING TO DO WITH ME. I'VE NEVER SEEN IT BEFORE.'

The two policemen flanking Dino pulled his elbows, causing the handcuffs to dig into his wrists. He was about to say something else, but that hurt!

Everyone in the room looked at Dino. Totally humiliated, he scanned the room for some support, but everyone averted their gaze until the Ispettore, in a loud voice, said, 'Scusi a tutti!', before breaking into song in the richest tenor voice: 'CHE BELLA COSA NA JURNATA E SOLE.'

Solveig's face lit up, and she suddenly bounced up and down like a little girl, making little short claps of delight. 'It's "O sole mio"!'

'N'ARIA SERENA DOPPO NA TEMPESTA.'

The string quartet seamlessly started to accompany the tenor, and five of the policemen moved to flank him, joining in with the singing.

'PE'LL'ARIA FRESCA PARE GIA NA FESTA.'

The look on Solveig's face was a joy to behold. She smacked and rubbed Sven's knee in her delight.

Dino's two guards immediately undid his handcuffs. One of them rubbed his wrist apologetically as he did so, muttering, 'Scusi'. Dino was just beginning to work out what was going on. It was all a bloody joke, a set-up!

The five policemen had now thrown their hats on the floor and were in full song, grouping themselves around the Ispettore.

'CHE BELLA COSA NA JURNATA E SOLE.'

The sound of their voices was uplifting, to say the least. Adam was stunned, Sven was grinning like a Cheshire cat, and everyone else in the room was totally transfixed.

'MA N'ATU SOLE, CCHIÙ BELLO, OJE NE.'

Adam did not know the first thing about opera, but he knew enough to understand that what he was hearing was of the highest quality. He was listening to six human musical instruments, each of them at the top of their profession. The Ispettore turned and sang directly at Dino, bowing and smiling at him, dedicating the song to him as best he could. Dino was not best pleased. He had been humiliated, but he was in show business and he knew that 'face' was everything. Be a good sport and pretend you enjoyed every minute of it. Knowing the words, he enthusiastically sang along to try and redeem some self-respect, but inside he was seething. The humiliation with Isabella and now these bloody, fake police.

When the sextet had finished singing, the whole room went wild; a standing ovation that went on for about two minutes, with shouts of 'Encore! Encore!'

So, with a little gesture of fake humility, the Ispettore led his choir in 'Hey Jude' by the Beatles. The string quartet perfectly accompanied every note with enthusiasm. The whole experience was a total musical masterclass just as it was meant to be. It had been planned in great detail.

Sunday 13th April

Sunday morning was sunny, breezy and cool. Adam decided that as it was his day off, he would have a wander around the city. The continental breakfast in the hotel was a sparse affair. Croissants and orange juice filled the gap. The sixteen-table breakfast room was an echo chamber, with couples, families of all ages and nationalities chattering away about their plans for the day, and kids running about excitedly. Adam took to the street. The milky yellow sun was just beginning to assert itself in the eastern sky.

A few miles away to the north in Parioli, at Luigi's house, a grey car transporter slowly winched two blue Alfa Romeo police cars one after the other onto the back of his lorry and tied the wheels off with nylon straps.

The short, smelly policeman who had searched Adam's table was walking down the Production Office corridor at Studio Lazio with eight shopping bags, four in each hand. Stopping outside the door marked Costumi (Wardrobe), he carefully placed the bags in his right hand on the floor and politely knocked on the door.

Ispettore Lucarelli came out of the door marked Contabile (Accounts), smoothing down the material over his left breast pocket, which was bulging with the contents of a brown envelope. His face said it all. A good evening's work, and for the musicians and the choir to be paid so early on a Sunday morning was most unusual. Luigi Mussomelli had style, no doubt about it.

At the party house, the black and white house cat posed on the newly cleaned windowsill, its eyes closed, bathing in the lukewarm light that came in through the freshly cleaned windows, lighting up the dust suspended in the air that had been stirred up by all of the noisy cleaning now going on. People were hoovering, moving furniture about, changing everything around. The cat was safer on the windowsill up out of the way.

A stream of backlit blue exhaust smoke followed the transporter lorry as it drove away up the slope of the tarmacked driveway.

By half past nine, three white-aproned men and one stocky woman who had been working since seven o'clock had nearly finished transforming the room back to its everyday comfort.

Adam had been given a very basic tourist map of the city by the hotel receptionist, Nello, and so headed south, keeping the sun on his left.

He thought back to his meeting with Production Manager Peter Dublin four days ago, on the Wednesday when the driver, Toni, had picked him up at Fiumicino airport.

The sign on the door read Production Office, with Portway Productions neatly underneath.

Toni knocked on the door, opened it a couple of inches and shouted, 'Permesso!' through the gap.

The female response from inside, in an undetermined English accent, bid, 'Come in.'

Toni stepped to one side, opening the door fully for Adam and his briefcase to enter the room. He pointed at the blue suitcase beside the far chair and, with a double nod of reassurance, informed him, 'It's okay!'

Adam stepped into the office and was surprised at how big it was. The light streaming through the huge window in front of him was softened by a thin, white, net material which caused the room to be evenly illuminated with a lovely soft, even light. To the left sat a middle-aged, brown-haired woman in a green, cotton, neck-high dress. Adam was about to acknowledge her when the silhouette of a man stood up from behind the large desk, at the window.

'Adam Kirby from Cinepan, I trust?'

Adam was obviously expected; you don't get into an office like this otherwise. Adam stared at the figure, but the window backlighted him, and he found it very difficult to discern any significant features apart from long curly hair.

'Yes!' Adam managed to get out before the silhouette stepped around the desk with an outstretched hand in welcome. The hand was smooth, not that of somebody who had ever done any manual work. There was a powerful smell of expensive eau de cologne and a whiff of coffee.

'Peter Dublin, Production Manager, and this is Gill, Production Secretary.'

Adam turned to greet her as she got up. As Adam was now between her and the window, he could see her a lot more clearly; her mouth gave a genuine, white-toothed smile, and she was bathed in a soft light. He suddenly understood the way the room lighting behaved.

Her handshake was cool, brief, cursory almost. 'Glad to meet you.'

'Do you fancy a coffee?' Peter said, gesticulating for him to take a seat.

'No, thanks, I'm fine.'

'Usual, please, Gill.' Peter directed his order over Adam's shoulder.

Gill scraped her chair on the wooden floor as she got up to obey his instruction.

Peter was in an almost complete silhouette. The brightness of the window behind him made it very hard to make out any of the finer details of his face, but the handmade silk shirt was apparent as was the expensive Rolex watch peeking out of his left cuff. His hair was light brown, almost shoulder-length and permed into hanging ringlets. The accent was very educated, very Oxford, Adam thought.

'So, Michael tells me that you are the best he's got to replace Barry Drinkwater. What happened to him exactly?'

There was a very loud, hissing noise from the coffee machine over on the far-left wall as Gill carried out her barista duties. A momentary thought flashed through Adam's mind as he prepared to answer Peter's question: who has an espresso machine in their office?

'We were shooting a winter sports show for ABC… Wide World of Sports*, ski jumping at Holmenkollen in Oslo. It seems he was halfway down doing the in-flight fly-by, and on the way back down, he lost his footing and slid about seventy-five yards into a tree, breaking his pelvis and nearly castrating himself.'*

Peter overacted a wince. 'Aaarrgh! Is he okay?'

'He was more than lucky there was a full team of doctors there because of the ski jumping. He was in hospital within a few minutes, but he's still in Oslo.'

'Castration is not something I would wish on Barry; he was a randy little bugger, like most of you Camera guys!'

There was footfall behind Adam as Gill brought Peter his coffee, respectfully placing it on the desk in front of him and turning the handle to the three o'clock position. He half nodded, more in acceptance than thanks.

'So young Adam, I know from Michael that you are good at your job, one of his best, but he would say that, wouldn't he?' He smiled and sipped his coffee. It was still too hot. 'But are you going to be able to work as part of our team? There are over forty key people here, and we all have to get along. You going to be able to do that?'

Adam paused for a second. That was pretty direct. 'I hope so. I've worked on a lot of different jobs and never had a falling-out. I've never been in a fight either!' he added, with a smile, that winning smile of his.

Peter was expecting the stock answer, but he was making a point. 'Well, it's important. This is a co-production, and we have producers from three different countries, a Scandinavian Director, Cameraman and Operator with the rest of the crew being mainly local. Do you speak Italian?' Peter took another tentative sip of his coffee.

Adam's hands were a little sweaty by now as he shifted a little awkwardly on his hard seat, which was at least four or five inches lower than Peter's so he effectively had to look up to him. He was aware that he was fully lit by the soft window light, and that Peter could see every muscle twitch in perfect detail on his face. He had this room set up for intimidation, or at the very least control of anyone on the other side of his desk.

'No, I don't. Just a bit of schoolboy French.'

'Well, matey, you will need to learn. If Gill here can pick it up, anyone can,' he said disparagingly.

'Pillow talk!' came the cool response from behind as she once again scraped her chair as she sat down.

Peter smiled, nodding towards her. 'She's married to a Chief Inspector of Police, very useful if we need to shoot in the city and park all the vehicles.'

There was no response, just the sound of Gill shuffling her papers as loud as she could.

It was obvious they bantered like this, but it was probably more biased towards Peter putting Gill down rather than the other way round. He was the head of this office and everything in it, particularly how it was lit and the way the seating was set up; everything was to his advantage. There was no doubt he was in total control.

'So, Gill has booked you a hotel in the city, and tomorrow you will start tests and meet the rest of your crew. One of the drivers will drop you off and pick you up in the morning. We have the filmstock in the fridge behind you. It's warm here and getting warmer, and we don't want any stock problems. Your Clapper is a local lad, Luca. Between him, you and Gill you are responsible for making sure that you have enough stock out of the fridge acclimatising for the next few days of filming.'

Adam was about to say something, but there was no pause in Peter's speech from the bridge.

'Today is the 9th. We start shooting on set on Monday 14th for two weeks, interiors, so that everyone can get to know each other. We will pay you a location allowance of two hundred dollars a week, and that is to cover your breakfast, lunch and supper. When we move out of studio, we will provide location catering, and you can lunch on us. Gill will take you down to see Tomassino to get your allowance. Your Grip is Anatra. He will help with the tests tomorrow. Any questions?'

'No, I don't think so.'

'Excellent. Well, try to learn Italian. All the Macchinisti, the stagehands, are local, and they speak very little English and... Oh! if you turn up late or drunk for work, I will put you on the first plane home, and you will paying for the flight, and then you will have Michael to deal with. Okay?'

Adam was a bit taken aback by the threat, but it actually made perfect sense. This guy was responsible for a multimillion-dollar movie and he was going to make sure it had as few hiccups as possible.

'Happy with that. I don't drink, so not a problem.'

Peter inwardly scoffed at the 'don't drink' answer; his experience of Camera crew was the exact opposite.

'Right, Gill, take our friend down to Tomassino and get some money in his pocket. When he's ready, get Toni or one of the others to take him to his hotel.'

Peter rose to his feet and leant forward to shake hands, but it was merely a touch of the palms, nothing more. Peter's attention had already turned back to his coffee.

Adam was brought back to the present day when he attempted to jaywalk through the traffic across the Via del Tritone on his way to the Fontana di Trevi. A carabinieri officer blew his whistle, pointing at him agitatedly. Adam waved back an apology to let him know that he had got the message. 'You don't mess with those carabinieri guys,' Jan, the Camera Operator, had told him last night at the party.

That party was something else. The whole setting was out of this world, incredibly prosperous, the people, the music, those cops that became a choir, bloody unbelievable, a long way from the world that he had grown up in Worcester Park.

As Adam wandered through the uneven, cobbled streets, voices floated out of open windows wrapped in the smell of fresh coffee. Rome was waking up. He turned a corner, pausing to allow a rattily chugging scooter to cross in front of him. He looked to see if the way was clear and crossed the road. A sunglasses seller was on his designated patch, with a little blue barrow that many years ago had been used to sell ice cream. He noticed Adam immediately, a tourist!

He shouted directly at him in welcome, 'Cinque mille lira, occhiali da sole, cinque mille lira!'

Adam was attracted by the array of cheap plastic laid out on the scratched plywood top. As he got closer, he was aware of the smell of dried sweat overlaying the unmistakable whiff of garlic.

'How much?' he asked, his face reflected in the vendor's sunglasses.

Five fingers shot into the air. 'Cinque mille, five thousand!' His black pullover had food stains down the front, his voice was gruff, his yellow teeth sloped inwards, a couple of the top ones were missing and his black hair glistened, certainly not someone you'd want to meet on a dark night.

The party house was nearly back to normal. The occasional tables and the upright, backed chairs had all been cleared away. The long sideboard had been cleaned and wax polished to remove any traces of food or white ring marks from the night before. The six crystal whisky glasses and four varieties of malt whisky were now back on their mats, close to the back wall where the cat couldn't knock them off. The two three-seater sofas had been brought back in, together with the matching armchairs. Two carved walnut occasional tables had been put back into their dimple marks in the carpet next to the armchairs. The windows had been cleaned, followed by the vacuuming of the whole room, carpet and rugs, and the lounge was finally back to normal. Nella, the housekeeper, was happy! Now for the next little job. She gave the lounge a final once-over before turning into the oak-panelled dining room that was to be the setting for that morning's meeting.

It was nice to be setting up for the Sunday meetings again, she thought. It meant that the house was busy again as it should be. It also meant that her employer, Luigi, was producing another film.

Nella had first started as a maid in the house when she was twenty-six, just before the war. Luigi had bought the house in 1950 – she remembered because that was the year that Fangio won his first Grand Prix at Monaco, and it was all over the papers. She had been offered the job of housekeeper and gladly accepted. There was not much work to be had at that time, particularly for domestic staff, so she was grateful. She was not married, preferring the company of a nearby lady who kept horses. They would go out riding together on her day off, which varied from week to week but became almost non-existent during film production. Luigi had never once 'knocked on her door'; he was a perfect gentleman. He may well have been aware of her sexual preferences, but he treated her with great respect, which, to be honest, was well deserved. Now, at fifty-two, half her life working in the same house, she was more than good at her job.

The gardener, Rino, had been roped in to help with the house cleaning and furniture work. However, he much preferred to be outside. He had been assisted in the heavier work by a couple of local men, who over the years had always been called in for any occasional extra jobs around the house or garden. All three were dressed in white shirts, black ties, and cream-coloured linen aprons over their grey flannel trousers. They all wore shiny black polished shoes. Nella inspected the group from head to toe before she would let them out of the kitchen to begin their day's work. She had standards, and they all knew it.

Luigi liked to hold the weekly Production meetings at his home. The Studio Lazio offices were utilitarian, concrete and characterless. His fifteen-foot, carved oak table, the ornate upright, backed, green, velvet-upholstered chairs and the covered sideboard with an ad-lib supply of hot coffee was, in his opinion, far more conducive to creative thinking. Nella would always set him at the head of the table, furthest from the door with his back to the partially opened window.

Earlier in the morning, she had overhead the most unpleasant row coming from upstairs between him and the American Producer, Dino, melon head, the man with no neck. She had taken an instant dislike to him the moment she clapped eyes on him. Baptised in dirty water seemed to spring to mind.

The argument was an absolute screaming match. Even the cat had decided to distance himself and walk out to the garden. The shouting American accused Luigi of totally humiliating him in front of the entire crew, destroying his credibility. She never heard Luigi's reply. He was always calm, always softly spoken.

She was setting the table for twelve plus Luigi, which was about right for a Production meeting. It varied over the years, each film a little different. They had held the initial Production meeting the previous Sunday, and many familiar faces were present. Producers, like Directors, like to work with the same people, develop relationships, work with friends almost.

Nella's favourite was Sophia in Make-up. She was always dressed in the brightest colours and had the most infectious giggle, like a thirty-five-year-old, naughty schoolgirl. Her long, light brown hair was always tied up with a colourful scarf, her make-up perfect. She was a real fun person and had been with Luigi for at least five films, probably more.

The Head of Wardrobe, Jose Villabianco, was one of the most charming, educated men she had ever met, certainly the best dressed. They shared a bond; they were both attracted to members of their own gender. He always greeted her by kissing her hand. He was a lovely man.

Peter Dublin, permed hair, English, loads of cologne, addicted to coffee, new for this Production. Allegedly married to a wealthy London society woman. He was 'a piece of work'. She didn't trust him. There was just something about him, too greasy! He never looked you in the eye.

Duke, First Assistant Director, had been with Luigi even longer than Sophia. Luigi said Duke was the closest thing he could get to a guarantee to finish within the budget, once confiding that he wouldn't do a picture without him. Duke was well-named; he was a rock of a man in every sense of the word, over six foot, with tight, naturally curly, black hair.

The Head of Art, Joe, was a jumped-up little painter. No social graces to speak of. Nella disliked him, and not without good reason; he had a way of looking down on her, always trying to put her down, with snidey little remarks, a worm of a man!

Last Sunday, she met the two Norwegians, the Director and his Cameraman, for the first time. They were both utterly charming, quietly spoken, and both had an air of calm about them, an air of humble confidence. She took to them immediately.

Gill, the Production Secretary, would be next to Luigi at the head of the table, taking the minutes. She had been with Luigi since 1966, so three years, and was married to a senior policeman. Nella had met him once, nice guy, but like most senior police officers that had come up through the ranks, he was full of his own self-importance. Gill, though, was undemanding, a pleasant enough woman.

Enzo Girosi, the gaffer, sixty-ish, lantern-jawed, mouth full of big teeth, had also been on the last four or five films, and his speciality was eating all the biscuits. So Nella used to spread them out over the table on four separate plates to give everyone else a chance. He was a very big guy, as most electricians were, and his long arms could almost reach across the table.

Carl, Sound Supervisor, and Dario, Construction Manager, were both new this year. They didn't have much to say and last week had positioned themselves near the door at the far end of the table, keeping out of the way. Lower down the pecking order, further down the table.

Rino, on Nella's instruction, had opened and clipped back the dining room window shutters. Together with his two assistants, he had cleaned the panes in the sash window, hoovered the floor and wax polished the table and sideboard so that the whole room smelt of carnauba. They had then precisely positioned the high-backed dining chairs, setting fourteen coasters, one extra just in case someone unexpected turned up. Nella had evenly placed down the centre of the table the four plates of biscuits, with a matching plate over the top to keep off any flies or deny a certain black and white feline vandal unwanted access.

When all the guests were assembled, the coffee would be brought in in thermos jugs and placed on coasters on the newly ironed, snow-white tableclothed sideboard. They all tended to arrive a few minutes early and all at once. Maybe it was the discipline of the business they all worked in.

Before the three men left the room, Nella asked Rino to check that the hot water in the urn for the coffee was heating up nicely in the kitchen. She added that she was grateful for his assistance and that all three of them could take a break in the service room, but they were not to wander off. Rino was very good at wandering off if he was not directly tasked with a specific job. He really did prefer to be outside in the garden where he was his own boss, that was his problem.

There was a spare chair beside the doorway on the left, and it looked inviting. Nella sat down for a short 'pausa', leaning her wooden tray against the wall. She had been on the go since seven o'clock; two minutes wouldn't hurt.

Above the sideboard, across the room, she looked at the wall lit by the silvery yellow, early morning sun coming in through the window. There were two large landscape pictures of the rolling hills of Tuscany throwing large diagonal shadows across the wall, but there was nothing in the dining room or the lounge that said anything about Luigi. The paintings on the landing of distinguished ancestors were not his; they had come off film sets. In fact, the whole house was a film set; there were no family photographs, nothing personal, nothing intimate. Had he ever been married or even in love? Did he have any children? He was a total enigma, a very private man. She knew that he was originally from Sicily, a very successful businessman. Allegedly he had made his money selling fish to restaurants and hotels all over the south of Italy long before the war. When Mussolini, in the 1930s, created a centre for the Italian film propaganda machine, grandly naming it Studio Lazio, Luigi had, several years later, in the fifties, become involved in some way with all of that. He was very creative, that was for sure. She doubted that he was a fascist and also doubted that he was involved with the Mafia, despite the fact he was from Sicily. As far as she was aware, there were no weapons in the house, no Mafia Tommy guns!

Rino, the gardener, had been a 'Black Feather' in the war, one of the elite Italian Alpini mountain troops. Even today, he was an incredibly fit man for someone in their late forties, usually out running most evenings. He had a German sniper rifle hanging up in his workshop at the back end of the garden, which he swore was deactivated. Still, a couple of years ago, there had been a few bangs from outside in the garden very early one morning, and four rabbits appeared a little later on the kitchen table, each one shot with a single bullet through the head. So, Nella felt that the jury was still out on the deactivation.

Luigi did have regular anonymous visitors, usually when she had a day off, but she had no idea who they were. There tended to be two of them, sometimes one. Their cups and plates were always left washed up and clean on the draining board, with no apparent clues to their identity. If she really wanted to, she could have listened in on Luigi's phone calls as the four phones in the house were all interconnected, but she was not that bothered. Her employer's business was his business, and no one else's. She did not want to lose her job. He always told her not to get back before nine, which she never did. Days off were to be treasured, and she was always very reluctant to leave her friend anyway. For her, the smell of the horses and hay was hard to walk away from. Certainly more so than the smell of carnauba polish, which most of the ground floor now smelled of.

Luigi was on time, as usual, wandering into the meeting room at around ten to ten. He liked to be early. Nella had set the table with her usual precision. The light, refreshing breeze from the slightly opened window brought in the timid smell of pine resin and distant woodsmoke that was soon overshadowed by the powerful smell of coffee waiting for the guests. He was upset that his welcoming joke with the police choir had gone down so badly with Dino. Everyone else, though, had loved it. It was not a good start to their working relationship, in actual fact a dreadful start. He wasn't very pleased about Dino's behaviour with Isabella either. This was the problem of having to involve the Yanks. The all-essential global film distributors had insisted on an American Producer to protect their interests. No American Producer, no financial backing. They had him over a barrel.

He looked out of the window. Each blade of grass supported a glistening water drop on its tip that glistened in the early sun; the dark red Acer in the weedless bed behind was in full leaf, revelling in the warming backlight. This was one of the many reasons that he held these meetings at home. A sight like that recharges one's emotional batteries, keeps one in touch with reality. His leather seat at the head of the table gave a gentle whoof of escaping air as he sat down. It was deliberately slightly higher, more luxurious than the others, the perfect place from which to chair the meeting. He opened his leather-bound notebook and took the top off his Parker ballpoint pen.

Peter Dublin was the first to arrive. You could hear the Porsche 911 coming down the drive like a precocious chainsaw gargling rivets that was crying for attention. Minutes later, he walked into the room, casually dressed in pale blue jeans and an ivory-buttoned denim shirt with flapped breast pockets. He placed his notepad on the table with a couple of biros.

'Good morning, Luigi. Great party last night, one of the best. Alex really enjoyed herself.'

Luigi smiled and gave a modest little chuckle. 'It was good, wasn't it? Help yourself to a coffee or an orange juice,' he said, waving his right arm at the sideboard.

Peter got straight down to business as he poured himself a coffee from the nearest thermos. 'Veronique Press was on to me again last thing Friday. *Casa News* want to run some article on Isabella, but they need more background.'

Luigi leant back. 'She really does not want her whole private life spread over the papers. Her story is that she came from stage school, started working as a young extra at sixteen, got discovered, and after that, the rest is history.'

'Well, they are saying that she is the person in the song "Where Do You Go To My Lovely" by Peter Sarstedt.'

'Yeah, well, they said it was Sophia Loren last week, so what do they know?' Luigi picked up his pen and pointed it as if to emphasise what he was about to say. 'We need to keep *Casa News* onside, but if Isabella wants her private life to be private, then we must all respect that. Allow them to interview her with Veronique Press present but never on her own. She is still quite naïve. In fact, any press interviews with any cast member have got to have Veronique present, I insist on that. It's essential that nothing untoward is ever printed.' He nodded firmly as if to add an exclamation mark to his instruction.

Peter nodded in agreement.

The sound of giggling outside in the corridor announced the arrival of Sophia, accompanied by the wide bulk of Duke entering the room. Peter walked around the back of Luigi's chair, sitting on the first seat, on his immediate left, where he had sat the previous week.

Duke was an imposing character, in his mid-fifties, with very wide muscular shoulders, like those of an Olympic swimmer. His voice was deep and authoritative, his small ears clung on the side of his head, and his short black curly hair was receding slightly and greying at the temples.

'Good morning, Luigi. Excellent do last night. I popped into the office on the way, saw Lucarelli. He wanted to thank you for paying him and the others so quickly. He said any time you need any singers just call him.'

He moved towards the aroma of coffee and the sideboard. The cups were small, delicate porcelain with a gold-leaf rim. Duke lifted one up towards Luigi, offering him another, but Luigi shook his head, muttering, 'No, fine, thanks,' almost under his breath.

From behind him came Luigi's favourite person, Sophia Make-up. He could always see the child in her face, such a happy person. Her long, light brown, bunched-up hair came up to Duke's shoulder; her red-and-green-painted doughnut earrings complemented her loose-fitting red and green patterned trousers that concealed her slightly short legs and Rubenesque bottom. She wore a gold crucifix; it was Sunday after all. Her face lit up when she saw Luigi, and she moved eagerly towards him, stretching her head forward and upward to greet him.

'How are you today?'

Luigi got up from his seat, reaching out to her shoulders, pulling her towards him, kissing her on both cheeks. Her open face beamed up at him. There was no hiding the fact she really liked him, her brown eyes danced all over his face. The feeling was mutual.

She giggled. 'You need a haircut, boss. Come by tomorrow lunch, and I'll give you a trim.'

Luigi laughed. She had cut his hair more times than he could remember over the years. 'We'll see, Sophia, we'll see!'

Gill, Production Secretary, had taken the seat at the head of the table on Luigi's right, ready to take detailed minutes. Duke had put himself next to her, with Lasse in the centre. Dino had still not appeared, and it was decided the meeting would start without him. He would, of course, be given a copy of the minutes.

All of the men apart from Jose had turned up in jeans and casual shirts; it was that sort of day. Peter had his sleeves rolled up, to make sure that his Rolex Oyster Perpetual watch was visible. Gill's make-up consisted of only mascara. She looked a little anaemic, kept her head down. Jose was immaculate in a pale grey suit and waistcoat, handmade, of course, no tie; it was a casual day. He had a lunch date later, so he was keen to get the meeting over by twelve-thirty. Sophia always managed to look a little bohemian with her detailed mascara and eyeliner. Was that a pencil holding her rolled and bunched hair in place?

Luigi was happy so far. Everyone seemed to be focused, and everyone was getting on. At the far end of the table, Dario from Construction touched elbows with Carl from Sound. Enzo, the gaffer, was helping himself to the biscuits as usual, with Joe from Art, on his right and an empty chair for Dino. Luigi was happy to let Lasse be the centre of attention as he had been the principal speaker at all of the meetings. He smiled a lot, this Scandinavian, careful to always check his notes.

Lasse looked up, holding his chin high, scanning the table, making sure he included everyone. 'I just want to make sure with the Art department and Construction that, when we do all of the boat arrivals at Civitavecchia, we are going to able to make one ship look like three different ones. One for 1918 when Eduardo leaves, another in 1921 when he comes back with Margaret, and the last in 1938 when Gina is packaged off to England, with that same ship arriving in England to be met by Alice.' He waved his biro enquiringly at Peter across the table. 'We still only have the one ship, is that right?'

Peter looked up from his notepad. 'We looked at trying to get another one, but it is cheaper to set dress the original. We have painted the stern half of the ship dark blue and the front half white, plus we have three different gangplanks.'

It was obvious from Lasse's expression that he was not convinced. 'I think that in fairness to everyone, I should go down to Civitavecchia with Sven, Joe and Dario as soon as possible just to make sure that we are making the best of everything…plus Sven and Enzo need to see the immigration hall.' He looked at Peter for confirmation, then at Joe and Enzo to record in his own mind their nods of agreement. Peter scribbled a few words on his pad and nodded.

Lasse looked up and down the table to let everyone know that he was changing tack. 'Now, for the submarine landing sequence, is the water deep enough for the submarine, bearing in mind that I want it close into the shore?'

There was silence. No one had thought of that.

Lasse continued. 'We don't have time to boat the circus a mile offshore.'

Duke on his left coughed slightly. 'Errh! We did a similar scene with the same sub a few years back, and where you are proposing to shoot is plenty deep enough. The tidal range is minimal, between four inches and a foot. I have organised two frogmen as safety standby, and an extra pair of hands to help get the camera kit onto the camera boat. The two English sailors with Gina in the rubber dingy are both qualified divers and know what they're doing. She will be in safe hands.'

Lasse nodded in confirmation as he took on each of Duke's points.

Dino was not at the meeting because he was upstairs in his room making a phone call. To overhear his conversation, which she never would, Nella could have picked up the hall phone, but she did not need to. His natural speaking voice, like most Americans, was so loud that it carried clear as a bell down into the hall. Nella was kneeling on the carpet, sweeping up ash from the lounge fire that the boys had dropped, and checked to make sure that she was alone. Everyone was in the meeting on the other side of the house, and the boys should be down in the kitchen. Dino's voice boomed through the slit in the nearly closed door.

'I want you to send Max over to me for a week or two. Charge it to my second account, yeah, yeah! A couple of his friends as well would be a good idea. Book 'em in somewhere in central Rome, not too flashy, near the station and fly 'em Pan Am, not first class. I don't want anyone knowing they're here. I'll phone you in a couple of days. Don't phone me, don't leave messages, you got that?'

Nella heard someone moving around in the kitchen down the corridor and, feeling a little guilty, stood up and walked down as casually as she could out of the hallway.

Lasse looked directly across the table at Sophia, tilting his head a little to his left, reducing his assertiveness. 'Sophia, we have Eduardo as a seven-year-old, an eighteen-year-old and then from twenty-nine to fifty. I think that it would help the audience if we could give him a small birthmark here.' Lasse rubbed his right-hand fingers across the left side of his face, jowl from his ear halfway forward to his chin, all the time watching her reaction. 'That will help the audience more clearly identify him through the years with the three different actors. What do you think?'

Sophia smiled and nodded. 'I think that is an excellent idea. The twenty-nine to fifty we will do with hair greying and a bit of latex around the eyes. Wardrobe and backgrounds will help as well, but we can do that, no problem.'

Lasse smiled. He liked this Sophia, she gave off an air of competence. 'Thank you. Now, Peter, the scenes in the shop with Gina: Luigi and I want a hand artist to do the fish gutting, needs to be very fast. So can we get a photo of Gina's hands and go down the fish market and find a female that is really fast at gutting and has similar hands, please?'

Peter Dublin nodded in acknowledgement, picking up his mini-cassette recorder from the table very slowly. He wanted everyone to see that he had the latest technology. He pressed the record button. 'Hand artist, fishmonger double for Gina,' he said, then pressed the stop button and placed it back on the desk. He looked around to see who was impressed.

Jose just smiled, his expression as he momentarily flicked his chin and eyes to one side giving away his thoughts. Sophia and Gill were head down, still making detailed notes.

Lasse looked around the table, up to Luigi at the head, before handing the meeting back to him, as the chairman. 'I think that's everything. Anyone?'

Sven put his hand up. 'Just a note for you, Joe,' he said, looking straight across the table. 'If it's not too late, can we have white tablecloths in the café? They will act as soft reflectors up on faces and make the scene a bit softer, more 1920s. I apologise for not mentioning it before. I made a note when I was lighting. If you can't though, it's not the end of the world.'

Joe frowned ever so slightly as if to convey this was a bit last-minute, but then he smiled and said, 'Yes, of course we can do that.'

Sven smiled apologetically. 'Thank you, Joe. Apologies, I will try to get my act together!'

Joe nodded in acceptance, then proceeded to write in his notepad.

Lasse nodded, waving his pen to bring the attention back to him. 'That will be nice, Sven, a nice touch, thank you. Now anything else?'

They all shook their heads; no further business. There was a pause, and Luigi gave a gentle cough to bring everyone's attention round to him. Sitting upright in his chair at the head of the table, he said, 'Just before we break up, I must remind everyone that we are on a very tight schedule here. We have to average three and a half minutes' screen time a day. These days Civitavecchia are only going to give us about four minutes so we are going to have to make up that six and a half minutes in the studio next week. There is little in the budget for overtime, and we can't afford to work weekend catch-up, apart from that. Thank you all for coming. It's been a very worthwhile meeting.'

Just as everyone was starting to gather up their papers and pens, Dino Burgio strutted into the room, nodding to Luigi and everyone else. He locked eyes with Peter. 'Peter, I wanna move out of here, get a place of my own, you fix that? Nice place, yeh know, minimum five bedrooms…up around here on the high ground. Plus, I need a Caddi, a Cadillac, any colour but black. My Caddi at home would take too long to ship over. So need to get one locally.'

Luigi cut in, 'We have provided you with a unit car, a driver, a Mercedes.'

Dino stared hard at him, his thin lips curled. 'Don't like Mercedes, German crap, want a Caddi, a Series 90, a V-16, like I've got at home, plus I want to be able to drive myself.'

'A Cadillac?' Peter said, turning to face him. 'That is going to be bloody expensive! Isn't that vintage, around 1950?'

Dino gave him a look of exasperation. '1940, 1941, one of the best motors out of Detroit. If you buy it right and sell it right, you can make a profit, that's what we do back home. Get the Art department to retrim it, increase its value, quality leather. I leave it with you. Thanks, everybody!' With barely a nod, he turned and quickly left the room.

Luigi looked at his bulky retreating figure, his mouth slightly open for a second in shock, almost lost for words. He felt like a cobra had fanged him.

Peter, seeing the expression on his face, attempted to take the sting out of the situation. 'I can look into all of that.' He stared down at Gill for support, but she was deliberately keeping her head down writing notes which said to him, 'That is your problem, sunshine!' He slowly picked up his mini-cassette recorder and pressed the record button, talking into his clutched hand as he followed Dino out of the room. 'Five bedrooms, high ground Parioli area, 1940 Cadillac, V-16, any colour but black.'

Luigi looked around the almost deserted table. Duke was still fiddling with his papers. Sophia was the last to leave. She paused in the doorway, and turned back.

'Boss, haircut, trim, tomorrow lunch time. Don't let me down!'

Luigi smiled. 'If I have time, Sophia, if I have time.'

She nodded and walked out of the room, leaving Duke still slowly sorting through his notes.

Rino, the gardener, mug of coffee in hand, walked over to the varnished wooden bench under the open dining room window and sat down. Looking at his perfectly weeded and watered flower beds, all just starting to come into blossom, he closed his eyes and lifted his head towards the morning sun, coffee cup firmly held in both hands resting on his lap.

Duke looked directly at Luigi, his frown showing his inner apprehension. He patted the air with his right hand, respectfully motioning Luigi to sit down, inferring that what he had to say was going to be quite serious and take more than a few minutes.

'Luigi, I need to tell you something, and I ask that you hear me out. I know that Luciano Scordia is putting up a lot of money into this film.' Luigi nodded, frowning momentarily in surprise as this information was not something that should be in the public domain. Duke leant forward, dropping his voice. 'He has approached me and asked me to be his eyes and ears on the production, to spy, basically, to report to him on a daily basis. Now you have shown me great loyalty over the years, and to my family, and I have a very substantial roof over our heads, thanks to you, so I wanted to tell you. I had little choice in the matter. He simply reminded me that I had a family and I would be foolish to put them at risk…'

Luigi put his hand up to stop the flow of confession. 'Duke, I really appreciate you coming to me and for being so honest. There is little that we can do about Scordia. His tentacles are all over this film, all over this business and many others in Rome.' Duke nodded. He was aware of Luciano's reputation. 'I have to live with him as a business partner, and there is little I can do to change that now, even if I wanted to. His style is to bully and frighten people, but I have wanted to make this film for many years. It may well be my last, so we need to get it done. There is a reason that you have such a good roof over your head. Because, my friend, you are the best First in Rome, and I need to work with the best.'

Duke leant forward even closer, increasing the intimacy. 'Boss, you really are a good man, one of the best. How do we go on? Difficult, eh?'

Luigi looked at the landscape paintings, the white-sheeted sideboard splattered with random splashes of spilt coffee and abandoned cups and saucers, like a medieval winter battlefield. He brought his gaze back to Duke, stared into his big face and nodded.

'We go on, we continue. There is nothing that I or you can do. Report to him every day. He will know from his other spies anyway how things are going, so always tell the truth, and if we have a problem, you never know, he may be able to make it go away.' He grimaced slightly. 'He has a way of making a lot of his problems just go away.' He nodded briefly to his right as if to signify a full stop.

Duke leant back, a little more relaxed. 'Thanks, boss. We'll make your film, and it will be your best yet.'

Luigi's face lit up. 'Yes, the best yet. That would be really something. It's very personal to me, very!'

Rino, the gardener, was rooted to his bench, hardly daring to breathe. He got up only after he was sure Duke and Luigi had left the room.

Monday 14th April

Adam's unit car had picked him up from his hotel at just before seven to take him to the studios. Being driven straight into the rising sun, Adam found the light very hard, almost blinding; he was glad he had a pair of sunglasses, even if they were cheap touristy plastic. Toni drove with his usual care, occasionally cursing some other motorist for their inconsiderate driving. Adam had slight reservations about the impending first day. He was unsure how it was going to be with the Wardrobe people Pia and Jose.

He thought back to last Wednesday when he arrived and had been taken by Gill to the Costumi department to sort out his laundry situation caused by having to come to Italy at such short notice.

Pia, the Wardrobe Assistant, had met them in the corridor outside the Production Office after the initial welcoming interview with Peter Dublin. Gill gently explained Adam's dilemma, asking her to help out, just the once, as they were not yet busy with production work. The slim, plain-faced, urchin-haircut girl was all smiles and only too glad to help, opening the door marked Costumi and then stepping to one side, allowing to him pass with his briefcase and bloated suitcase.

The room was the same size as the Production Office, with a long bench to the left and to the right against the walls.

Two hunched, dark-haired seamstresses were sat in front of a couple of sewing machines in the middle of the room, both intently flipping and sewing garments. They gave Adam no more than a superficial glance. Their work required too much concentration. There was a smell of laundry soap and the sound of a washing machine sloshing its soapy way through its programmed task.

The windows at the far end of the room were draped with very luxurious red and gold ornate curtains, giving the whole space a very opulent look. The drapes had obviously come off a film set and been put up to give the room a homely feel. They protected the room from the sun's rays which are not compatible with racks of expensive clothes.

On the far left stood a line of three washing machines; only the middle one was working, the other two had their doors open, inviting hands to fill them up and give them something to do. Past them was a small open door, and Adam caught a glimpse of a few items of coloured washing hanging out to dry in the sun. There was no wind so the clothes simply hung motionless.

Between the sewing ladies and the open door were a couple of singed, buff-topped ironing boards, each with its own iron. The centre of the room was taken up by about a dozen or so shoulder-high, heavy-duty, black metal clothes racks. In front of that, about a third of them were populated with clothes of all different colours, each one catalogued by a large rigid vertical label with some notes and a number. The rest of the racks were empty. No five hundred extras this week, thought Adam.

Pia had not fully understood Adam's South London mumblings as they had walked down the corridor and so decided to revert to sign language, motioning Adam to place his suitcase on the bench on the right. Adam swung it up, causing a firm 'boof' as it hit the scratched wood; it was heavy. Pia stood back to allow him to select what he wanted to be washed.

Pia picked up a large wooden tray from the many that were under the table, placing it next to the opened suitcase and indicating that this was for Adam to put his selection on. Adam was not a precise packer of suitcases, and it was a little embarrassing for him to let Pia see the chaos of shirts, pullovers, jeans, socks and pants that had all been thrown in like ingredients in a cake.

Pia watched with some amusement at his embarrassment, but this is what she had chosen to do for a living. She loved her job. This was her third film as a Wardrobe Assistant, and it should be like all of the others, well paid, good fun, and hopefully she would get a chance to shine, meet some stars! There was a lot of work in the studios, at least two other films in production, one just finishing off, and another two due to start later in the summer. It was good times at Studio Lazio, and everyone was happy.

Adam was piling up his embarrassment of soiled clothes, while Pia took to folding them very neatly onto the tray, showing no signs of squeamishness, but she was, Adam noted, more than a little compulsive about the way she folded them: gently, firmly, placing one on top of another and patting them down with a businesslike tap to reduce their height and get the air out of them.

He pulled out a pair of jeans by the leg and lifted them onto the bench. Pia immediately picked them up, automatically searching the pockets. From the left pocket came a rather stiff hankie, and from the right she produced, like a conjurer, a brand-new pink Durex, and held it up to his face. Her eyes had changed; she was not happy.

At that exact moment, the door opened and in walked a thousand-dollar, blue suit with a very well-groomed man inside it. His timing could not have been more perfect; it was like an action freeze frame. Adam went bright red in embarrassment.

'Eh? Che fai?' were the first words to come out of the newcomer's surprised mouth, followed by a wide grin of recognition, a sort of 'I've caught you' look.

Pia was stunned. She just looked totally dumbstruck. Adam, stammering for the right words, had no idea who he was, but sensed his importance by his suit and her reaction. Oh! Shit!

'Pia was helping me with my washing...'

'Was she now?' came the perfect purring English reply. 'Was she now?'

Pia dropped the contraceptive down on the bench next to the suitcase, like it was dog poo, then very deliberately folded her arms. Never a good sign when an Italian woman folds her arms like that – the Italian pout added the exclamation mark!

The blue-suited man took in the whole scene, his eyes darting from Pia to the chaotic, empty suitcase, to the pile of clothes on the tray, then to Adam's face, to the contraceptive and back to Pia's unhappy face, her folded arms and finally slowly back to Adam, in his redness now trying to think of the right thing to say. He was totally tongue-tied, for a change.

'And you are?' the newcomer asked quizzically. Was he actually enjoying this moment?

'Adam Kirby, Focus Puller from Cinepan.'

'Ah! Adam. Jose Villabianco, Head of Wardrobe. What an entrance, Adam. I shall dine out on this for weeks.'

His words were precise, enunciated, very smoothly spoken with only the slightest trace of an Italian accent. This guy had lived in England or been educated there; you do not get to talk like that doing a language course or watching American films.

'Adam! It would seem that you have embarrassed young Pia here. Italian girls do not take kindly to contraceptives. It is against the will of the church!'

Pia did not fully understand what was being said, but she got the gist of it, slowly unfolding her arms when she realised that she was not the one in trouble; Adam was! The two seamstresses had stopped work and were now straining their ears to find out what was going on while trying not to make it obvious they were eavesdropping.

The cologned Jose was the same height as Adam, a chiselled face, small neat moustache and large dark brown eyes, and that suit, all hand-stitched, no doubt! The silk shirt completed the fashion statement, helped by the blue patterned cravat. Sunglasses were tucked into the top breast pocket. His brown eyes were mischievous; he seemed to be flirting with Adam.

'Well, my testosterone-filled young friend, I will leave you with the lovely Pia and look forward to meeting you again.' He turned to leave. 'Ciao, bello!' Clearly, he did not wish to stay any longer, possibly to avoid further embarrassment, or more likely he was off to tell the story to someone else, as quickly as he could. The Italians love a bit of gossip.

The second encounter on the Thursday morning when Adam had gone to collect his clothes had gone just as badly even though he had brought Pia an Easter egg from the little studio café as a peace offering.

The door to the Costumi department was open when Adam arrived. He tentatively looked into the room. The first person he saw was Jose, standing almost in the doorway. Oh, shit, thought Adam. He was hoping he wouldn't be there.

'Adam, my lovely boy, how are you today? Full of the joys, I trust. You must be looking for our Pia,' he said, turning to shout at the same time, 'Pia, Adam's here.'

Pia appeared at the back door, her slim body silhouetted against the bright light.

Jose turned to Adam. 'So, what have you been up to, young man?' He was all smiles, obviously amused, some inner joke maybe, but he was definitely flirting. His eau de cologne attempted to wrap itself around Adam, smothering him almost.

'Tests. Camera tests, down the corridor.'

'Sounds boring! No fun! Have you had any fun since you got to Rome?' It was a question loaded with sexual innuendo.

Adam decided to play it straight. 'Not really. A meal on my own, and that's about it, really.'

'You shouldn't dine alone, Adam, a good-looking boy like you. We'll have to see if we can arrange something for you. Ah, Pia!'

Pia had appeared beside him, clutching a bulging pillow case close to her slim body. Adam noted that she did not seem that displeased to see him, which somewhat surprised him. What he did not know was that when she had told her family about him the previous evening, they had all laughed so much, they cried. Italians, it would seem, have a sense of humour. She had a pouty smile that suited her delicate face, framed by the large curl of brown hair hanging down to her left eyebrow. Jose took a pace to his left to allow her to approach Adam. He was going to enjoy watching this interchange. His whole expression was one of anticipation, as he looked from one to another, like watching a table tennis match.

'Your lavandaria...washing!' Pia softly explained as it was pretty obvious what she was holding.

Adam moved forward, offering her last week's Easter egg, but her hands were full, so Jose stepped forward and gently accepted it on her behalf, grinning even more as he did so. The gesture was not lost on Adam; this guy fancied him, his whole body language said so, and now he was holding Adam's peace offering like it was intended for him.

Adam firmly took hold of the pillow case with both hands, making absolutely sure that he did not touch Pia's slim little body. That would be all he needed: a fumble, a grope, touching of any kind, unintentional or not, would not go down well.

Jose turned to Pia, offering her the Easter egg. 'Un regalo, Pia, a gift for you from Adam.' His gesture was overacted, exaggerated, but Adam had to admit, he had a lot of style, not to mention his handmade grey suit. He really knew how to dress, this guy!

Pia smiled coyly and muttered, 'Grazie' under her breath. 'Thank you, Adam.'

'Well, thanks for doing all of this, much appreciated. I have to get back to work now, so thanks.'

Pia nodded her acceptance, but Jose was always going to have the last word.

'If you ever need to dress up, just come by. I'm sure we can fit you up,' he said, gesturing to the racks of clothes with their catalogued labels. The way he said 'fit you up' was not missed on Adam.

'Thanks, I'll bear that in mind.'

Hugging his washing almost as a protective barrier, he hurriedly left the room only to hear halfway down the corridor: 'CIAO, BELLO!'

Jose was always going to have the last word.

The loud screaming klaxon of a passing lorry that buffeted them with its aggressive slipstream brought Adam back to the present day as Toni turned the Mercedes off the main road and approached the now-familiar, peach-coloured studio entrance blockhouse.

The barrier was down as they approached but the security guard raised it when he recognised the familiar car, allowing them to respectfully trickle past, waving like royalty as they did.

Toni immediately turned hard right as he had done on the previous Thursday and Friday mornings, moving away from the Production block to the now-familiar collection of small wooden buildings in the shadow of very mature pine trees.

These humble, old wooden sheds had no grand signs, no flashing neon. These were where the actual workers like Toni came for breakfast. Inside the small café, the patterned, brown lino was worn cream in places bearing the most footfall. Some of the nine or so tables were occupied by men in rough jackets and shirts. No flash suits here. The smell of cheap cigarette smoke that greets everyone that enters gives way to the more pleasant aroma of fresh coffee as one nears the glass-topped display counter, topped with croissants, bread rolls and snacks.

The owner was a stocky, thick-set woman with a slight moustache, grey-veined blackish hair cascading down to the middle of her back. She always greeted Toni with her customary, 'Buongiorno, Toni', automatically placing a small white cup of coffee on the countertop. Turning to Adam, she asked, 'Aranciata, ciabatta, proscuitto?' She had quickly learned that Adam, like most English crew, liked a bacon roll.

Adam nodded. 'Yes, please,' he said as he watched her pull firmly down on the presser arm to extract every drop of juice from three large oranges and one lemon. A very nutritious and cheap way to start the day, and the lemon juice helped wake you up! Adam looked along the counter. There were no more leftover Easter eggs. He must have bought the last one when he bought Pia's peace offering last Thursday morning. He looked at his watch. It was seven forty-five. On camera at eight-thirty. He had to get his first day right.

Toni dropped him off at the main doors. There were cars parking up, and a lot of people milling about. Adam walked into the Production corridor, his eyes adjusting to the change in light, as he tucked his sunglasses into the top left breast pocket of his faded denim shirt. The castanet clicking of heels caused him to look to his left and find a surprise: a familiar face, a young actress that he had worked with several times over the years.

Striding towards him, head high, in a full flowing white, maxi dress, one of those lucky or talented actresses, one of the top ten per cent who were always on the screen, her clacking heels accentuating the flowing image of an art deco porcelain dancer. Adam remembered a night shoot for London Weekend Television when she spent virtually half the night in an argument scene in a parked car, crying her eyes out. How she did it for so long amazed him, take after take, she must have been totally emotionally exhausted by dawn when they finally called wrap.

He didn’t like to see a woman cry; it didn’t sit well with him for some reason. He seemed to recall her name was Belinda. He waved at her.

‘Belinda?’ he said, not too loudly in case he was wrong.

Her face lit up. She recognised him but didn’t remember his name. ‘You’re a long way from home!’ she said, genuinely surprised to see him.

‘I might say the same!’ he said, then, with a dead straight face and in a perfect cockney accent, added, ‘Are you okay, darlin’? You look absolutely dreadful.’

She was totally taken aback for a second, just the sort of thing that any actress without any make-up would want to hear first thing in the morning. Adam stood back, a smirky, pouty smile on his lips, waiting for her reaction. He remembered that she had a great sense of humour, a lovely laugh. She clenched her jaw and her pale grey eyes went very hard for a second, then, seeing the smile on his face, punched him on the arm.

‘Bastard!’

He smirked again. ‘It is Belinda, isn’t it? Adam, Adam Kirby. I’m Focus!’

She tapped her foot, almost impatient to move on. ‘Yes, Adam. Belinda Sharp. I’m playing Margaret. Look, I’m a bit late. Can we meet up later? Don’t want to keep Make-up waiting on the first day.’

'Yes, of course,' Adam said. Then, once again reverting to his cockney accent, added, 'I hope you get better soon, darlin'!'

She just shook her head, smiled and muttered 'bastard' under her breath, still shaking her head in disbelief. She turned, heels clacking, white dress flowing, and strode into the Make-up department.

Adam looked at her retreating form. The last time he had worked with her, her hair had been every colour and hue of curly fallen beech leaves; now it was dull brown, straight, just hanging down the side of her very pale face, the perfect canvas on which to paint a new character.

Beatrice Mosena was the Third Assistant Director, lucky to have such a job at only eighteen. Black leather jacket zipped right up to her chin against the early morning chill, astride the vibrating yakety yak of her aged scooter, she smelt the Mercato Tuscolana through the traffic fumes long before she got there. Its smell was unique: fresh fish, hanging poultry and cheap plastic toys. One of the black-suited unit drivers, late the previous evening, had delivered to her three pictures of Isabella Marco's hands. Now she was tasked with finding a female fishmonger who wanted to be a movie star for a day. She really did have a job like no other, she thought, smiling to herself.

Coming to a shuddering, jerked halt into a parking place to the left of the grey concrete entrance, she eased off her helmet, taking the heavy-duty padlock and chain out of the boot box. She needed to make sure that her family hand-me-down was still there to get her back to the studio by nine, or Duke would not be happy. It was never good when Duke was unhappy, even if he was the best boss in the world.

Anatra, the Grip, had got in early and loaded all of the camera equipment into the large white Fiat van. He was waiting in the Camera department with Luca, the Clapper Boy. Adam wished both of them 'Good morning', shaking each of them firmly by the hand, reinforcing it with good eye contact and a smile, something he had learned was an excellent way to start the day when working in Europe. Luca led the way to the parked van outside. Opening the passenger door, he eased himself across to sit in the middle on the handbrake, unperturbed by the discomfort.

Anatra went back into the Camera room. Luca just sat, looking out of the windscreen, obviously not a morning person. Adam's thoughts travelled back to when he had first met his little crew.

He had first come across Luca last Thursday sitting on a canvas-backed chair in the Camera room reading a newspaper, a long cigarette holder stuck in his mouth. His hair was black, but it looked dyed; the whole image was that of a faded French actor in a Hollywood B-movie.

The reading figure leapt enthusiastically to his feet to acknowledge Adam's entrance. 'I'm Luca Clapsticks!'

The handshake was rough; the nails were chewed. This guy was used to manual labour, lives on his nerves, thought Adam. A handshake tells you a lot about a person. The warmth of Luca's greeting, the smile with the cigarette holder, the double clasp as he brought his left hand in to reinforce his welcome – everything said this guy was okay. Well, apart from the dyed hair! He was obviously trying to hide his age, which Adam put at about fifty. His front teeth were stained with nicotine. His sideburns showed signs of grey. He was a mature Clapper Boy, that was for sure.

Before either of them could continue the conversation, the door into the Production Office corridor opened and in stepped two brown, safari-style jacketed men with large leather shoulder bags. One was slightly stocky, powerful, mid-thirties, and a full blonde bushy beard matched his short fair hair. The other was taller, slimmer with red hair going grey at the temples, who Adam instantly recognised as Sven Lungren, the Norwegian Director of Photography, his boss in effect. So the bearded man must be the Camera Operator Jan Mattias. Two Vikings had arrived, and they looked the part!

Handshakes were warm; the Camera crew was together for the first time. People who earn their living working with a professional cine camera are few, probably numbering less than five hundred from all over Europe and Scandinavia, which made their skills very niche. It was a very difficult business to get into. Often son followed father; you would see the same surnames cropping up in film credits decades apart. That was probably why the greetings were so warm. They were part of an elite; they were all going to have to depend on each other's very special expertise. As was the way with any art form, they were also going to learn from each other.

When Sven spoke, it was like a grandfather talking to a grandchild; slow, soft, every word carefully enunciated. 'Adam, nice to see you again. This is Jan Mattias, the operator.'

Jan stepped forward, offering his hand in greeting. 'Glad to meet you, Adam.' He also spoke slowly, with hardly any trace of an accent. His hands were small, very dry, but the handshake was firm; there was a lot of strength there, a good first impression.

Sven gently swung his shoulder bag onto the nearest black box. 'Adam, I'd like to shoot tests on all of the lenses, in particular the zoom. I want to see how it compares quality-wise to the primes.'

Adam was about to respond when two silhouettes appeared in the doorway to the car park behind him. The taller one with dark grey hair in a brush cut spoke first, revealing a large full set of teeth, in a prominent jaw.

'Buongiorno, Sven, do you need more lights?' The accent was a mixture of Italian and American English.

The shorter man hung back. He was obviously lower down the pecking order. Sven had the most charming way about him; he was, without doubt, a real gentleman, smiling a genuine smile of thanks.

'No, Enzo, these two pups are fine,' he said, gesturing at the two lamps standing like sentinels on their heavy-duty stands, guarding the thirteen camera boxes that had been delivered from the airport the day before. Sven turned to Adam. 'This is Enzo, our gaffer. Adam, meet Enzo.'

Enzo nodded. 'Glad to meet you. If you need anything, just call twenty-seven on the phone over there. We are nearly ready on set, pre-light. If you have time and want to come over, it's Stage three.'

'That would be good, Enzo. Jan here can run the tests with Adam. He is a cameraman also!'

'Okay! For sure, good! See you in a while, Stage three!' Nodding respectfully to Jan and Adam, he turned to the door, and the smaller man who had been waiting patiently in his shadow stepped forward and smiled as he introduced himself. 'Anatra, the Grip.'

Jan suppressed a giggle; he was plainly quite amused at something. Anatra just smiled; he was, for some inexplicable reason, obviously used to it!

Adam held his hand out in greeting. 'Glad to meet you, Anatra! Good!'

Luca shuffled his feet as if to say, give me something to do. Adam made to pick up a smaller lidded box of varnished plywood and nodded to imply that its contents were for him. The box was labelled 'The unit box, cans, tape, neg report sheets'. Luca took hold of the handle, nodded and started to undo the lid clips.

Sven, seeing that work had begun, turned to Jan and in Norwegian gave his instructions for the day. Bidding his farewells, he went off to Stage three, to his pre-light with Enzo.

Jan watched Anatra as he walked away to the far side of the room, pulling a large blue dustsheet off his pride and joy: the Moviola crab dolly. It was a very old model and very heavy. I hope we don't have to carry that bloody thing up any stairs, thought Adam. Jan was grinning again as he watched him. Adam had no idea what was causing him such amusement, apart from the fact that Anatra had a very ploddy way of walking.

Later in the morning, around eleven, Jan decided to call a break for half an hour. Anatra and Luca had wandered off, leaving them alone. Adam was curious.

'Have you worked here before?' he asked him.

'Last year for about two months – May, June. Great place, great city, couldn't wait to get back, it's warmer here!'

'So, do you speak Italian then?'

'A bit. Enough to get me into trouble in a restaurant.'

Adam knew that meant more than just a few words, a great many more than him. He looked around to make sure that it was still just the two of them in the room. 'Jan, what is it about Anatra that amuses you?'

'You see the way he walks, plod, plod plod? Anatra is Italian for duck. He walks like a duck!'

Adam was inwardly grinning. That was his kind of humour, funny, cruel, but bloody funny.

Adam was brought back to the present day by the wriggling of Luca beside him, trying to make himself more comfortable on the handbrake. Anatra, the 'duck', was finally on his way, slamming the Camera department door behind him and quickly locking it with a long brass key.

Luca leant forward and pulled the driver's door latch to speed up Anatra's progress. Anatra apologised for the delay as he climbed up into the driver's seat, citing turning off the lights and locking up as the excuse.

Adam looked at his watch. It was ten past eight; they were ahead of time.

Anatra drove the van the few hundred yards to the stage, the three of them squeezed into the two front seats. Luca was obviously uncomfortable, his tenseness revealing that he regretted sitting on the handbrake. The aged, rust-spotted shuddering box was running on borrowed time, giving off a blue cloud of unburned diesel as it moved off. It was painstakingly kept on the road by the studio mechanic Alessandro Mosena, Beatrice's father. Success is obviously relative. The more success, the more relatives.

The three-storey windowless block of soundproof concrete painted the ubiquitous Studio Lazio pink was to be their workplace.

There were six men of various heights and sizes by the side door waiting like dockers for a ship to come in. Three were seated on a large, eight-foot-long handcart, dressed for physical work in jeans, black shoes and an array of shirts, pullovers and one black leather jacket. Before the van had come to a stop, they were like a swarm of bees to the back and the side door, twelve tentacles, grabbing the thirteen camera boxes plus all the Grip boxes and loading them onto the handcart before Adam had even realised what was going on. The fully laden cart with its precious cargo was soon disappearing, then gone, into the building, pulled, pushed, enthusiastically shepherded by what was obviously a very well-organised, experienced team.

Adam slid down from his seat and walked round to the back of the truck. It was empty, save for a torn airline luggage label on the mutilated, deeply scored plywood floor.

Anatra saw the astonished look on his face as he proudly closed the rear doors and said, 'I miei Macchinisti, la mia crew.'

Adam was lost for words. If you saw those six somewhat scruffy individuals waiting on a street corner on a dark night, you'd consider walking the other way. But they had just swamped the job. Amazing!

Peter Dublin was on the phone. 'Paddy, me old mate, sorry to call you at home but I need a favour. Need to get hold of a V-16, Series 90 Cadillac, around 1940, in total running order, reasonable nick, any colour but black. If anyone knows where I can find one, you can.'

He listened, nodding as the boss of O'Connor Action Vehicles in Iver Buckinghamshire give him the usual spiel, 'Yeah, can look at that for you…not going to be easy…going to cost you…you'll owe me a big favour', and all of the usual monologue you would expect from someone who operated on the very fringes of legality in the motor trade on the outskirts of London.

Peter ended the call a little impatiently. 'Okay! Okay! Okay, Paddy, I know it's not a Ford Anglia, but will you get back to me, pronto, please? Thanks!' He placed the phone back in its cradle and turned to Gill. 'It's a bloody limited edition, for God's sake, only four hundred and fifty ever made!'

She grimaced, raising her eyebrows. He was not the only one with problems; she was waiting for the estate agent to open so that she could organise a new rental for Dino. Not a good start to the first day of production. They didn't need this!

The hangar-like space of the studio smelt of fresh sawn wood, emulsion paint and dust being cremated by burning hot studio lamps. The space was sparsely lit by a few working lights from high up in the ceiling forty feet above them. There was an audible deadness, not the reverberation of sound that one would expect with any regular building of such a vast size. The eighteen-inch, insulated, soundproof hangar doors on the way in told the full the story. It was a sound stage, covered from floor to ceiling in hessian insulation that entrapped every sound vibration in its dusty fibres. It was unexpectedly cool, a little chilly, but Adam knew it would warm up. The lights would do that.

The set was the interior of a twee Lyon's style 1920s English Tea Room with ten or so square tables with white tablecloths in a double line, each with three wooden hoop, double-hooped-back chairs and a central walkway. The outside wall was missing. Joe Art was just finishing off the set, dressing the last table with its white tablecloth, sugar bowl with tweezers, white china cups and saucers.

It was twenty past eight. The camera boxes were neatly laid out on the floor, guarded by one of Anatra's Macchinisti. The set was a mass of milling people. Adam moved to box one, the camera box. Duke held up his hand, signalling him to stop, and with not a great deal of grace, climbed onto the camera trolley that had now been unloaded, and turned to face the set. He clapped his hands two or three times to get everyone's attention.

'Ragazzi, ragazzi! I have a few words to say before we begin.'

The noise level dropped but not completely; there were little clusters of whispering here and there, mostly from behind the set or somewhere in the anonymous shadows.

'RAGAZZI, SHUT UP! BE QUIET, SILENZIO!'

The studio got the message eventually.

'Ragazzi, I am Duke, the First. A few things: this film is a co-production, business on the set will be conducted in English. For those of you who don't speak English we have arranged for an interpreter. His name is Petros Theophilus. Show yourself, Petros.'

A short, round-headed man in his forties wearing large, black, round-shaped spectacles, which gave him a somewhat owl-like appearance, stepped towards the set to be lit a little better, stuck his hand in the air and waved unenthusiastically.

'Petros speaks nine languages and will translate for you anything that you are unsure or unclear about… Use him; he is one of us.'

Petros's body language inferred that he was not that happy to be the centre of attention. After his initial wave, he put both his hands down at his side and looked absently at the floor, retreating back into his considerable intellect. Duke looked around, staring into the darker corners making sure that the first bit of his speech had got through.

'We will be shooting live sound on set, not guide track, so we will need silence. What's that in Italian, Petros?'

Taken totally by surprise, and dragged back out of his reverie, Petros blinked then, almost with no thought, hooted 'Silenzio', shuffling uncertainly as he did.

Duke paused for a second, hoping that all of this was sinking in. 'Silenzio. We cannot go back to the old ways. We will be shooting live sound. Okay, finally, our Director, Lasse Norstad, would like to say a couple of words.' He gestured to the tall figure standing a few feet to his right next to the camera boxes.

Lasse smiled and nodded as if to convey thanks. He turned towards the set and the majority of the crew, lifting his chin as he did. Precisely in time with his movement, a light from high up in the lighting rig suddenly came on, covering his head and thin, grey-shirted torso in a circular pool of hard yellow light which caused him to blink momentarily. Now he really was the centre of attention.

'Good morning, everybody, good morning.' He had a very slight Norwegian accent, but his voice was loud and crystal clear like an actor on a stage. 'Our film is the story of four lives that begin for us in the 1920s in Sicily and end in the present day. We have to shoot very quickly – we have to average three and a half minutes a day, every day, so we will not have the luxury of time to be self-indulgent. But shooting quickly can cause problems, particularly because we will not be shooting in continuity. Mistakes can happen, sometimes big mistakes.'

A whispering like trickling water started up from behind the scenery, and Duke clapped his hands. The rippling voices petered out and stopped. Lasse nodded and spoke even louder.

'Every day I will tell everyone what we are doing that day, and when it is. When we are shooting 1920s, if anyone sees anything modern in the background like a flash car or a donkey and cart that should not be there, tell Duke, not me… Duke will then look into it. We do not want to make ourselves a laughing stock. We are all a team making this film together. I want it to be a friction-free shoot, a huge box office success. Did you get all of that, Petros?'

Petros was momentarily caught off-guard but quickly replied, 'Yes, of course. Hvert ord!… Every word.'

Lasse smiled. 'You even speak Norwegian?'

Petros nodded. 'Yes, of course, but not Albanian!' Entering into the spirit of the exchange. Petros, the owl, had just proved his credentials.

Lasse wrapped up his speech. 'Thank you, thank you all!'

The light on Lasse clicked off, and the show was over. The chatter in the studio immediately returned to its previous levels, if not a little louder. Lasse smiled to himself, nodded to Sven a few feet to his right, pointing down to the floor foot marks, and gave a thumbs up to acknowledge the lighting effect that he and Enzo had rigged for him. Exactly what was wanted.

Beatrice Mosena stood at the fresh fish counter watching a rubber-aproned woman working alongside her red-faced husband, serving their customers. She had surreptitiously been watching her work for about three minutes. Her gutting was fast, very fast in fact. She was about forty-five, slim with drawn features, greying brownish hair trapped under a blue headscarf. Hardly film star material. She was missing a couple of teeth, and the breasts that had once fed her four children were empty, flaccid on her chest. Not at all like the lady she was meant to be doubling for. But her arms, hands and nails were in good condition and a reasonable match to the photos Beatrice was holding. It must be all the fish oil.

Decision made, Beatrice approached her. She was about to make her day, and give her something to talk about for years to come!

Anatra had helped Adam lift the Arriflex blimp camera onto the heavy-duty O'Connor pan and tilt head firmly bolted to Anatra's Moviola dolly. Luca had with due ceremony handed Adam the first loaded magazine, four hundred feet of Kodak's best. It was now laced up in the camera and ready to go. A new chamois leather eyepiece cover had been fitted to the viewfinder. It was just before eight-thirty, and the show was about to start. Adam had laid down the law the previous week about keeping the camera and lens boxes absolutely spotless: no drinks near them, no food, no standing on them. They were to be kept immaculate. So now in the shadows, they were all being watched over very diligently by Anatra's Chief Macchinista Andrea, he of the black leather jacket and cackling laugh.

There were about nine canvas-backed chairs in a semi-circle on the edges of the light glow from the set. Four of them were filled, and there were many more in the audience, in the studio. Many eyes were watching, their influence and importance diminishing the further away from the set and the further back into the darkness they were. Those in the lit area of the set were the key performers, and everything hung on what they did.

The camera dolly was parked off to one side, literally waiting in the wings for its cue to perform. Two young, grey-coated female stand-ins were sitting like statues opposite each other at the café tables in total silence. They were the focus of attention.

Lasse, Jan and Anatra, in the middle of the café set, were doing what appeared to be a little dance. Lasse was stooping, his right eye glued to his Tewe viewfinder, staring at the two seated figures, making very small steps forwards, back, to the side, back, to the side again, trying to find the optimum position for his opening shot. Jan and Anatra followed every move, all the time keeping about three feet from him. Eventually, Lasse stopped, stood up, then looked down at the setting on his Tewe viewfinder and called out, 'Forty.' Anatra chalked an X on the floor between his feet. Adam reacted immediately, turned to Luca and said, 'Forty'. Luca turned to the senior stagehand, Macchinista Andrea, waiting patiently beside the camera boxes. 'Quaranta,' he whispered.

Within a couple of minutes Adam had fitted the forty lens onto the camera, checked that the front glass of the blimp was spotlessly clean, then allowed Anatra to position the dolly and camera with the lens centred exactly over his chalk mark on the floor. Jan was sitting on his seat on the dolly.

Beatrice Mosena's short figure, chin up, strode confidently across the hard concrete floor, walking straight up to Duke's towering figure.

He smiled at her, pleased that she had got there in time. 'Everything okay?'

'Yes. I found someone, dropped the details into the office.'

'Good! Where is Ben?'

'He's outside chasing up two of the crowd.'

'Right, get him in here, call Belinda and Anita, Fulvio can stay in Make-up. We will be going for rehearsal soon, and we have got to get this place silent. Ben will do red light, door lock. I need both of you behind the set to break up the talkers, okay?'

Beatrice was already turning on her heel before his final words; she knew what a challenge it was going to be to get total pin-drop silence.

Sven came over to the camera and crouched to the same height as the lens. He looked at the selected scene, lifting up his monocle like dark pan glass and checked the lighting contrast of the set.

Adam had set the focus for the scene from his seat on the dolly. Jan took his eye away from the viewfinder. They knew there would be a pause now while the real actors were brought on to run their lines before going for a take.

Jan whispered, 'Easy first shot for you, wide angle. Lasse likes wide lenses, so you will not have to work too hard today.'

Adam was about to reply when a woman dressed in yellow, with shoulder-length brown hair walked up to them. Adam recognised her as one of the spectators from the viewing circle of canvas-backed chairs.

'Hi! Morning! I'm Grace, Grace De Mattais, Continuity.'

Jan smiled a welcome. 'I'm Jan, and this is Adam.'

Grace moved in a little closer in order to make the conversation more intimate. Crouching slightly, she said, 'I have not worked Cinepan before and am not sure what lens gives what view. I know that it's wider than Techniscope, but would it be possible to have a peek through the camera just before a take so that I can get my eye in?'

Jan nodded. 'Yes, of course.'

Grace looked around to check that no one else was privy to their conversation as she stooped a little lower. 'I won't need to do it all of the time, just to get used to what lens gives what view.'

Jan nodded as if to convey that he understood exactly what she was trying to say. His facial expression became more serious. 'The only thing is if you wear eye make-up, it'll come off on the eyepiece, and I could end up looking like a one-eyed Panda.'

Grace's laughter was an explosive splutter. 'I don't wear make-up for work.'

Jan nodded. 'That's fine then!'

Adam leant forward. 'Have you ever had conjunctivitis?'

Grace frowned, taken by surprise by the question. 'No! Not for many years.'

Adam's eyes hardened. 'Well, you will have soon.' He gently tapped the chamois, leather-covered eyepiece. 'Because we've all got it.'

Grace's almond-shaped, hazel brown eyes widened in surprise, trying to read Adam's expression. She turned back to Jan. The same deadpan, serious face, slightly arched eyebrows. She looked back to Adam, still looking at her matter-of-factly. Then suddenly, spontaneously, he burst out laughing and patted her lightly on the back. She looked from one to the other. They were both killing themselves laughing. She had been set up!

'You bastards,' she said, under her breath.

Adam smirked. 'That's the second time I've been called that today! Must be doing something right!'

Jan touched her shoulder, giving it a light rub of reassurance. 'Yes, of course, Grace. You are welcome any time, never a problem. We are all in this together. Any time!'

Grace stood up, trying to retrieve her dented self-esteem. 'So, boys, that's how it's going to be, is it?' she said, smiling.

Jan smirked, his laugh lines creased in a smile. 'Any time, Grace, any time!'

Adam nodded, smiling. 'You're English?'

'Half and half!' She was about to continue, but their attention was drawn to Duke on the set telling the two stand-ins to go as he ushered into their places Belinda and an actress that the call sheet named as Anita.

Behind them, carrying two brown overcoats, came Pia from Wardrobe, her virtually non-existent bosoms making little impression on her loose, yellow T-shirt. She looked straight at Adam, knowing that she would find him next to the camera. That's where he could always be seen; the clapstick ran all the errands.

Their eyes met. She nodded very slightly in greeting, showing no emotion. She had seen him at the party, hiding in his dark corner with his Camera people, but they had not spoken. She had stayed in her little social circle and he in his. When she had come to leave the party, he was gone.

Grace noted the surreptitious interchange but said nothing, just filed it away.

Benito, the Second Assistant Director, led a procession of seven extras onto the set and sat each of them down more or less randomly on the seats at the tables. The café had its customers. Pia moved obsequiously into the shadows and was lost from view.

Grace, noticing that the set was starting to get busy, turned to leave, smiling ruefully. 'Thank you, boys…appreciated!'

Adam watched her not-unattractive backside meander back to her canvas chair where she would resume her set-watching.

Luciano Scordia was an outdoor person. The moment that the spring weather warmed up in April, he was out in his 'square', sitting in the leather seat that was carried out for him every morning and placed next to the vast, fifteen-foot English oak table. As a creature of habit, he was settling down to read the morning papers that had been placed for him in a fanned array next to his coffee, orange juice and croissant. He liked to be well informed on all matters, local, national and international, and the papers were his way of keeping abreast of what was going on in the outside world. He didn't go out much, and when he did, he never left the little piazza by the same exit and never partook of any activity on a regular basis. His life outside had no predictable pattern. He had made many enemies in his seventy-one years, which was why he chose to live the life he did.

The square was entirely enclosed by tall sandstone buildings on all four sides. Back in the fifties, when he had first bought the small, three-sided piazza together with its three large houses, the front had been open to the street. He had built a line of three-storey properties across the front, joining the houses on the right and left, thus sealing off the small piazza from the road. To get into the square now, the only access was through the 'new' fifties' houses or through locked wooden doors backed by a steel plate on the backs of the houses on the other three sides.

Five years ago, the carabinieri had assessed what they would have to do to effect an arrest in what they nicknamed the 'Vaticano Nero'. The research estimated that it would have taken eighty men all moving in simultaneously on four sides. That assault would inevitably be noisy. By the time they would eventually gain access, Luciano and his cohorts and any incriminating paperwork would have scuttled down into the ancient catacombs straddled by the houses. The whole site had been chosen and modified with meticulous care; it was inconspicuous from the road but nevertheless an impregnable fortress. Luciano's family, and some of his staff, none of whom were friends, lived in the buildings. In his small city within a city, he was to all intents and purposes, almost above the law. But he was cunning. No illegal activity could ever be traced back to him, he made sure of that. His close family adored him, his beautiful daughter Sylvania and his son Vinincio.

During the day, he could be found at the table, reading and taking things easy. But at seven-thirty every evening except Sunday, he cleared everyone from the square and conducted his 'business' with his very close 'neighbours' from the courtyard, plus a trickle of invited people who came in through the fifties' houses from the street. That was his time for 'business', and every man, woman, child, dog and cat in the complex knew and observed that.

The early morning light was catching the top of the western building, which acted as a vertical sandstone, ochre-coloured reflector, illuminating the whole area in a warm golden glow. That light would remain fairly constant all day as the buildings tracked the sun through the sky. It was tranquil; the hubbub of the city beyond the walls did not really interfere. The sound of gentle water jetting started up as a tall, long-haired youth in a grey shirt and blue jeans turned on a tap to commence his morning watering of the huge terracotta pots of flowers, ferns and herbs that were scattered around the edges of the ancient cobbled courtyard. Luciano paid him no mind as he sipped his orange juice, nibbled the end of his croissant and picked up the copy of *Variety* magazine that had been flown in from London overnight. As a Film Producer, he needed to keep abreast of the film industry gossip.

From one of the doors over to his right, a tall, voluptuously shaped woman in a tight-fitting, grey suit stepped out into the square, putting down her briefcase so that she had both hands free to pull and lock her front door. As she walked to the centre table, she dropped the key into her glossy, leather, designer shoulder bag.

'Morning, Papa!' she said, leaning forward to kiss him affectionally on his forehead. 'I'm off to the office for the day. Is there anything that you need?'

Luciano looked up. A couple of croissant crumbs were stuck to his chin, which he brushed off with the back of his right hand. 'Sylvania…morning. No, I don't think so. The film is starting today, so this evening I want to discuss how we might increase our interest should things be going well and mitigate our losses should things appear to be going badly. Plus, I hear on the grapevine that Burgio is bringing in some heavies from LA and that he is moving out of Luigi's villa. We need to know where he is moving to so that we can keep an eye on him. I also hear he has instructed Dublin to get him a Cadillac, the jumped-up little prick!'

Sylvania listened in silence. She was used to her father's expletives. She nodded in agreement, bringing her left hand across her body to help with the weight of her briefcase full of documents. She smiled as she looked around, checking that they were not being overheard.

'We can look at various options regarding the film. The contracts are well-worded, tight, but, we believe, as far as we can gather, that Luigi is at the limit of his budget and maybe can't borrow any more. The Yanks will not commit another dollar, so there may well be opportunities if he starts to run over, *for whatever reason.*'

Luciano smiled, revealing a gold, diamond-studded front tooth. He understood exactly where she was coming from. 'Three and a half minutes a day, not easy to achieve, even with Duke driving it!' He nodded repeatedly. 'Okay. Okay, Talk tonight at seven-thirty… Have a good day.'

'You too. Try to spend a little time in the gym, if you can.'

Luciano nodded. She said the same thing every day, but he hated exercise, his obesity bearing witness to the fact. He watched her swinging gait, as her high heels navigated the ancient cobbles on her way out to the front entranceway that would be dutifully opened up for her.

He was more than proud of his daughter, thirty-five years of age, a legal degree with honours, a mind like quicksilver and the ability to put the family business before everything else. She more than made up for her useless brother. He was such a disappointment. It was hard to believe that he had sired him.

Luigi twisted the brass key, letting himself into his office next to Production. He flicked on the fluorescent lights that spluttered and glowed into life. The room was the same size as the one next door, but there the similarity ended. The walls were papered in a dark red and gold flock wallpaper that did not reflect the light. The red buttoned, leather, high-backed chairs around the large circular table matched the wallpaper. There was a large, softly murmuring fridge next to a long sideboard that had a collection of various bottles of alcohol that catered for most tastes. Inverted clean drinking glasses sheltered under a white dust cloth. The shutters on the far window were closed, but thin shafts of bright light shimmered and trickled, wriggling their way through the nearly closed slats. His desk had a green in tray on the right, and a red one on the left, both containing a few sheets of paper.

The handset cables on the two phones on either side of his red leather blotter were twisted; he did not have any compulsion for tidiness as his housekeeper Nella would heartily endorse. She had been given the day off, and riding boots in hand and jodhpurs on, she was on her way to her friend who owned a stable and livery yard up in the hills, about twenty minutes away.

There was a knock at the door. After a few seconds, it opened a few respectful inches. It was Peter Dublin.

'Luigi, you in? Can I have a moment?'

Luigi placed his case on the nearest chair. 'Yes, come in, come in.'

The Production Manager firmly closed the door and lowered his voice, adding an air of conspiracy to the conversation. 'I've been looking into the Cadillac, hoping to get an answer this morning, but it's going to be a lot of money and will really dig into our cash flow.'

Luigi, realising that the conversation was not going to be a short one, pulled out a chair and sat down, gesturing for Dublin to do the same. Somewhat irritated, he said, 'I know, I know. Moving out of the villa, wanting his own place is not helping either.' He paused.

Dublin looked at him enquiringly. 'Do you think he's doing it deliberately, trying to stretch our budget?'

Luigi pursed his lips then shook his head. 'I have no idea what his plan is, but he's certainly up to something. Look, when you've got something concrete, car wise, we'll talk. Later today, you say?'

'Hope so, should be!'

Luigi looked down at his watch. 'Right, okay. Now, I've got a press call this morning with Isabella and Veronique. Tomorrow, my usual Tuesday, I'm going to the Casa Annunciata at twelve, and most likely Isabella will come as well. Veronique thinks that it's a good photo opportunity, but I'm not sure. Kids in wheelchairs, is that good publicity?'

Dublin smiled, his left hand flicking his long-permed hair back behind his ear. 'You are well known for your charity work. The kids will be over the moon to meet Isabella, and if she wears a low-cut dress and is photographed leaning over a kid in a wheelchair, you'll hit the front pages!'

Luigi's nostrils flared momentarily in indignation. 'I find that a bit cynical, Peter.'

Dublin leant forward. 'Cynical maybe, but the reality of the business that we work in is that any publicity is good publicity,' he said, nodding to reinforce his point.

Luigi looked away to the slivers of light squeezing through the dust-covered slats as though trying to distance himself from the realities of the conversation. 'Yeah! Okay! We'll see how Isabella feels about it, and I'll speak to the home. Thanks.'

Dublin rose, easing his chair compulsively back to exactly where it had been when he first came in. 'You know, Luigi, I sometimes wonder if you are too nice for this business.'

Luigi stared up at his condescending face. 'You may well be right, Peter, but don't ever mistake my kindness as a sign of weakness. I can be a complete and utter bastard if I have to be.'

Dublin nodded, a bit taken aback by the way the conversation had turned. Nervous, he unconsciously flicked his hair back behind his ear. 'Okay. I'll get going and be in touch when I've got news. Thanks.'

Luigi simply nodded and looked back to the shutters as a chugging lorry slowly drove past, momentarily casting a dark shadow that blocked out the shimmering light.

The set had settled down to a rhythm. The first four set-ups had gone well, apart from the fact that the Assistant Directors had a lot of trouble getting the set quiet and keeping it quiet. The Sound man, Carl, threw a tantrum a couple of times in frustration. Eventually, Duke stopped everything, and in a very loud voice, read everyone the riot act, saying that if they needed to talk, then not to do it during a take, and if they didn't need to speak, then shut up! In the end, he cleared the set of everyone but the shooting crew, which helped, but it didn't completely cure the problem.

Belinda had smiled sweetly at Adam every time that he had run his tape out to her eye. But she was an actress; you can never tell what they are thinking. Anita, playing her sister, was a continual gossip, never stopped talking, and Adam noticed that both of them vied with each other to get a word in edgeways. It seemed they had a lot of catching up to do.

Lasse had a lovely way of working, directing the actresses by using their first name followed by the name of the role that they were playing, a technique that Adam had never witnessed before.

Jan and Lasse had always got on really well; they were definitely on each other's wavelength. Adam found Jan to be a very experienced cam op, very decisive, knowing immediately after a take exactly what could be done to improve it, or if he was happy he immediately said so. Lasse had insisted on having him on the crew, bringing both him and Sven over from Norway. It was obvious they all had mutual respect for each other, which made working together a much richer experience.

Just before each take, Grace had come up and looked through the camera. Jan and Adam always remained on their seats, just swinging slightly to one side to allow her to access the all-important, chamois-covered eyepiece. She always came slowly, deliberately between them, supporting herself with a hand on Jan's left shoulder and Adam's right. Never there longer than a few seconds, just long enough to see the left, right, top and bottom of the frame and record it in her mind. She seemed to be a very tactile person, putting hands on shoulders, so naturally, touching was second nature to her.

Adam enjoyed her visits; he liked the feel of her hand, which once placed never moved, warm, reassuring. The very scent of her, the touch of her stirred something in him, something he couldn't quite put his finger on. Whatever it was, the memory was very faint.

Belinda had been made up to look like a twenty-year-old, as had Anita. Adam was in awe of the Make-up department; how these people transformed someone quite plain and pale into the various characters never failed to amaze him.

Jan's thoughts, though, were elsewhere. 'Oh my God! A two-beer girl,' he said, staring at Sophia in Make-up as she did her final checks, gently brushing a dusting of face powder onto Anita's nose.

Adam hadn't a clue what he was mumbling about. 'What's a two-beer girl?'

But before Jan could explain, Duke called, 'GOING FOR A TAKE. SILENZIO!' which was echoed behind the set by the Assistants Ben and Beatrice. The latter had a voice that could shatter glass a kilometre away. She may be young and petite, but she knew how to belt it out.

A loud bell rang over by the main entrance doors, and two-foot-high, red-lit signs denoting 'Silenzio' lit up either side of the main doors. They were now in lockdown, and the set was starting to get the message.

At the end of the take, Adam gave Grace the focal length of the lens, the distance, the lens aperture stops and the fact that Sven had decided not to use any filters.

Five takes, number two as a 'hold', four and five as the prints. Adam's gate checks were clear. As he closed the silver clip up on the camera blimp door, he could see that Jan was slightly flushed, buzzing.

'So, what's this two-beer girl business?' he asked again.

Jan looked at him with a smile, clearly animated. 'It's a scoring system for women, how many beers you need to fancy them!'

Adam shook his head. 'I don't understand, Jan.'

Jan made a drinking motion with his right hand. 'When you drink, the more you drink, the more beautiful the women in the bar become. So after ten beers, even a really ugly girl is beautiful, because drink makes your standards lower… Get it? So, a one-beer girl is so beautiful that you fancy her only after one beer… Get it?'

Adam struggled to understand the Norwegian analysis of female pulchritude. Jan just stared at him, smiling, waiting for the penny to drop. Adam nodded, running the information through in his head. Eventually, it sank in and he burst out laughing.

'Got it, got it. Got it!'

Jan flicked his eyebrows up and down in delight.

'So who's the two-beer girl then, Jan?'

'The Make-up girl, with the coloured earrings, don't know her name… Got a call sheet?'

Adam reached down to his green canvas bucket diddy bag. He pulled out the call sheet and scanned down the photocopied page. 'Her name is Sophia Mandini,' he said, handing Jan the sheet. 'She's the senior Make-up supervisor and a lesbian.'

Jan scanned the sheet then looked up, perplexed. 'Lesbian? How do you know that?' he said, frowning, facially overacting the fact that all his hopes and dreams were now in tatters.

Adam smiled. There was that smirk again.

'Bastard!' Jan said, instantly relieved.

Third one today, thought Adam. 'She is wearing a ring, though!' Adam tapped the third finger of his left hand.

Jan looked deflated. 'Oh! Never noticed that. Need to find out if she's married.'

Adam fluttered his eyebrows. 'Really? You've really got the hots for her?'

Jan smirked. 'Ahh! Let's wait and see. She may be a lesbian after all!'

Adam leant forward. 'I've had a brainwave… Duke'll know.'

Jan held up his hand. 'What? You must be joking!'

Adam decided to offer more information. 'She wasn't with anyone at the party, just a couple of dolly mates, but she left before you arrived, got dragged away by a huge guy in a raincoat.'

Jan was now nodding and frowning, emotionally confused, when suddenly the woman of his dreams appeared beside him.

'Excuse me, can I introduce myself? I'm Sophia.'

Jan gulped like an animated cartoon rabbit, flushed and flustered. 'Errr! Jan! And this is Adam.'

If Sophia noticed his reaction, she gave nothing away.

'I don't need to look through. I hear you've all got conjunctivitis anyway, but Anita has a wig, and we're on to her close-ups after lunch, so I just wanted to ask you to check before you roll that there isn't any lace showing.'

'I always check anyway! But sometimes, sometimes the light can catch them, and it shows on camera,' Jan said hurriedly, eager to please. He rambled on, 'No problem, Sophia, no problem, I'll keep an eye out for you.'

'Thank you, Jan, you are very kind. I always come to camera side, before we run. But four eyes are always better than two. Thank you.'

Adam leant forward. 'I'll keep an eye out for you as well, Sophia.'

'Thank you, Adam,' she said, beaming, the laugh line around her eyes creasing as she added, 'I hope your eye gets better…darlin'!' She looked him deadpan in the eye and then giggled, a mischievous smile revealing her small white teeth.

Jan was transfixed, just grinning from ear to ear. Adam was taken aback at her cockney accent. Belinda had obviously turned into a dialogue coach while she was in Make-up. They both watched her walk away with very different thoughts. Jan's were more to do with procreation; Adam's more to do with the fact that this studio seemed to run on gossip, which meant that everyone but everyone already knew about his encounter with Pia, the Durex, the Easter egg and the libidinous Jose. Oh shit!

Adam looked at his watch. The morning had flown past, and the set was now winding down. Before the set was cleared,

Grace was going through the ceremony of the polaroids, taking one of each artist sitting at their table, a couple of the whole set, and the positions of all of the extras. She finished with a standing shot of Belinda and Anita for Wardrobe. There was a pause after each photo while she waited for the camera to give birth to its embryonic image.

She checked each print and waving the last one backwards and forwards to assist its drying, eventually walked back to her chair, nodding to Duke that she was finished. It was obvious that she and Duke had worked together many times before because their work processes were by now reduced to very subtle nods, with nothing extra to be said.

Enzo had set up a small Inky Dink working light on a stand behind Grace to light up her little workspace of the camping table and the portable typewriter. She was the only one with such a light, but it was customary to look after the continuity girl.

Duke looked around, visually checking with a thumbs up the other key players, Lasse, Sven, Carl Sound, before thanking everyone for a really good morning and calling lunch until two prompt.

The set started to empty. Grace, polaroids spread out on her table, was typing up her notes with clattering efficiency. Beatrice and Ben moved into a huddle with Duke for a debrief. Adam looked round to the camera boxes. Macchinista Andrea had got hold of a huge chicken feather duster from somewhere and was doing a mime show of a maid dusting the camera boxes, a flick here, a flick there, a further flick for effect. He was bent double, miming the serious effort that any ancient servant would have recognised. Adam, Luca and Anatra were spellbound; it was hilarious. Every now and then, Andrea looked at Adam, nodding as if to ask, is this okay? Am I being thorough enough? Adam realised his demand for spotless camera boxes was being sent up, mischievously, yes, but hilariously as well. Andrea obviously had a great sense of humour.

Adam, still laughing, turned to Luca, and said, 'Camera cover, please.' Then, turning to Anatra, instructed, 'Drop the arm, please. Check the lock off.'

Anatra twisted the small handle on the back of the dolly, and the camera gently eased down on its arm to its lowest point. He checked the flip lock on the head, giving it a little tug to confirm that it was firm.

Adam turned to Andrea. 'The camera cover sheet.'

He responded quickly, striding confidently past Anatra and handing it respectfully with two hands to Adam, as he said, 'You go lunch, me stay here with camera!' Pointing his dirty-nailed fingers from his right eye to the camera and the camera boxes, he signalled he would watch over all of the equipment until Adam got back.

Adam was impressed. He was being very well looked after by these Macchinisti, piss-taking mime artists or not. They may be the poorest paid on the set, but they were very professional.

Jan, Lasse and Sven were in deep Nordic conversation in the shadows on the far side of the set, presumably, like Duke with his two Assistants, reviewing the first morning's work.

Pia stood alone with her thoughts, far back in the shadows, intently watching Adam for a couple of minutes. She picked up her shoulder bag and headed out through the large thick studio doors now being watched over by the gum-chewing security guard lounging in his canvas-backed chair.

Duke noticed Ben had forgotten to turn off the large red 'Silenzio' light, and made a mental note.

Luigi studied the proposed press handout that Veronique had handed him as soon as she had casually plonked her brown, stitched hide shoulder bag on the table. She was, as usual, straight to the drinks sideboard, helping herself to a mid-morning brandy. She stood very upright; four years at the Sorbonne did that to a girl.

She had known Luigi for years and regarded him as an equal, totally unwilling to comprehend the fact that he paid her wages, not the other way around.

Luigi put the press handout on the table. 'Isabella will be here in a minute. Who's the journalist?'

'It's Max, from *Cinema Nuovo*. Bi-monthly. He's been around for years.' She had a deep, earthy voice floating on a caricatured French accent that would have seduced a monk. 'They're a bit left-wing but fairly harmless.'

Luigi nodded, tapping the typewritten sheet. 'This release only tells about the first third of the story. You happy about that?'

She took a sip of brandy, savouring the experience as if it were the first of the day. 'It's more about Isabella not giving away the plotline. You know what actors are like: once they start talking, they can't bloody well stop. Before you know it, they have given away the whole bloody plot, and no one wants to see the film.' She took another sip. 'Next month we'll tell him a little more. You are restricting script release, aren't you?'

Luigi grimaced. 'Yes, of course, I am!' he said, waving his right hand as if to convey he was not a total idiot. She really was a character, this Veronique, fifty-ish and well preserved. The Almighty had not been very kind when he put her together. She had a slightly bulbous nose, ears that stuck out and a somewhat lopsided mouth. But there was something about her, the way she held herself, the rumpled jacket. The casual voluminous blue silk scarf, the art deco brooch, the culottes that flapped as she walked, and her light musky perfume, all giving off a very strong sensual presence. It was doubtful that any man lucky enough to spend a weekend with her would remember it with a grin for the rest of his life.

There was a gentle tap at the door. Isabella's smiling face slowly came into view. 'Permesso? Permesso?'

Luigi pulled on the side of the table to ease himself up. Veronique stepped back, knowing that Luigi and Isabella would be pleased to be in each other's company again. Their eye contact and the warmth of their embrace confirmed this. Veronique used the distraction as an opportunity to pour herself another brandy.

Peter Dublin was staring at about eighteen inches of printed fax paper. He half looked over his shoulder at Gill. 'They've found one. It's in bloody Toulouse! Luigi has got to approve this. I can't sign this off. It's bloody ridiculous!'

Gill looked up. 'Be grateful it's so near, could have been in London or Dublin! Hah!'

Dublin smiled ruefully, accepting her play with his surname. 'Give Luigi a call. See if he's available.'

Gill reached for the phone, dialling the two-digit number.

Dublin picked up his sunglasses from the desk and patted his back pocket to check his wallet. Turning, he stared at Gill's unmoving, hunched listening figure.

'There's no reply!' She looked at her watch. 'He's probably in the canteen by now. He's got a press call, and he always likes to provide lunch. Isabella may be there as well.'

Dublin walked over to the large mirror beside the door, checking his appearance, ruffling his hair around his ears.

'I'll go to lunch now then. Back in a few, okay?'

Gill nodded. She was used to having late, short lunch breaks.

Adam knew that lunch in the canteen of any studio is always enjoyable. You see people from different productions all gathered together to eat in the middle of the day: Production staff, Editors, Make-up, Wardrobe, all of the trades. Plus, of course, actors and crowd artists, all in a wide variety of different costumes, many with bibs to protect their fronts, issued by the Wardrobe department. Some had their theatrical wigs removed for comfort for that precious forty-five minutes but looked very 'clipped' with their hair pinned up and back. Then there were always the child actors and extras, with their chaperones trying to keep the precocious little monsters in order.

The Studio Lazio canteen comprised two sections: one carpeted closed-off area with waiter service that was frequented mainly by management, and the larger, main self-service area where the vast majority sat down randomly at any one of the fifty or so tables. The air smelt of boiled vegetables and coffee, and it was very noisy. The big floor-to-ceiling windows and white tiled floor reflected the sound of scraping seats and animated chatter.

Adam decided that he liked Italian food as he selected Prosciutto, melon, a ciabatta roll and butter, a Coke, and he was off, wooden tray in hand, looking for a spare seat anywhere. It was absolutely heaving; they had broken late, and there was virtually nowhere to sit. He decided to wander back outside and sit on one of the long, sparsely populated benches that were backed up to the low wall of the raised flower bed.

He balanced his tray on his knees, not very romantic, but this was the way of it. He was used to eating alone being the only Englishman on the job, apart from Peter Dublin. No circle of local friends, no socialising after work. Everyone scatters to their houses and flats, and there you are, Adam, a pocket full of dollars and no one to spend it with. Which is why he was surprised to see a cream envelope tucked in the top of his canvas ditty bag when he returned ten minutes early to make sure that the camera was ready for two.

He was the first one back apart from a couple of electricians who were changing a large lamp bulb on one of 2ks on a heavy-duty, high lift stand on the far edge of the set.

He picked up the envelope and cautiously sniffed it – nothing discernible. It was thin, sealed, with his name 'ADAM KIRBY FOCUS' written in copperplate. Probably Production Office, tomorrow's call sheet maybe? Bit early for that, though, he thought. He tore it open and drew out a single page folded in half. He unfolded it, hand a little damp, with anticipation.

I will come to your hotel room. 9 tonight.

There was no signature. Adam looked around. People were starting to come back onto the set. Duke's voice could be heard issuing instructions to Ben and Beatrice, and Jan appeared from the shadows, chatting to Sven. Adam stuffed the paper as deep into his jeans hip pocket as he could. He undid the rubber bungee strap holding the dust sheet on the camera. Andrea was nowhere to be seen and neither was Luca. So much for keeping an eye on the camera gear!

Grace appeared immediately, sitting down at her typewriter, carefully rolling in four sheets of paper sandwiched by three black carbon papers in preparation for the details of the next shot. She didn't look up.

Sven came over, smiling as he always did. He was rubbing his monocle pan glass with a handkerchief, something he did a lot. Perhaps it was a form of worry bead. Maybe he was not as cool and calm as he would like people to think.

'Adam, when we do Anita's close-up will you remind me to look at a number one diffuser, please? She may need a little softening, just a little.'

'Yes, of course. Anything else?'

'No, that's all, thank you,' he said, with a smile as he turned towards the set where Lasse was in deep conversation with Jan.

There was a clacking noise from the dolly as Anatra pushed and pulled the handle that pumped up the air pressure in the reservoir. He had magically appeared from nowhere and was keen to make sure that his presence was noted. Luca appeared, carrying his report sheets and a magazine case, which he placed with the camera boxes. Adam walked a couple of paces towards him.

'Where's Andrea? I thought he was keeping an eye on the equipment.'

'Son had an accident at school, had to go, cut head,' he explained, grimacing in pain and wiping his left-hand fingers across his head as if he was trying to create a parting.

Adam nodded. 'Okay! Okay! Thanks.'

'Adam, a seventy-five, please.' Jan's voice floated over from the set, cutting through the hubbub. Adam had already tuned his ears to listen out for Jan's and Sven's voices, and waved to let him know that he had heard.

'On its way!' he said, slightly shouting.

Grace did not look up. She heard everything, saw everything, missed nothing, made a note about the seventy-five-millimetre lens. It could change, but it was unlikely with this crew. They seemed to know what they were doing.

Beatrice was bringing on Anita and Belinda, and the rhythm cycle of the set had begun again, at three minutes past two. Ben was a few paces behind with the extras.

Peter Dublin strode back into his office. Gill turned and smiled at him as he entered. His nostrils flared momentarily as he looked from left to right. She had closed the shutters and put on the fluorescents. He strode petulantly past her, straight to the back wall, around his desk and yanked open the shutters with as much energy as he could muster. They crashed back against the wall with a deafening double clack that reverberated around the room. Gill jumped and winced from the extreme assault on her eardrums as the sheet over the windows suddenly turned bright white as light flooded into the room, catching the refugee columns of now homeless dust fleeing and falling from the ancient slatted woodwork.

'I'm sorry, Peter, that may well work for you, but it's not so good for me. You were out so—'

'Fine! Fine! Whatever! What news on the house?'

Gill was shaken, hesitant, unsure. 'Errh! Donna…the agency only have one short-term. The owner recently died, it's part-furnished, just north of Parioli.'

'Have you seen it?' he barked, tapping his foot, agitatedly licking his bottom lip.

'No, Peter, I've been stuck here…but I can go up this afternoon. If you're going to be around.'

'Okay, okay. Luigi has gone for the car. Where's Dino?'

'He's in the city at a meeting.'

'In town? What the hell's he doing holding a meeting? He doesn't know anyone. He's only been here ten days!' His lips became even thinner with frustration.

'I don't know, Peter. He doesn't tell me anything. I'm just the secretary!'

'Well, I can't go ahead with the car unless Dino says he wants it. Then we've got to organise getting it here and getting Mosena to check it over.'

'Could we send one of the drivers?'

'What! None of them own a passport. They barely earn a bloody living. Do you honestly think they can afford holidays abroad? Most of them have never left Rome,' he said, shaking his head. 'Shit! Leave it with me. Leave it to me. You go and see this house. If it's any good, get Dino to view it. Then get the Art department to dress it. Keep all the bills separate from Production. I'll try to get him to pay a contribution.'

'Good luck with that. Any point in asking Veronique? She's French. She may have a nephew or something?'

'You have no bloody idea, have you, Gill? No bloody idea at all. She's from Paris, Toulouse… Toulouse is the opposite end of the bloody country. Like London and err, Aberdeen!'

Gill stood up and turned away to try to defuse the situation. She picked up her shoulder bag from the floor. 'Fine! Just trying to help. I'm off. Be back as soon as I can.'

'Cretin,' he said, under his breath.

She heard the insult, saw the contempt in his eyes. She moved quickly, grabbed her handbag, almost lunged at the clothes stand to grab her lightweight coat and left the room as quickly as she could. The door clicked closed like an exclamation mark behind her.

The corridor was cool, quiet; everyone was on set. She took a couple of paces, stopped and drew a deep breath, trying to get her heart rate down. Deep breaths, that's the way to do it.

'Whoo! What an arsehole!' she muttered.

The click-clack of footsteps focused her attention on Jose walking from the entranceway towards her. Damn!

Jose was, as usual, all smiles as he greeted her. 'Gill, my dear. How are you?'

'Fine, thanks, Jose. Just off to—'

'You don't look fine, my dear. Are you okay?'

She was almost in tears. She bit her lip, trying hard to hold them back.

'I'm fine… Fine… I must…'

'Gill, look at me. Tell me what's happened.'

'No, it's nothing.'

'Nothing. You are shaking, woman, close to tears, that's not nothing.'

'I'm fine, Jose, I'm fine,' she repeated, lifting her shoulder bag onto her shoulder, then digging her nails into her palm as hard as she could to take her mind off it all.

Jose looked around to see who else might be a witness, but they were alone. 'Gill, this is not right. Who has upset you? Peter?'

'No, I'm fine… I must be going… I'm fine. Thank you.' As she grimaced and tried to move past him, Jose stopped her, firmly placing his hand under her left elbow.

'Okay, Gill, but if Luigi saw you this upset, he would want to know why, and I want to know why.'

'I'm fine, honestly! Thanks, Jose. It was just one of those silly things, you know.'

Jose's eyes went very hard, something that she had never seen before in 'Mister Charming'.

'If he is upsetting you, Gill, he needs to be very careful. Here in Italy, we treat our women with respect, and from what I have seen, you are not well treated.'

Footsteps from the entranceway heralded the arrival of a broad-shouldered, slim-waisted man with a crew cut, who gave them no more than a passing glance as he turned down the corridor towards the Wardrobe department.

Jose took hold of both her hands and squeezed them tight. 'Lift your chin, Gill, lift your chin. People notice a low chin but never a high one. Lift your chin, my darling. I have to go. He is for me!' he said, nodding towards the retreating figure with a sideways nod of his head. He gave her fingers an extra hard squeeze of reassurance then slowly let go, smiling. 'Lift your chin, my darling.'

'Thank you, Jose. Thank you.'

As he turned and walked quickly after his visitor, Gill momentarily paused, took a deep breath and straightened herself up. Then taking her sunglasses out of her bag, she placed them firmly on the bridge of her nose and followed him down the corridor and out into the bright sunlight.

Adam was kept busy all afternoon with little time to guess who would 'come to his room at nine' between set-ups. His mind wandered, though, as it was the only time he had to think about it. It was like a soap opera coming to him in instalments, three minutes here, two minutes there, thirty seconds. He had the sort of job that required a lot of concentration, and wandering minds led to mistakes. Adam Kirby could not afford to make mistakes.

He hardly knew anyone in Rome. Solveig, Sven's wife, would be his first choice. Blond hair, blue eyes, very mature. Maybe she and Sven were swingers. He laughed at the thought.

He had wandered casually over to Grace's desk when she had nipped out for a coffee to check her handwriting to see if it was copperplate, but all her notes were in squiggly shorthand, which looked like Chinese to him. She had hazel eyes and was quite a bit older than him. He wasn't into dark eyes, preferring the archetypal Scandinavian Solveig look. Lovely cool hands though. He liked her touch on his shoulder when she checked through the camera, nice long fingers as well. She had an aura about her, plus something that stirred a faint memory in him that he could still not get his head around.

He hadn't mentioned anything to Jan because he didn't know him that well yet and was unsure if he could keep stuff like that to himself. At that thought, alarm bells starting ringing. It could be Jose! Oh, shit! 'Ciao, bello', still rang in his ears. That could be very awkward. His experience of Wardrobe boys back home was that they all had a great sense of humour, were always fun to be with and were invariably quite loud. But they made terrific loyal, caring friends. Nonetheless, did he really want a one-to-one with Jose? No, not really.

Beatrice was a significant presence on set, very loud, not very tall, but a lovely figure that she kept well hidden under her leather jacket. She was still very young though, and he was not into young women – jailbait. The glass-shattering, high soprano shout was the ultimate turn-off.

Anita and Belinda, the actresses, now that would be an experience, an Adam sandwich! That was really quite an arousing thought, a very arousing thought, although demand would soon outstrip supply. What a way to go, though. But he was not that lucky.

The thing that was really nagging him was who would know what hotel and what room he was in. The only person he could think of was Gill in the office, and Duke, because Duke knew everything about everything. Gill from the office, she was in love with her policeman husband, she had said so in so many words on the first day he met her. He thought back to that day when Peter Dublin had finished with him and handed him over to his secretary.

'Right, Gill, take our friend down to Tomassino and get some money in his pocket. When he's ready, get Toni or one of the others to take him to his hotel.'

Peter rose to his feet and leant forward to shake hands, but it was merely a touch of the palms, nothing more. Peter's attention had already turned back to his coffee.

Adam turned towards Gill as she got up from behind her desk and ushered him with an exaggerated bowing gesture towards the door, offering in some gentle way an apology for the grilling that he had just experienced. In the corridor Adam looked down at his suitcase and stooped slightly to pick it up.

Gill paused for a second. 'You never been to Italy before?'

'No. Mainly work in England or around London, Carnaby Street, the swinging West End, but I know the cameraman, Sven Lungren, met him last summer, took some Cinepan gear over to Norway to demonstrate it. He was shooting some concentration camp scenes, amazing guy, minimal use of light, a real gentleman!'

'They all are, these Scandinavians. The Director, Lasse, is a dream of a guy.'

As Gill said the words 'dream of a guy,' he suddenly identified her accent: Australian.

'You're Australian?'

She smiled coyly. 'Yes, many years ago!'

'How come you're married to a policeman?'

Gill stopped. She was obviously keen to build bridges. 'Oh, you know, eighteen years ago doing the world tour as we all do... I was jaywalking across the road in Via Veneto, and this young policeman stopped me and tried to fine me, as they do!'

Adam put down his case outside the door labelled 'Luigi Mussomelli, Producer', and adjusted his stance to face her directly, as she obviously had a tale to tell.

She was about mid-forties, he guessed, with high cheekbones and the most amazing bright green eyes that danced as they looked into his face. But she was animated now, happy to be speaking in her mother tongue.

'It was love at first sight. I met him later when he came off duty at the same place where I jaywalked, and we have not been apart since. We have two sons. I'm now a Roman Catholic. Oh, and we also have a cat!'

'Wow! What a lovely story.'

'That's how you learn Italian, Adam, fall in love. It's the easiest way!' She laughed. Her eyes told the whole story. She was still in love with the policeman.

The chatter and footsteps of a group of four people entering the building to the right became the full stop that ended her reminiscence, as their chatter and clatter reverberated off the hard concrete walls.

Through one of the many square windows overlooking the car park, Adam could see Toni, the driver, standing beside a black Mercedes, talking to another black-suited driver as he dusted the bonnet and windscreen in the bright sunlight. Got to keep them clean, boys! thought Adam. A few more paces and they arrived outside a door marked 'Contabile, Tomassino Molveno'.

Gill paused and pointed to the sign. 'This word means accountant and is probably the most important word that you will learn today,' she said, smiling and stooping slightly as she knocked on the door and opened it a few inches. 'Permesso?'

'Si! Si! Si!' came the enthusiastic response from within.

Gill opened the door to reveal a similar-sized room to the Production Office, but the shutters to the large rear window were closed, and the lighting was the usual hanging fluorescents, giving a much more even light.

But it was a bank! Adam was totally taken aback. There was a long counter with four serving positions and steel bars from the countertop to the ceiling. It was a bank, no doubt about it.

Behind the bars was one of the happiest-looking faces that Adam had seen all day, apart from maybe Toni the driver.

'Tomassino, this is Adam Kirby, our Focus Puller. Is it convenient to draw some expenses for him?'

'Si! Si! Certo, of course!' Even more smiles in welcome. 'I have your paperwork here, just a moment.'

His accent was very slight, but with an American twang, something that Adam would notice more and more during his stay; the influence in Italy of the American film industry.

On the other side of the bars there was an office area with half a dozen desks, most of them littered with papers and files. Two female bookkeepers were intently adding up figures on adding machines and did not look up lest it ruined their concentration. Tomassino headed for the furthest desk, towards a number of box files.

Adam turned to Gill. 'I came away in a bit of a hurry, as you know, because of Barry, and I don't have a lot of clean washing. How do I get that—'

Gill swiftly interrupted, sensing his embarrassment. 'No problem, Adam, we can do that here for you otherwise it'll cost a fortune if you ask the hotel to do it. I will get Pia, our Wardrobe Assistant, to come and sort you out. When you are finished just go outside and Toni will take you to your hotel. It's all paid for. We'll see you tomorrow morning. Toni will pick you up at eight. We can do your washing now because production has not yet started, but you will have to make your own arrangements for next week as we will be too busy.'

Tomassino was returning to the well-worn counter at position three. He was beaming all over his face. Adam had never met an accountant who enjoyed giving money away, but this one obviously did. Gill tapped him gently on the shoulder.

'I'm off now, but I'll get Pia for you. If you need anything, I am in the office.' Her green eyes still sparkled and bounced. She liked Adam for some reason, and her body language said so. Little wonder she had captured a policeman's heart when she was younger. With a final smile, she moved quickly towards the door, her business with him now finished.

Adam was in her debt, and he knew it. He half turned as her hand reached for the door handle. 'Thanks, Gill, you've been great!'

With a smile, she was gone.

Tomassino's left hand was full of money, and in his right hand, he had a form for Adam to sign. He was not going to part with any of his lira without a signature.

'This is up to the 19th, Saturday. After that, you come here, and I give you more... good, eh?'

Adam had never seen a set-up like this before. He still couldn't get over the worn counters and the bars and was trying to work it out in his mind when it suddenly dawned on him. It was all about paying large numbers of extras when they had crowd scenes.

Tomassino was quickly counting out the money. 'We do twenty-eight dollars a day for ten days, 600 lire to the dollar. I give you one hundred and sixty-eight thousand lire, Adam... Va bene?'

Adam was amazed to see so much paper money coming his way. It felt like Christmas. 'Great. Thank you very much!'

'You sign here.' Tomassino was smiling even more as he saw the pleasure on Adam's face. He pushed the receipt form under the metal bar, placing a biro on it as he did.

Adam gave the form a cursory glance. It seemed to tally up with what Tomassino had said. This guy was a pro. He knew what he was doing. Adam signed the form and eased it back under the bar, and Tomassino pushed through the handful of money.

'You count it!'

'I trust you, Tomassino. You do this for a living.'

'Thank you, Adam.' He beamed even more at the compliment and was about to continue when the main door to the corridor clicked, opening slightly.

A soft female voice asked, 'Permesso?'

Tomassino nodded, answering, 'Si, si,' to a young, short, dark-haired, elfin-figured woman of about twenty, wearing a yellow woollen pullover buttoned up the front and faded blue jeans, who now came into the room.

'I look for Adam? I am Pia. Wardrobe?'

Tomassino looked a little puzzled.

Adam turned around. 'Yes. I'm Adam.'

Pia stepped into the room. 'You have washing, yes?'

'I have, but…' Adam turned back to Tomassino, who by now had grasped what was going on.

'Just a second, Pia, we nearly finished.' To Adam, he said, 'Adam, this is a lot of money. You be careful. There are pickpockets and ladri in the city. Keep your money safe, different pockets, yeah?'

Adam took the money and eased it as deeply as he could into the back pocket of his jeans. He had no idea what ladri were, but they sounded dodgy. He offered his hand through the bars to Tomassino in thanks. Tomassino's face lit up as he shook his hand. It was unusual for the English to shake hands; they were usually more standoffish. Maybe he had had too many dealings with Peter Dublin.

'You be careful, Adam. A lot of money... thieves, yeah?'

Adam understood and nodded a couple of times to let the accountant know that he had got the message. Thanking him with another nod, he picked up his briefcase and suitcase and turned to face Pia, who was holding the door open. They walked out into the corridor, and Pia indicated to turn to the left, pausing for him to come alongside her. She turned her face to him. Her hair was a work of art, glossy, light brown, silky smooth, very fine and cut in a 1930s bob cut, flapper style, down over her left eye, no make-up except for a bit of mascara. When she spoke, she revealed perfect white teeth. Her large, enquiring brown eyes were very gentle, very dark, almost black.

'You 'ave some washing. Lavandaria, yes?'

Adam was a million miles away until a nudge from Jan brought him back to the present moment.

'He's here now,' Jan said, nodding towards the set as the actor Fulvio Cortese, in a white shirt and brown breeches, was marched onto the set by Beatrice.

Jan got up from the dolly seat and slowly walked the few paces to be ready for Lasse to tell him how the scene would run. He, like Anatra, was prepared for the dance of the viewfinder. The latter was stood off to one side watching in anticipation, his white shirt half hanging out of baggy, chalk-marked trousers, the unpolished dusty black shoes dispelling any air of fashion sense. He rolled his chalk stick around his fingers, poised, ready to mark the floor with the camera position. He may look scruffy, but as a Grip, the mover of the dolly, he had an excellent sense of timing and movement. Plus, he always hit his marks.

They had done a tracking shot just before lunch, and Jan was so pleased to have got it first take that he turned around in his seat and shook Anatra's hand in thanks. That small gesture made the 'Duck's' day.

Fulvio was barely out of his teens, very nervous, slightly in awe of his surroundings. He looked around everywhere, taken in by the size of the place and the huge scaffold lighting rig above the set. The two electricians silently watching up in the rig looked down like a couple of sweaty birds of prey, watching every movement beneath them. Everyone had forgotten they were there, apart from Enzo and Sven. They observed the young newcomer, sensing his nervousness. The older, bald one grinned at his moustached companion and whispered somewhat disparagingly, 'Televisione.' 'Si!' was the nodded, smirked response.

The dance of the viewfinder ended in a wide angle, forty-millimetre, one of Lasse's favourite lenses.

'We have paid for the set. Let's see it,' he repeatedly said throughout the day.

Grace noted it without even looking up.

Jan returned to his little round seat on the dolly and nodded confidentially to Adam as he said, 'Young Fulvio's a television actor. Saw him in a soap opera on TV last year when I was over. He's nervous though, he was shaking earlier. He didn't have that birthmark on his face, though, must be a Lasse thing. He does that sometimes to make actors more remarkable.'

Adam smirked. 'Don't you mean memorable, Jan?'

'Yes, sorry, memorable! Not my first bloody language, be fair!'

They both laughed. Adam pointed to the set. 'Belinda and Anita will look after him. Can't be easy suddenly walking in here and being the centre of attention unless you have a massive ego.'

'Most actors have, Adam. I couldn't do what they do.'

'Course you could. Think of all that money, all the champagne and all those Make-up girls like Sophia falling over themselves to bonk you.'

'Bastard!' The smile turned into a laugh. 'You really are a bastard, Adam Kirby! A real bastard!'

Jose was carrying a tray with three glasses of orange juice. He placed it down on the outdoor table with the large faded tan umbrella sited at the back of the Wardrobe department.

His two guests nodded, smiling in appreciation. Joe's white pallid skin did not like sunshine. He positioned his chair to the most shadowed part of the table. His oversized, blue-lensed sunglasses accentuated his pointed face and the fact that he needed a shave. The sun momentarily reflected off the moving tray as Jose placed it in the centre of the table for them to serve themselves should they desire. As Jose sat down, he appraised his other guest: the clean, white, ironed shirt was tight over a muscular upper torso, the biceps totally filling the short sleeves, the undone three top buttons revealing a brown hairy chest.

'Captain Steve, thanks a lot for coming in. We need your expertise.'

The lined, sun-carved face beneath the brown crew cut nodded. 'You're welcome.' The brown tattooed arms bore testimony to forty years spent mainly outdoors. His blue eyes were unflinching, quite cold. He didn't wear sunglasses, never saw the need for them.

Joe from the Art department spread out his notepad and put down his pen. This meeting was for him as much as Jose.

The muscular figure smiled. 'Glad to be of help. I've done some research.' There was a slight, lilting trace of a South Wales accent. He gently waved three sheets of stapled paper before him. 'Uniforms and badges are always tricky. The army units in Sicily in early 1943 were mainly the 16th Italian corps. The 4th Livorno, the 54th Napoli, the Assietta and the Aosta…

There were two German battalions, the 15th Panzer Grenadier and the Hermann Göring Division, plus a load of coastal defence units mainly run by old local Sicilians.'

Jose nodded, grimacing. 'I suspected that it would not just be one regiment, but that's an awful lot of choice.'

Captain Steve gave an encouraging smile. 'Well, my advice, for what it's worth, is to get the military department of Bermans and Nathans Costumiers in London, get hold of Malcolm and get him to send out a couple of each uniform for the close-ups. As for the guys in the background, no one will notice specifics; all of that can come from here.'

Jose pointed his right index finger skywards. 'We have to get it right. There are an awful lot of old soldiers and military buffs around.'

Steve acknowledged his concern. 'If you speak to Bermans and Nathans, they will have actual old uniforms, and they will be correct. Malcolm really knows his stuff but be aware, though, when you're casting extras, these World War II uniforms, particularly from the area of southern Italy, tend to be on the small side.'

Jose made a note. 'Excellent point, thank you for that.'

'Because the script calls for the exact correct regimental badges, you really need to speak to Malcolm to see what he's got, but he should have them in stock. Then you can take it from there. This list is all yours!' He handed Jose the paperwork.

Joe looked up, checking with a bit of a lean-forward that it was okay to interrupt. 'What about weapons, Steve?'

'As a registered armourer, I can provide any weapon you want, within reason, or I can ship them in from London, Munich or the States. Background rifles and holster fillers will all be wood as usual. Foreground stuff – non-firing – is not a problem, and anything that you want to go bang I can provide, but on set, I need thirty minutes' briefing time beforehand to ensure safe usage. Blanks can blind, and some weapons have to fire a wooden round to work. So work out what you need and let me know as much in advance as you can.'

'Any idea of cost?'

'Tell me what you need, and I will give you a price. If you need a lot, I will need to bring in someone else to help. Because if a weapon goes missing, there is hell to pay, and I could lose my licence. You have no idea how many forms there are to fill in if you lose a rifle.' He smiled ruefully.

Joe grinned. 'Ever lost one?'

'Not yet. I make it very clear from the beginning that you can't mess about with guns. Treat 'em with respect and remember what they're designed to do.'

Joe looked from right to left, overacting being furtive. 'Can you get me a Colt automatic?'

Steve's look hardened slightly. 'For a film or personal use?'

'Personal, private use.'

'No, Joe, I don't deal in unregistered firearms. I would lose my licence, but if you really want something like that, go down to Porte Portese market on a Sunday morning. There are a couple of guys up the back end who may be willing to help. It's rumoured they can get anything from a pea shooter to a Sherman tank, but it's highly illegal, and there are undercover police wandering around, so I wouldn't recommend it.'

'Oh! Okay, just thought that it would be fun to shoot up a few trees up in the hills.'

Jose interrupted. 'All this talk of guns is far too macho, boys! I think it's time to end this very productive meeting and thank both of you for coming. We will let you know what we want and when. Okay?'

Captain Steve stood up, leant over the table and shook Joe by the hand. His grip was intense, making Joe wince slightly. Jose saw the man's strength and simply waved his hand, quickly grasping the tray of glasses to avoid having his very delicate hand crushed. He was a flute player, after all.

Grace's visits to the camera became less frequent. It had not taken her long to get 'her eye in' for the forty lens and the fifty. Jan and Adam both enjoyed her little visits, her polite 'Thank you, boys' as she left, leaving behind a faint scent. It was nice to have a bit of female company in a predominantly male environment.

Fulvio was very well cast. His part was to chat up the English rose, Belinda, a skill that seemed to come easily to him. He was a real charmer, with naturally curly hair, perfect teeth, flashing eyes and little fleeting tactile touches. Adam was always fascinated by how little performances of quality drama were played out, sometimes repeatedly with slight variations, the difference between a printed take, a hold and a 'No! no! no! One more time! Please take'. Fulvio earned respect very quickly. He hit his marks and gave Lasse what he wanted performance-wise. Even the vultures in the lighting rig gave him a nod of approval.

There was a pause for a few minutes when the artists disappeared for a wardrobe change, and the two set dressers made some minor set changes to denote a different day. Sven took the opportunity to change the lighting in the set to make it look later in the day, creating shadows by hanging a slat in front of the main key light that threw subtle shadows across the back wall. All of the background artists had changed, except the serving girl in the tea shop.

Grace went through the ceremony of the polaroids before anyone was allowed to leave. After that, the set virtually emptied, leaving Adam and Grace almost alone. Luca had gone off to the loading room over in the back corner to reload, and Anatra had asked Adam's permission to nip outside for a fag.

Jan, Sven and Lasse were sitting down in the café set in deep conversation, but they were all smiling. That was a good sign.

Adam decided to wander over to Grace's little lit work area. She was typing feverishly. He was amazed at her speed.

'You're very quick!' he said, gesturing at the typewriter.

She stopped typing and looked up at him. Her clearly defined eyebrows, high cheekbones and full lips curling at the corners didn't go unnoticed by Adam. She placed her hands on her lap, lifted her shoulders up and down and took a deep breath, indicating she was taking a break along with everyone else.

'Oh, Adam! Yes, it helps being a pianist.'

'Your notes, Grace, they're all squiggles.'

She smiled and pointed to the paperwork on her desk. 'It's shorthand, with a combination of Pitman shorthand and ballet notation for body position. You know, left hand on hip, right knuckle closed, head looks high right, all of that sort of stuff!'

'Bloody clever, Grace. Have you got your eye in yet?'

She laughed. 'Nearly. I suppose you've got all of that in your head, page one for you.'

Adam nodded. 'Yeah! Well imprinted by now.'

'How long have you been doing Focus?'

'About ten years. I started as a floor sweeper, became a Clapper Boy, and within six months, the Focus left to work on

Supercar with the Andersons, and I stepped into his shoes. It's been downhill ever since.'

'I think you're being modest, Adam. You wouldn't be here unless you were very good. A lot of people would give their right arm to have your job.'

'Maybe, Grace, maybe. What about you? You said you were half and half – what's all that about?'

'Oh! It's nothing. My mum was from London, my dad from Sicily, and I am dual nationality. That's about it, really.'

'What skin do you like to live in, Grace? What nationality is your heart?'

She paused and frowned, somewhat taken aback. 'That's a profound and intelligent question for day one, Adam. I don't really know how to answer. I have never given it any thought. I think in both languages, even dream in both languages. Can't give you an answer, I'm afraid.'

'Apologies, Grace, didn't mean to pry. You just strike me as, well… a very interesting person.'

'Thank you, Adam. What about your skin? Where is your heart?'

'Back home, in a garage in Worcester Park with my Anglia rally car.'

She laughed. 'Typical man. No deep psychological answer from you either then?'

'No, Grace.'

‘I will think about your question, Adam. If I ever come up with an answer, I’ll let you know. How does that sound?’

‘I’m sorry, Grace, you’re right. It was a bit deep for day one, but it just seemed to be the question to ask.’

‘You impulsive, Adam? Always just go with your instincts?’

‘I don’t know. Never given it any thought.’

‘Touché, Adam, touché!’ She smiled and nodded. ‘Anyway, I need to type these up, otherwise I’ll fall behind. It’s been nice talking to you.’

‘You too, Grace… good. I’ll let you get on.’

Adam looked around and saw people were starting to drift back. He noticed Duke heading towards the Norwegian delegation still sitting in the café set. As Sven spotted the approaching figure, he pulled out his pan glass and polished it with his hanky. Adam read the signs: back to work, boys! He looked down at Grace who was now head down, typing furiously in her own world, almost oblivious to his presence.

‘Cheers, Grace!’

She looked up, nodded momentarily, smiled, looked back down and continued typing.

The older bald electrician in the lighting rig had fallen asleep against a couple of old dusty cushions that provided a modicum of comfort in the world of steel tubing. His moustached companion kicked him in the ankle.

'Attenzione!' he said, pointing down to the set, now busy with people.

Ben walked on, leading eight café customer extras onto the set, setting six of them down and holding two back for action walk-in. Belinda and Fulvio were sitting on a couple of the canvas-backed chairs in the semi-circle next to Grace.

Jan strolled back to the camera, patting Adam on the back as he did so. 'You all fixed up then?'

'What?'

'Grace. You all fixed up, dinner for two, romantic evening?'

'Christ, no! No. She's old enough to be my mother.'

'Many a good tune played on an old violin.'

'No, Jan, no, we were just talking. About Sophia, actually.'

'What? What about Sophia?'

'She's definitely a lesbian. Lives with another woman, lots of tattoos, has been for years!'

'Oh! Damn. Are you sure?'

'No, Jan, I'm not. I'm just pulling your leg. I was talking to Grace about how she's half English, half Italian. We never mentioned Sophia. That's for you to sort out. But if it's okay, I'll just wind you up at every opportunity, if that's okay, yeah?'

'Bastard, you really are a bastard, Adam. It's going to be good working with you!' Jan couldn't help laughing.

'Got to do something to keep us sane!' Adam smiled.

Luca was standing a few feet away, slightly behind them, as he listened in on their conversation and watched them. He came to the conclusion that these two were more than a bit odd, but they were undoubtedly on each other's wavelength, that much was true. He stepped forward.

'I can tell bout Sophia, if you interest.'

Jan glanced at the set to check that he had time. His quick look told him that he had.

'Okay, Luca! Go ahead, carry on.'

'She was married but husband die. Cancer, a few years ago. She very sick afterwards, very unhappy. No boyfriend.'

Jan looked at him very seriously, regretting the flippancy of his earlier comments about her.

'Oh, shit. Luca, I didn't know that. That's really sad.'

'She very laugh outside, but inside not good, very sad.'

Duke's voice suddenly boomed, 'OKAY, RAGAZZI, SETTLE DOWN. GOING FOR LINE-UP!'

Jan flicked his eyes quickly back to the set and then back to Luca. 'Don't say anything, Luca, please, nothing.'

'Okay, understand, capito!' He smiled and nodded. His expression became serious as he realised the information he had just shared had had a very sobering effect on both Jan and Adam.

Luigi watched the retreating figure of the journalist who had just run up a pretty substantial restaurant bill by choosing the most expensive items on the menu. The amount of wine he had drunk probably accounted for his slightly meandering exit. The waiters were now clearing the tables around the three remaining diners.

He looked across at Isabella. 'That went well. You happy?'

She smiled. Most of her lipstick was on the serviette that she was dabbing her mouth with. She raised her eyebrows in agreement.

'Yes, I'm okay with him. What do you think, Veronique?'

'You'll get a good write-up. We virtually wrote his article for him with our press handout, and he's eaten and drunk us out of house and home so he should be happy. Still wanted your back story, though!'

Luigi interrupted. 'If Isabella wants to keep her private life private, then we should respect her wishes. Anyway, it makes her more interesting?'

Veronique held her head to one side, scowling slightly in disagreement. 'I don't know, it works both ways. I suppose if there are gaps in the background, you can always fill them in later when the star starts to fade, bit by bit, to get yourself back in the headlines.'

Isabella opened her mouth in genuine surprise. 'What are you saying, Veronique?'

'I'm saying, ma chérie, that all female leads have just a few years, and as the wrinkles come and the bosom falls, there is a queue of younger, more vibrant flesh waiting in the wings trying to push you out of the way… a sorry fact of life!'

Isabella snorted. 'That's so unkind!'

'Maybe, chérie, maybe, but early nights, stay away from the booze and drugs, never be a drama queen on set and your longevity increases proportionally. Like Loren.'

Isabella turned to Luigi open-mouthed.

He looked wistfully at her. 'Loren. If only we could have afforded her.'

'Luigi!' Isabella exclaimed, waving a hand at him.

Como Trani lovingly wiped his not-so-clean rag across the gleaming top brass engine tube of his pride and joy.

His hands told his story: no wedding ring, a deeply ingrained patina of grease and oil that had built up over many years, fat, dirty-nailed fingers, flesh burned and scarred by countless encounters with scorching hot metal.

The screwdriver in the top pocket of his old stained overalls had just tightened up double clips on a water hose for the drinking water tank. He was about to leave the one thing that he loved more than anything else: the submarine he had maintained since 1946 when a group of twenty or so ex-Regia Marina officers had decided to preserve and rescue her from being lifted as scrap by the yard down the road. She had been shot at, bombed at and was half submerged when the committee headed by a local ex-admiral decided that she should be saved. Thus the Acciaio Preservation Trust came into existence.

Como, the lead engineer, was the only member of the Trust to receive a modest income. The rest just signed cheques on a very regular basis, usually for quite large sums of money. Their compensation was to dress up in their old naval uniforms, which the kind years had now made very tight around the middle, and take guided tours of school kids from all around northern Italy. Three or four times a year, they would take her to sea and recapture their youth. The old girl's venom had been removed. The torpedo tubes were now welded and sealed, and the gun on the deck was rusted beyond salvation but still substantial enough to hang on to if the swell became a bit rough. The insurers would not allow her to submerge much below periscope depth. But she was beautiful, really looked the part, with long flowing lines, a retired predator from another age. Plus, she was going to be a film star again.

In ten days' time, she was going to sail about three hundred kilometres down to Civitavecchia, for a very substantial fee, all fuel paid, to star in a film. In her prime, fully submerged, she would have murmured down there in twenty-two hours; on the surface taken about thirteen hours. But she was no longer in her prime. Hence, the committee planned for eighteen hours with the Italian flag flying proudly from her conning tower. They had already drawn straws for who was going to sail on her.

Como had things to mend on shore; he had a small metalwork shop nearby and was the local go-to man for the repair of anything made of metal. He would always use more metal plate than necessary, more rivets, more welds, creating a restoration that weighed twice as much as it should. But he was cheap, only worked for cash and drove the local school bus morning and afternoon. Moving his precious cargo carefully, no one took offence at his long, ragged beard and the half-lit roll-up that he always had stuck in his nicotine-stained lips. He did, though, have an air about him in more ways than one.

Before he left, he stroked the rocker cover on top of the starboard engine, something that he always did as a ritual, then paused to listen to the hull talk. She had a language all of her own, a creak, a slight groan from the stern that echoed, amplified by the vast megaphone-like tube. No sound of the wind or the gentle slap of waves on her thighs penetrated from the outside. She was a solid old girl. He went out, as always, through the front hatch and pulled himself up into the light salty breeze. She was moored rent-free just outside of the Muggiano navy yard where her keel had first been laid. It really helped that the chairman was a retired Admiral – free mooring – plus she would have been melted down to create a line of Fiats many years ago if it wasn't for him.

He carefully closed the heavy hatch, clipping the padlock firmly shut and picking up his rust-tinged steel toolbox, walked across the pitted deck down the gently bobbing gangplank to terra firma.

Duke looked at his watch. It was five thirty-five. He shuffled his feet as Grace walked back to her seat, waving the last polaroid. He noticed her nod to say that she was finished.

'Thank you, ragazzi, thank you for an excellent first day. It's a wrap. Call sheets are in the tray at the door. Tomorrow morning, eight-thirty. Thank you.'

One of the drivers had appeared on set with Joe from the Art department. Lasse, Sven and Enzo quickly walked over to them, exchanged greetings and walked off into the shadows. The inadequate metal blue glow of the working lights high up in the room were starting to come into their own, as the lights on the set were slowly going off one by one as the two electricians high up in the world of scaffolding went about shutting down their end of the business.

As Duke walked over to Grace his voice carried across the floor. 'Grace?'

She was looking down at her polaroids and typed notes. 'I know what you're going to ask me. How much?'

'Well?'

'About three fifty, something like that.'

'That's not bad, Grace, not bad at all for day one!'

'It's excellent,' she said, smiling and nodding at him in agreement.

'Nearly four minutes,' he added, giving her one of his cheeky grins.

'No, Duke, three fifty-ish, not four minutes. We'll know more tomorrow, but that's a rough, okay?'

He looked at her for a second. 'You're right, Grace, three fifty is not four minutes. As usual, you're right.'

'Always, always,' she replied with a smile as she gathered up her notes.

Adam watched the encounter. He was right. She was an interesting woman.

Duke patted her affectionately on her shoulder and turned to pick up his shoulder bag from the chair next to her before he slowly walked away, shrugging his broad shoulders to relieve the tension that had been gradually tightening up all day.

Adam actually felt a bit funny seeing someone else chatting her up. No reason for that; she was old enough to be his mother. Then it hit him: her smell, her still cool hand on his shoulder just before every take as she looked through the camera, getting her eye in. It was jasmine. The childhood memories suddenly all came flooding back. As a child, every morning before he left for school, his mother would always hug him with her hands on his shoulder on the front doorstep, every school day, without fail. Next to the front door had been a huge jasmine bush. Grace had just completely, unknowingly, rekindled all of those memories. The smell of her, the jasmine, was linked to the hand on the shoulder. Adam bit his lip. Twenty-nine years old now, sunshine, not a kid any more! Get a grip. He looked over to Grace's workstation. She had packed her notes into her briefcase and was in the process of clipping the lid back on her portable typewriter.

One of the electricians appeared beside her. 'Finito?' he asked.

Grasping the switch on the cable to her work light, she turned and replied, 'Si, grazie. Ho finito. Grazie a Lei.'

The electrician nodded. 'Di niente,' he said as he switched off the light and lowered it down on its stand.

Adam had not heard her speak Italian before – he always thought of her as English – but from what he just heard it was clear she was naturally bilingual, or half and half, as she called it.

Anatra, with a couple of his Macchinisti, had loaded up the camera trolly. After lifting the last box, he turned to Adam with a little wave to get his attention. 'Adam? We are ready.'

Adam looked around the set, checking for anything that may have been missed. It looked totally different now. All of the lights were off. It was characterless, uninteresting. The cold, shadowless glow of the high working lights made it look almost derelict. It was bland, resting, asleep until tomorrow when once again it would become the centre of attention.

His experienced eyes double-checked the set. He nodded to Anatra to confirm he was satisfied and they could all leave. Lifting his green ditty bag onto the trolley, they all followed Grace across the flat, smooth, concrete floor, the tyres of the trolley making a rubbery, squelchy sound in protest at the pile of camera cases.

Adam and Anatra picked up their call sheets from the tray on the small table beside the lolling unit driver sitting in the security man's chair. He was waiting for the clapstick to give him the fruits of everyone's hard-earned labours so that he could deliver them to the film processing labs on the other side of the city.

But he knew it would be a forty-minute wait, if not more. Clapsticks were always the last to leave. That was how long it took to unload the magazines, label all of the cans and write out the report sheets. There would usually be a pile of around six to ten cans, all taped together with the instruction sheets sandwiched in between the first and second tin.

He liked that evening run. There was a lovely coffee shop next to the labs; his reward for having to drive across the city in rush hour.

Duke stopped at the payphone kiosk just outside the building, dialling a number that he had scribbled on a piece of paper in his shoulder bag. The response at the Vaticano Nero was prompt and polite. He could come at seven forty-five, and Luciano Scordia would be available to see him personally.

He put the phone back in its cradle and grimaced. He was not looking forward to the meeting, but Scordia had insisted. He wanted to know in detail everything that had gone on during the first day. The copy of the continuity sheets would only tell him so much, and anyway, they wouldn't arrive till tomorrow morning after the Production Office had copied and delivered them, so Duke had to make a personal appearance and be interrogated. He just hoped that Scordia's daughter, the scorpion-like Sylvania, would not be there. He positively disliked her. She was a jackal, always looking for weakness, for any opportunity to better her position, the heir to her ageing dad's throne. She was determined to make sure that it would be worth inheriting.

Adam was at a loose end. He had no idea what to do, whether to eat, not eat, dress up, dress down. The evening was now an unknown quantity. Biting his lip in uncertainty, he wandered along the outside of the building up towards the Production Office.

Three unit cars were gleaming in the late afternoon sun. One of the drivers saw him approaching. He got out, waved and called, 'Adam, hotel?' signalling him to get in. Adam acknowledged with a confirming finger pointed in the air. He opened the front passenger door and plomped himself down.

The driver smiled. 'Hotel?'

'Yes! Yes, please, hotel.'

The smell of leather polish filled his throat for a few seconds until the engine started, and the heating system blew a draught of warm air straight into his face. Adam leant forward and directed the airstream over to his side window.

Nine o'clock was two and a half hours away, and he still didn't know what to expect. Fortunately, the driver was the strong silent type, so Adam didn't have to engage in monosyllabic, broken English chit-chat.

Lasse looked out of the rear seat window as they turned onto the coast road for Civitavecchia. The sun was still a presence in the sky, but it was on its way to far-flung places, and its reducing warmth and warm tinge were giving fair warning.

The Mediterranean horizon was clear and dead straight level. A couple of small yachts bobbed their way north. Further out to sea, in the distance absorbing the detail was a commercial freighter on its way south. No one spoke. It had been a hard day, and the hour-plus drive was an opportunity to wind down. Sven, in the middle, closed his eyes every now and then. Joe, to his right, just stared out of the side window, mind in neutral, seeing nothing, noting nothing. Enzo, in the front, was wrestling with some minor inner demon, head tilted to one side as he chewed gum.

As they neared the outskirts of the port, a red Porsche 911 with English plates tore past them at well over the speed limit, horn blaring, lights flashing, its violent slipstream buffeting them, causing their driver to mutter something under his breath to do with sex and mothers. Dublin was on his way to open the gates and ensure that all went well with the recce.

Adam decided to take a shower while he tried to work out what to do. He dressed, put on clean underwear and strolled down to the lobby. He looked around for somewhere to sit and wait. There was the bar, but there were two entrances to the hotel so he might miss whoever was coming to see him. Plus, he had no idea who was coming so how would he know whether he missed this mystery person or not! Sod it, he thought, he'd have a light supper and then go back to his room and just wait.

The traffic outside the hotel, as usual, did its best to hospitalise him, but he had got used to that and waited for a minor break before taking a dignified trot to the other side of the road, looking to see which of the half dozen or so little restaurants looked the most appealing.

It was happy hour at Trattoria Rosa and the place was heaving, but the one next door was quieter. There were about eight tables outside on the pavement. The white-aproned waiter was guarding the menu stand like a fisherman waiting for a bite.

'For one?'

Adam just smiled. They always knew he was English. They always bloody knew. Fact is they always knew the nationality of any passer-by just by their clothes and accessories. It's how they got their business, called the punters in and earned their tips.

'Yes, for one, thank you. Grazie!' he added, making an effort to use the language. As usual, he sat with his back to the restaurant so that he could observe the procession of people and vehicles. Watching the lifeblood of the city that ceaselessly ebbed and flowed over every cobble and ancient walkway from dawn till dusk fascinated him, and he never tired of it.

He ordered a Coke and a small pizza, avoiding the garlic just in case Solveig Larsen turned up later. Her husband was away, after all, a hundred miles away on a recce at Civitavecchia… Dream on, Adam, dream on!

Duke walked up the few steps to the faded green-painted door. He looked up and down the small street, but didn't notice anything out of the ordinary. No loitering policemen, no parked cars with dark windows. Just a few scooters and the occasional van or private car. It was dustbin night, and several houses in the street had put their bins out. A few doors down on the other side of the street, a fat, old, grey and balding man in braces was dragging his very dented, stained, lidless and no doubt odorous, receptacle from the narrow, pebbled alleyway to the side of his house.

Duke knocked on the door. It had no bell or knocker, so he rapped hard a couple of times. Immediately two dogs started barking inside, one from the left and one to the right, very deep, intrusive, authoritative; these were not lapdogs.

A small eye-level hatch slid open with a soft oiled metallic *shhuh, donk* just below the never-used keyhole. One and a half eyes with bushy black eyebrows appeared, and a muted voice enquired, 'Si?'

Duke peered into the slot. The dogs were now in full song, the small aperture acting as a loudspeaker.

'Duke from Studio Lazio.'

'Si. Wait.'

The hatch closed, the dogs were shouted at and doors inside were slammed shut. A couple of whimpers and then the canine kerfuffle stopped.

The sound of a metal bolt at the top of the door being slid across was followed by one at the bottom before, finally, the door opened. The black bushy eyebrows belonged to a curly, black-haired man who was every bit as big as Duke. He put his big hand up to stop Duke stepping forward and leant out past the door frame to check that the visitor was alone and that the street was clear. Satisfied, he beckoned Duke into a small room, which smelled of pizza and dogs, that oily unmistakable unwashed dog smell. Dark spots of water from two large, half-filled dog bowls were spattered on the carpetless floorboards.

Duke stood motionless in the centre of the room as the steel-backed front door was closed behind him and the bolts were slid back into their secure position.

The doorkeeper came from behind and stood in front of him, well within his personal space. There was a whiff of dried sweat, pizza breath. The eyes were cold and challenging.

'Gun? Knife?' he said, gesturing him to raise his arms.

Duke forced a smile and extended both arms outwards, his right fingers nearly touching the wall.

The frisk was very firm, very businesslike, even down to both of his ankles checking for a leg holster. A large dog could be heard breathing and snuffling from behind the door on the right.

He looked around the room: two small fluorescents lit the small square space, a desk and chair were set on the left, the cords to the two telephones were all twisted, there was a half-eaten segment of pizza on a plate and a capless beer bottle. The big, rough hands had finished their work. Satisfied, Pizza Breath grunted and turned. His scarred knuckles knocked hard on the green-painted, steel door. The paint at face level had long since given up trying to survive such treatment; it was worn thin and patchy, revealing the pitted steel plate underneath.

The voice on the other side was higher-pitched, muffled. 'Va bene, va bene.'

More metallic bolts could be heard sliding back before the door was opened with a heavy, unlubricated, metal-on-metal screek, revealing another room. This one was of a similar size but brighter, cleaner, with white walls and varnished dark brown floorboards. A small, low, wooden table with an empty plate and a high-backed, leather chair shadowing a dog-eared girlie magazine on the floor.

As Duke stepped forward, a smaller, older, balding figure in a white shirt smiled a toothy grin. A strong smell of cheap chain-store aftershave filled the air.

'Duke, welcome. Follow me, Luciano is expecting you,' he said, with a slight bow, almost as an apology for the compulsory welcoming treatment a few minutes earlier.

He opened the only door to reveal a cobbled square populated by large terracotta tubs, each filled with a different kind of green flowerless vegetation. The smell of herbs filled the air, such a natural clean smell. Duke was able to pick out mint, thyme, rosemary, sage. The evening sun was still casting its light on the top of the back building, the sandstone and blue-grey windows helping to reflect an even shadowless warm light down into the square.

There was a huge oak table in the centre, almost like a design statement. At its head sat a plumpish figure in a clean, ironed, white shirt. He waved to Duke to take a seat on the nearest bench next to him. Underneath, on the cobbles, was spilt food, small pieces of bread. It was now time for the sparrows to eat, and half a dozen or so pecked and darted, retreating like a fluttering brown wave as Duke approached.

Luciano offered no hand in welcome. He just nodded a few times as Duke made himself comfortable. There was hardly any sound of the city, just a barely perceptible hum, reflected like the light from high up on the buildings. Sparrows chattered, reminding each other that night was on its way.

'Evening, Luciano. A lovely setting, truly lovely. This would make for a fine restaurant.'

Luciano snorted and leant forward. 'Tell me about the first day, your impressions.'

Duke was not affronted by the blunt, friendless welcome. He had met his host a couple of times before, and his conduct had always been the same: emotionless, cold and impolite. He looked up at the mottled sandstone buildings, at the mature beige-painted wooden window frames; such a lovely setting for such an evil man.

'It went very well. We got just under four minutes.'

'What's the Director like?'

Duke paused for a second, looking up to his right as if trying to recall each visual image from the day.

'He's very good with people. He made an excellent speech first thing, the crew liked that. Very considerate with the artists, gets the best out of them, doesn't waste film. Does a couple of rehearsals, gets the mistakes over, then just goes for a take, gets it on film. Nice guy!'

'Cameraman?'

'From the same school, very competent. They are friends. Very much on each other's wavelength. They eat out together most evenings.'

Luciano's technique was interrogative rather than conversational. The moment Duke paused for breath, he asked another question.

'This television actor Flavio.'

'Fulvio. He was the surprise of the day. He was excellent, very well cast. Looks and sounds the part, going to have great future.'

'So you've given me no bad news, everything's rosy, right?'

An unexpected voice from behind slipped around Duke's throat like a garrotte.

'Not true. They had a lot of trouble getting quiet on stage and wasted a lot of time.'

The scorpion had struck! Sylvania, the heir apparent, slowly came into Duke's peripheral vision, drawing level with his left shoulder but keeping a couple of metres away, her movement silent, barefooted.

Duke was taken aback. Luciano had given no indication of her arrival. How long she had been there was anyone's guess.

Duke turned to look at her. 'Sylvania, good evening!'

'Set problems?' Luciano, now alert, leant forward.

'No! No! No problems. It's just that the crew are used to shooting guide track when everything is dubbed afterwards, and Lasse doesn't work that way. He shoots live sound, no after dub. The crew are getting the message, settling down; it's just a stricter discipline. The way of the future is much cheaper in the long run.'

'You going to be able to keep a handle on that, Duke?' Luciano sucked in his cheeks, paused, then added, 'You need a couple of guys on set to keep quiet, I've got a couple.'

'No! No! No need for that. I've got two good Assistants. We're on top of it.'

Sylvania curled her lips as she walked round to her father and affectionately placed her left hand on his right shoulder. She gave a little squeeze to indicate she wanted to take over the conversation. Luciano eased himself back in his chair, happy to take a more submissive role.

Duke noticed that there was still no wedding ring on her left hand. Her light summer dress accentuated her voluptuous shape, and her make-up had been thickly applied. She was a good-looking woman. She looked down at Duke for a couple of seconds, studying him, trying to read him.

'How do we slow things down, Duke? Push Luigi over budget so that we can increase our investment?'

Duke couldn't believe what he was hearing, and yet he could; it was the way she thought.

'You are asking the wrong person. I have no idea.'

'Come now, Duke, the best First in Rome, and you don't know where the weak points are?'

'I think that we need to establish some parameters here. Luigi has shown me great loyalty over many years. I am not now going to stab him in the back. As you ask, I will report to you, but I've told Luigi that I am doing so.'

Sylvania sensed a pause coming. 'You are very vulnerable, Duke,' she said, with a knowing nod.

'I am very aware that an unmarked car could knock my son off his scooter on the way to college, or my family be hurt in some way. But respect loyalty, Luciano, respect loyalty. Don't ask me to turn because I won't. I would rather leave the film, resign and go to work on another production than let Luigi down. I get a lot of offers, believe you me. I'm one of the key ingredients in this production that ensures that your investment is well spent and that you profit from it. If someone else comes in, another First, you could be signing cheques like an octopus!'

Sylvania tensed. She did not appreciate being patronised.

Luciano felt her grip on his shoulder tighten. He knew her well enough to know that it was time to reassert himself. He patted her hand.

'Duke, you are from a bygone age, you really are, but I hear what you say. Loyalty, we could all do with some of that. Let us leave it there for now. Call me every day after work and leave a message with the office here. Let's meet once a week so that I can see the colour of your eyes.'

Sylvania's expression was as hard as stone, her dark eyes cold and unblinking. She removed her hand from her father's shoulder and flicked her hair behind her left ear. She was displeased; Duke had been let off too lightly.

Duke read what was going on between them: the old blood not quite ready to let the young blood take over. He slowly stood up, looked from the pouting direct stare of Sylvania down to Luciano, who simply nodded, signifying that he could leave.

The wall downlights around the courtyard were starting to come on one after the other, highlighting the uneven building stonework and the shadow-casting terracotta pots and their leafy green aromatic contents.

Duke nodded. 'Sylvania, Luciano,' he said, before turning and walking towards the same door through which he had entered. He noticed the rifle barrel with telescopic sight sticking out of the upstairs window, only because it moved as he went to leave. Otherwise, he would not have spotted it. Luciano obviously didn't take any chances. The door opened in front of him when he was three paces away from it. He turned and looked back. Luciano and Sylvania were engrossed in a heated but quiet conversation. She was not happy, and he was patting the air, trying to calm her down.

All the lights halfway up the buildings were now on, totally altering the little courtyard. Everything above the lights disappeared into the darkness, and everything below was wrapped in a warm yellow glow. It was a beautiful setting, a lovely place to dine. It was a shame that the only thing on the menu here was sinister manipulation.

Adam wanted the bill for his meal, but waiters knew all about keeping diners in a half-empty restaurant to make it look more appealing, busier. They had all mastered the art of walking by tunnel-visioned. Eventually, Adam got up and went to the service bar, waving his wallet to try and get somebody's attention. He left a tip because he knew he would be coming back regularly so there was no point cutting your nose off to spite your face.

Time was marching on, and this nine o'clock 'appointment' was looming. Crossing the street back to the hotel was a little more leisurely as the traffic had quietened down – as much as it ever could in the city that lives with the honking of horns and squealing rubber tyres eighteen hours a day.

Adam had a good look around the hotel, around the bar, the seats in reception, but there was no one, no one that he knew or even anyone just hanging around. He wandered up to his room. It was cool and odourless but he had grown accustomed to the smell of it; now it was just neutral and bland. A widdle and a teeth clean seemed to be the order of the day, finished with an extra-large splash of Old Spice aftershave. He looked at his watch. Five to nine. He opened the shutters, letting in a puff of warm traffic fumes and the rattle of badly silenced scooters. The sun had virtually disappeared, and the street lights had taken over. This was like waiting for the dentist!

A quick check in the full-length mirror to make sure his flies were done up and his hair looked okay. A wander back to the window to glance at the usual traffic and trendies on their way to the Spanish Steps to promenade.

Then a *tap tap* on the door. Adam's pulse rate shot up. His hand shook as he gently opened the door to reveal…Pia!

Fully made-up, perfect mascara and eyeliner, quiff perfectly over her left eye. Vodka bottle in her right hand, low-cut, tight-fitting, green mini dress, tilted head and a smile that was a joy to look at. Adam was rarely lost for words, but she looked utterly stunning. Her figure was a lolly stick, but her face and dress were a work of art.

A 'Good evening, Adam' floated from her pale pink lips. 'May I come in?'

'Yes, yes, of course!'

As she walked forward, she gently placed the neck of the vodka bottle in his right hand. The smell of her as she brushed past him was delicate, light and feminine. She walked into the small space between the bed and the small dressing table desk, then turned to face him, deliberately placing her shoulder bag on the bed.

'My English, Adam, is slow. If you use easy words, speak slow, I can understand. Shall we have a drink?' she said, gesturing at the bottle that Adam had forgotten he was holding.

He looked at her, taking in the whole image. She looked straight back at him, smiling, gently biting her lip. Her presentation was faultless, her make-up, dress, smile, lipstick, she was from another age. An elfin-like, 1930s flapper, and she was in his bedroom.

He looked at the dressing table desk. There were two upside-down glasses on small paper doilies. Pia walked casually over to the window. Her heels clacked on the wooden floor, the noise drawing attention to her slim ankles and small feet.

'There's no ice, Pia, is that okay?'

She half turned from the window, looking over her left shoulder. Another smile. 'That's fine, Adam, good.' She turned, sauntered back towards him, lifting her face up towards him and taking the offered drink in her right hand, easing forward so that she was within his personal space with barely a foot between them. She flicked her hair over her left ear and bit her lip gently. Her eyes were unblinking, but she was shaking slightly. She looked very vulnerable.

Adam eased away a little to try to increase the space between them, which seemed to make her more nervous. He noticed little red stress blotches on her chest above the top of her dress.

'Why are you here, Pia?'

She brought her glass up to her lips and took a gulp. She tried to hide the fact that she did not like the taste, but her reflex reaction gave it away, as she bit her bottom lip again.

'To make love, Adam, to make love with you. You have contraceptive, we make love, be nice…'

Alarms bells were starting to ring. There was something not right here, the shaking, the nervousness, the stress blotches on her chest, the hair-flicking, the lip-biting and her obvious distaste for vodka. None of this added up.

She closed the gap between them, offering her face up to him. 'You find me pretty, Adam, we make love.' Her eyes were wide open as she scanned his face. She moistened her lips, pouting slightly as if preparing to kiss him, but she was shaking, visibly trembling.

Adam put down his glass, took her glass from her shaking hand and put a hand on each of her shoulders. 'Pia, making love to you would be fantastic, but I need to know you a little better, and I think that we should go out and have a drink and a bite to eat first, don't you?'

'No, Adam, we can drink, stay here, make love.'

Adam gripped her a little tighter as he saw she was shaking even more now. Her eyes were pleading with him, and tears were starting to form. She lifted her head up and closed her eyes, offering her face up to him. Tears ran gently down her cheeks.

Adam let go of her and reached over to the bed to pick up her shoulder bag. He turned and stepped quickly to open the door. She stood there for a second, surprised by the suddenness of his movement. Her mascara was running down her face. Adam held the door wide open to let her out.

'Let's go out and have a drink!' he said.

She gulped back a tear, paused, accepting the fact that he was waiting for her out in the corridor. 'Please let me do make-up, no go out like this.'

Adam handed her back her bag and smiled, happier that the door was now open. He walked slowly and deliberately into the corridor and turned to face her.

'I'll wait out here, Pia. Leave the door open and come out when you are ready.'

She was not shaking quite so much now, as she bit her lip again, trying to control her emotions. She walked up to the full-length wall mirror and took a small, cloth, make-up bag out of her shoulder bag.

Adam looked down the corridor. At the far end, a family of four were fumbling their way into their room. Adam's mind was in turmoil. What the hell was going on here? She really wanted to get laid, but something was not right. She was so nervous. His thoughts travelled back to a story he had heard from his best mate, Geoff, a couple of years ago about a guy who had bonked a young girl, who afterwards had changed her mind and accused him of rape. All hell had broken loose, police, courts, probation for three years, an absolute nightmare. Adam was a firm believer in loving older women – they knew what they wanted, what life was about and how to enjoy themselves – but the body of a woman, mind of a child had never floated his boat.

He looked into the room. Pia was leaning forward into the mirror. She looked so delicate, so vulnerable. She turned, sensing his presence, smiled sheepishly, then turned back to the mirror to finish applying her lipstick with a slow definite stroke.

She looked at him again, checked her make-up one more time and placed the lipstick back in her bag. She ambled out into the corridor. Adam paused to lock the door while she waited beside him, timidly, uncertainly. Once the door was locked,

Adam relaxed. Now they could go and have a drink and a bite to eat.

He turned to her. ‘Are you happy to go to the little restaurant over the road?’

She smiled, a little shamefaced, humiliated, bit her lip again and replied, ‘Yes, Adam, that will be good.’

The road had quietened down. Before crossing, Adam offered her his arm, which took her by surprise, but she accepted, and they became like all of the other promenading couples on the Spanish Steps, walking in step along the cobbled street.

Trattoria Rosa had thinned out. Happy hour had been and gone, so Adam, seeing an empty table at the end of the row, steered Pia towards it, gesturing her to sit down with her back to the other diners. If there were going to be more tears, Adam wanted her to have some privacy and not be in full view of the rest of the restaurant. The table was smeary from spilt drinks, but at least they were sitting comfortably.

‘What would you like? Wine, beer, Coke?’

She smiled, a smile that showed the child in her. She had a beautiful face, her brown eyes were large and round, accentuated by the mascara and eyeliner. She had slight dimples, and her pale pink lipstick somehow took away the voluptuousness of her lips. He noticed that the red blotch stress marks on her chest had almost disappeared.

'I don't know, Adam. A small wine, maybe… rosé?' She bit her lip again and looked upwards as if trying to clear her mind.

Adam smiled. She had a long neck, long fingers. He had never really studied her before. Her skin was blemish-free, the whites of her eyes very clear. She was, without doubt, a gorgeous young woman.

A waitress appeared from inside the restaurant. Adam waved his left hand to draw her attention. Pia took this as a cue to get a grip of herself, sitting upright, lifting her chin and forcing a smile.

The waitress, a similar age to Pia, with curly brown hair, a white apron, white blouse, cloth in hand, was attentive, quickly wiping the table clean.

'Something to eat, drink?' Barely a trace of an accent.

Adam smiled inwardly. English again – he must have it stamped on his forehead.

He looked up at her and smiled. 'A Coke and a glass of rosé, please.'

'Nothing to eat?'

'Maybe later. Just the drinks for now. Thanks.'

She nodded. 'Va bene,' she said, sucking in her cheeks, a little disappointed that she was not getting a food order out of it.

Adam watched her go, then turned to Pia and spoke softly, whispering almost, 'Why do you want to make love to me, Pia?'

She looked down, staring vacantly at the wall for a couple of seconds before bringing her eyes back to him. She smiled. 'Because you nice, Adam. You always joke and laugh, very good at your job, *simpatico*.'

Adam leant forward and gently took hold of both her hands. 'I think that it was your first time, Pia.'

'No! No! Not first time.'

'I don't believe you, Pia. I think that it was your first time and I think that you were very frightened.'

'No! No! Adam!' She gently fidgeted her hands free from his hold.

'Why me, Pia? There are lots of boys who would love to go out with you. You are very attractive.'

'Studio Lazio Macchinisti boys, they talk, all talk each other, compare you. You different, Adam, no talk, *esperto*, gentle, kind, Adam.'

'Pia, when two people make love, they should know each other, like each other, be kind to each other, because if that's not the case, afterwards you can feel dirty, do you understand? Pia, do you understand what I am saying? It's not just knickers off and whoopee! There has to be more to it than that, particularly the first time. Pia, the first time is so important. You remember it for the rest of your life.'

She didn't really understand everything that he was saying but got the gist of it. She was being lectured!

'You say me not nice, not attractive?'

'It's not that, Pia, you are missing the point. When I first made love, my first time, I had been going out with the girl for three years, we were in love.'

'You still in love, Adam, still love girlfriend?'

'No, we parted, but I think of her every day or so and… well!'

'You still love her, Adam?'

'No, Pia, I'm over her now. We broke each other's hearts.'

'You sad, Adam, you sad?'

The waitress returned with their drinks on a small tray, placing them on the table along with an aluminium ashtray that she gently laid on top of the till receipt.

Adam nodded. 'Grazie! Grazie!' Overacting the smiling thanks as usual.

Pia just smiled, looking down to avoid eye contact as Adam slid her glass of wine to her. There was condensation on the outside of the glass. She gently ran her finger down it, causing water to trickle down the stem.

'Are you going to have something to eat, Pia? Anything?'

'No, Adam, no food. Me no hungry.'

Adam leant forward, almost whispering, 'So, okay, then, Pia, where does this leave us? I cannot make love to you because we know nothing about each other, never been anywhere together, never been to a movie or a club—'

A very noisy, virtually unsilenced motorbike thundered past, causing them both to wince at the noise that had cut short his little sermon.

She looked at him, eyes wide, a little tearful. 'You no tell anyone bout this…no one?'

'No, Pia, I'm no Macchinista boy, I no tell anyone. This is just between the two of us.'

'You promise, Adam…promise?'

'I promise, Pia. We have a big secret, a very tender, lovely secret.'

'You very kind, Adam. Thank you, I think I go now, go home, metro.'

Adam looked at her. She was still shaking. There was no way he was going to let her go home on the metro.

'Finish your drink.' He sipped his Coke, exaggerating the motion to encourage her.

'No, *me* go home, thank you, it's best.' She started to get up.

'Wait a second, Pia. I'm paying for you to go home in a taxi, no argument!'

'I'm fine, Adam!'

'No, Pia, a taxi, I pay, you don't argue. Otherwise, I tell everyone!' he added, with a wink and a smile as he opened his wallet and paid for the drinks, tucking a note under the ashtray.

She smiled, laughed at herself and took a sip of the wine. Resignedly, she stood up, lifting her bag onto her right shoulder, which meant that her arm was not accessible for Adam to take to reassure her. They walked now like brother and sister instead of a courting couple as they crossed the road to the far pavement. Adam was looking for a taxi, but they all seemed to be taken. Pia just walked silently beside him. Her expression told him that she was rebuking herself and seemingly regretting the whole encounter. She frowned, often slowly biting her lip and staring upwards to maybe try and clear her head. They both lost track of distance and time.

Eventually, a taxi appeared. Adam waved like a demented tourist, and the taxi effected a squealing turn and came to an abrupt stop a few yards in front of them. Adam took hold of Pia's shoulder. She turned to face him, unable to look him in the eye.

'I pay full fare plus tip, Pia… no arguments. Tell me how much he wants.'

She smiled wanly and leant through the opened passenger window, speaking quickly in her mother tongue. Her lean into the vehicle accentuated her very short skirt and slim figure. She looked very vulnerable as she straightened to face him.

'Dodici mille lire, Adam, twelve thousand, it's a lot!'

Adam already had his wallet out and gave her a ten and a five.

'Fifteen, Pia, to cover the tip.'

She took the notes slowly. Without a word, she leant forward and kissed him on the cheek, taking him completely by surprise.

He smiled, shook his head and smiled again. 'Pia, before you go home, check your make-up. Have a clear head, yeah?'

'I will, Adam, I will.' She looked him straight in the eye, her big brown eyes slightly moist again, frown lines appearing on her forehead. 'Adam, don't tell anyone, please! Please!'

He opened the rear door for her. 'No, Pia, I don't tell anyone. An Englishman's word is his bond, you can rely on me… it's okay!' He patted her gently on the back as she got into the taxi, turned and sat into the seat, twisting her knees in, finishing with a nod to confirm that she was settled. He closed the door, and within a couple of seconds, the taxi had revved up and bumped its way down the cobbled street.

Adam stood watching the retreating vehicle until it was out of sight. What in blue blazes was all of that about? His mind was in turmoil. He had no idea where he was. He slowly turned and walked back the way that they had come. Eventually, he reached familiar surroundings, but he didn't know whether to eat, drink, or just go back to his room and collect his thoughts. He decided on the latter.

His room smelt of the city as he had left the shutters open. The opened vodka bottle and the two glasses were where they had left them on the dressing table. He picked up the one with her pink lipstick on. It was a thick lip print. She had treacled it on, no doubt about it! He sniffed it. There was no smell, just the raw smell of the spirit. He screwed the cap back on the bottle as if trying to put a full stop at the end of one of the most unforgettable evenings of his twenty-nine years. Sleep was not going to be easy to come by that night with so much going round in his head.

He was right. The alarm at twenty to seven was most unwelcome.

Tuesday 15th April

The early morning sun was starting to refresh the sandstone buildings. The city was buzzing; scooters were scooting, cars were rumbling over the cobbles; everyone was charging enthusiastically into the new day. Adam felt jaded and off-balance from lack of sleep, and hungry because he had only had a light meal the evening before.

A few minutes after seven o'clock, Toni's car swept up beside him. Adam reached for the front door handle, but it was locked. Adam leant down, and Toni waved for him to get in the back. Taken aback, Adam was about to open the rear door when it was opened for him, from the inside. He peered in to see Jose smiling at him.

'Adam, apologies for hijacking your car. Mine is in for a service today, and so I asked Toni to pick me up. I hope you don't mind. I only live a couple of blocks away. You okay?'

Adam settled into his seat and pulled the door closed. He was a little surprised, to say the least. 'No, it's fine! Not a problem. Nice to see you, Jose.'

Toni smiled and waved at Adam in his rear-view mirror. 'Adam, morning,' he said, before pulling out into the procession of traffic.

Jose eased himself even more to his left to give Adam more space. 'How are you getting on here, Adam? Settling in?'

'Yes, fine, thanks, fine. Friendly crew, lovely bunch of people.'

Jose smiled and nodded. 'How's your Italian coming along?' He reached into his jacket breast pocket and eased out a folded piece of paper, which he waved gently. 'I have written down all of the swear words for you, Adam, phonetically, of course, with their approximate meanings. Mainly they are to do with God, mothers, sex, and excrement in any combination, or more likely a combination of all four, but they say that swear words are the first that you learn in any language so, here you are, my gift to you, *mio regalo*, my gift!'

Adam took the piece of paper and gently unfolded it. His jaw dropped in shock. Line after line of perfectly phonetically written words, with the translation underneath. But the writing was perfect copperplate; he had seen this hand before. He swung round to Jose, speechless.

Jose just sat there, saying nothing, watching his every reaction and his obvious discomfort.

Adam looked down again at the paper, then back to Jose. 'I have seen this writing before, Jose.'

'Have you, Adam? Where would that be?'

'On a note stuffed in my diddy bag. A nine o'clock meeting.'

'Really?'

'Yes, and I think that you wrote that note.'

Jose smiled, sat back in his seat and turned away from Adam to look out of his window at the passing traffic.

'Yes, Adam, I did. I wrote the note for a young friend.'

'Pia?' Adam frowned. He was even more confused now. What the hell is going on here? This was not a normal start to the day.

'Yes! Pia. How is she, by the way?'

'She's fine, as far as I know, fine. Why, Jose? Why write the note?'

'I can tell you the whole story, but you must keep it to yourself. All of it, every detail. Do I have your word, Adam?'

Adam was in a mild state of shock. He looked at Jose and then to Toni as he stared ahead, focused on driving. He indicated with a nod that Toni would hear everything. Jose smiled, stroked his moustache with his right index finger to indicate that he was wholly composed and in charge of the whole situation.

'Toni is Pia's uncle. He knows everything. In fact, it was partly his idea.'

Adam looked at Toni's eyes in the rear-view mirror. He nodded back in agreement.

Jose turned to Adam, the light-heartedness now gone from his face.

'Pia is the youngest of five sisters; two are married with children, and one is engaged. The other is a tart who would like nothing more than to be locked up for a few days with a randy football team. They regard young Pia as the runt of the litter. They call her the "ironing board" because of her figure. No boyfriends, still a virgin, and they constantly taunt her, constantly! Siblings can be very cruel, very cruel! So we looked for someone to help make Pia a woman, and you popped up. An Englishman, very sexually experienced, kind, considerate, great sense of humour, so you were cast for the part. We hope you don't mind. The English are renowned for keeping secrets.'

Adam was lost for words. He looked at the back of Toni's head and his reflected eyes in the mirror. He was concentrating on his driving, but he didn't need to as the road ahead was clear. He was keeping out of it. Adam turned to Jose.

'This meeting this morning, your car being serviced, it's no accident, is it?'

'Absolutely right, Adam, what a smart guy you are. We just wanted to make sure that you continue to be discreet. Studio Lazio is a gossip mill, and Pia will not become the centre of gossip. Is that okay? How is she?'

'How is she? Okay, as far as I know. Okay, look, nothing happened, we went out for a drink, and she went home in a taxi.'

'Nothing happened,' Jose repeated, his eyebrows raised in surprise. 'What do you mean, nothing happened?'

'I mean, Jose, that she was so nervous, so frightened, that I took out her for a drink and sent her home in a taxi.'

'Well, well, Adam! You really are English, aren't you? Anyone else would have bonked her senseless.'

'No, Jose, you're wrong. I am not into vulnerable young women. It was best that she was treated with respect and sent home.'

'Adam, you amaze me! Nothing happened? She went home in a taxi?'

'Nothing happened, Jose, nothing.'

'Shit! Back to square one!' he replied, grimacing as he turned to look out of the window.

'No, Jose, not back to square one. She is outstandingly beautiful, a virtually perfect face. This is not about sex and virginity; it's about…about respect, and her standing as a person. She has the look of the sixties. I should know! I spend most of my time filming in London's West End. She is outstandingly beautiful. In London, Kings Road, Carnaby Street, she would stop the traffic. Take some photos of her, get her an agent, you know people, don't you?'

Toni looked up at him in the mirror. He had been listening to every syllable and now nodded agitatedly. 'Si, si!'

Jose paused for a second, smacked his thigh with a loud slap. 'Of course you are right, you are so right, she is lovely, very beautiful. Yes, I know agents, photographers, I can ship some Quant frocks. That's a great idea, great idea. I can even put her pictures up in my shop. Yes!'

Adam looked surprised.

'You don't know about my shop. I sell clothes and an eclectic range of objets d'art, down in Trastevere. You must come by, Adam. I'd love to fit you up, particularly now I know that you're not into women.'

Adam raised his right hand as if to say something, but Jose cut across him.

'Only joking, Adam, only joking. The offer is there, nonetheless. Come by. I'm there on Saturdays. I'll get a visiting card put in your diddy bag,' he added, laughing.

The gates of the studio loomed before them. Jose, realising that he was running out of time, looked Adam hard in the eye, his eyes as cold as ice. The speed at which his mood changed was chilling. 'Say nothing about any of this to anyone, Adam, not any of it. They make wheelchairs in your size, and you have no friends here to push you. Do I make myself clear?'

Adam, startled by the sudden change in tone, backed away slightly. 'Yes, I understand.'

Jose's expression changed again, like a switch suddenly being pulled. The ensuing smile was instant and genuine. 'Thanks, Adam, glad we understand one another.'

Toni turned right through the gate and gently eased the car to a halt outside the café.

Jose opened his door and eased himself out of his seat. 'Enjoy your coffee, Adam. It's a bit too working-class for me, but Toni is going to buy you breakfast and give me the bill, so enjoy. Ciao, bello!'

The door slammed, and Adam was left holding a page of swear words that was in places damp from the sweat of his hand. Well, that was an interesting start to the day!

Luigi was in his usual seat in the dining room with his back to the barely opened window. Nella was in her element, proudly striding towards him with a laden breakfast tray. The early morning sun was just about to floodlight the room; it was already lighting the window frame and getting more confident by the minute.

She spotted Rino, the gardener, through the window as he walked past, pushing a wheelbarrow towards the rising sun and some little job that he had devised to keep himself busy, or apparently so.

Luigi pulled his serviette from the table onto his lap. 'Buongiorno, Nella! How are you today?'

'Fine, thank you, sir. I've done you a herb omelette to stock you up as you are out today. Does Mister Burgio want breakfast later?'

'I have absolutely no idea, Nella, no idea!'

She placed the tray down in the middle of the table and lifted the silver cover off the plate. Luigi leant forward and gently took the plate, lifting it towards his face to smell the steaming plateful as Nella placed a knife and fork in front of him. The smell of fresh coffee filled their nostrils as Nella lifted the spare saucer off the top of his cup and saucer.

Luigi smiled at the smell. He liked Nella's early morning coffee. 'Thank you, Nella, this is lovely. Mister Burgio may well be leaving us. This morning, he is looking at renting a house higher up the hill, a few minutes up the road, so he may well be moving out.'

'Oh, that's sad, sir. Such a nice man.'

'Nella, you are too diplomatic. We both feel the same way about our house guest. We should be grateful that he might be moving away and that we can get back to normality.'

'I understand, sir. Will you be back for supper?'

'Busy day today, Nella. Casa Annunciata at twelve as usual with Isabella. Then hopefully first rushes viewing at three, so most likely be back around six or six-thirty, providing everything is okay.'

'Oh, I'm sure it will be, sir. You have such a friendly crew this time.'

'I always have a friendly crew,' he said, smiling as he tasted the first mouthful. 'Mmmm! This is lovely!'

'Oh, thank you! Is there anything else I can get you?'

'No, I'm fine, Nella. I am sorry that Mister Burgio has not let you know what he wants. I'll have a word with him.'

'Oh, it's okay, sir, no trouble. I'll rustle up something for him when he comes down. Will that be all, sir?'

'Thank you, Nella, this is lovely. I am well taken care of.'

'A pleasure, sir.'

Veniero Frattari had been a film editor for almost twenty-five years, working virtually consistently on productions with American backers. Studio Lazio was the go-to place in Europe for American money; it was a cheap place to make a movie but not as cheap as it used to be in the hard days immediately after the war. The thing that brought the Yanks back time after time was the sets. The Italians were incredibly talented at making everything look extremely realistic, and the labour was cheap, too cheap in his view.

The unit driver had just handed him the film prints of the first day's work that had been processed overnight at the lab across the city. The sound house next door had then transferred in real-time all of the recorded sound from Carl the Sound man's quarter-inch tapes to 35mm sound striped film. Over the next few hours, Veniero would syncronise all of the sound to pictures, ready for the producers to view at three in the projection room. He was not particularly keen to go to this room because it absolutely stank of cigar and cigarette smoke, and as a recent quitter, he really disliked the smell of the place. He still kept his old pipe on the shelf above the edit machine, perhaps as a souvenir of temptations past. But also because it defined his personality in a way, a quiet, contemplative, organised person who spent most of his working life sitting down, working in the spirity smell of film cement.

His room was where the film came to life, took shape, where the story unfolded. He would, of course, work with the Director and follow his instruction. Still, he always managed to put a piece of himself in, bring something to the party, which is probably why he was rarely out of work. He knew from past experience that Grace's continuity notes would be very detailed, as they had always been over the years. He opened up the envelope to take stock of what went where and when. He pulled down his window, blind immediately halving the amount of light in the room. He was ready to work on the harvest that had been created on the first day, and it would be him, and only him, who decided whether they had shot three minutes fifty.

As the set was starting to come alive and the lights were one by one starting to come on, Adam saw the unit driver hand Sven the report sheets from the lab. He knew what the letter contained because of Sven's body language as he tightened up. This was the way it worked. It was something that happened first thing in the morning on virtually every film set around the world: delivery of the lab report.

He watched intently as Sven opened the envelope and unfolded the two printed pages. Jan walked over towards him but kept a respectful distance. Being a Director of Photography can be a very lonely place to be when the lab paperwork arrives. Sven read each line, slowly and carefully, the serious set to his face slowly transforming into a grin of smug self-satisfaction as he read the final few lines. He turned to Jan with a broad smile, and an upbeat conversation took place, which ended with Jan patting him gently on the shoulder.

Thank God for that! thought Adam. Out-of-focus shots or unreported hairs in the gate were a plane ticket home for him as far as he was concerned. He knew only too well if there were anything wrong, he would get the dreaded eye flick to flag up the fact there was a problem; he had received a few of those in his ten-year career, not a pleasant experience. But Sven turned to him, nodded and smiled. He didn't have to say anything; the nod and smile said it all.

Pia appeared briefly in the distance in and out of the gloom and shadows. At least she was up and about and seemingly okay, Adam observed with relief. There was quite a dark undercurrent working its way into the production, and it just made Adam think very carefully about his behaviour. Maybe he needed to be a lot more circumspect and a bit less of a wind-up merchant!

Gill stopped at the top of the sloping drive to the old, yellow, stone country house surrounded by large, mature pine trees. The driveway was full of ruts and bumps, the stone scalpings over time having been pushed up to either side, leaving a somewhat high middle that was covered in sparse grass. She was the first one there. She switched off the engine and wound down her window.

The smell of pine resins and damp vegetation drifted in, and cockerels could be heard in the far distance, encouraging the hens to get on with their day. The wealthy owner of the house had recently died, and the family were looking for a short-term let of a few months until the estate was sorted out, which was lucky for Gill because quality houses in this affluent area were hard to come by.

Gill decided to freewheel down the slope, which was probably the most sensible decision, bearing in mind the state of the track. The slope was steep, and she had to brake most of the way down. The bumps were as bad as they looked in the early morning cross light. The car silencer grated a couple of times in protest as the raised centre repeatedly hit it. As she neared the house, she was aware of another small, pale blue vehicle turning off the main road and following her down. She watched in the rear-view mirror as it bumped and lurched about, eventually coming to a stop just behind her.

The house agent was true to type, all teeth and tits, as they say back home in her native Australia. How she could drive in such a short tight dress was hard to comprehend. They were both there for Dino Burgio. The house agent was very keen to meet him, Gill less so. She found the man to be mannerless, physically repulsive and more than a little dangerous. There was something icy about him.

They had to wait three-quarters of an hour before the black Mercedes unit car could be seen turning off the main road down onto the track. By this time Gill had heard virtually the entire twenty-two-year life story of the house agent and her desire to get into movies. Like a sponge, she absorbed a forty-five-minute monologue of ego and self-interest. She could barely get a word in edgeways.

It was beneath Dino to open his own car door so he waited for his driver to hastily get out, walk around the car and obsequiously let him out. Gill watched from a few paces away as the house agent launched herself towards him. Before she could say anything, he held out his hand.

'Dino Burgio, international Film Producer.'

Gill couldn't believe her ears. What a creep!

'Donna Tavazzi, Donna, very pleased to meet you.'

Dino couldn't take his eyes off her cleavage, which bounced gently as she moved forward to shake his hand. Dino took her hand and simultaneously gripped her right shoulder with his left hand.

'Nice to meet you, Donna. Very nice!' He held her gaze. 'Need to get that track fixed though. I have a Cadillac, and it ain't gonna get on well with that track. You can do that, yeah?'

'Yes, of course, Mister Burgio, anything to help, anything.'

'Good, Donna. You got a great attitude, great attitude, I like that. Shall we see the house?'

'Yes, of course, of course, it's all open. I'll take you round.'

Dino looked briefly at the house, the open front door and then back to Donna's cleavage before he reluctantly looked up at Gill.

'No need for you to come in, Gill. Donna can see me round.'

'Yes, fine, Dino, absolutely, fine,' she said, forcing a smile, as she watched Dino put his hand on the agent's lower back just above her ample buttocks as he gently eased her towards the open door.

Gill shrugged her shoulders and let out a deep breath, looking up at the clear sky. The unit driver appeared beside her, sensing her discomfort.

Neither of them enjoyed being anywhere near Dino. Gill's Italian was totally fluent, which was good as the driver preferred to speak in his mother tongue rather than use her to practise his English. The conversation was light, gossipy, as was usual for the unit drivers; rather like hairdressers, they shared similar lines of communication.

The one piece of gossip that quite surprised Gill was that yesterday, the son of Andrea, one of the Macchinisti, badly cut his head at school. The kid had been treated that afternoon at the American Hospital, which, it would be fair to say, was not cheap! Before Gill could glean more information, a smiling Dino and an equally smiling Donna appeared. The driver immediately walked over to the car, and as quickly as he could, reversed and turned it around, ready to drive away. He got out and stood holding Dino's door open for him.

Dino beamed at Gill. 'It's great, great. Donna here has shown me around. I like it. The Art department need to come in and tidy round and give the main bedroom a coat of paint, and there's a dripping tap in the downstairs toilet. Once I'm in, we'll get Props and Art to come in and see what extras are needed. Can't tell till I've been in a few days. You okay with that?'

Gill nodded. 'That's fine, Dino, absolutely fine. What's happening about the driveway?'

'Leave that up to you…Donna and the owners. I ain't going to pay for it, but it needs to be done as it lets the property down. Oh! And the chickens round the back need to go. Ain't gonna have no rooster telling me when to wake up!' he added, with a grin.

Donna was all smiles, positively glowing, just nodding in agreement, as she muttered, 'No problem!'

Dino, by now, was walking towards his car. He stopped, turned and smiled at Donna. 'Car will pick you up at eight. Eight okay?'

Donna blushed and smiled like a schoolgirl. 'Yes, fine, Mr Burgio.'

'Dino. Call me Dino. Looking forward to it, thanks!'

Gill tried hard to hide her shock. She stood and watched Dino leering at Donna as he eased himself into the car. His driver gently closed his door before he walked around the back and nodded respectfully at the two women who had now gravitated together.

The women watched as the Mercedes slowly bumped its way up to the main road, occasionally emitting a scraping noise as the exhaust silencer argued with the track.

Gill turned to Donna, deciding to ignore Donna's social life and just stick to business. 'The track, the chickens and the bit of decorating. Will the family be happy with that?'

Donna was miles away, watching the retreating Mercedes, thoughts racing through her head.

'Sorry, yes! No, all that will be fine. They don't want it to stay empty, and as Mr Burgio says, the track has got to be done anyway.'

'Okay, fine. Get the contract and bank details over to me at the studio this afternoon, and our accountant will sign it and set up the payments. Tenancy to commence immediately. Mr Burgio is a very impatient man.'

Donna was on a high. It was evident that meeting the Film Producer had fulfilled all of her dreams. 'Yes, yes, of course, fine, I can do that!'

Gill nodded a closing smile and slowly walked to her car, grateful for the fact that she was not a point of interest for Mr Burgio. She was very tempted to warn Donna, to give her some motherly advice, but her body language told her that her words would fall on deaf ears. That young lady was going to learn a lot about life in the next day or so. Now all that remained, apart from the everyday challenge of administrating a major film, was getting a Cadillac from Toulouse to Rome in one piece before the end of the week.

Adam had a leisurely morning, focusing on close-ups mainly of Fulvio and Belinda as their relationship slowly matured and became less overt, more subtle, and more of a love affair. It was a pleasure to see good actors working, and the little subtle touches and nuances that they put in, a smile here, a nod there, a little touch, was lovely to watch!

Pia kept her distance from Adam even though she was on set to look after Belinda. She had no reason to come to the camera side and never did. Grace just did her thing, only coming to the camera a couple of times to look through. Adam devised a signalling system whereby he held his hands, one above his head for the headroom and his left hand to signal where the bottom of the frame was against his body, and she was happy with that. It was approximate but it seemed to work for her.

Jan was still going on about Sophia, watching her intently every time she fussed over Belinda. What she did was as much about keeping the artist happy and feeling important as to whether they actually really needed that little dab of face powder just before every take. She was like all of the best make-up artists, an expert in the science of emotional support, no doubt about it.

Jan leant forward to Adam during a brief pause in the proceedings. 'I'm going to ask her out. What do you think?'

Adam, mollified by his recent experiences, decided to play it straight. 'You have to be very discreet, Jan. This place is an absolute gossip mill, and if you are indiscreet, it won't be long before the whole of Western Europe knows. She might not be happy with that; she's a local, a Catholic, judging by her crucifix, and you believe in a god with a big hammer. Not a lot in common!'

Jan leant back in surprise, banging his head slightly against the camera. 'Thor? I don't believe in Thor. I'm just unconvinced by the whole God thing.'

Adam leant towards him. 'I can't tell you what to do, mate, that's a decision you have to make for yourself. My only advice is to be very discreet and don't expect an easy lay because you ain't gonna get one!'

'No! All joking aside, I really like her… really… I do!'

'You're a lost cause, Jan! Good luck. Write her a letter, stick it in her make-up bag, or I can, if you want. That seems to be the best way forward. I'll deliver it for you, if you want. No one notices me wandering around the set all the time, chatting everyone up.'

Jan smiled and clapped Adam gently on the shoulder as Duke called out, 'Going for a line-up!'

A plan was starting to form in his mind.

Luigi was totally at home at the Casa Annunciata, down in the old factory area at the back of the railway. It was a place full of wonderful people and sick children, the former caring for the latter. Isabella had gone down a storm. All of the carers had dressed up for her visit, and Luigi noticed a lot of them were wearing more make-up than usual. It was a really fulfilling way to spend a morning, and it was also an excellent opportunity to see how his regular charitable donations were being spent. The amounts varied over the years, but usually a percentage of the profits from each of his films was written into the contracts for the home. Having no children of his own, the charity filled a gap in his personal life.

A few paparazzi had gathered outside, ready for Isabella's departure, but Luigi's driver, Bruno, let no one past the wrought-iron gates into the grounds. Because of his size and general demeanour, no one was prepared to try their luck. One of the more voluptuous journalists did try fluttering her eyelashes and pouting her lips at him in an attempt to get past and get an exclusive photo sequence inside the home with Isabella and some of the kids, but she might as well have chatted up a statue; she got nowhere.

Isabella had really entered into the whole spirit of the place and had ended up with her hands and forearms spattered in water paint in her efforts to encourage others to follow her lead. Luigi watched her with joy as she played and giggled with the kids. He could see the child in her again, which he recalled wasn't that long ago. She had always been a happy child, an absolute joy to be with, like her mother.

It was coming up for lunchtime, and as he usually did, Luigi went to the kitchen and collected a couple of trays of food to feed to the kids, nearly all of whom were not blessed with the ability to feed themselves. Both he and Isabella felt the same way: it was a privilege to help those who could not help themselves.

Leaving was a relatively long, drawn-out affair with all of the kids and some of the carers wanting a hug or some physical contact with Isabella before she left. Her visit had undoubtedly brought a considerable amount of joy to a lot of people.

As the front door was opened for them to leave, the paparazzi, now numbering ten or twelve, all surged and became agitated, buzzing agitatedly like bees around the main gate. Luigi's driver opened it halfway to let them out, which exacerbated the activity. The sound of camera shutters clicking, flashbulbs popping and a cacophony of requests for photographs and personal information filled the air.

Luigi's driver literally swam through the crowd, as he had done many times before, with Isabella right behind him in the shadow of his bulk. Luigi followed up at the rear, the little procession resembling a three-person conga all the way to the car, which they all managed to get into without any significant incident apart from a lot of shouting and jostling. The drive off was protracted as the more determined tried to get one final photo before they eventually were able to pull clear and accelerate carefully away. All three of them breathed a sigh of relief at the same time, which made Luigi laugh.

'They never turn out for me, Isabella. Must be something to do with you being here today… Seriously though, thank you for coming, it was really appreciated. They will talk about this morning for months to come, believe me.'

'Luigi, it is always a pleasure, even if I have got paint on my dress,' she said, pointing to a spattered blue thumb-size blob on her sleeve.

Luigi looked hard at her sleeve, then back up to her face. 'Loren would never complain, Isabella!'

'Luigi, you are so cruel!'

Peter Dublin paused for a second in the doorway of the office, pleased to see that Gill had not altered the lighting by closing the shutters. She did have the fluorescents on, though, which he deliberately switched off with a quick flick, before walking past her to his desk by the window.

'You had anything?'

Gill, ignoring the light change, looked up from her typewriter and forced a smile. 'No, not yet, been waiting for you to come back.'

'Okay, what's happening about the Caddi?'

'Just come off the phone. I've organised for the vendor to drive it down, all expenses paid. I've insisted on fully comprehensive insurance, though. He reckons he'll be here Friday, maybe Thursday evening.'

'Good, Gill, good. Will he require a train fare home?'

'No, don't think so. He is coming down with a mate, and they are going to do a few days' sightseeing, so hopefully not.'

Dublin picked up the eight or so pieces of paper on his desk, had a quick shuffle through and dropped them disdainfully back down, then walked purposefully towards the door.

'Well done. The moment it gets here, get Mosena to check it over. I don't want Dino going ballistic because it's not firing on all cylinders. Talking of the wonderous Dino, I have a rushes viewing with him and Luigi in a few minutes, so I'll walk over, take a bit of fresh air, okay?'

Gill just looked up and smiled. 'Okay. Enjoy.'

Dublin nodded and slammed the door with considerable force behind him. She winced at the noise and looked over at the light switch. It was becoming a bit of a battleground, that little square piece of metal.

The assembly of film and sound had gone well for Veniero Frattari. As far as he could tell on his Steenbeck edit machine, the pictures looked good. They were all now laced up and ready in the viewing room projector, awaiting the arrival of the big wigs. As predicted, the little theatre stank of cigar and cigarette smoke; it was woven into the fabric of the room, into every one of the sixty-four flip-up red seats and the matching red floor-to-ceiling curtains down either side. That silver-screened space entertained a lot of very nervous people on a day-to-day basis. Careers were ended in that room; rows over artistic interpretation were an almost daily occurrence.

The whole space had a very negative energy about it, which magically changed to one of positive euphoria when the viewed material was technically fault-free, visually and artistically pleasing, to all of those watching. An air of self-congratulation could fill the air, or an air of deep depression in the case of required reshoots.

Veniero had seen the dramas in that little sloping room unfold many times and in many different languages over the years. It was a very volatile, mercurial business. Viewing rushes (the Americans called them dailies) was always the cause of a lot of nervousness, whatever you called them. Still, he had a system. He sat up the back, right next to the door and kept out of it. Let them all fight it out down in the stalls down the front.

Dublin was the first to arrive and was standing by the water machine in the foyer. Luigi's car drew up, followed a few seconds later by Dino. The latter never paused his step as he walked straight past Dublin and the door that he was holding open, striding down to the front row to sit in the middle seat.

Luigi was in less of a hurry. He nodded at Dublin and said, 'Good morning, Peter, everything all right?' He noticed

Veniero standing quietly to one side. 'When you're ready, Veniero, when you're ready.'

Veniero nodded and leant upwards to tap the glass window to the projector room. As Dublin took a seat in the front row, the lights dimmed. Within a few seconds, the screen was illuminated with the focus leader. A large circle cut into thirty-six white and thirty-six black tapering segments, all meeting in the centre, flickered its way onto the screen. The image moved very slightly in and out of focus as the projectionist checked his lens setting.

Apart from the murmur of the projector, it was so quiet you could have heard a pin drop. The clapper board clapped, and you could hear Lasse's off-mike voice clearly call 'ACTION'.

Veniero was happy. The little café scene looked absolutely spot on, transporting him back to the 1920s. His good mood was short-lived as Dino suddenly shouted up from the front, 'It's soft, bloody soft. Sharpen it, can yah?'

Luigi looked alarmed, and Dublin was aghast.

'It's bloody soft. Can't you people see it's out of focus? Soft! Bloody soft!' By now Dino was standing up in the flickering projected light, the image of the set flashing all over his face and white shirt.

Veniero stood up and tapped the projector room glass. The lights came back on, followed a few seconds later by the projector light onto the screen and Dino fizzling out.

Dino waved both hands in frustration and turned to the small projectionist window. 'It's soft, bloody soft! Can't you people see that?'

Dublin was open-mouthed. Luigi frowned as he said, 'It's okay, seems fine.'

'It's not! There's no bite to the picture. It's either shit camera work or crappy dirty lenses. Cinepan always send their crap stuff to Europe and keep the best at home!'

Luigi stood up. 'Hold on, hold on here, Dino. Let's look at this logically. You think that the pictures are not sharp, they lack definition, is that right?'

'Yeah! That bloody cameraman has used too much diffusion, ruined it, need to get rid of him!'

'I'm sorry, Dino, that's not the way I work.'

Dino cut across, 'Well, it bloody well should be. He's ruined a day's work, and we need to stop him before he ruins the rest of today's too.'

Dublin stood up and eased his way backwards, trying to make himself as inconspicuous as possible.

Veniero's voice rang out from the back. 'May I say something?'

Dino scowled, but Luigi held up his hand. 'Please, Veniero, please.'

Veniero walked down a few rows towards the two protagonists.

'There may well be something in what Mr Burgio says. This is a very old screen and a very old projector, and the prints from the lab here are on local Ferranticolour film, which gives a much softer look than the American filmstocks that he may be more used to. May I suggest that we try to get a viewing in theatre one, which has just been recently modernised and if you want, send the outtake negatives to Lumaxfilm labs in London for a high-quality graded print as a check? Also, I have read all of the continuity notes, and the cameraman did not use any diffusion at all during the first day. I understand it's not his style; he prefers light, to tell his story.'

Luigi held up his hand again. 'Okay, Veniero, okay. I think that's a sensible way forward. Try to get a booking and send the negatives to London.'

Dino stamped his foot and repeatedly shook his fist in frustration, like a petulant child not getting what it wants. 'I've never known such a set-up. Crappy theatres, old projectors, crappy labs, you people are stone age, stone age! Run the bloody film anyway, and let's see what we can make of it!'

Dublin stood uneasily, almost hyperventilating, sucking in his breath through pursed lips. 'I'll take the film to London, personal baggage, tonight. Be back tomorrow morning.'

Luigi nodded and smiled. 'Thank you, Peter, but can't you just ship it?'

‘No. There’s no guarantee it will be put on any particular plane. It has to be accompanied baggage. I’ll take it and bring it all back tomorrow.’

Dino sat down and waved his hand in the air at the projectionist. ‘Just get on with it, stop talking, run it, run it!’

Veniero tapped the projectionist’s window glass, and a few seconds later, the lights dimmed, and the screen spluttered into a colourful moving picture. Veniero’s pulse rate was right up, and he thought of his old pipe on the shelf. This Dino was enough to make him take up smoking again.

Adam knew immediately that something was up when Dublin sidled his way on the set and signalled to Duke that he wanted to speak to him and Lasse. Duke walked towards him, the noise on the set slowly increasing like an orchestra reaching a crescendo, as the instruments of speculation, intrigue and gossip all started to play. Dublin waited for Lasse to join them. The directorial smiles were all gone, replaced by a curious frown. Dublin flicked his hair nervously behind his left ear as he murmured to Duke six inches above him. Duke, like Lasse, was stone-faced. Neither betrayed any emotion; they just nodded and nodded. Everyone on set was watching, some trying to lip-read and get a head start on the gossip. Eventually, Dublin finished speaking and stepped back, looked around and was most displeased to find himself the centre of attention. Duke nodded, then nodded again as if digesting a lot of complex information. Finally, he stood up to his full height, his face emotionless.

'Okay, ragazzi, going for line-up. Ben, ease the red and let's try to keep the noise down…keep the noise down…we have work to do.'

Adam watched the whole encounter from a safe distance, knowing deep in his core that it was not good news. His suspicions were confirmed when Duke and Lasse beckoned Sven to join them, and a stone-faced, three-headed nodding match took place at the edge of the set.

The vultures in the lighting rig heard most of the conversation as they sat quietly above, but neither of them spoke good enough English, and all they were able to pick up was Dino and projection, but it was a start, enough to begin a rumour.

Lasse was the first to break away and signal to Jan that he was ready for the dance of the viewfinder. Anatra plodded towards them, chalk in hand, spare chalk behind his ear and a snowlike dusting of it down the front of his trousers. Adam knew that he would probably have to wait until the end of the day to find out what was going on. The rumour mill had already started to work; it just hadn't reached him yet.

Gill wasn't the least bit surprised to hear that her beloved Production Manager was bunking off to London. He was incredibly agile at getting out of the way when the shit hit the fan, or some disaster loomed. He seemed to have a sixth sense for it. She had already dispatched Veniero in a unit car to the labs to identify the outtake negative that was stored in their vaults for security. She had also organised the shipping agent to get underway to the lab as well. The beloved Peter was booked on the eight o'clock Alitalia flight to Heathrow and also booked into the Aerial Hotel on Bath Road right outside the airport. Fortunately, the world's best film lab was just a mile and a half to the west, down the same road, not a surprise really as a large percentage of their business flew into them from all over the northern hemisphere night after night.

The set had become jittery; you could sense it, the Production Manager and the First in deep, deep conversation. Something was definitely wrong. The fragile world of the self-employed was in a state of uncertainty, insecure, vulnerable. Adam was as concerned as everyone else. They hadn't even seen the rushes yet; that was not due to happen until after wrap. Jan was not able to offer any clarification, and Sven was polishing his viewfinder every couple of minutes. Grace came over to the camera and bent down to put her head between them.

'You boys all right? What was all that about?'

Jan checked the set to make sure that he had time to talk. 'No idea, no idea at all. Maybe someone's been hurt?'

'Well, if I hear anything, I'll let you know, and if you hear anything, you let me know.'

'That's fine, Grace, fine. Thanks.'

Adam looked at her for a couple of seconds, wondered about her story. She was like a still lake, very calm on the surface. Still, he sensed, very deep, the deeper you go the colder it often gets, but equally so, there are often very interesting things below the surface. She was a total enigma to him, as many of the women on the set were. As she turned and walked back to her desk, he watched her. She had a lovely gait, very measured, sure-footed, confident. The only one that Adam had a handle on was Pia, and she appeared during the day a couple of times, just giving him a neutral nod, no more than any other person. She was obviously determined to keep her secret.

Dublin breezed back into the office to pick up his well-thumbed address book from his locked top drawer and spent a few minutes on an international call to London, to his old mate, Paddy, the car dealer, inviting him to come to his hotel at the airport and bring along a couple of girls so that they could have a party.

Gill busied herself with her notes and paperwork, wondering what presents he would bring back to his bejewelled, hawk-faced wife, Alex. It was hard to respect a bully who was a coward without a moral compass. It was a shame though. Everyone else on the payroll was absolutely charming. It seemed to be just the Production Office that had drawn the short straw.

Adam sensed the jitters on the set; it was much quieter between takes, much more subdued. Duke carried on as usual as if nothing had happened, as did Lasse, but Sven was a lot quieter than normal, only smiling tightly at Jan whenever they approached one another. Jan never asked him what had gone on, and there was no time for a confidential chat as Duke kept up a relentless pace, getting through set-up after set-up, crisply, cleanly, moving on. They had to finish on the café set that day, as they were moving out to the back lot for exteriors, while the stage was re-rigged for fresh upcoming interior scenes. The big man did not like overtime; it was against his nature. Also, the weather forecast for the next few days was good, which was always an added bonus when working outside.

It was only when Duke called out, 'Ragazzi, children, listen. Tomorrow we are on the back lot. Read your call sheets. Last scene is under rainmakers so Camera, Sound, Wardrobe, Make-up, Props, bring your waterproofs. Read your call sheets. Rain, *piove*, final scenes tomorrow. Thanks, everybody, it's a wrap,' that Sven came over to the camera and beckoned to Jan, Adam and Luca, leading them to a quiet, dark corner.

He explained as best he could what had gone on at the Producer's rushes viewing and how displeased the Producer Dino was with the quality of the pictures. After he had finished, a sense of gloom descended over all of them as they took on board the fact that they could all be looking for a new job in the next twenty-four hours. Adam was particularly glum because he knew that the set of lenses that he had brought out with him from London were first-rate, absolutely pin-sharp. Plus the fact he had checked through the camera before every take to make sure that everything was exactly as it should be. There was something not right here. Still, it certainly wasn't the quality of the kit or any cock-up on the part of the Camera crew.

The only person who smiled momentarily late that afternoon was Grace. Four minutes, ten seconds screen time. The boys done good!

Luigi was waiting tight-lipped in the cinema foyer for the crew as they trickled in just before six. The entire production crew was there: Make-up, Wardrobe, Continuity, Construction, Props and Camera. The mood was very sombre, people were tight-lipped, barely smiling, all having by now heard about the earlier row. Even Sophia was quiet, which was most unusual. Jose just nodded at everyone, with a forced smile. Dodgy pictures were the sole problem of the Camera crew, everyone knew that, but these sorts of issues could introduce significant change and affect everybody. An air of unease hung in the air.

One of the larger viewing rooms had just finished its rushes viewing, and twenty or so happy, chattering crew from another production tumbled out into the foyer and mixed with Adam's crew. It was like a winning and losing football team sharing the same dressing room. The atmosphere could not have been more marked as the victors swept through and out into the sunshine.

Adam and the rest of the crew trickled like naughty schoolchildren waiting to see the headmaster into the all-enveloping smell of nicotine. Everyone spread out and took a seat in the sloping viewing room, isolating themselves from each other, except for Lasse, Sven and Luigi, who sat together down the front.

Adam sat halfway to the back; he didn't want to feel cold hard stares on the back of his neck. He felt very alone as Jan, his only possible ally, moved down to the end of the front row a couple of seats away from his compatriot Sven. The lights dimmed, the projector flickered, and the show began. You could have heard a pin drop.

Gill looked at her watch, gave her desk a final look-over and slowly ran her finger down every line on her daybook to make sure that she had not missed anything. Satisfied, she respectfully closed the book. It was her Bible, her lord and master.

When her phone rang, she knew who it would be. It was his time of day; he rang, each and every day. Ispettore Alberto Consalvo rarely asked his Sovrintendenti to do this, unless his police work was absolutely crucial and he couldn't get away. Speaking to his wife after work was one of the pleasures of his life. A love affair that still burned bright after nearly twenty-five years.

'Supper out, tonight, my dear!'

A little celebration of the successful conclusion of a case this afternoon that had been going on for some six weeks. He felt that they both had earned a reward. Like many of the cases he worked on, this one had affected Gill too, with some of the unsociable hours he had to work, coming home late, sometimes going out very early. It was difficult being a policeman's wife, but the downtime when it occurred was precious and, in their case, usually quite romantically intense. They worked hard at their marriage, and it paid dividends.

Adam came out of the viewing room none the wiser and undoubtedly frustrated. If there were a can to kick down the road, he would certainly have kicked it. As everyone else exited the room they kept their distance. The mood was as sombre as it had been before they'd entered the room.

The pictures did look a little soft, but Adam had seen worse. Not that his opinion counted but he thought that it was probably the projection. Sven looked back and studied the projection room window a couple of times and wiped his handkerchief down the silver-beaded screen to see if it was clean. Apart from that, they all went their separate ways, waiting for the morning and the results of the Lumaxfilm graded prints from London.

Adam decided to go out for a really posh meal because he had a feeling that he could be on a plane home in the next couple of days. He decided on Jan's frequent recommendations to cross the Tiber and go to Trastevere under the Janiculum Hill and sample the culinary delights away from the main tourist route.

His driver was the strong, silent one, who spoke virtually no English. Still, he understood the word Trastevere, and after twenty minutes or so, eventually turned him out on a street corner. Mimicking a knife and fork action with both hands up and down to his mouth a few times coupled with multiple repetitions of the word 'buono' convinced Adam that this was the place.

Jan had always advised him to seek out shabby, badly painted places with no tablecloths and waiters without aprons because that was where the locals ate. Adam hadn't a clue where he was. He decided to make a mental note of some of the street names he passed: Via Luciano Manara, Via Luigi Masi. He wandered down cobbled streets, trying to retain some sense of direction but failing miserably. He gave up in the end. There was the occasional passing taxi, so he was not overly concerned. It was obviously a very bohemian part of town. The sound of voices and the smell of cooking food wafted out of open windows. The occasional shop, the odd small restaurant, quaint guest house hotels and residential apartments were all sprinkled haphazardly down each and every little lane, some of them barely wide enough for a car. It was undoubtedly his type of place.

Eventually, he decided, with a bit of trepidation, to sit down at a small trattoria with just five bare, wooden, outside tables. The waiter spoke no English and handed Adam a well-thumbed, typewritten sheet on which Adam recognised 'Prosciutto e melone' and 'Spaghetti alla Carbonara', to which he pointed and smiled. This seemed to have the desired effect. His request for Coca Cola was also understood. And there he was, all on his own as usual, thousands of miles from home, Billy no mates.

The food when it came was superb, a total surprise. Adam should have had more faith. He had never tasted Italian food so good. He was tempted to order a second Carbonara, but he'd had to wait for nearly twenty-five minutes for the first one and so decided against it. He looked at his watch. It was almost nine. The sun had given up trying to light the maze of little streets, and the sparse street lighting was starting to take over, intermittently illuminating little patches, here and there, leaving the rest in shadow. He paid the bill and left a generous tip. He had been very well looked after, cracking food, and it hadn't been that expensive. Certainly a lot cheaper than around his hotel at the Spanish Steps.

He decided to walk back the way he had come and would get a cab if he saw one. He wasn't in a rush. People travel halfway around the world to see places like this. He was about to follow his nose up a little alley when he was aware of footsteps behind him, clacking on the cobbles. He half turned, just checked out of the corner of his eye. A fluttering, cream patterned dress, female, so no threat.

A few clacky steps later, a voice rang out, 'You okay, darlin'? You look absolutely dreadful!'

Adam turned in surprise to see Grace striding towards him, chin held high, dark blue blouse, leather shoulder bag across her body, looking every inch a local. He smiled.

'Grace, what a surprise!'

She touched him gently on the shoulder. 'What are you doing out here? A bit off your beaten track?'

'Oh! Been to a restaurant, thought I'd come out for a good ethnic meal here before I get sent home.'

She laughed. 'You're not going to get sent home. It's a storm in a teacup. It'll all be sorted by tomorrow. Where are you going anyway? You lost?'

'Yeah! Slightly. Looking for a cab rank.'

'Well, you're a long way from one of those. I'll take you there if you want.'

Adam smiled and nodded in thanks. 'That would be nice. Saves me getting lost, wandering in the wrong direction.'

She indicated with a flowing motion of her left arm for him to start walking.

'What are you doing here, Grace?'

'Oh, it's where I live, just a few streets away. I've been with Sophia. We both play piano and guitar and we have a little performance on Saturday. It's a friend's party in a restaurant. It saves them having to pay a professional.'

Adam nodded, slightly surprised. 'Jan has a bit of a crush on Sophia, but don't tell anyone. He's pretty besotted.'

She indicated for them to turn right into a narrow alley, which was barely eight foot wide, and the cobbles were uneven. You had to be a local to know this route.

'Well, good luck with that, Adam. She has cut herself off completely since her husband died. No one can get near her, which is a shame. She is one of the world's friendliest people, make a lovely—'

A figure suddenly appeared out of the gloom in front of them. He walked forward and blocked their way. He raised his right hand, which was holding a gun. He was barely six feet in front of them now. He pointed the gun at Adam and waved it from left to right. 'Money, wallet!' he spat, from yellow teeth.

Grace paused for a second, stared hard at the would-be assailant, a short, long-haired youth, dark-haired and unshaven, who was becoming increasingly agitated.

'Money, wallet, money!'

Adam was frozen to the spot. He had never been held up before. Grace stepped in front of him, bending down to open her shoulder bag.

'Money…money. I've got money, money.'

Adam stared in horror as she began to walk towards him.

'Please, please, money, yes!' she said. By this time, Grace was right in front of the youth, in front of Adam, almost acting as a barrier.

The youth was surprised and pleased by her obvious demonstration of panic and fear and momentarily stopped waving the gun as he focused on taking the money that was about to come his way.

Adam, to this day, still did not know what happened next, but suddenly Grace stopped and slowly removed her hand from her bag. Then standing bolt upright, she hit her assailant repeatedly with her left hand. At the same time, she seemed to quickly lift her right knee up very high and bring her foot down on his leg. The ensuing ejaculative scream of pain was ear-splitting, the gun wavered, and the youth fell to the ground, blood oozing from his nose. As he fell, the gun clattered onto the cobbles, and his attention moved to his left knee. He was in absolute agony, screaming, 'BOGDI, MARKU, BOGDI, MARKU, BOGDI!'

Grace turned to Adam. 'Run, Adam, we must run. Give me your jacket.'

She pulled hard at his dark blue denim shoulder, dragging him back the way they had come. In the distance back down the dark alley, they could hear above the screams the sounds of running feet and voices shouting, 'RADUT, RADUT!'

They reached the end of the alley and Grace waved him to the right. She pulled at Adam's jacket. 'Jacket, give me your jacket.'

Adam slowed down as he awkwardly pulled his right sleeve out. Grace leant towards him and grabbed the scruff of his neck, pulling very hard. The force of it surprised him. She was almost dragging him along the road, moving faster than he was. He was finding it hard to keep up. He pulled his white T-shirt down around his midriff to prevent it from lifting off with his jacket.

Behind them, the street walls echoed with the sounds of running feet that seemed to be getting closer. The fading screams of injury were turning into groans. Eventually, by holding out his left arm, she was able to pull the jacket free. It floated in the air for a second until she took hold of it with both hands and started to tie it tightly around her waist. The bag across her shoulder flapped up and down on her right hip. The steps behind them were getting louder. Grace pulled him left into a wider alley with a feeble attempt at street lighting. There were apartments with little stone steps leading up to the doors. Grace slowed down and stepped up to the first front door, pulling Adam with her. Standing on the top step, she roughly twisted his jacket around her waist, totally concealing her white dress.

'Kiss me, Adam, kiss me!' She bent her neck down to him and pulled him towards her. Taking her face in her hands, she roughly, urgently pulled him even closer.

The running steps were nearly upon them. Just around the corner, they could hear panting, heavy breathing.

Adam tentatively moved his face towards her pouting lips. Her right hand roughly grabbed his left wrist and thrust his hand onto her right breast.

'Commit, Adam! Commit or get us both stabbed.'

Their lips met, her left arm pulled his back towards her, forcing his groin into hers. Her right arm went round his neck and forcibly pulled his head tighter towards her. Two running figures suddenly appeared at the end of the alley, panting like jackals. They paused momentarily, staring hard at the couple kissing on the doorstep. Grace's tongue fluttered lightly across Adam's top lip. He responded by putting his right arm around her back and pulling her closer to him. The anonymous figures were uncertain, hesitant. They watched the lovers for what seemed like an eternity, then ran off, continuing their vengeful search up the alley. Adam and Grace both held their pose, but listened and listened, their ears straining. They didn't say a word until it was clear that the footfall had faded and they were out of danger.

Grace gently pushed him away with her hands on his shoulders. He stepped tentatively down off the little step back into the road. She let out a long breath, looked him in the eye and said, 'You all right?'

They were both blushing.

'Yes, yes, fine, Grace, fine!'

'Sorry, Adam, that was no way for a lady to behave, but those little bastards knife half a dozen people a month and some of them die. We could never outrun them.'

'It's fine, Grace, fine, absolutely fine.'

She flicked her hair nervously back behind her ear and let out a deep sigh. 'We have to get out of here, Adam, get back to the main road, where it's lit.' She put her right hand on his shoulder and pushed him gently, guiding him up the alley. 'This way. It's a couple of streets away.'

Adam was silent for the first dozen or so paces, gathering his tumbling thoughts. Eventually, they fell into a rhythm of walking together. He turned to her, panting, trying to get his breath back. 'He had a gun, Grace…he had a gun. What possessed—'

She cut across him, 'It was fake, Adam, it was plastic.' She paused to take a large breath. 'Didn't you hear it rattle when it fell on the road? It was plastic.'

'How did you know it was—'

She smiled a tight smile as she cut across him again, 'Real guns are not red inside the barrel, and he had the safety on, an amateur. It was you he was after. They leave the locals alone. You look like a well-heeled English tourist, Adam…which you are!' She snorted lightly.

'How do you know about guns? You're a girl.'

'Girl?' she hooted. 'Girls don't know about guns, is that what you're trying to say?'

'Well, I guess so.'

'Well, young Adam, if you are a script girl working in film in Rome, guns are on set almost every week in some way, shape or form, and you have to learn about them. Thanks for the "girl thing" though. Glad you noticed!' She smiled, looking him up and down, and took another deep breath, still panting slightly.

He inwardly chewed his inner lip. All this alley running was like a scene from *The Third Man*. He felt out of his comfort zone, out of his depth. He certainly wasn't in control. The minor cobbled roadway was beginning to get brighter, wider, and their in-time footsteps echoed less. The smell was starting to change from musty stonework to exhaust fumes. A small piazza opened up before them, the occasional car rumbled by. The odd scooter added to the gentle activity of the late evening atmosphere. On the far side were three restaurants, all nearly empty. Adam nodded towards them.

'Drink?'

'I think so, Adam. I think we need to come to a little pact, don't you, after all that's gone on!'

As they crossed the road, he tried to assert his masculinity by holding up his hand to slow her down as a car appeared. She suppressed a giggle, said nothing, just smiled, keeping her thoughts to herself. There was no waiter to welcome them, so they just sat down opposite each other at one of the tables.

She looked at him. 'Would you like your jacket back?'

He looked at her properly for the first time, seeing her in a totally different light. She had hazel eyes, not dark brown, and they were almond-shaped. They looked straight at him. He was not the only one seeing someone in a completely new light. There were light laugh lines stretching part way to her temples, her brown hair was tousled, messed up by his hands.

Her lips moved again. 'Jacket, Adam, jacket. Would you like your jacket back?'

He nodded and raised his eyebrows in affirmation as she stood up, unknotting the sleeves tied around her waist, pulling until the blue denim floated free. She raised her right arm to prevent the hanging sleeve from touching the ground, flicking it towards him with a smile. He decided not to wear it and instead placed it on the seat beside him.

She lifted her chin up. 'I'm sorry, Adam, for the forced snog and the boob fumble, but I couldn't think of anything else. It must have been like kissing your auntie!'

Adam leant forward and took hold of both of her hands. Her long fingers were warm. They naturally curled into his, and their eyes locked.

'I think, Grace, that you just saved my life.'

The waiter slowly appeared behind Adam. Grace saw him coming and pulled her hands quickly back towards her, breaking the hold, a tight smile of embarrassment touching her face. She blushed suddenly like a naughty schoolgirl then looked up at the now attentive waiter.

'Azzurro, per piacere… Adam, what would you like?'

'Oh! A Coke, Grace, just a Coke, thanks.'

The waiter nodded, noting his request. Grace smiled and very deliberately put her hands under the table onto her lap. 'I expect now there's some woman somewhere that wants my guts for garters, sorry!'

'No, Grace, there is no woman, no woman anywhere, and I have to say I have not been kissed like that for a very long time.'

Grace ignored the compliment, looked around to check if there was anyone within earshot, and, satisfied, she tilted her head to one side. 'Why? No wife, girlfriend, fiancée, Adam? You gay?'

He snuffled. 'No, Grace, not gay. Been working away in Europe since Christmas, winter sports shows for the Yanks ABC *Wide World of Sports*, Wengen, Interlaken, Kitzbuhel, Oslo. No time for relationships, never home.'

'A guy like you obviously needs a bonk now and then, so what do you do, pay for it?'

Adam was taken aback. 'That was pretty direct! No, Grace, I've never paid for it. I do computer dating, Dateline. I get four matches, four girls' addresses, phone numbers waiting in an envelope on my door mat when I get home, then, Chinese meal out, Worcester Park high street, back to the house and bit of hi-fi and up to the bedroom. Keeps Jolly Roger happy!'

'Jolly Roger! Jolly Roger! Are you saying what I think you're saying? You're joking. You're kidding, right? It can't be that easy.'

'No, Grace, that's what it's like now in swinging London. All the girls are on the pill.'

'I find that hard to believe, Adam, hard to believe. You must catch something nasty.'

'No, Grace, never have. They're nice people, all of them, just out to have a good time and enjoy life.'

'I'm astonished, absolutely astonished. No commitment…barmy!'

'No, Grace, you can't commit to someone who's away all the time, never around. But what about you, Grace? Married? Mother of five?'

She flicked her hair back with her hand. The look she gave him told him that she was happy to ask the questions but not so keen to answer them. She shrugged.

'Oh! No! Widowed, years ago, had a daughter, died of meningitis when she was two, got the stretch marks, wide hips and crashed boobs to prove it.' She smiled and looked away momentarily.

Adam respected her pause. She was obviously uncomfortable.

She looked at him, trying to read him. 'You're the first man I've kissed like that in years, a bit of a shock…feeling you stirring against me!' She was smiling and starting to blush.

'The boobs didn't feel crashed to me, Grace.'

'The miracles of a wonder bra!' A fleeting grin then, 'Look, can we change the subject, please? I'm not comfortable with the way this is all going. I think that we both need to blot out the last hour and everything that happened in it and get back to normality.'

'Okay, Grace, okay. I fully respect that, but before we put it all in the basements of our minds, I need to know what you did to that mugger. One minute he's waving a gun at us, the next minute he's lying on the ground screaming. What did you do?'

Grace noticed the waiter coming back to the table with their drinks. She nodded and flicked her eyes to the waiter to convey that they were about to be interrupted. She smiled as two glasses were put down and two chilled bottles placed in the middle of the table. The waiter trapped their bill under the glass ashtray, nodded and turned away.

Grace shook her head slowly, smiling. 'Oh, you know, bit of karate when I was a teenager. Like riding a bike, you never forget!'

Adam paused, digesting the answer, nodded a couple of times, then decided to move on. 'Look, I'm sorry about your husband, Grace. Losing a child, can't imagine what that must be like.'

'You get to live with it, Adam, you just get to live with it. They say time heals and that it gets easier. Does it? Does it really?' She winced slightly.

'I don't know, Grace, the big love of my life is now walking around with another man's baby in her womb.'

'Is that why you are a gold-plated, Oscar-winning seducer of women, then?' Smiling, mocking slightly, as she gently swigged at her beer.

Adam paused, looked her directly in the eye. She couldn't hold his gaze. She looked away, watching a car bump slowly down the cobbles on the other side of the road.

'I know what you think of me, Grace, but I never lie, never deceive, never lead people on. What you see is what you get.'

'Silver tongue, Adam, silver tongue.' She looked him in the eye.

'Grace, you're the one with the silver tongue. I've not been kissed like that in years.'

'Adam, I thought we agreed to change the subject?'

'No, you decided to change the subject, not me, Grace. Look, I know that we both have a lot of stuff hidden, festering in the basements of our minds, but when we first sat down here, you held my hands and an energy charge… Something, I don't know, happened.'

She cut across him, 'Near-death experience, Adam,' she said, forcing a smile, trying to put a full stop to the conversation.

'No, Grace, it wasn't that…it was a reflex…on both our parts. I think we're missing something here.'

She reached up with her left hand to the small gold crucifix nestling on her neck, felt its shape, almost trying to drawer strength from it. The fingers of her right hand were around the neck of her beer bottle, slowly stroking the moisture upwards and downwards. Adam read the conflict.

'Grace, I am going to say that I want to meet you again, just the two of us. I'm not looking for a leg-over, not looking to suckle your crashed bosoms, kiss your stretch marks or anything like that. I just want to find out what that energy charge was about when you put your hands in mine.'

She picked up her bottle with the intention of banging it on the table to stop the conversation, changed her mind, took another swig instead. 'Adam, this is ridiculous. Let's just draw a line under this evening, be discreet, tell nobody and keep the secret, okay? Okay? Promise me!'

Her eyes were starting to well up. She was agitated and had had enough. 'I'm going home now. Get the waiter to call you a taxi. They take about eight minutes.' She stood up. 'Night, Adam.'

'Whoa, hang on, you can't walk home!'

'I'm fine, Adam, I'm fine. I'm only a few minutes away, and I look like…like a local…not a loaded English tourist! Thanks for the drink.'

'Thanks for saving my life, Grace.'

She pursed her lips and smiled. 'That may well be something I regret. Be discreet, Adam, tell no one, keep the secret.'

With that, she turned and walked back across the road.

Adam watched her go. He muttered under his breath, 'Turn round, Grace, turn round, look back.'

She didn't. He just watched her disappear down the road and turn into the little narrow alley between the buildings.

Alberto Consalvo sat with his wife Gill at their regular window seat of the little trattoria and watched with a childlike grin as two dark blue Alfa Romeo police cars went screaming past, sirens blaring, blue lights flashing. He nodded, smiling in approval. He had no desire to rush round the corner, wave his badge, get involved. The Rome night shift was more than capable of looking after any minor incidents that occurred. He would, though, check the night incident log when he got in to work in the morning, just to find out what was going on in the near vicinity of one of his regular haunts. Not that he ever felt at all vulnerable. The sight of the badge in his breast pocket stopped a lot of trouble before it even got started. Then there was his Beretta in the underslung shoulder holster, never fired in anger in over twenty years, waved, yes, used as a threat, yes, but never actually fired.

Gill didn't like it, hated guns, but never said anything. After all, it was a tool of his trade, and she understood that. The upside was that she had a trained, armed bodyguard every time she went out with him.

Another set of blue lights winked up the street, the blaring siren bouncing off the narrow brickwork as a large white box-like ambulance rumbled down the cobbles. It must be serious.

Wednesday 16th April

Solveig Lungren, her short blonde hair in disarray, was sitting up in bed, the sheets pulled up to her neck, hugging a pillow. She was watching her husband in his dressing gown, collar sticking up, on the phone to London.

The man that she loved had kept her awake most of the night with his constant tossing and turning and intermittent mumbling and teeth grinding that he always seemed to do when he was wound up.

He had hardly slept, and now he was sitting hunched over, elbow on the dressing table, knuckles white around the brown plastic handset. She could see the reflection of his tense face in the mirror as he stared unfocused at the floor, waiting for someone to talk to him.

Eventually, the handset made a click.

'Hi, Ed, it's Sven Lungren, Sven Lungren from *The Script Girl* in Rome. We sent some negatives to you overnight for checking. How was it?'

She watched him nodding slowly as he listened carefully. Slowly his body language changed, and she could see the tenseness leaving his face.

'Really? Really! Oh, that's good, excellent, Ed. Great.' He was starting to sit up. He turned and nodded to her and smiled, giving her a thumbs up. 'Thanks, Ed, thanks. Very kind, very kind. Thanks again. Bye!' He turned and gently put the phone back in its cradle on the dressing table.

'He said that it's all fine, some of the nicest pictures to come in overnight, very nice, sharp. Even got the exposure right, bang in the middle. He was very complimentary, nice guy.'

She flicked her gaze to the red numbers on the alarm clock beside her. Smiling, she slowly turned and looked up at him, scarecrow-like, his red hair all standing up, pyjamas all crumpled, a lopsided grin on his face.

'Would my clever man like me to take some of that tension away before he goes off to work?' Smiling, while slowly and deliberately licking her top lip, she slowly, with her right hand, lifted her huggy pillow onto the floor.

Luigi's bedside phone rang. It was Dublin phoning from London, detailing the results of the lab report. The news was good, very good in fact, no technical problems at all. Luigi asked him to fax every positive detail to the office so that he had a hard copy to give Dino. The more positive the detail, the better.

The cockerel at the end of the garden crowed, welcoming the day. There's a thought! Perhaps he could ask Nella to knock up a couple of boiled eggs for breakfast to celebrate.

Ispettore Consalvo cast his eye over the night log from the previous evening. There was not a lot from the area around the restaurant in Trastevere. A couple of domestics, a fight at a bar in the small hours, and a young man, a foreigner, attacked by a couple of tourists, a woman in a white dress and a guy in blue denim. His story was that the woman attacked him. Alberto reread the report, visualised the area, the dark street. He had patrolled the area years ago as a Sovrintendente. The case didn't ring true.

More likely, our foreign friend was one of the little gang of gutter muggers that had been polluting the area for the last six months, a mini three-man crime wave. No weapon was found on him, but that came as no surprise as his mates probably cleaned him up before running off. There were no visual witnesses, only local people who heard screaming, shouting and the sound of someone running. So this little criminal mastermind probably just tried it on with the wrong tourist… Tough! He looked at the injury report.

It took his mind back to the year before when four blade-wielding gutter muggers had, late one evening in the same area, held up the unarmed combat training instructor for the SAS in Hereford, who was there on holiday with his young wife and eight-year-old daughter. The results had been catastrophic. All four were hospitalised, one nearly died, and one still walked with a limp and now street begged for a living near the Piazza

Barboni. Last night's injured youth got off lightly; at least he didn't have his ribcage smashed into his lungs, but apparently his assailant was not the man. He said it was the woman in the cream or white dress. A bit odd, that!

Isabella Marco, a bit itchy in her well-worn khaki army fatigues, sat looking out of the window of the Make-up Winnebago. She was bathed in the familiar, comfortable smell of eau de cologne and make-up. The electricians had laid on power from seven o'clock, so all the multiple dressing table mirror lights were on, as was the kettle, and she had nearly finished her camomile tea.

Sophia had not needed to do much to her, just a light bit of mascara; this was a natural look day. The initial scenes were a bit of head acting, so she didn't need the leather belt to protect her back, elbow pads, knee and wrist supports probably until after coffee. She had, though, had her nails cut right back because of the almost certain risk of ripping them off on the assault course, one of the hazards of having to act the part of a trainee spy.

She looked out over the assault course. The Props guys were hosing water into the wading trench, the mud crawl they had finished swamping just as she arrived at seven-fifteen.

Over at the shooting range set, she could see electricians pushing into place two giant, tiltable, three-metre square, double-sided reflectors mounted on an old car chassis. The cameraman Sven was with them. That was obviously where they were starting. Lasse, lovely Lasse, the Director, was talking to Duke and his two Assistants nearby.

A creaking white van drove slowly by and turned into the course. Isabella recognised the driver as Anatra, the Grip. He had been on her last film. Nice guy, knew his job.

No sign of Sound, but they were always late, so, the cast assembled, it was time for her to go and introduce herself, bring everyone to her side and increase her fan base. Initial impressions count for a lot, Luigi had taught her that.

The steps down from the Winnebago were quite steep. She was just about to step down when a sizeable suntanned hand suddenly appeared from nowhere, gently taking her left hand to guide her down. She smiled in surprise.

'Captain Steve, how kind.'

'Good morning, Isabella, how are you today? Ready for another day of pain, guts and glory?'

He looked every inch the part of a Marine commando captain, in his khaki shirt, army webbing belt and khaki trousers, his green beret neatly folded into his left epaulette. Isabella was unaware that Duke had tasked him to keep an eye on her all the time that she was on set so that Bruno could run some errands.

Isabella headed straight for Sven, who, for her, was the most important man on the set. His lighting could show every fault on her face, make her look like a dog or highlight all of her beauty. For her, he was the go-to guy.

As they walked, Steve noticed the direction that she was heading in and strolled naturally along beside her. 'Now are you happy with all of this, Isabella? You've spent the last week working here, familiarising yourself. The judo guys have trained you up, they're happy, and you no longer jump out of your skin when you fire a gun, so no worries, right?'

She looked at him with the look that a young pupil gives a teacher: respect, coupled with a touch of wonder. 'The swinging rope bridge, the fights, it's very well-rehearsed, and I'm happy with that, but the swinging rope bridge, I don't like the swinging rope bridge. I feel I run across it, like, like a silly girl, can't help it.'

He patted her gently on her shoulder. 'Still? Okay. I'll have a chat with Lasse. He'll most likely get your stunt double to do it, but either way he'll find a way round it.'

Sven turned as he saw her approach. Captain Steve nodded a respectful farewell and headed over towards Lasse and Duke with his two Assistant Directors.

Isabella thrust out her chest, walked as tall as she could, put on her most adorable face and lifted her chin. 'Sven, good morning. How are you today?'

His smile said it all. To be in the presence of such an outstanding natural beauty was always a pleasure.

'Isabella, you look absolutely radiant, lovely. Looking forward to your first day?'

'Yes, very much, very much. I've been here all last week practising with Captain Steve. I feel like a real squaddy!'

Sven smiled and nodded. 'Oh! Respect to you for that, always better if you can practice, it always shows, looks much better on camera.'

She nodded, looking around at what was to all intents and purposes a virtually full-size military assault course. 'It's big, isn't it?' she said, biting her lip, making her eyes big, acting the little scared girl look.

Sven smiled. He sensed her insecurity; new film, new role, strange crew, no way of knowing whether it would be a success or a flop. He decided to change the subject. 'You happy with these reflectors?' he asked, nodding at the two huge shiny silver boards which looked like two silver sails, and as such totally out of place in such a military setting.

'Yes, fine, it's par for the course, here. Don't squint even if they're burning your retina to pieces. I'd prefer them scrimmed, softened though!'

Sven laughed. 'Okay, I hear where you're coming from.'

She sensed that it was time to move on and continue her tour rather like a queen at a garden party. 'If you'll excuse me, I'd like to go and say hello to the Camera crew, let them know I can hit my marks.'

Sven smirked. 'He'll be glad about that. His name's Adam. Do you want me to—'

'No! Fine, thanks, Sven. I know the Clapper and Grip but not Adam, so see you later.' She paused before adding, 'You will look after me, won't you?' giving him a mini head shake and raised eyebrows, like a teenage girl trying to appear endearing.

Sven smiled a gentle, fatherly smile. 'Yes, of course. You're in safe hands.'

Adam watched the encounter from a distance. He couldn't hear what was being said, but their body language told him that the well-endowed, pretty young woman in the khaki fatigues was trying to do a job on Sven, and he was enjoying every minute of it. She turned, smiled in farewell and headed towards him. Her voice rang out.

'Adam? Are you Adam?' She had a tonal voice, quite throaty, sexy with an intertwined Italian accent. She covered the ground very quickly, obviously a very fit young woman, but also the star of the film, the La-di-da, as they say at home.

Adam put on his best smile. 'Yes, I'm Adam. Glad to meet you.'

She walked right into his space and tilted her face up to him. The clean soapy smell of her filled his nostrils.

'Adam, I'm Isabella. Pleased to meet you. I hear that you are a bit of a wind-up merchant, that you have conjunctivitis, true?' she said, smiling, big-eyed at him.

Adam was taken aback. This was a real red-blooded woman, bloody hell! 'No! No! Not actually…'

She laughed, stepping backwards out of his space. 'Your reputation precedes you, Adam. I hear though that you are very precise, very good at your job!'

Adam swayed on his feet slightly. 'Oh, really? Thanks.'

She leant forward to overemphasise what she was about to say, and her clean soapy smell wafted over him again. 'You'll be glad to know that I've been taught to hit my marks. I'm very precise, like you!'

Adam had got the measure of her by now. She was more than a bit of a character, to say the least. 'I'm glad about that. Anglo-Italian relations are very important.'

She laughed. 'Adam, I look forward to working with you. Stay on your marks! I'm just going to say hello to Luca and Anatra.'

Adam nodded a smiling, polite farewell. She turned and walked towards the group. Were her overalls meant to be that tight around her curvy backside, or was Jose Wardrobe showing a little poetic licence?

Jan appeared in the distance, walking down from the Make-up and catering vans up to Lasse and Duke, giving a hearty 'Morning, Adam' as he crossed the uneven grass. Seeing him approach, Duke nodded and turned to Lasse, handing him a small handheld megaphone.

Lasse took it eagerly and blew into it to make sure that it was turned on. A muted *WHOOF! WHOOF!* filled the air.

'Good morning, everybody, good morning, buongiorno a tutti. Today we are filming Gina, Isabella, at the army training camp in Scotland. It is 1942, it is a montage sequence, no scripted dialogue, but we will be recording sound. The last sequence of the day will be under rainmakers. First scenes are over behind the assault wall. Thank you. Oh, and there will be gunfire.'

Petros, the owl-like interpreter, relayed what had been said to a small disparate group of Macchinisti and Props guys, most of whom had already roughly gleaned all the information that they required.

Duke took over the loud hailer and shouted, 'OVER HERE, GUYS, RAGAZZI! LINE UP, LINE UP!'

Adam looked around. There was no sign of Grace, bit early for her anyway. He had noticed that her fold-up table and chair were still leaning against the large grey Props pantechnicon on their way in. Pia appeared back on the approach road with a short, dark-haired woman in khaki army fatigues, who from a distance looked exactly like Isabella's twin – the stunt double, most likely.

Peter Dublin and Sven Lungren were not the only people from Production on the phone to Ed, the contact man at Lumaxfilm labs in London, early that morning. Veniero Frattari, the Senior Editor, had beaten all of them to it and had gleaned all of the detailed information that he could regarding the reprints. He was now in the process of typing out a multi-carboned detailed report.

Those who knew him well, particularly his assistant, regarded him as a pedant, more than a bit anal in his desire for detail. He had written a book on the history of Studio Lazio since its inception in 1937 when Mussolini had resurrected the Italian film business by building a movie empire that still stands today. He detailed every aspect of its construction and expansion in the twenty or so chapters, including every film ever made within its concrete walls. Plus, as much gossip about the stars and people who had worked there as could be mentioned without being sued. Not many people knew, but he was a non-executive Director of the studio management board, and his report was as much for them, as the movers and shakers of the film *The Script Girl.*

What he was writing was not going to go down well with the management, but it had to be said and he was the one to say it. At least if he wrote it before anyone else did, he could phrase things in such a way that no one would actually get fired.

As soon as Isabella had finished chatting to Adam, Sven walked over to him and let him know that the London reprints were all okay and that it was now highly unlikely that he was going to be sent home in disgrace. The editor would edit the Lumaxfilm reprints back to back with the original locally made prints so that there would be an immediate comparison and no further dispute. They were out of the woods.

Jan joined them and said it was a pity that Adam was not being sent home and that he'd have to put up with him for a bit longer until Production finally sussed him out. Adam took the wind-up on the chin with a self-deprecating smile. It was good that Jan gave as good as he got. It would seem the South London boy and the Viking had bonded.

Luciano Scordia, sitting at his long table in the square centre, looked down at the note that Sylvania had left him after her conversation with Duke the previous evening. It did not please him. It was not the problems with the pictures, the definition or lack thereof; that was easily solved with a change of crew, change of processing labs or even a change of equipment. No, it was the fact that on day one, they had shot three minutes forty, and on day two they had shot even more: four minutes ten, well above the three and a half minutes that they were scheduled to do. They were already slightly ahead of schedule after only two days. This Director and his crew were fast, and they were most likely going to get even faster with each passing day of working together. Duke would not slow things down, so if he was going to push Luigi over budget, push him into debt, Luciano was going to have to do something about it.

He picked up the handset of his phone from the little table beside him and carefully dialled two numbers. A phone could suddenly be heard ringing out from the open shutters of the house's second floor, high up behind him.

A little interference was called for, and he knew just the person to carry it out.

Adam really enjoyed the morning. It was all *Boy's Own* stuff; he learned quite a bit about guns from watching Captain Steve, who on camera demonstrated the various weapons to the four trainee spy actors and Isabella. The smell of cordite filled the air as Isabella fired her Sten gun at the targets in front of the sandbank. Great stuff! And he was being paid to film it.

Grace had been well cared for by the electricians as usual. They had tied a wide umbrella to a heavy-duty light stand and placed it right behind her little fold-up table and chair. She was the only one of the crew to be working in the shade.

She smiled at Adam in a non-committal way, just as she did to everyone else on the crew. When it was time for a coffee break, the rest of the crew wandered over to the small white catering van parked next to the Make-up Winnebago in the lane, while she continued working, busily typing away.

Anatra was doing camera cover duty, so Adam wandered over to her as casually as he could, his pulse rate rising with every pace that he took towards her. She looked up and looked around to make sure that no one was in earshot.

'Adam, how are you today?'

'Fine. Thank you, Grace, fine. I was wondering if we might—'

She quickly nodded to the left and the right and said, 'I know what you're going to say. Adam, a relationship with you is going to be like jumping out of a plane without a parachute: a bit of initial euphoria, then a dawning reality, followed by a cataclysmic end. I – we – do not need that.'

'I'm sorry, Grace, but I still feel the same, I can't help it. Can't we at least talk?'

'No, Adam, we can't. If I'm seen speaking to you like this more than once a week, tongues will start wagging.'

'Grace, it's not going to go away. We have to talk.'

'Adam, there's nothing to talk about. Let's drop the subject.'

'I'm sorry, Grace, sorry, but I think that we are missing something here.'

'Damn you, Adam, damn you, why are you so bloody persistent?'

'You know why, Grace, you know very well. That touch, fleeting as it was, was so real, so natural.'

She pursed her lips, looked angrily at him for a second but started to blush. She looked confused. 'Okay! We'll talk, we'll talk. I'll cook you an unappetising supper at my place, and we can thrash it all out there and then, after which, hopefully, we can both get on with our lives. You happy now?'

He looked down at her and saw the fire in her eyes. He had no idea what emotions were running through her head. One of the electricians was coming back from the coffee wagon with a tray and a cup, heading straight towards them, presumably for Grace. Adam nodded towards the approaching figure.

'Your coffee's coming. I need an address, Grace, an address.'

She stood up, half turned to the approaching electrician, then turned back to Adam. 'I'll leave an envelope on the desk here at lunch, just pick it up. I'll make it out to, oh, I don't know, to…to Jay Roger. Don't bring him with you tonight and don't get any ideas. We are going to have a chat and nothing more, do you get that? Really?'

Adam looked up. The old, moustached vulture electrician from the lighting rig was now within earshot. Adam smiled broadly. 'Oh! Great, Grace, that's very funny. I like that! I never knew that. Thanks, mate.'

She turned to take the offered tray with the polystyrene cup. 'Grazie, molto simpatico, Alberto. Grazie.'

The electrician bowed respectfully. 'Prego, Grace, prego,' he said and continued his gentle perambulation towards the unattended reflectors.

She turned back to Adam, faking a smile and raising her voice for the benefit of the departing figure. 'Cheers, Adam. Cheers, nice to talk to you. Let me know about that lens when you have time, thanks.'

Her eyes, however, were still blazing, unsmiling; she was not happy. She turned back to her desk, placed the tray next to the typewriter and sat down. The interaction was at an end as far as she was concerned

Peter Dublin breezed into the office, holding his blue linen jacket casually over his shoulder. Gill was at her desk and stopped typing as he entered. She looked up with a smile.

'Morning, Peter, good trip?'

He ignored her as he looked around. The fluorescents were on, and the shutters were closed. He strode past her, walked around his desk, threw his jacket over his chair and clutched at the shutter handles, twisting and pulling them open. A light puff of warm air flooded into the room, causing Gill to blink and momentarily jerk back at the sudden change.

Dublin turned back to his desk and surveyed all the papers that she had laid out for him to look at. Without looking at her, his head tilted down, he muttered to himself, 'It's all okay, get the fax?' It was the local print. 'WHAT'S THIS?' he shouted, suddenly looking up, his nostrils flaring.

She was taken aback. 'I don't know what you're looking at!'

He was snarling now. 'THIS! This report crap from the editor!'

He looked down, his eyes staring hard as he read down the first page, angrily turned to the second page, looking from side to side in frustration, then snorting as he read the final few lines on the third page. He could barely contain himself.

'WHAT IS THIS? WHAT IS THIS?'

Gill looked up, feeling the tension in the room. 'It's Veniero's report about the rushes viewing yesterday, stating what has happened, the results of the reprint and his advice for better practice in the future.'

Dublin was apoplectic. 'HE CAN'T DO THAT! IT'S SOD ALL TO DO WITH HIM. IT WAS ME WHO TOOK CHARGE OF THE WHOLE BUSINESS, ME WHO WENT TO LONDON, TOOK, EVERYTHING IN, ME WHO REPORTED BACK EARLY IN THE MORNING, IT'S ME WHO BROUGHT THE REPRINT BACK. IT HAS ABSOLUTELY NOTHING TO DO WITH HIM. IF A REPORT NEEDS TO BE WRITTEN, IT NEEDS TO COME FROM ME, NOT HIM…BLOODY UPSTART! I'M THE BLOODY PRODUCTION MANAGER. IT'S ME THAT SHOULD BE WRITING ALL OF THIS!'

He banged his fist hard on his desk, with a thunderous clump. The small cappuccino cup bounced up in the air and fell onto the floor with a clatter as its small handle broke off. He was visibly shaking with rage.

'WHO'S SEEN THIS? WHO'S SEEN THIS?'

Gill leant forward, very tense, unsure what to do. 'Heads of department. I photocopied it, and internal mail collected it an hour ago.'

'WHAT? WHAT! YOU BITCH! YOU HAVE ABSOLUTELY NO RIGHT TO DO THAT, CRETIN! CRETIN!'

The door to the office suddenly opened and Luigi entered the room, standing in his rolled-up shirtsleeves, black braces holding up his slightly bulging trousers. His entrance was like a bomb going off. He smiled at Gill.

'The walls of these offices are not as thick as you think they are. Gill, will you leave us for a few minutes, please? Go to the canteen, get yourself a drink, put it on my account.'

The look on Dublin's face was an absolute picture. 'I…I…'

Luigi held his hand up. He gently stepped to one side as Gill pulled her bag from the coat rack and with a tight-lipped smile, whispered, 'Thank you,' as she went out into the dark corridor. Luigi gently closed the door behind her.

'Sit down, Peter. Sit down.'

Dublin moved to sit down. As he pulled his seat away from his desk his foot unexpectedly trod on the broken cup and he tottered slightly off-balance for a second.

'Luigi…I—'

'QUIET, PETER, QUIET! Your behaviour here is of great concern to me, great concern. I have heard you on many occasions, shouting and screaming, here in this office. It's not the way we do things here in Italy. You came over from London, highly recommended, very experienced, but I'm afraid I have to disagree with all of those recommendations now. I feel that we have been misled.'

By now, Dublin's lips had gone dry. He moistened them surreptitiously with his tongue. His underarms were starting to sweat. He lifted his chin as if to speak, but Luigi held up his hand to stop him.

'I am giving you a first and final warning. I am now looking for any excuse to fire you. If you continue as you are, you will be asked to clear your desk and get out. Do I make myself clear?'

Dublin took a deep breath. 'Yes. Yes, Luigi. I, I…'

Luigi held his hand up again. 'You have in Gill one of the best Production Secretaries in Rome. If you don't have the wit to work with her, use her local knowledge and expertise, then you have, as they say in London, blown it, baby. And that report from Veniero was spot on. Detailed, constructive and extremely useful, not only to us but also to the management here at the studio. You, Peter, could never have written anything so detailed, so technical, so useful in a million years. You do not have the wherewithal. That is all I have to say on the matter.'

Luigi turned, put his hand on the brass handle, calmly twisted it and left the room, closing the door behind him with a gentle clunk.

Dublin just sat in his seat, a silhouette completely backlit by the white light window behind him, sweat running in a trickle down his forehead. Sweat marks starting to appear as he began to leak into the armpits and onto the front of his handmade silk shirt.

Coffee on set was normally meant to be taken on the run, but Duke knew that a crew working outside in the sun all day needed to drink and often, plus the fact Isabella had to pad up for the unarmed combat scenes and that would take a few minutes. So he had called fifteen minutes.

Adam was one of the last to get to the little catering van with the two white tables covered in thermoses of coffee, milk, sugar, polystyrene cups, jugs of orange juice and small plastic bottles of water. The tables looked like a swarm of locusts had been through, and the caterer was in the process of clearing away the empties into a black polythene bag. Adam grabbed a bottle of water and, as he turned, nearly crashed into Captain Steve.

'Whoa, sorry, Steve, apologies.'

'No problem, Adam, no problem. I could tell from the look on your face that you almost enjoyed the morning. Did you do national service?' There was a very slight, South Wales accent, almost imperceptible. The dark blue eyes were set deep in his face, hypnotic, constantly moving, missing nothing.

Adam smiled. The guy looked every inch a professional soldier, standing bolt upright, stomach in, chest out, biceps to die for with a skin that looked like brown sandpaper.

'No. Just missed it. 1960, wasn't it?'

'Shame, Adam, shame. It's a great experience, think everyone should go through it. Look, mate, fancy a beer one evening? My wife's away, and a chat about the old country is always good for the soul. WODJA FINK, SON?' he added, his head jerking forward in a pecking motion that London cockneys are renowned for.

Adam burst out laughing. 'That would be great, Steve, great. I'm fed up of dining alone. Chat later, need to get back, okay?'

Steve nodded. 'Well, I'm on set for the rest of the week, either on camera or as technical advisor, and also to make sure that the judo guys don't damage Isabella. Just let me know. Any evening. Up to you, mate. I'm gonna wait here for her highness. See you later!'

Adam smiled, then nodding in farewell, strolled back towards the reflectors, looking very incongruous in the middle of the Scottish country training area; background tree leaves spray-painted to resemble the brownish tones of early autumn. Concerned that people were starting to collect together and chatter, he began to walk much faster. He was, after all, a key player.

Jan was beside the camera, watching him, smiling, waiting for him to arrive. Anatra was poised frozen like a statue, holding the corner of the white cloth camera cover, which he gently removed with a theatrical flourish to coincide with Adam's last couple of strides. Always miming the piss-take, these guys!

Adam couldn't help but laugh.

When Gill got back to the office, it was empty. The lights were off and the shutters were closed; it was eerily quiet. The small fridge behind her desk gurgled momentarily. The external line on the phone on her desk began to ring insistently. She flicked on the fluorescents, which spluttered, made a couple of muted donking noises and eventually flickered into life. She picked up the handset and dropped her shoulder bag onto her seat.

It was Donna Tavazzi, the house agent, wanting to know when her screen test was going to be.

Gill's eyes glazed. She could not believe what she was hearing. She asked her to slow down, as she lifted her bag off her chair and sat down. The monologue continued. She started to take notes. The door suddenly opened and Peter Dublin strode back in, shirt changed, top buttons undone. Noting she was on the phone, he simply nodded and walked over to his desk, walking around the back, and gently opened the left-hand shutter.

Gill continued to listen for another couple of minutes. Dublin sat down, picked up the papers on his desk and slowly started to read through them. Gill came off the phone, slowly putting the handset back in the cradle.

'You're not going to believe this. The house agent, a Donna Tavazzi, says she spent yesterday evening and half of last night with Dino. She said that he promised her a screen test and that she had all of the assets to have a great future in the business!'

Dublin looked up, a look of disbelief on his face. 'What! You're joking!'

Gill grimaced. 'She's a very well-built girl, pretty determined, but she says that if she does not get a screen test and isn't booked to appear in the film, she is going to go to the papers and make formal charges regarding rape, last night in his hotel!'

Dublin was speechless. 'What! Shit! She can't do that—'

Gill interrupted. 'She says that it was like having a wardrobe fall on her with the key still in the lock. She's deadly serious!' Gill shook her head in disbelief. 'She has given him twenty-four hours, until noon tomorrow.'

Dublin's phone rang. He picked up. Within seconds his eyes had glazed and his lips tightened. 'Sally, how nice. How did you get my number? Oh, Paddy. Great.' He shuffled awkwardly on his seat and glanced at Gill, wishing she was not there.

'Oh! Sally, I don't think that's a good idea. I'm absolutely swamped here. I'm not going to have time, hiring extras. If you come over, it's not down to me, love. We have to go through an agency, it's all very strictly controlled here. No, Sally, I can't put you up as my house is being used as a film set for the next three weeks. I'm moving out into a hotel.'

Gill watched in silence, totally engrossed in the fact that the pigeons from last night's little party with Paddy, the car dealer, at Heathrow's Ariel Hotel had all come home to roost. She was not a spiteful woman, but she thoroughly enjoyed watching him squirm. Let's just hope that there are no more little surprises in the pipeline, biologically speaking.

On the backlot, lunch from the caterers was nothing special: a polystyrene lunch box with a bit of melon and three large pieces of pizza, which, it was fair to say, looked like and tasted like speckled cardboard. Adam had deliberately hung back, miming fiddling with one of the essential items in his diddy bag, his Kelly lens depth of field calculator. His only thought was to collect the promised envelope from Grace's desk. The Macchinista sitting guard over the white draped sound and camera kit was conveniently facing away, more interested in his car magazine.

Before wandering off to lunch along with everyone else, Grace had put all her paperwork into her briefcase, leaving just her lidded typewriter holding down something white.

Adam wandered casually over to her desk, constantly looking around to make sure no one was nearby or watching. He picked up the envelope and stuffed it firmly into his jeans pocket.

Next stop the location toilets. He couldn't wait to tear it open. He was shaking slightly in anticipation, but the handwritten information was sparse: eight p.m. and an address in Trastevere. That was it, but at least she hadn't slammed the door in his face…yet.

The early scenes after lunch confirmed the fact that Isabella was not a bimbo sex symbol. The amount of effort she put into every scene was a pleasure to behold. They only had to do a couple of takes on virtually every set-up. When she bayonetted the helmeted straw figure, she meant it. She was out for blood, her unarmed combat training scenes were like a ballet, she rolled, twisted, thrust, disarmed, elbowed and kicked. Everything she did was incredibly energetic, thoroughly believable, as were the performances of all of the extras. Luca told Jan, Sven and Adam that all the extras were members of the Rome Judo club and that the little, short guy was a third dan black belt instructor, none of which came as any surprise. They were all like little bouncing balls.

Isabella did the under barbed wire mud crawl with utter determination, and likewise weighed down by a large rucksack the flooded trench wade, all without hesitation. She ended up virtually covered from head to foot in thick, gooey, brown, black mud, hardly the *Playboy* centrefold, but her energy, radiant personality and sheer beauty shone through. In the film business, respect is very hard-earned, but virtually everyone who was on set that day fell in love with that young lady. She was going to be a joy to work with. Watch out, Loren!

Duke called another break while Isabella went off to clean up and change for the final scene under rainmakers. Sven strolled over to Jan and Adam, handing them three pages of typewritten paper. It was the report from the editor. He stood beside them, silently watching them as Jan read the first page and gave it to Adam, followed by the second and third.

Adam was impressed. It was very detailed, very comprehensive. The report put the blame fairly and squarely on the local film stock print and a smoky, dirty projection room, with the nicotine-stained screen and dirty projector lenses that should have been upgraded years ago like the other two viewing theatres.

Adam felt as if a huge weight had been lifted off his shoulders, and both he and Jan smiled as they handed the report back to Sven. Their smiles of relief were short-lived as the noise around them suddenly increased dramatically.

Macchinisti on the move is never a silent process; it always involves lots of shouting and arm-waving. Under Anatra's direction they were moving all the kit back to the van. Luca was reloading in the front seat, black cotton, light-proof loading bag on his lap, magazine inside, along with the roll of new film. Adam sympathised; he had been a Clapper for three years. Hot hands in that zipped bag on hot days makes your hands tacky, which sticks to the film emulsion, so you have to be quick and very dextrous. You very quickly learn to see with your fingers. People banging and shaking the van do not help!

Gill tried phoning Dino, but he was never in his office, and he had not yet collected the keys for his new rental house up on the high ground above the city. She decided against leaving a note as things like that could easily fall into the wrong hands. The last thing anybody needed was for someone to have a hard copy of the allegations, all of which could be traced back to her. Dublin had found some excuse to go out, telling her to sort it, as he usually did with any problem. Clearly, a manager in name only. She was just about to talk it through with Luigi next door when Ben, the Second Assistant Director, knocked politely on the door.

'Permesso? Permesso, Gill!'

'Come in, Ben, come in. What can I do for you?'

Ben walked in tentatively, checking the desk at the far end of the room to see if Dublin was there. He relaxed, smiled, and put his right-hand fingers gently on her desk.

'Gill, the lunch, on the backlot, no one like it. Beatrice and I had thirty complaints, over half the crew. They said it was cheap, insulting! Duke asked you to have a word with the caterers. The coffee was fine, he's happy with that, but lunch was…he said that you'd understand the word "crap"!'

Gill smiled. Duke always did have a knack of coming straight to the point. 'Okay, Ben, okay, I get the message. Tell Duke I'll look into it, try to sort it for tomorrow. Thank you. Anything else?'

'No. Unless the call sheets are ready? I can take them.'

'Yes, they are actually. Just finished. They're in the box on the chair outside, ready for internal mail. You're welcome to take them. Yes, take them. Please do!'

Adam looked up. The rain bars were set high, about twenty feet up, which was never a good sign. It meant they were in for a real drenching. Also, a sizeable five-foot wind machine was sitting on top of a small zip-up tower: another bad sign.

The set was an army checkpoint, with a stripey wooden barrier and a small wooden guardhouse that looked like it had been there for ten years. The action vehicle was an old black Wolseley, right-hand drive, of course, with English plates and a Taxi sign stuck on the roof. The Props guys were just finishing masking up the headlights with black gaffer tape to create a thin black slit, as per the wartime blackout regulations. The car reminded Adam of the one his dad had owned when he was a kid; the darn thing was very prone to breaking down, and always just before a major trip. The thing was a bloody liability.

To the right, just to one side of the approach road, Sven had a large arc lamp rigged up high on a tower, peeking over the top of some low trees. The Macchinisti had rigged a plywood roof over the top of the camera with a blanket tacked to it so that the rain would make no sound. It was sloped from front to back to shed water. Adam was impressed.

The rehearsal went well. Isabella arrives right to left in the taxi, up to the army sentry box, four sentries all in army greatcoats, their rifles fitted with bayonets. One of them checks her papers, then the barrier is raised and she is allowed to pass. A couple more rehearsals, minor adjustments, reposition the car down the track, put Isabella in. Clear the set.

Duke stands well back, behind the camera. 'OKAY! TEST, TEST. PIOVE! MAKE RAIN!'

The result is instantaneous. The Props guys open the valves. The water lines had all been primed half an hour ago. MONSOON! Three fire hoses running six rain bars. The wind machine is gently panned left and right by the two electricians up in the lighting rig.

The arc light on the tower to the side subtly side-lights the cascading droplets. It was hard to comprehend the amount of water that fell in those few seconds. Lasse and Sven both study the scene, and both seem happy. Lasse nods at Duke to stop.

Duke shouts, 'BASTA! ENOUGH! BASTA!'

The rain instantly stops. Jan takes his eye away from the eyepiece. 'Wow! That looks amazing.'

Adam leans around the front of the camera to check that the front glass is spotless. Duke gets the confirmatory nod from Lasse.

'GOING FOR A TAKE. GOING FOR A TAKE. START THE TAXI. START THE TAXI!'

Beatrice, standing beside the Wolseley driver's door, gives a hearty thumbs up and quickly runs back to the shelter of the light tower.

Duke bawls, 'TURN OVER!'

Adam flicks the camera switch.

Jan squints to check the circular speed counter on the back of the camera, then shouts, 'SPEED!' and quickly jambs his eye into the eyepiece.

Carl Sound calls, 'SPEED!' from the sound desk set ten feet behind the camera.

Luca holds up the clapper board four foot in front of the lens, holding the clapper open. The Sound Assistant in full waterproofs stands just on the edge of the frame to the right to get the car door slam effect.

Jan calls, 'MARK IT!'

Luca firmly claps the board. 'Sixty-eight, take one.' Then scuttles back to behind the camera.

The four sentries brace themselves. One of them bites his lip; he knows what's coming.

Duke shouts, 'PIOVE! PIOVE!' and the deluge commences.

The sentries are totally soaked within seconds.

Duke calls, 'ACTION, TAXI!' and waves at the Wolseley in the distance.

Grace starts her stopwatch. The little black car bounces down the track, up towards the barrier. The sentry holds up his hand, signalling it to stop. Isabella gets out, bending her face downwards to protect herself from the fan-assisted downpour, closing the door with difficulty against the wind. She then opens the rear door and pulls out a small briefcase, putting it down in the mud to slam the door shut before picking it back up and walking as quickly as she can, head into the gale, to the waiting sentry with the rain pouring off his red cap, to get her papers checked.

Lasse watches tunnel-visioned every move, every nuance right through to the little soaked suitcase-carrying figure being escorted by the sentry past the barrier and out of frame.

'CUT!' he shouts.

Grace stops her watch, notes the time. The wind machine is immediately panned off to the right, away from the set. The deluge stops instantly, with just a few watery leftovers dripping intermittently. Adam immediately leans around the front of the camera and bellows to check his front glass. 'Clear!' Thank God for that!

Duke moves closer to Lasse. 'How was that for you, sir?'

Lasse looks up at him with a grimace. 'One more time, please. I want to see that permit-checking more clearly with the sentry. He needs to turn to camera more. I don't want to do it as a close-up. We'll rehearse it.'

Duke looks around. 'RESET! RESET. REHEARSAL.'

Sophia was already offering Isabella a towel for her hair with another over her arm should it be needed. Pia was standing behind her, trying to get her wet coat off, with the exact dry matching replacement draped over her shoulder.

A Props guy was wiping down and drying the mud-spattered suitcase.

Adam decided to check the camera gate and make sure that everything was as clean as it could be in his little world.

Grace wrote down: 'HOLD sentry permit check, not clear enough'.

The Wolseley car refuses to start. Adam was not surprised; fan-powered rain gets everywhere.

In the viewing theatre, Luigi did not feel the need to sit next to Dublin. He was not in his good books. He sat in the second row, leaving the front row for him. Dino had not turned up yet so Luigi decided to go ahead without him and nodded to Veniero to begin.

The memo-creating editor tapped the projection room glass from his customary seat at the back of the viewing theatre, and the lights dimmed. The show began.

Gill strode into the canteen. All of the chairs were upside down on top of the tables. The floor looked shiny in places where it was still damp from being mopped. The antiseptic smell of cleaning fluid hung in the air. The marble floor echoed with her footsteps. It was virtually deserted, except for two of the white-overalled female serving assistants cleaning down the hotplate area on the serving counter. The catering manager, Fausto, a red-faced balloon of a man in a shiny black suit, came out of the restaurant area to greet her.

'Signora Consalvo, to what do I owe this honour?'

Gill kept her distance, her hands at her side. She was not in the mood for having her hand grabbed by a sweaty palm and given a slobbery kiss, as was his habit.

'Fausto, the location lunch, we have had complaints.'

'Oh no! I'm sorry to hear that. I did tell Mr Dublin that our bronze option was very basic.'

Gill frowned. 'I'm sorry, Fausto, I don't understand. I was not part of the initial deal-making.'

Fausto beamed a conciliatory smile. 'Well, Gill, we have four packages, four options: bronze, the very basic, the cheapest; silver, a good mid-range; gold which is very, very good, excellent in fact; and deluxe which is, well, haute cuisine. Five star! Usually just for the actors, the stars.'

Gill nodded. Slowly it was all starting to make sense. 'I see, I see. And Mr Dublin booked the bronze option, the cheapest, right?'

'Si. Yes. He said that he had a very tight budget…'

'Thank you, Fausto. I was not aware of any of this. I will get back to you. I will speak to Mr Dublin. Thank you.'

'A pleasure, Signora, always a pleasure.' He smiled a sweaty smile but knew from the expression on her face that he had not heard the last of it.

Adam could not wait for wrap to be called, rushes to be over and to be in that taxi outside Grace's flat. But life was not that kind.

Lasse insisted they do another three takes under rainmakers before he was happy. It had taken the Props guys over a quarter of an hour to get the Wolseley action vehicle to eventually start, using virtually a whole can of WD-40, a great deal of swearing and lots of arm-waving in the process. Isabella was drenched from head to toe, as were the four sentries, their coats providing very little protection against such a prolonged, four-time onslaught of water. The late afternoon sun did little to warm them up.

The rushes viewing, unlike the previous day, was an uplifting experience. There were no technical problems, it was all in focus, lovely lighting; there was no doubt that Sven was a master of his craft. The difference between the London Lumaxfilm print and the local print was very marked, chalk and cheese. You get what you pay for in that game. Veniero, the editor, was as pleased as punch as Sven thanked him for his report. It was nice to be appreciated.

Toni drove Adam back to his hotel, never once mentioning Pia. Everything else, the rainmakers, the spartan lunch, tonight's football, the traffic, but never Pia. But the kind smile that he gave him as he dropped him off told Adam that he had earned some respect for the way that he had conducted himself with regards to his niece.

Adam looked at his watch. He didn't have long. Just time for a quick shower and a change of clothes. Grace rarely went to rushes. She would have had a head start of over an hour. The hot water in the hotel always went cool about this time of day as everyone showered before going out for supper. Adam just had to grin and bear it, giving himself an enthusiastic soaping down. There was no way he was going to turn up sweaty. Before leaving the room, he looked at the pack of contraceptives in his suitcase and chuckled to himself. If only… Something told him he was not going to need them this evening, and probably not for quite some evenings to come, if ever.

Adam's luck changed with regards to the taxi. One had just dropped off some guests at the hotel as he was walking out.

His little piece of paper with the address written on it caused the driver to frown and pause for thought as he tried to remember where it was. Eventually, he nodded. 'Ah, si! Si!' he said and waved for Adam to get in the back. This said to Adam that his destination was not on the main drag.

He could not have been more right. The last few turns down the little cobbled streets got progressively narrower and narrower. When they eventually came to a stop, the driver had to pull hard over to his right, the wing mirror nearly touching the wall, so that Adam could open his rear door to get out.

The ancient metal sign high up on the wall, Via Cigno, told him that he was in the right place. All he had to do now was find number five. The taxi gently drove off, leaving him with the smell of exhaust fumes, which soon cleared, replaced with the dry, musty smell of ancient sandstone. He wandered down the street, looking at the numbers on the buildings. He found number seven, then meandered along a little alley about fifteen feet long and four foot wide before he saw a dark wooden door at the end, and a small white glazed tile with the number five in red glaze.

There was a white illuminated bell push on the peeling, brown-painted door frame. Shaking slightly, he gently pushed the button. He couldn't hear any bell ringing inside. There was a peephole set in the door, just above the number tile. He heard a scratching sound and was about to ring again when the door opened, and a waft of roasting fish wafted momentarily towards him.

Grace leant around the door, a smile of welcome, just standing there for a second, looking at him. He did the same, just looked at her. She was dressed in a high-necked green and white blouse, adorned with a thin gold necklace and crucifix, and blue jeans with a large, brown, buckled leather belt. Not a trace of make-up, except for maybe a little mascara.

'Come in, Adam, come in. You found it all right then?' She held the door open for him as he entered the narrow hallway. As he brushed past her, there was a slight whiff of subtle jasmine that he had smelt on her on the first day. 'Go on through, go on through!'

Adam continued up the white painted hallway past the door to the kitchen. The air was warmer for a couple of paces; the aroma of hot baked fish, now even stronger, wafted out, filling his nostrils. He walked on into a small squarish lounge about seven metres square. To the right, up against the wall, was a large, white, leather, three-seater sofa littered with a few large, coloured scatter cushions. In front was a small low coffee table, and to the left, dominating the wall area, a sizeable dark oak dresser with a couple of blue Delft design decorative plates on the top shelf. The other two shelves were empty. Next to it, on the left, was a shiny black upright piano with the lid down. The top was adorned with folds of paper, presumably sheet music. The small television in the far right corner on a small table looked old and unloved. Adam hesitated as she came up behind him.

'Have a seat. Have a seat,' she said, pointing to the sofa. 'Drink? Beer, tea, water? I got in some Coke, if you fancy?'

'Coke would be lovely, Grace, thank you.'

'Ice?'

'Yes, please. Thanks.' He moved to sit down, watching her walk back to the kitchen. 'Bloody hell, Grace, you've got legs right up to your shoulders. You kept that well hidden!'

She stopped and turned back to him. 'Behave, Adam, behave. You're here to talk, nothing more.' She held up her right index finger like a teacher ticking off a child. There was no smile.

Adam pushed his chin forward. 'Sorry, boss!' He looked to his right. The windowless room continued through an archway into a well-lit conservatory area where there was a round dining table, set for two. She came back holding a white mug and a glass of Coke with clinking ice cubes that she placed carefully on one of the leather placemats on the coffee table in front of him. She slowly put her mug down in front of her.

'I've done you fish, chips and peas, to remind you of home…but…but I've got no chip fat, so it's baked and roast frittes, if that's okay. Be about half an hour.'

'Thank you, Grace. You are very kind. I like fish and chips.'

She sat down next to him, put her mug on the table and, leaning back, picked up one of the cushions. Hugging it close protectively to her body, she stared forward at the dresser, not looking at him.

He turned and looked at her. She was tense, almost strangling the cushion. She spoke, slowly as if from a rehearsed script. 'This idea of yours, Adam, is crackpot. It is just going to cause a shedload of pain. I'm a widow, a Catholic widow, living on my own, in Catholic Rome, a great deal older than you. In a couple of months' time you will bugger off back home, and I will be left here to pick up the pieces. Not very smart, eh?'

He looked sideways at her tense figure. 'Grace, I'm not asking for anything. I have no idea where any of this is going to lead, but I sensed something special, just for a few seconds. Sorry, I—'

She cut across him, raising her voice slightly, 'Adam, you don't seem to realise that it is really easy here to get a bad reputation and be called "puttana", whore. Once labelled, it is impossible to shake off. I live here. I have a social life here. It's too risky, not for you, for me.'

He looked at her but she continued to stare at the dresser, avoiding his eyes. He was about to say something, but she squeezed the cushion even tighter.

'You've only been here just over a week, and already there's something gone on between you and Pia. I don't believe it's sexual, but you've had a row with her or hurt her in some way.'

Adam was shocked but tried not to show it. He decided to adopt her method of staring straight ahead, vacantly, into space.

'What makes you think that, Grace?'

'Adam, it's the way people look at you, not when you are looking at them, but when you're not, when your back is turned. They watch you. They give the game away. Belinda is a case in point. She's like a spider watching you buzzing around her web, waiting for her last couple of days here so she can invite you back to her room, to help her pack most likely and then, then do what spiders do, suck every gram of moisture out of you, before going home engorged to a boring hubby and two labradors in the Home Counties.'

He turned to her. 'That is… You amaze me.'

'It's true, Adam. I don't want to be one of many, another score on your card. You haven't even discovered the Venus club yet. There is so much hot flesh down there, from all over the world. You'd be like a kid in a sweet shop!'

'Stop, Grace, stop! You obviously have a very low opinion of me. You obviously think that I am totally dominated by my trousers. But you're wrong. Let me ask you a question, Grace, a simple yes or no answer. Do you think that we may have something going here that is worth exploring, even though the world is stacked against us?'

She flashed him a quick look. 'I don't think so, Adam.'

'Is that a yes or a no?'

'I don't know, Adam. I just don't know.'

'Are you denying that something clicked with us?'

'Adam, I don't know. NO!' She held the cushion even tighter.

'Okay, Grace, okay. Let me put a few ideas forward. I'm happy if you ignore me and keep staring at the wall. Look at things another way: we begin a relationship, both of us totally aware that it has a shitty ending, but because we're both a bit stupid, we decide to meet up two or three times a week, just to enjoy each other's company and just to see how it goes. No Belindas, no Venus club, no Anitas.'

At that, Grace turned to him and smiled, sniffing disparagingly. 'Anita has the sex drive of a dodo. She never stops talking. I don't see her as a threat.'

Adam picked up a cushion that was to his right and hugged it to him, mimicking her body language. He looked straight ahead.

There was silence. They seemed to have reached an impasse.

'Adam…Adam, I'm forty-six, I have hot flushes. How old are you, thirty? There's no point.'

He turned to her, pretending to be insulted. 'If you don't mind, I'm twenty-nine!'

She laughed. 'Twenty-nine. That makes it even worse, even worse. Cradle snatching.'

He gently placed his cushion back onto the sofa, twisted himself round towards her and leant forward, his chin level with her shoulder. 'Sorry, Grace, but I still want to kiss you. Sorry, need a kiss.'

She turned, twisting her body towards him, all the while keeping the cushion as a barrier between them. Their faces were a few inches apart. She stared into his eyes, trying to read him, searching for reassurance. She was close to tears.

'This is madness,' she said, as a single tear ran down her cheek. She then slowly, deliberately let go of her cushion, and with both hands, used her long cool fingers to very, very slowly and gently ease his head towards her. Their lips met. It was very different to that first time on the steps with the panting hyenas watching. This time it was incredibly tender, unbelievably gentle. There was no need for vice-like grips. She gently cradled his head as all of the tension of the last few minutes were washed away. Her hands were soft, cool. Adam didn't know what to do with his hands; her cushion prevented him from holding her, so he just gently took hold of her wrists.

Eventually, after what seemed for her an eternity, she very slowly and gently opened up her fingers and let go of his face, easing away from him slightly.

'Whoa!' She let out a deep breath. 'Whoa. What are we doing?'

Adam just looked into her moist eyes. 'I think that we just proved a point, Grace. There was a special moment. We've just proved it.'

She nodded slowly in affirmation and stared unfocused at the floor for a few seconds, arching her eyebrows as if accepting a new reality. She turned back to him. Her hazel eyes flicked backwards and forwards, taking in every detail of his face. She smiled. 'Adam, you had me from "Have you ever had conjunctivitis?" From that moment, laughing boy, I have been fighting a rearguard action to keep you at arm's length, physically and emotionally, but I failed miserably. You remind me of my dad, always teasing, always joking. This is so wrong, Adam, so wrong, so bloody stupid.'

Adam looked into her damp, vulnerable eyes. 'Sorry, Grace, you shouldn't be so bloody attractive. It's all your fault. Do you think that we can make the next kiss last until supper?'

wanted to contact her, that would be the first place they would try.

Putting her best foot forward, she gathered herself together, took a long shower in an effort to clean herself up, both physically and emotionally. After nine, parking anywhere near her office was nigh on impossible, so she decided to hail a taxi.

When she arrived, she was surprised to find someone waiting outside her office – a long-haired, tall, slim, thirty-ish, very good-looking, trendy young man. She unlocked the door and beckoned him in and to take a seat. She walked around the back of her desk and sat down in her leather chair.

He gave her his card. 'Donna, I understand that you have a story to tell about the American Film Producer Dino Burgio?'

She looked down at his card. He was from *Insight News*. SHIT! He pulled out a pen and a notebook from his jeans pocket. His smile was warm and friendly.

'How do you know about Dino?' Her mind was racing. This was not part of the master plan. It was screen tests she was after, not to carry out her threat, not to talk to the press.

He smiled engagingly, speaking slowly, calmly. 'We believe that you are in a relationship with him and that he is going to use his position to make you a star. That sort of story always has a huge public interest, an in-depth story can really help you on your way, happens all the time!' he said, finishing once again with a warm smile.

Thursday 17th April

Donna Tavazzi was not one to let the grass grow under her feet; Gill's phone was ringing insistently when she walked into the office at nine o'clock. Signorina Tavazzi wanted to know why Mr Burgio had not been in touch. Gill explained that she had not seen Mr Burgio. In fact, no one had seen Mr Burgio and he was not answering his phone. Gill made it clear that she did not want to leave written notes all over the place, due to the fact that the matter, because of its sensitivity, was best dealt with face to face.

Donna was not appeased. She gave a time limit – until noon – regarding her original demand. After that, she was going to the papers to tell her story. Gill hung up and tried dialling Dino's extension; it rang out, which came as no surprise as he was rarely in his office.

The first thing that Adam did when Grace walked onto the set was to try to catch her eye, get some kind of a sign. But her behaviour was completely normal. The same nod, the same smile that she gave to everyone. How she did it, he had no idea. The intensity of the previous evening had had such a profound effect on him he was now looking for something from her to let him know that she felt the same way, but there was nothing. She gave nothing away. He remembered what she had told him about people watching you when your back is turned, and so he decided just to play it cool and almost ignore her. They were due to meet late on Saturday afternoon after she got back from playing at some party somewhere. He would just have to wait until then, but he hoped in the meantime that she wouldn't change her mind. So bloody frustrating that she would be only a few feet away from him all day.

Veronique Press did not do door-knocking. It was unnecessary in her view, not her style. She simply cruised into the Production Office, bracelets jangling like castanets and walked straight up to Gill's desk. If Dublin had been there, she would have totally ignored him, but he wasn't. It was far too early.

'Bonjour, chérie, 'ow are you today? Oh! I like your top.'

Gill looked up. The perfume was already starting to envelop her. She smiled politely. 'Morning, Vee. Thank you. I'm glad you like it. It's one of Jose's…'

'Ah! The little shop, with a big heart. Good.' Without pausing for breath she continued, 'Look, chérie, I've got a photographer outside. I need two set passes so I can get a few snaps of Isabella playing soldier this morning. Luigi knows about it. Okay?'

Gill looked around and pursed her lips, deep in thought for a couple of seconds. 'Vee, that's no problem. Passes coming up…but…but can I ask you your opinion on a very delicate matter? Very hush-hush, top secret.'

Veronique's eyes opened wide, her eyebrows raised in faked surprise. 'Of course, chérie, of course.'

Gill leant forward. 'It's very private, Vee, it's not to go outside this room. I just need your advice.'

'Je comprends, chérie. If you knew half the secrets that I know…' she said, raising her eyebrows. 'I am trustworthy! Absolument!'

'We have a young lady, a very voluptuous young lady, a Donna Tavazzi, the house agent, who was bedded by Dino last night after she was promised screen tests and a part in the film. Now, today, she wants her screen tests and threatens to go to the papers, ready to claim that he raped her if she doesn't get them.'

''Ow do we know she was bedded by Dino?'

Gill raised her eyebrows. 'Oh, I believe her, Vee. I don't doubt her at all. I was there at the house-viewing when greasy Dino promised to send a car for her.'

Veronique was wide-eyed. 'Shit! How stupid can anyone be? Is she serious?' she asked, looking around to see if there was any brandy like in the office next door. Gill noticed her distraction but let it pass.

'She is very determined, Vee, very determined, says it was like a wardrobe falling on her. Could it become a PR disaster, do you think?'

'Don't know about disaster, ma chérie, but she is going to look pretty dumb. It will certainly get her face in the papers! Does she have any witnesses?'

'No idea, Vee, no idea, but I can't get hold of Dino. She says she's going public this afternoon.'

Veronique paused and stared vacantly into space for a few seconds as she computed all of the options. Decision made, she turned back to Gill.

'Right, tell Luigi, and my advice would be to offer her money to shut her up, but she needs to sign a legal non-disclosure contract before she gets even a sou! Discuss it with Luigi. He'll know what to do.'

Gill nodded. 'Thanks, Vee, thanks, I will. Now, I'll get you those two set passes.' She took a book of pre-printed block out of her top drawer, tore off two, then signed and dated them before handing them to the somewhat impatient Veronique.

'Thanks, Vee. Keep mum, yeah?'

'Certainement, chérie, of course. Did Jose have any more of those tops?'

'He did, Vee, he did.'

Veronique raised her eyebrows, and with a 'Goody good!' turned and castanetted her way out of the office.

Her photographer was nearly asleep, slouching on one of the seats outside in the corridor. She should have smelt a rat when he asked to stop and make a phone call on the way over to the backlot, but her mind was on other things. And she wanted to get to the film set before coffee break.

Isabella's final day on the backlot was a more sedentary affair: five desks, with fold-up wooden seats and a large blackboard on an easel. Captain Steve supervised the trainee spies loading gun magazine clips, blindfolded, before moving on to handling wired detonators and sticks of explosives. Many of the male crew members gathered behind the camera line and just listened and watched each scene being filmed, even though it was all in English, albeit with a trace of a South Wales accent.

The morning was a masterclass in the art of sabotage, how to blow up bridges, where to place the charges, the best way to blow train lines to ensure long-term damage. It was totally absorbing. The Marine certainly knew his stuff. When he finally finished, after Lasse called 'CUT' at coffee time, the crew all gave Steve a round of applause – something that would never happen at snobby Pinewood!

As the clapping faded, the hovering Veronique immediately moved in, requesting the extras in army uniform to stay in the background while they took pictures of Isabella holding a Sten gun in front of the camera. Adam decided to stick around, simply to make sure that no one messed with the camera, his pride and joy. It was okay to use it as a stills prop in the background, but not to touch it. Captain Steve wandered over to him as Veronique and her stills man plied their trade with Isabella. Sophia fussed before every shutter click. There was no way her leading lady was going to have a shiny nose or a single hair out of place, particularly when the picture could end up on a fifteen-metre hoarding or become the centrefold of a magazine.

Adam sensed that Steve was also protective. He never took his eyes off the little actress. He was tense, like a coiled spring, ready to jump in if anything untoward should occur.

Adam nodded to him. 'Is this all for real, Steve? World War II, young female spies trained in sabotage, unarmed combat and stuff?'

Steve nodded, never taking his eyes off Isabella. 'Very much so, mate! Very much so! Young men and some women, part of Churchill's secret army, the SOE. They were used all over Europe. Many of 'em captured and tortured. But they did a frightening amount of damage before and after D-Day in France mainly, liaising with the local resistance groups, blowing up railway tracks and cutting phone lines, radioing back information. They made a difference, a big difference.'

Adam raised his eyebrows. 'Well, you learn something new every day. Were you involved?'

'No, mate, not me. I was just Marine commando. Spent most of my time training in Scotland for things that never happened. I never went anywhere!' he added, smiling and turning fleetingly to look hard-eyed at Adam before focusing back on the pantomime of the stills session.

Adam looked at him for a second. There was something about that answer that did not ring true. He couldn't put his finger on it, but he knew from the set of Steve's jaw that there was no point in pursuing the matter.

Eventually, as the rest of the crew started to sidle back, plastic cups in hand, Veronique announced that she was finished. This was Steve's cue to step crisply forward and take back his gun from Isabella, breathing a sigh of relief as he did so. Steve automatically, almost unconsciously, unclipped the empty magazine, making sure that the weapon was pointed all the time firmly at the floor. He offered it to Adam.

'Here you are, matey! Good old Sten, the biggest load of mass-produced crap in World War II. You around tonight…meal…beer?'

Adam smiled. 'Cracking idea, Steve, cracking. Whereabouts?'

Steve smiled. 'Come to my place. I'll show you the armoury, give you a guided tour. There's plenty of places nearby. Say, about seven-thirty, eight? I've got a card in my bag with the address.'

Adam looked down at the Sten. It was heavier than he was expecting. But he now understood where Grace was coming from when she'd said there was always a gun on set in the Italian film business.

Within five minutes of Veronique flaunting out of the office, Gill was on the phone to Luigi at his home. He listened intently, took down Donna's phone number and work address and instructed Gill to leave the matter with him, requesting that she made no written note and told no one. Gill crossed out the two lines in her daybook immediately after putting the phone down. She didn't mention the fact that Dublin knew.

Donna Tavazzi was a depressed young woman and believed that she had been used, taken advantage of. Promises had been made, but none of them seemed to be coming to fruition. She was beginning to feel dirty and more than a little abused.

When she had woken up in the hotel bed some twenty-four hours ago, her head was splitting. She was alone, totally alone. She knew that she had participated in sex, she remembered that. But there was no note, no 'give me a call, thanks for a great time, we need to speak about your screen tests', nothing. She had called the Production Office, the only contact number she had for him, but Gill, the secretary, had fobbed her off, saying that Dino was unavailable. Because she didn't have a phone in her one-room flat, she decided to go into her city office. At least if people

Donna's head was crystal clear now. Alarm bells were ringing. His notebook was open, his pen poised, head tilted attentively engagingly to one side.

'How do you know about that?' She was agitated now. 'How do you know? Who told you? Has Dino spoken to you?'

His reply was slow, softly spoken. 'No, we haven't talked to him yet, but he's on our list obviously. Look, care to tell me all about him? How did you first meet?'

He left a long pause, like all experienced journalists, waiting for her to fill the uncomfortable silence. She didn't disappoint. This was unfamiliar ground for her.

'I first met him the day before yesterday. He's a client, and I managed to find a house for him. How do you know about him? I want to know how you know.'

He smiled, nodded in sympathy and paused again to give her a bit of time to gather her thoughts as he held a look of complete interest and that engaging smile.

'It's information that's just out there, you know. This sort of stuff just comes in all the time… Look, how about we change tack. Tell me a bit about yourself, where you're from and the like, bit of background information.'

She looked at him. He was really sympathetic, really interested in her, attentive, kind eyes. Shame it wasn't him that had been in that hotel bedroom. He had such a warm, genuine manner, lovely teeth. She was happier to chat about herself, tell him her life story. He was obviously very interested. Then her phone rang.

'Excuse me.'

As she listened, her eyes glazed. She nodded, looked at the smiling eyes across the desk, nodded again, slowly understanding. His look was changing to one of polite curiosity.

'Okay! Okay! I hear what you're saying. Yes! Thank you. I'll wait. Yes, of course.'

She slowly placed the handset in the cradle. She was now panicking slightly, adrenaline flowing like a mountain torrent.

'That was the film production lawyer. She's on her way over here, says she'll be here in half an hour.' Donna was visibly agitated now. She looked from left to right, not knowing what to do. 'She has instructed me to say absolutely nothing to anyone until she has spoken to me. She doesn't know you're here, but she was adamant about not saying anything to the press. I'm confused.'

The journalist leant back, giving her a little more space. 'Oh, Donna, you are about to be steamrollered, happens all the time. Can we get something down, some story, something, because the rumour mill is wildly inaccurate, rubbish can be printed because...because... other...other journalists...literally, just make up stories, any stories just to fill print space. At least if I have your account, it will be the truth. I won't publish anything unless I have your permission, you know that. A good exclusive will always hold sway over rumour.'

Donna looked at him. She instinctively knew that she could trust him. He was just so sympathetic, so genuine.

Loretta Alonzo was not that familiar with rushing. It was something that was not really in her repertoire of skills; her style was slow, careful and methodical, but as the lawyer, the legal eagle for *The Script Girl*, when Luigi Mussomelli, the Producer, said jump, she jumped.

Within ten minutes of receiving his phone call she was in a taxi heading across the city to meet up with a Donna Tavazzi, who Luigi's fellow Producer Dino Burgio had allegedly bedded. The lady was now attempting to put the story into the public domain, which is the last thing that any business enterprise wants, particularly a film in the early days of production in the biggest gossip mill in the world, outside of Hollywood. A non-disclosure agreement was the order of the day here, a thousand dollars and shut up, fifteen hundred if there were witnesses. Should all be done and dusted by lunchtime.

The traffic was horrendous, solid. She could almost have walked it quicker. But she sat tight, being more than a bit overweight. The diabetes didn't help either. She didn't like walking, and every time she reluctantly thought about getting out and taking to her leather platform soles, the traffic cleared a little, and they made a hundred yards' progress or so. When she eventually arrived and paid the taxi driver, it was nearly an hour since she had left the comfort of her office.

Donna's office was a drab little affair, with paint peeling off the dark window frames. Sited in a small back street amid a line of small single-trader businesses, lawyers, hairdressers, a small dressmaker and the ubiquitous coffee bar, it was certainly not the poshest part of town.

Clutching her briefcase, she walked purposefully up to the door. It was shut, and she pushed gently to open it, but it was locked, firmly locked. It rattled a little in its frame when she pushed, but it was definitely locked. The lights were not on inside, it was dark, uninhabited. She lowered her head and shielding her eyes to kill the strong outside reflection, she pushed hard up against the glass to attempt to see in. There was a desk covered in papers, a low-backed seat on either side of it and two feet sticking out from under the far side of the desk. She stared. The legs, the feet were not moving. There was something not right here. She pushed harder against the glass, attempting to look around the small room. There appeared to splashes of something dark down the light brown wall behind the desk. She looked around, but there was no one lurking about, just the usual trickle of people going about their business. She looked again into the little room. The legs were still in the same place. She decided to go up the street into the little café and call the police.

It was not her place to attempt to force the door. Breaking and entering was not in her job description.

Luigi collected a cup of coffee from Gill. On arrival at the office, they exchanged pleasantries and nothing more. He did not want to discuss anything until he had heard from the solicitor. There was still no sign of Dublin. Gill had no idea where he was; he had kept a very low profile since Luigi's threat to fire him. His office attendance since then had been minimal, to say the least.

As Luigi left the room, Gill's phone rang. It was Como Trani, the mechanic from the Accacio submarine restoration society, three hundred kilometres up the coast. He was gabbling, near to tears. His pride and joy, his beautiful submarine, which was due to set sail over the weekend to be positioned ready for filming at Civitavecchia first thing on Monday morning, had been subject to a major fire and was not going to be seaworthy, let alone move under its own power. It had been sabotaged. The lock to the entrance hatch on the main deck had been forced. A fire had been deliberately started using rags and a flammable liquid in the engine compartment, and the damage was substantial. It was definitely sabotage, and not a very subtle job at that.

Trani was beside himself, half a life's work up in flames. The insurers had insisted on an automatic extinguisher system which had stopped the fire from spreading out of the engine compartment, but the damage was still considerable. The restoration committee had ruled out towing the craft down the coast because the damage to the engines meant no pumps would be operable, and that made the vessel unseaworthy and the insurance invalid. So, in a nutshell, the main action prop for half of next week's filming was not going to turn up bobbing just off the coast at Civitavecchia as per contract.

Gill put the phone down, pursing her lips, not believing how badly her week was going. A firm knock at the door and her husband, all six-foot-two of him, suddenly appeared, the look on his face one of great concern.

'My dear, it would appear that you may get dragged into a spot of bother. A Donna Tavazzi has been found murdered in her office.'

Gill jumped in pure shock, disbelief written all over her face. 'What! I spoke to her on the phone earlier this morning.'

'Well, she was found in her office, by this film's production lawyer, with her head smashed in, and your name, your phone number, that phone number, is all over her notepad.'

Gill was wide-eyed. 'I can't believe it!'

'Sad but true, my dear. I know that you had nothing to do with it, but another Ispettore will be taking the case. I can't be involved obviously due to a potential conflict of interest. I just wanted to let you know to prepare you for the interrogation that is to come. I know that you had nothing to do with it.'

'No, I didn't. This is horrible, horrible. She was such a nice girl, head in the clouds, but a friendly kid, really nice kid. Who would do such a thing? Who would kill a twenty-year-old house agent? She was just a kid!'

'My love, I have to go, but my advice is to tell them everything you know, every tiny detail, however obscure, to help us catch the bastards that did this. The truth and everything that you know is always best. The investigating Ispettore is Paulo. You can tell him that I dropped in to let you know what's going on. I've nothing to hide here. He's not my cup of tea, bit pedantic, but he is an excellent, honest cop, very persistent. He will get to the bottom of this.'

Gill stood up, slightly tearful and walked around the desk to her husband. 'I need a hug,' she said, holding her arms out to encircle his large frame.

He smiled, a reassuring grimace, and held out his arms and pulled her to him. The force of his hold drove the breath from her, but she needed that, that physical feeling of strength and support and the reassuring kiss to her forehead.

The last few shots before lunch were less visually exciting than the assault course sequences, with Captain Steve demonstrating the use of the mobile radio transmitter, in his words the Beloved Type three mark two, or Bee two, to its friends. A very neat affair in a small leather suitcase. He droned on about frequencies and voltages, finishing his briefing with a chart on the lecture board displaying all of the Morse signals dot and dashes.

Lasse did all he could to make things more interesting with close-ups of Isabella and the other spies listening intently. Plus close-ups of the Morse key being tapped, the knobs being turned, all of which made the whole sequence more visually interesting. But when it was all over, Adam, like many others on set that morning, was a lot wiser and respectful of what these agents behind enemy lines had to go through to be effective.

Grace maintained her decorum, stayed focused on her job and nothing more, which Adam found more than a little disconcerting. The amount of tender emotion that had flowed so freely between them the evening before had been something new for Adam. They were both so caring with each other, so gentle, not the everyday rough and tumble knicker-ripping that had been the hallmark of most of his previous encounters with members of the opposite sex. Maybe it was because she was older, more experienced. He had no idea, but she had accused Belinda of having the ability to weave a complex spider's web to trap men, and yet that was exactly what she, Grace De Mattias, had done to him. Woven her web, spun her charms around him, trapped him in an emotional spell, and he could not have been happier. He would like to believe that the feelings were mutual, but he could not be sure. She gave nothing away. There was undoubtedly a suppression of the sexual side of the relationship; it was more about tenderness with her. She was very much in control. He knew from the way that she had used the cushion to protect her body that she was not suddenly going to throw herself on the floor, legs in the air and scream, 'Take me! For God's sake, take me!' He laughed inwardly at the very prospect. That, if it ever happened, was a long way off. But if it ever did occur, he knew that it would be one of the highlights of his life. She had caught him, hook, line and sinker.

As he occasionally momentarily flicked his eyes over to her to look at her now very familiar face and mannerisms, he hoped that he was at the beginning of a really meaningful episode of his life. Still, he would have to wait and see.

Luigi did not have a problem with police officers. In his eyes, in the main, they help to maintain the society that he wanted to live in. Being mainly law-abiding, he did not have any issues with an Ispettore and his Sovrintendente being in his office and asking him about his movements that morning. But he did not like being talked down to and being treated disrespectfully. He was not from the back streets, and he had done nothing wrong.

He decided to stand up and assert himself, but he was at a slight disadvantage because he was not wearing his very expensive, hand-tailored jacket. That was on the back of his chair. Instead, he was in shirtsleeves, and his thin black braces were working hard to hold up his slightly bulging trousers. He was acutely aware that he was not cutting an imposing figure.

'Ispettore, I fully respect your need to garner every available piece of information regarding Miss Tavazzi, but as I have explained, she was attempting to exert pressure on this office, to gain a foothold in the film business, something that I was unaware of until this morning. I suggest that you speak to Mr Burgio and try to elicit from him as to what promises he made to her and what went on when he met her. As to me sending our solicitor to her office, that was solely a fact-finding mission and nothing more. As I said, we do not know what she was trying to achieve exactly. Speak to Mr Burgio. I'm sure that he will be able to provide you with a lot more information than me.'

The Ispettore was a praying mantis of a man, grey-skinned, thin, gaunt, slightly sunken eyes and chest, and long, slender arms. His Sovrintendente hung back over his left shoulder, notebook out, pen poised. The opposite in stature, squat, powerful, unshaven, greasy black hair parted in the middle, early thirties. His small dark eyes never blinked; they panned like two telescopes, constantly scanning for any small detail that may be of interest in the small space, flitting from papers on the desk to drinks on the sideboard, pictures on the wall, taking everything in, missing nothing.

Luigi now stood incongruously in his braces, right-hand fingers balanced lightly on the desk, trying to give the impression of composure and control.

The Ispettore leant forward. ‘You say that your solicitor was on a fact-finding mission. What do you mean exactly?’

‘I understand that our Production Secretary Gill took a call from Miss Tavazzi asking when her screen test was going be because she believed that she had been promised one by Mr Burgio. Miss Tavazzi threatened to go to the papers and drag Mr Burgio’s name through the mud in the process, should that screen test not be forthcoming. I merely instructed our solicitor to evaluate precisely what Miss Tavazzi was trying to achieve, and that is it, pure and simple! Nothing more, nothing less.’

The Ispettore scowled. ‘I’m not convinced. I think there’s more going on here than meets the eye. I will speak with Gill, the secretary, next. In the meantime, where is Dino Burgio? Do you know?’

Luigi relaxed a little and took his hand off the desk, sensing that the pressure was off him for the time being. ‘Gill Consalvo is next door, and as for Mr Burgio, I have no idea. I have not spoken to him or seen him for a couple of days. I understand that he is in the process of moving into a new property, and that is how he met Miss Tavazzi.’

The Sovrintendente's eyes flashed at the mention of the name Consalvo. He said nothing, just scowled slightly as he mentally filed the information.

His superior grunted. 'We will continue this conversation in a few days, you can be assured. Thank you for your time.'

'It's a pleasure. Always happy to help.'

The Sovrintendente opened the door for his superior while staring back hard at Luigi, who had already taken a couple of paces towards the drinks sideboard. Then with notebook still in hand, he nodded knowingly before closing the door behind them, leaving Luigi to pour himself a brandy to help take away the nasty taste in his mouth.

Alessandro Mosena, the Studio Lazio car mechanic, was impressed at this two and a half tons of Detroit steel. The little Frenchman and his pal who had delivered the red-painted Cadillac were, like many vintage car collectors, more than a little vintage themselves. Very anorakish and, more often than not, showed little or no interest in the opposite sex. This pair were definitely true to type. The upside of those vehicular obsessions was that the bulbous-bonneted vehicle was in concourse showroom condition. The old goatee-bearded vendor had even stopped somewhere near to the studio, and washed and buffed every trace of the journey down from Toulouse off the car. It positively gleamed. There not a squashed fly in sight, the chrome work and window glass were brilliant and the paintwork was immaculate. The smell of the leather upholstery completed its appeal.

Alessandro was not going to have a lot to do; the V-16 engine, all seven litres of it, gargled silently away, trying its best to empty the fuel tank. After the anoraks had gone, he stood back and looked at his new charge. An almost grotesque heavyweight, very luxurious of course, but ponderous, heavy and incredibly expensive to run. Very different to the Italian way of designing cars with beautiful, aerodynamic long flowing lines. The difference to him between a slim fiery Italian woman and a short fat-necked American gangster. But he would take it for a road test that would undoubtedly turn heads. Then he would check every single lock to make sure that it was as difficult to steal as possible. After all, this was 1960s Italy, and the criminal fraternity would regard a vehicle of this weight and incredible power as the absolute go-to vehicle, ideal for ram-raiding a bank or shop.

Peter Dublin passed the two departing detectives in the corridor just outside the Production Office. They were unfamiliar to him, but he gave them more than a passing glance. They, in return, gave him the once-over, also probably curious to know who he was.

Gill was lost in thought, her hands tightly gripping the desk, trying to float away some of the tension in her body. She appeared tight-lipped when Dublin strode into the office and stopped in front of her desk.

Looking down at her frowning face, he said, 'Who were they, those two? They looked official.'

Gill looked up. 'They were very official – policemen investigating the murder of the house agent Donna Tavazzi. She was killed in her office this morning. They believe that her murder is linked to this film production, and to Dino, in particular.'

'Shit! That's not good news, not good news at all.'

'Well, they will get round to you too, don't worry.'

'What! Why me? I've nothing to do with her, never even met her. You're the one who has had all the dealings with her. It's got nothing to do with me, no way!'

'Well, thank you for your support, Peter. I mistakenly thought that we were a team, but anyway that's not the only news. The submarine has been sabotaged and will not be coming down here next week, or any time in the near future. A fire broke out on it and now it's not in working order. It's going to take months to fix.'

'Well, let's get another one! Get another one!'

'Peter, World War II submarines do not exactly grow on trees. It's one thing to pay a small fee to a charity to sail down the coast, give everyone a weekend jolly. It's quite something else to get a functioning sub for us to play with within a couple of thousand miles from here, for virtually no payment. We just don't have the budget. And another thing: the crew have complained about the location lunch. It seems your bronze package did not go down too well.'

Dublin was becoming increasingly agitated, looking wildly around the room, trying to find some inspiration. Gill just looked up at him, writhing in his incompetence. It was hard to have any respect for this man.

'Oh, bloody hell! Bloody hell! This production is turning into an absolute bloody nightmare. I'd be better off back home doing a bloody detective series for Euston Films, a lot less bloody hassle. Look, I've got business in town. You sort it! You sort it!' He turned and headed back towards the door.

'What? You're kidding me! The unit food, the sub, the murder investigation, you want me to deal with all of it?'

'Yes! Yes! You sort it! You have my full backing.'

'You're joking!'

'You'll be fine, fine, just use that female intuition that you think you've got in abundance, and you'll be fine. Absolutely fine! Sorry, got to go! Needs must.'

'You must be joking, Peter. I'm just the secretary, not the Production Manager. This all needs managing. That's what Production Managers do!'

'Don't you bloody preach to me, telling me how to do my job. I'm telling you to sort it, so just bloody sort it. Luigi is always banging on about how bloody clever you are, well, prove it!'

Gill was incredulous, staring open-mouthed as she watched him yank open the door and slam it closed behind him with as much force as he could muster.

Luigi came out of his office to see the figure of Dublin almost running down the corridor towards the exit doors. Within a few seconds, he was standing in front of Gill, concerned.

'What was all that about, Gill?'

Gill looked up, with a grimace. 'Where would you like me to start?'

Ben, the Second Assistant Director, was surprised to see one of the unit drivers suddenly appear on the backlot with an envelope for Duke from the Production Office. Call sheets late afternoon, yes, but envelopes containing messages did not bode well. Was another crisis brewing?

He waited patiently for the end of the take and a lull in the proceedings before going up to Duke and casually handing the envelope to him. He did everything he could to make light of the gesture because he knew that half the set would have seen the driver arrive and hand him the envelope.

Duke just smiled and sniffed it as if smelling for scent or perfume. His raised eyebrows let everyone know that it smelt nice. He opened it carefully and read the contents, all the time smiling.

'Fantastic, fantastic! Thank you, Ben.'

The set watchers relaxed; there was nothing to worry about.

Duke firmly tucked the letter into the back pocket of his jeans and looked up with a smile. 'Okay, ragazzi. Next scene over here, going for line-up!'

Not all the best performances on set take place in front of the camera. Duke, for very good reason, was regarded as the best in the business, and hiding bad news from the crew was second nature to him. He knew how fragile the business could be, and he had no intention of causing alarm, certainly not on his set.

An emergency meeting had been called by Luigi and Gill, for immediately after rushes. Summoned were Lasse, the Art department and the Construction team. Supper would be delivered to the meeting room. It was obviously not going to be a two-minute affair.

Como Trani, the naval engineer, was not often in his workshop, but he was moping about, fed up, more than a bit grumpy and could think of nowhere else he really wanted to be. The old grease-marked phone rang, and he hoped it was the insurance company. It wasn't. It was the secretary from the film production in Rome asking for his advice.

What followed was one of the strangest telephone conversations he had ever had. He came off the phone nodding his head in disbelief. They were something else, these film people, they really were.

Adam found the doorway in the cobbled street. The paint had faded to a pale green-blue with a whitish powdery coating. Peeling in places, particularly around the key lock and along the bottom, it looked very inconspicuous, very run-of-the-mill.

There was a small electric push button on the door. Adam looked at the faded name card with S. Lewis on it. This must be place, he thought, as he pressed the button. There were sounds from inside, and a muffled voice shouted, 'UN MOMENTO'. A blue Fiat 500 chugged past, filling the air with its fumes. Adam heard a couple of bolts being slid open. Eventually, the door opened, and Steve's smiling face appeared. He was dressed in a patchy, oil-splattered, grey overall.

'So, you found it then?' He wiped his hands vigorously with a rather dirty, grey cloth.

'No problem, just followed your directions.' He waved the small visiting card before stuffing it back into his pocket.

Steve opened the door more fully to allow him in. 'Come in! Come in! I'm not quite ready, just need to put on a clean shirt. Come on in.'

Adam walked in and was confronted by a grey-black set of railings that went from floor to ceiling. The railing door was open, framing Steve as he continued to wipe his hands. There was a very large key hanging out of the lock. It was just like the doors that you see in prison films.

'Sorry! Sorry! It's all a bit cloak and dagger. It's my job, being a registered armourer!' Stuffing the rag in his hip pocket, he turned to close the front door. There were two very substantial bolts, one at the bottom and one at the top.

Adam walked through the barred 'prison' gate into the living room. Steve followed, pulling the railing door closed behind him. He locked it, removed the key and kept it in his hand. The fluidity of movement that he showed in all of the door-locking process told Adam it was a well-rehearsed habit.

'Sorry, Adam, it's what you have to do if you have guns on the premises. Lots of bars and locks to keep out the ungodly!' He very deliberately placed the large key onto a small sideboard with four or five assorted framed photos on it, all of them needing a bit of a dusting. There were also a few letters piled up, one of them apart from the others, which looked to be unopened.

Steve looked around the room as if to say, 'This is me'. Turning to Adam, he said, 'I'll be about five minutes. A beer while you're waiting?'

'No, I'm fine, thanks.'

Steve nodded and waved his arm motioning for Adam to take a seat anywhere he liked.

Adam walked towards the centrepiece of the room: a five-foot, square, oak table covered in a yellow cotton, flower-designed tablecloth, and two chairs on either side. In the middle of the table stood a substantial circular upright vase containing a large collection of flowers, which were beginning to wilt. The water at the bottom was a browny pink colour, only about two inches deep, which explained the flowers' desire to give up on life. They had been at their best more than a few days ago.

Steve noticed Adam looking at the flowers and the slightly puzzled look on his face. 'My wife's!' he explained, gesturing towards the flowers. 'I'm married. Maria, local lady, she's a stewardess, away at the moment. She's always away!'

Adam read a lot from that, the pauses, the turning slowly away to move to the corridor. His body language said it all: a marriage that had faded in its intensity, maybe?

'She's back at the weekend. Sunday, sometime in the afternoon. New York, Washington via Los Angeles.'

Adam nodded, smiling in understanding, attempting to cheer up the conversation. Steve obviously missed her.

'I'm going to change. Have a seat. I'll be five minutes, then I'll show you the armoury.'

Adam nodded. 'No problem.'

With a final nod, Steve left the room through the doorway that led into the dim corridor. There were no other doors.

The sparsely furnished, dark cream painted room was quite large, squarish, about twenty foot or so. The wall opposite the barred entrance wall had four tall, thin windows with the dark brown, metre-high shutters half-opened, sticking out into the room. The view was that of a sunlit external sandstone brick wall, about twenty or so feet away. They were certainly not overlooked. The bright reflected light from the wall silhouetted the substantial steel bars in each window frame, going vertically every four inches or so from top to bottom. The room was, to all intents and purposes, a prison.

There was a green armchair with an occasional table beside it to the left, and scattered across the top and on the floor were a few magazines. Before sitting down, he looked once more around the room, at the barred and locked entranceway. It was very substantial, obviously designed to stop any uninvited guests from coming in, or leaving for that matter. On the other side of the table was a long, three-seater sofa, with a sand-coloured cotton throw over it, together with a couple of red cushions.

Adam was interested in the magazines; things like that tell you a lot about people. Sitting down, he started to rifle through the colourful collection. He smiled inwardly to himself. He should have known. They were all firearm related: *Gun World*, *Guns*. Adam settled for the February edition of *Guns and Ammo* magazine with an article about the infamous Thompson, 'The Fact and the Fiction'.

Adam soon lost track of time. These magazines were absolutely fascinating, all American, but you could buy virtually anything in the classifieds if you had the dollars, even a World War II Sherman tank.

Steve came striding energetically back into the room, transformed by a faded blue denim shirt with matching jeans, a red kerchief tied loosely round his neck and sunglasses clipped to his left breast pocket.

'Right, sorry to keep you waiting, mate. Would you like to see the armoury?' The way Steve said the word 'armoury' conveyed the fact it was his pride and joy.

'Yeah, that would be great.' Adam really did want the guided tour; the gun magazines had kindled his interest.

Steve beckoned him to follow. He turned into the first room on the left in the corridor, flicking a light switch on the wall as he entered. Four fluorescents flicked into life and, after a few seconds, flooded the four-metre square. A windowless room in light. What Adam saw amazed him, and the smell of gun oil filled the air. Steve saw his nose twitch.

'The perfume of weaponry!'

Adam was totally taken aback. The far white wall facing him was covered in grey, black pistols, sitting in their metal clips. Two per weapon, but some of the larger, longer ones had three. There must have been forty guns up there, all different. Below the hanging pistols at waist level was a glass display case containing even more. These ones looked like Wild West guns in light brown, polished leather holsters with filled bullet clips around their ornate carved belts. The left wall had about ten or so rifles of various lengths, each held up by three or four cradle clips. The right-hand wall was the same. There were guns everywhere.

Steve said nothing as he watched Adam's expression, probably with more than a bit of pride. Everyone he had brought into the room over the years was stunned, speechless, and Adam was no exception.

'Bloody hell, Steve! You could start a war!'

'Not really, mate, these are all deactivated. They're props for films. There's virtually a gun for every war: American colt automatics, Italian Berettas that the local cops and carabinieri use, British service revolvers, German lugers, and even Russian and Israeli stuff.'

Adam was stunned. 'How do you get all of this stuff?'

'I buy it. Mainly from the States. Having an armourer's licence here means that I can own virtually anything, even machine guns, but I have to let the government know exactly what I've got, and they do random inspections. If I've got anything here that I'm not meant to have, I go straight to prison, and they confiscate the whole collection. Downstairs in the basement, I have a lathe and workshop. If any guns need to fire, I can activate them just for when they are on set, and then deactivate them when I bring them back home. Now you understand all the bars and locks on the front door!'

Adam walked over to the display cabinet with the western holsters. They were, without doubt, a work of art. Steve moved in beside him, noting his interest. He tapped the glass.

'Colt Peacemaker, one of the guns that won the Wild West, or so they say.'

Without taking his eyes off the display cabinet, Adam asked, 'Which one is your favourite?'

Steve shrugged. 'Difficult question. Most of them do what it says on the tin, with varying degrees of success. Some are beautifully engineered, some mass-produced. Big bullets, little bullets, all for a slightly different purpose, but my particular favourite is the first pistol that I ever fired, this one, the British Enfield mark two.' Steve pointed to a revolver in the middle of the display, tapping it with the back of his not-so-clean nail. 'Quite heavy, only six shots, but soldierproof. Forget to clean it or get it dirty, and it will still go bang when you pull the trigger.' He waved his hand towards the pistols on the right, automatics with wooden handles. 'No point in having twelve or so bullets in a clip if the bloody things jam after two. Anyway, shall we go and eat? I'm starving.'

Adam was still transfixed. He had no idea how many different varieties of pistols and rifles there were. He gave one final look at the gun-oiled Aladdin's cave and gently shook his head in amazement. Steve was waiting at the door, his hand on the light switch.

Leaving the house was a ritual, but the locking of the prison bar gated entrance and then the locking of the outside front door were carried out methodically. Steve checked each sequence with a push and a pull to ensure that the locks were all fully engaged and functioning. As he gave the front door lock its final push, he looked up and down the street, checking for anything that was out of the ordinary, something that he obviously did every time he left the building.

As they walked, Adam was full of questions like a schoolboy, curious and fascinated. 'Do you carry a gun when you go out?'

'No, Adam, it's illegal. They lock you straight up, but I'm a registered lethal weapon, so I don't need one,' he replied, laughing.

Adam laughed too, but the significance of the remark was lost on him. 'Is your place alarmed?'

'I don't discuss security, Adam, sorry. I'd have to kill you if I told you.' He burst out laughing. It was a very old joke, that's what made it even funnier, or so Steve thought.

Steve knew where he was headed. After walking for about five minutes, they came to a small square with about thirty tables, all with various coloured umbrellas that denoted which table belonged to which restaurant. It was a truly atmospheric setting.

Friday 18th April

Sovrintendente Mauro Sofri had little time for journalists. He regarded them as one of the lower lifeforms of society. Sanctimonious, self-interested, parasitic scavengers of people's woes, particularly this fairly typical specimen that he now had seated in front of him. A young, frightened creature named Franco Cialente from *Insight News*, a tittle-tattle publication with a small circulation and of little literary merit.

The grey-painted, six-metre-square room smelt of stale cigarette smoke. If rooms had an energy vibe, this one had fear and apprehension in abundance. It was virtually featureless, apart from a small table with a cheap light wooden chair on either side. A third chair off to one side, against the wall, supported the skinny frame of Ispettore Paulo Gatti. He watched the suspect's body language, every breath, when he took it, how often he took it. Every sigh, every twitch, every physical movement was noted and saved to memory. He just watched, said nothing, preferring to leave the initial fact-finding conversations, as he always called them, to his Sovrintendente.

To the journalist's credit, he had presented himself voluntarily at the Viminale headquarters within half an hour of reading their police press release regarding the murder of a Donna Tavazzi the day before.

The two lights in the room on either side of the solid-looking door were both pointing at him, lighting him up like a deer in headlights. The rest of the windowless room was in shadow.

Mauro stood up and walked around behind Franco, lightly touching him on the right shoulder, making him jump.

'You say that Miss Donna Tavazzi was up on your wallboard as a potential news item from ten-thirty yesterday morning?'

Franco half turned to answer Mauro behind him, but found himself staring at the hunched, shadowy expressionless figure of his superior, the Ispettore.

'Ten-thirty, maybe eleven. I got sent out about eleven-fifteen.'

'Who sent you?'

'The duty editor, Giovanni.'

'This wallboard, what does it have on it, exactly?'

'Potential stories. Names, addresses, contact details and story outline. Hers was, if I remember rightly, "young actress seduced by Film Producer Dino Burgio. See Giovanni for more info".'

'So Giovanni put this information on the board then?'

'Yes. Either him or his secretary.'

'How many people would see that board, see that information?'

'Fifteen, twenty, plus any visitors to the building, or cleaners.'

'So this information was on virtually public display for forty-five or so minutes, or longer. Is it still there now?'

'No. It would have been taken off when we went to print.'

Mauro remained calm. 'Went to print?'

'Yes. We went to print overnight with her story. It'll be in all the shops now. No one knew she was dead; you never let the news out until this morning!'

Mauro looked anxiously at his superior, who shrugged and shifted his position in his chair to lean forward. He spoke slowly, calmly. His voice was thinner, higher-pitched than the gravelly tones of his Sovrintendente.

'This Giovanni seems to be of interest in all of this. Where did he get all of this information regarding Miss Tavazzi's alleged seduction from?'

Franco was confused now. He did not know who to answer. He tried to turn more in his chair, but Mauro walked from behind to stand in the shadows beside his Ispettore.

He stammered, dry-mouthed, 'I have no idea, no idea. They never told me. They just said get there! Get her story, get back, write it up! And push it under the nose of one of the editors.'

Paulo stood up. 'Do you have all of your original notes and a copy of the printed article?'

Franco pointed down to his shoulder bag on the floor. 'I have my original notes, all of them. I haven't seen the printed piece; that was all done overnight.'

Paulo walked towards the small table and sat down, forming an almost total silhouette against the two intense spotlights.

'Franco, you are a crucial witness here, a vast potential source of information and maybe even a murderer. I hope that you don't have any appointments for the rest of the day. I will leave you with Sovrintendente Sofri here while I go to have a chat with Editor Giovanni. Let us hope that he corroborates your story.'

Adam was left to his own devices when Toni dropped him off at the little working men's studio café, after asking him if he was happy to walk over to the Camera department on his own. Toni had been tasked late the previous night to drive up the coast to the naval base of Muggiano, collect an engineer and bring them back to the Hotel San Giorgio at Civitavecchia. Why, he had no idea, it was all a mystery. Most of his runs were around the city, with the occasional one out to the coast. It was totally unheard of to drive a thousand-kilometre round trip, particularly in a day. It was going to be a very, very long day. Toni just hoped that the engineer was a pretty lady with a nice perfume. Little did he know that he was going to spend half the day chauffeuring the exact opposite.

Peter Dublin drove with his usual aplomb straight at the studio gate barrier, which he expected to rise as it did every morning the moment that he came into view. This morning, however, it didn't, and he was forced to come to a very undignified noisy crash stop, with his shiny, red bonnet ending up nearly touching the stationary, striped, steel bar.

He glowered at the security guard who had deliberately left the barrier down as he slowly walked out of his small office then round the back of the car to the driver's side. He lent down as Peter Dublin wound down his window.

'Mister Dublin, we have been asked to take back your studio entry permit, and for one of us to escort you to Luigi Mussomelli's office. Would you please leave your car here on the left.'

Dublin was shocked, taken aback, to say the least. Confused would be a good description. He slowly leant forward and removed the small blue Studio Lazio car pass from his windscreen. His pulse rate was increasing. A trickle of nervous sweat ran down his temple.

Fausto, the human balloon of a catering manager, looked up as Gill Consalvo, chin held high, strode towards him. The noise in the canteen was considerable, as the eight or so staff were clearing up after the breakfast service before turning their attention to mid-morning coffee.

'Signora Consalvo, how nice to see you! To what do I owe this honour?'

Gill kept her distance as she handed him an unsealed white envelope. 'Fausto, the Production team would like to change the specification for the location meals on the backlot. Raise the quality from bronze to silver. Here is a letter of authority to cover today. And if you would be so kind as to draw up a new agreement, we will sign it for you. Is that okay?'

Fausto smiled as he took the envelope, quickly opened it and slowly read it from top to bottom. 'I see that you want ten per cent extra food and drink with every meal layout.'

Gill nodded. 'Yes, please, Fausto. A film crew marches on its stomach, and if they are properly fed, and there is a bit extra to go round, then everyone is happy. It's a small price to pay for flexibility and goodwill. The bronze package caused more harm than good. I need your personal assurance that the quality of the silver package will remain high. Do I have it?' she asked, tilting her head gently to one side and smiling.

Fausto looked up from the letter. There was something different about her today. She was more assertive, more confident. 'Yes, of course. I will speak to the chefs. They will be under no illusions. Top-quality silver service. Top-quality.'

'Thank you, Fausto. The numbers are as Ben gave you last night, no change. Thank you!'

'A pleasure, Signora. A pleasure, always a pleasure.'

Gill nodded and turned. Her retreating figure was different, less hunched, her stride longer, more determined.

Dario, the Construction manager, was in his office early. He looked across the large drawing desk at his chief carpenter, his face half-lit by the square dusty window that partially illuminated the room.

'You should have been at the meeting last night, Cesare! We have lost the submarine, and we are going to construct one from a milk tanker!'

'What!' Cesare's eyes opened wide. 'Are you mad?'

'It's true. The submarine for next week has been sabotaged, and by next Thursday, we are going to have to create a floating facsimile of a World War II English sub from a milk tanker or a petrol tanker, whichever comes first.'

'Okay! Okay! How are we going to do that?'

'We had a meeting last night. Gill, the Production Secretary, is Australian, originally from Cairns, Great Barrier Reef. Well, apparently, her dad was a dive captain who ran a business taking tourists diving. It would seem that he had a very large pontoon diving platform a mile off shore, based on a couple of old milk tankers. You know, the ones that go round the farms collecting all of the milk and then taking it back to the dairy for pasteurising. For our film, the Director says that we only have to construct from the conning tower, halfway to the bow. Just for the launching of the rubber dingy with the rowing sailor and the female spy.'

'How the hell are we going to do that?'

'Oh, we have help! A technical advisor, the navy engineer from the sub, is coming to Civitavecchia. He's being picked up as we speak.'

Cesare frowned, and stroked his finger across the dusty desk. 'This is a bit of a challenge, Boss.'

'Oh, it gets better, Cesare! We are not going to even try to find an old tanker rotting in a metal scrapyard Australian style. We are going to buy one in good working order. Drive it to Civitavecchia, lift the tank off, which we can make watertight by welding on a few plates and brackets. After that, when we are finished, and the rushes are all cleared as OKAY we will remove all our fixing plates and lugs and then drop the whole thing back on the lorry. And here's the clever bit: we'll probably sell it for more than we paid for it because the Art department will do one of their totally fabulous paint jobs on it.'

Cesare just shook his head. 'Boss, I am lost for words. Lost for words.'

Dario smiled confidently. 'Oh, it'll work. We have two pipeline welders joining our team, you know. Guys that can make every weld gas-tight, and watertight. The Art department reckon that they will have a tanker, either milk or more likely a petrol delivery tanker, at Civitavecchia by Monday morning or even earlier if they get lucky, so we have three days, or more. It's a walk in the park!'

'Boss, whose idea was all of this?'

'Gill Consalvo. They've made her the new Production Manager. Very, very bright lady, she came out of her shell yesterday. Watch this space; it's going to get very interesting. In the meantime, I have to contact the marina down at Civitavecchia and ask if we can beg, borrow or steal one of their sling cranes that they use for launching yachts.'

The door to Luigi's office had been deliberately left slightly ajar. Bruno, the driver bodyguard, was sitting just outside in the corridor. His large, heavy frame was uncomfortable on the small, cheap, high-backed chair.

English was not his first language, but he got the gist of what was going on. He was there just in case Luigi needed him, which in no small way he hoped that he did. It would be an absolute joy to punch Dublin hard in the guts after the arrogant, dismissive way he spoke to all of the drivers. A little of what goes around comes around never did anyone any harm.

Dublin was agitated, his voice raised. Bruno felt uneasy as he listened in.

'You can't fire me, Luigi, you can't. I have a legal contract of employment until six weeks after filming ceases.'

Luigi spoke softly, assuredly. 'That's where you are so very wrong, Peter.' He paused momentarily. 'Had you bothered to read the document properly before you signed it, you would have seen that it mentions things like conscientiously making every possible effort to manage the various issues that come up. And not bunking off the moment a crisis looms. Telling the secretary to, in your words, "Sort it, just bloody sort it" in my eyes is a complete dereliction of your duty to simply carry out the very job you are paid to do. Plus your charge off to London to take the film to the laboratories was totally unjustified in my view, not to mention costly and unnecessary.'

Dublin protested, 'I don't agree with any of this. I think it's all shit, and I don't agree with any of it. I believe you are well out of order. I HAVE A CONTRACT, A BLOODY CONTRACT, LUIGI!'

'Peter, you are not listening. It is no coincidence that I have the office next to your Production Office. The walls are paper-thin; I hear everything that goes on. Your bullying, intimidation, outright rudeness, complete lack of respect for women and most other people, for that matter. The manner in which you are expected to conduct yourself is also written large in the contract. You're actually not a very nice person, and I have already talked this through with our solicitor, Loretta Alonzo, who agrees that you don't have a legal leg to stand on. You are in breach of contract on multiple counts. You are due one month's wages and no reference. We will all be well rid of you, and my only regret is making the mistake of hiring you in the first place.'

Dublin started to panic. 'You can't do this, you can't.'

Luigi grimaced. 'I can, Peter. I can and I just have. Bruno will escort you to your office to collect your personal effects and escort you from the premises. Bruno!'

Dublin stamped and gesticulated more violently. 'You greasy little spic! You have no right to treat me like this. You haven't heard the last of this. Your shitty little film is going to bomb and hopefully ruin all of you! This is all a load of crap!' The final word came out more as a whisper, as a vice-like grip from behind suddenly gripped his left shoulder and an arm thrust into his right armpit. The next second, his feet were no longer touching the floor, and he was being turned and lifted like a rag doll towards the now open door.

Lasse had started the day with his usual briefing speech, this time getting up onto a large, felled log covered in moss.

'Buongiorno a tutti. Today we are filming the beginning of the relationship between Danilo and Eduardo. It's 1905 in the country in Sicily and it's where Danilo hurts his knee, which causes him to have a limp for the rest of his life. I would like to say that the job that the Art department has done here is amazing…absolutely amazing! Thank you! Clever people. Thank you.'

Unlike the old show business standing joke of never working with children or animals, Adam was not scared of working with children. In his experience, child actors while on set, are in the main, very well disciplined and eager to please. The two kids in rehearsal that morning were a joy. Both were about seven years old, similarly dressed in short trousers. One of them had a birthmark on his left-side jowl, which meant that he was playing the younger version of the lad who chatted up Belinda and Anita in the first London café scenes. They were both from the local drama school, so Lasse had to work with the interpreter Petros to make sure that they understood his direction. That was a strange process that Adam had never witnessed before: a Director having to go through an intermediary.

Isabella had three days off, and the crew had moved to another part of the backlot where a small, turn-of-the-century, country cottage was set in a lovely flower garden, the whole scene set in a meadow full of bushes and trees.

The dance of the viewfinder resulted in a very long camera track, surprisingly not looking at the little cottage but concentrating the other way on the meadow and the collection of small trees and bushes. The two kids were to be tracked by the camera for around twenty metres as they noisily ran in and out of the vegetation.

Anatra and his six Macchinisti had already brought onto the set a pile of the steel track railway for the Elemack camera dolly to roll on. Once Lasse and Jan had decided the beginning and end positions, it was up to Anatra and his Macchinisti to lay down the temporary railway on small wooden boxes and level the whole thing up with small wedges. Adam was impressed. Twenty metres of track put down in just over thirty minutes. The speed at which these guys worked was impressive. They were a true team, noisy, as always, but very efficient.

While Anatra, with his spirit level, was checking the final levels, Andrea the comic, duster-waving clown of a Macchinista walked casually over to Duke. The latter was standing on his own off to one side, watching the whole process, waiting for a sign that he could begin rehearsal.

Andrea nodded and spoke softly to Duke to avoid anyone overhearing. 'Duke, I have a message for you from Signor Scordia. He wishes to remind you that you have not called him for two nights and he is very eager to hear from you this evening. He asked that you give the matter your most urgent attention.'

Duke looked Andrea directly in the eye, not blinking, as he smiled broadly. 'Thanks, Andrea, very kind, much appreciated. I can do that. Much appreciated. Thank you.'

Andrea nodded, also giving a broad smile for the benefit of anyone watching and strolled back towards the track, casually picking up a couple of wooden wedges that were laying on the grass surplus to the track levelling requirements. Duke watched his retreating figure, expressionless. He had always had his suspicions about Andrea. Particularly when he had heard that the man's son had been treated at the American Hospital when he fell over and cut his head at school. That was a typical Scordia way of saying thank you, and keeping his foot soldiers onside.

Adam looked over at Grace as she arrived to set up her typewriter on her little desk. She smiled her good mornings even to Adam, but that was all; he was just one of the crew, and she greeted him no differently to everyone else. Adam felt insecure about the relationship, which was new ground for him. Usually, he held all of the trump cards, but not this time. She had him just where she wanted him, and that made him uneasy. He wasn't in control.

Gill's phone rang. It was her husband.

'How did it go? Did he give you a hard time?'

Gill snorted. 'No, not at all. The Ispettore said virtually nothing. He left his Sovrintendente Mauro somebody or other to ask all the questions. He seemed pretty respectful. Have you said anything to him?'

Alberto laughed. 'No, but he's up for promotion, and I sit on his selection board. He is well aware who you are married to. Everyone here knows about my foreign, show business wife. You are a legend, my dear, a legend!'

Gill laughed. 'I've got to go, got a meeting with the boss Luigi in a couple of minutes. Take care. See you tonight. Thanks for calling. Love you!'

Duke, like all good First Assistant Directors, pushed his luck with the crew regarding breaks. Sometimes he called them early, sometimes he called them late. This one he called early because he wanted to save crew time while Sophia Make-up gave the second lad a very bloody left knee. Ben, the Second Assistant, would be taking their coffee and croissants to the Make-up trailer to make sure nobody missed out.

Adam made sure that the dolly was double-wedged so that it would not move on the rail track, and watched Anatra check the head lock and carefully drape over and tie off the white camera cover. He wandered slowly over to Grace's desk to give her the lens and filter settings for her continuity sheets. She didn't look up even though she was aware that there was no one else about; she had checked the moment he began his overtly casual walk.

'I get damp just watching you, Adam. Tomorrow, five-thirty. Don't keep me waiting and don't play games. Bring a bottle of Monte P with you if you can.'

Adam was taken aback by her words. She was obviously finding it as hard as he was. He smiled. 'Monty Pee? What's that?'

'Montepulciano. It's red wine, dumbo, red wine. Can you get someone to bring me a coffee? Not you, too obvious, someone else. Thanks. Until tomorrow. Keep cool, look cool, keep the secret!'

Adam nodded. 'No problem, Monty Poochano.'

Grace still did not look up but she was trying hard not to laugh. 'Pull chee arno, Montay Pulcheeano, beautiful mountain. God, you're thick!'

Veronique Press stood in the place that she felt most comfortable, next to the drinks sideboard in Luigi's office, with a brandy in her hand. She was holding court. Luigi and Gill, both seated at the oak conference table, were listening attentively.

'The story is out. It started in a little tittle-tattle rag, but now it's in print, and the fact that she's been found dead means it's in the public domain. The guy that wrote the piece was probably one of the last people to see her alive. The broadsheets will be queuing up to get his story, and he can sell to the highest bidder. The fact that he will be in breach of confidence with his paper may or may not shut him up. I somehow doubt it; money always wins out.'

Luigi pursed his lips. 'What should we do, issue a press release?'

Veronique looked down, in deep thought. 'No. We need to more passive, less reactionary. Plan an answer to every question that we are likely to get asked when the phone rings, and it will ring, believe me. Construct answers, neutral responses, stating that there is no way that the killing has anything to do with this production. It is a random event. She was a talentless fantasist, who had been pestering the life out of casting directors over many years, and had a reputation in the business as a bit of a nut job.'

Gill held up her hand to stop her. 'That's not true, Vee, not true. She was just a naïve kid who wanted her fifteen minutes of fame. She wasn't a nut job.'

'Ma chérie! I am a publicist. It's my job to publicise good stuff and reduce negative stuff to inconsequentiality. That's what we do.'

Gill looked at Luigi to gauge his feeling on the matter, but he avoided her gaze, looking only at Veronique. He nodded.

'I agree with Veronique. Let her construct a very comprehensive hymn sheet that we all sing from. Let her deal with all of the calls. Make bloody sure that Dino has a copy and sticks to it, but I agree with Gill that we don't want to paint the kid in a bad light. Unless we are forced into a corner, of course. She will have family somewhere who have lost a daughter. This is not a pleasant time for them, so let's not make things worse. We'll set you up in an office down the corridor and let the switchboard know to forward all enquiries to you. Happy with that?'

Veronique sipped her brandy, nodded and smiled. 'Oui, mon brave, oui! I'll get straight on it. Is there a typewriter?'

Gill smiled as she rose, sensing that the meeting was at an end. 'You can have Peter Dublin's. He won't be needing it. He never used it anyway.'

The old electrician, Alberto, had brought Grace her coffee. He was the one who always set up her chair and table and rigged her umbrella to shade her from the sun. He was a bit of a grandfather figure.

Duke never left the set, instead casually sitting down with Lasse and Sven on a trio of canvas-backed chairs next to the track as they drank the coffee that Beatrice, the Third Assistant, had brought them on a tray. The sun was warm, and it was a pleasant day. The first, very long track of the film had gone well.

Anatra and two of his Macchinisti, replete with coffee and croissants from the catering truck, walked purposefully back towards the camera dolly trackline. All three bent down and began to undo the twist clamps that held the sections together.

Duke waved. 'Leave it, ragazzi, leave it. We are going to use it again. Leave it.'

Adam heard the instruction and was surprised. He thought that the scene of the kids running and playing tag up the meadow was in the can and that they would be moving on.

Gill had been able to get hold of the two landscape gardeners at short notice to level up the track down to Dino's rented villa. However, both were now beginning to wish that they had not taken on the job.

The client, some American Film Producer nut job, was a complete and utter pain in the proverbial. He had a ball, a small, grey, leather American baseball, signed by some star player that they had never heard of, that he insisted on rolling down the track towards the house. If the bloody ball bounced out of line, they had to go back and painstakingly shovel stone and gravel from their flatbed truck into the now almost imperceptible hole until it was absolutely level. All because of having to mollycoddle the big, fat, old, red, American car, currently parked ostentatiously in front of the villa.

Salvation came when a police car turned into the drive and the American and his tall thin compatriot retired to the villa with their plain-clothed visitors, leaving them to turn the drive into a sloping bowling alley and ponder what misdemeanours their objectionable client had been up to.

Adam had never in his whole life seen a track used twice, but it happened. The second scene was the kid with the birthmark carrying his disabled mate on his back, who was in agony due to his injured, bloody knee.

Jan just turned the camera the other way and tracked the kids up the opposite side of the meadow and through the little cottage doors.

Just before the take, Sophia came and squirted fake blood, Kensington Gore, all over the kid's knee, his hands and even put bloody streaks on his face. It looked horrendous and excruciatingly painful. The kid was a great screamer. The whole scene had a great deal of painful trauma and urgency about it. It took three takes, but eventually, Lasse was happy with it.

The crew then moved on down the meadow to film a thirty-year-old, very diminutive stunt double in shorts fall out of a tree onto an airbag which the Stunt Director had buried in a deep hole and then covered in leaves, thus explaining how the kid hurt his knee.

As they packed up for the move down to the tree, Adam reflected on the fact that Lasse and Duke had saved the production at least forty minutes of production set-up time through their fastidious planning to use the same track for two different sequences. One pointing one way, and one pointing the other. By eleven-thirty they already had over two and a half minutes in the can. The only person who did not seem pleased about the whole thing was the Macchinista Andrea.

Saturday 19th April

The hotel receptionist, Renata, was very courteous as she took Adam down into the basement and unlocked the door to the guest laundry room. Adam smiled his thanks and gave her a small tip. It was not his favourite task of the week, but laundry had to done.

He had not been sitting down that long, watching his clothes slosh around the scratched circular plastic window, when the clatter of heels could be heard coming towards him down the corridor.

A young female voice rang out. 'Hi, there. How're you today?'

Adam turned and looked up to see a very attractive young lady smiling at him. Her mode of dress denoted what she did for a living. A very short skirt, white ankle socks and a red top that barely concealed her voluptuous figure and bulging black bra. All were telling the same story. There was a waft of chain-store perfume.

She looked at him sitting down. 'That looks boring. Fancy a bit of fun?' Adam was taken aback, but she continued. 'Looks like you could do with a bit of fun. Here, back up in your room, where would you like it? Right here would be nice, exciting. What do you think?'

She had a slight European accent, but she was, without a doubt, a beautiful woman with short, brown hair, large, false eyelashes and an over-enthusiastic application of rouge and lipstick. 'China Doll' sprung to mind.

Adam smiled at her. 'No, I'm fine, thank you.'

'My name's Susie. What's yours?'

Adam tried to show as little interest as possible. 'My name doesn't matter, Susie. Thanks, but I'm fine.'

She walked up to him, invading his private space. 'C'mon, Mister No Name. You don't know what you're missing.'

The smell of cheap perfume was now almost overbearing. Adam stood up to assert a bit of authority. As he did so, she overacted, open-eyed, as to how tall he was.

'Thanks, Susie, but no thanks. I'm fine, fine. Thanks all the same.'

She looked shocked, as if he had just slapped her. 'Oh! Okay, Mister No Name, if you really aren't up for it today, just call reception anytime and ask for Susie. I can get here in half an hour, but for you, I'd really hurry. Okay?'

Adam stepped back to put a little fresh air between them. 'Thanks, Susie. Nice to meet you. Have a good day.'

She smiled, then nodded. She had done her best, acknowledged that she had a 'no sale' and gave one last smile and pout before clacking her way off down the corridor. Adam watched her tightly skirted, curvy bottom swing down the corridor and turn right before finally disappearing.

Adam sat back down. The washing was sloshing, and his thoughts turned to Pia.

She had not had a lot to do with him since their evening encounter. She nodded to him on set and smiled a rather shamefaced smile whenever they were close to each other. Few people noticed. Apart from that, they had had no contact except for just before wrap when she came up to him and, with grand ceremony, presented him with one of Jose's visiting cards for his little shop. She waved it so that everyone knew that she was a delivery messenger. The card was bright pink and red, not exactly subtle, but everyone on set had been presented with one, at one time or another.

Adam thanked her and waved it at shoulder height. A muted cheer went up. After the first week, the Englishman was obviously totally accepted by the rest of the crew as an all right, okay guy.

After watching the ageing tumble dryer clunk and rattle away for another few minutes, he decided out of sheer boredom to find out where Susie had gone. The little corridor was obviously the working girl route in and out of the hotel. Posh hotels don't have call girls wandering around reception and in the lifts; it gives the place a bad name. So the oldest profession in the world had to have another means of entry and exit.

Adam slowly followed the now fading smell of perfume down the corridor, past all of the heavy, oak, locked doors to the end where it turned right and continued for another twenty metres or so before coming to a stop at a slightly ajar door.

The door eased open easily. Adam walked through it and slowly up a short slope that was apparently a delivery area, before the smell and noise of traffic told him that he was in an alley off one of the more minor local roads.

When he got back to his laundry, much to his relief it had finished washing and started its drying cycle. So after another thirty minutes of sheer boredom he decided to dump the now clean clothes back in his room, grab a light lunch and take the bull by the horns and try to find the little shop that everyone was talking about.

On the way he stopped off at a small news-stand and picked up a tourist map of Rome, noticing as he did racks of sunglasses just like his but for half the price that he had paid his smelly, yellow-toothed street vendor. But hey ho, can't get it right all of the time.

His hike took him down to the south through the Piazza Barberini and the now-familiar Fontana di Trevi and across the River Tiber at the Ponte Garibaldi. An hour-long but fascinating wander through the heart of one of the most significant capital cities of the world. The whole place just oozed history and culture. He was a long way from his home in Worcester Park, that was for sure. The little shop in Trastevere was actually reasonably easy to find just off the Piazza San Calisto, the whole area being a collection of trendy little bars, restaurants, and shops with tiny apartments above them.

The shop exterior was the same colour as the visiting card, a very unsubtle pink and bright red. There was a dark-skinned mannequin on either side of the open door. The one on the left was an Indian lady dressed as a bride, in a gold sari with henna tattoos on the backs of her hands and tastefully draped in small items of what looked like gold jewellery. The head was adorned in the most ornate gilded scarf, with a hanging jewel-encrusted white pearl draped in the centre of the forehead. The figure on the other side of the door looked like a North African version of Twiggy in a light tan, leather mini dress and white, high-necked blouse, set off by a colossal chromium crucifix on a heavy chain. The face was very eye-catching, with big brown eyes and a short haircut with the falling lop of hair across the forehead. Very, very unusual, and very eye-catching.

The chain and padlock from the leg of each of the mannequins to the shop window sill reminded one that the ungodly were everywhere. The painted make-up on both models was more than professional; it was outstanding. Adam looked at the bride's face. It actually had a presence; it was riveting, staring straight at him.

A familiar voice rang out from inside. 'Ah! Adam, dear boy, you've come to be fitted up at last. At last! Welcome.'

Adam turned to see Jose walking towards him with his sunglasses on the top of his head and wearing a bright, patterned, orange shirt, covered in a design of palm trees, bananas and exotic fruit. A red handkerchief was tastefully draped out of his breast pocket.

Adam smiled. 'Good afternoon, Jose. This is all very impressive, amazing, in fact!' he said, pointing at the sari-clad mannequin.

'Oh! She's all glitter and no substance, dear boy, a tribute to the fake jewellery trade and Sophia's make-up.'

Adam was taken aback. 'What, Sophia did that make-up?'

Jose ran his finger down the mannequin's cheek. 'She doesn't usually paint in oils; but an artist is an artist, right? Come in, come in, spend a fortune on things that you don't really need, fill your boots, as they say. I actually have some genuine Texan cowboy boots in your size, if you're interested.'

Adam faked open-mouthed, wide-eyed wonder as he walked in. To say the stock was eclectic was an understatement. The faint smell of a joss stick fought for dominance with the more earthy aroma of fresh new cotton cloth, and of course,

Jose's all-pervasive eau de cologne. There was a small till counter near the door. The shop was about fifteen metres by ten metres and appeared much larger on the inside than it first seemed. A huge, gilded glass mirror on the left-hand wall gave the illusion of even more space. Shelves of random stuff filled all of the walls. Multi-coloured fabrics cascaded off random chairs of all shapes and sizes onto the floor. Mannequins of all genders and colour tones were dotted around, here and there, reflecting every possible taste in clothes, from the flapper look of the 1930s through to the pencil-thin, short mini dresses of the modern day. Jose had a lot of stock, no doubt about it.

Near the door was a shelf of the most delicate art deco bronze and glass artwork, naked or partially draped female figures by someone labelled as Lalique, through to a thin-necked wine glass tightly encasing a hand grenade.

Adam was more than taken aback. 'What's this, Jose?'

'Thirty thousand lire to you, dear. Oh, as you're so lovely, how about twenty-five?'

'No, Jose, it's a hand grenade. A British hand grenade!'

'Oh, it won't go off, dear boy, the glass is stopping it.'

Adam stepped back. 'What? You're joking!'

'Of course I'm joking! It's deactivated. It's a talking point, impulse buy, a bestseller, in fact. You can buy them for half the price down Porta Portese market, but mine is set in crystal, so you get what you pay for. Now what can I interest you in?'

Adam looked around and then back to Jose's smiling, enquiring face. 'A wallet, a nice leather wallet to keep my money in and have my old one virtually empty ready to hand over to the street muggers, should the occasion arise.'

Jose grimaced. 'Oh! You've been mugged already, have you?'

Adam flustered internally for a second. 'No, not yet, but I hear there's a lot of muggers about, so best to be careful.'

'You need to dress more like a local, Adam. Get a pale blue suit and stick sunglasses on the top of your head. Look the part, walk the walk. But first, a wallet for you, my lovely friend. Would you like me to give you a hand to get your change out?'

A large marina boatyard just after Easter is always a busy place. All the boat owners are either nagging the marina staff to get their boats off the hard and back in the water, or they are busy fiddling, doing those last-minute little jobs before their fibreglass pride and joy is launched for the summer season.

All around the large yard were yachts of all sizes up on their temporary steel chocks. Flashy, high-speed motor cruisers were all getting a visit from their owners. Pressure washers were squirting, and the smell of antifoul paint filled the air. Over the far side, away from the boats on a large piece of hard standing stood Dario Construction with his chief carpenter together with Joe from the Art department all standing looking up at an Agip Supercortemaggiore petrol tanker complete with the six-legged, flame-spitting dog logo. On the way in they had collected a bearded, roll-up-smoking engineer from his hotel, complete with two very large, heavy, steel toolboxes.

Joe pulled down the brim of his Australian bushman's hat to try to protect his pale face from the all-pervading sun as he squinted through his blue sunglasses at the three people stood with him.

'Right then, the submarine we are going to copy is the British S-class which is about sixty-five metres long. Our tanker here is about eight metres long. Sooo, we are just making the conning tower and a bit of the front deck. Studio interiors and a model shot will cover the rest of the sequence. We only see it from the starboard side, and it will now be a night shot instead of day for night. So we have more than a bit of licence. It only has to hold together for the shoot and then just a couple of days until we get rushes clearance.'

Como Trani grinned, smiling a brown, toothy smile. 'Easy' was the only word he said.

The other three looked on with glazed expressions, alarm apparent on all of their faces. They knew that he had given the mini bar in his hotel room a total clear-out because they could still smell elements of it on his breath. Como bent down to his nearest toolbox and took out a huge adjustable wrench, then undulated in his oil-daubed, baggy, grey overalls over to the tanker, looking up underneath it, squinting hard at the underbelly of the tank, pausing only to tap it hard with his spanner to check that it was actually empty.

He shouted at the underneath of the tank, 'Eight bolts front, probably ten at the back. Hold this onto the chassis, we need to flush it before we weld it or we will all be blown to bits, so can someone get a hose and a small crane and we'll have this off in an hour!'

Dario just shook his head in disbelief. 'Is he for real?'

Joe smiled an uneasy smile. 'He did tell me he's not very good with drawings, does everything by eye. I believe old-school was the term he used!'

Dario knew then that the next few days were either going to be a masterclass or a ginormous cock-up which could easily result in a not inconsiderable hole in the film's budget and all of them being fired.

At twenty-five past five, the taxi once again had to pull right over so that Adam could get out. The sandstone smell of the alley up to the dark, wooden door was like a perfume to him. He had smelt it when he had last left her, and its musty odour had remained with him. Funny how just a basic earthy smell reminded him of her, her little house and their first encounter. He lightly touched the doorbell.

A gentle, scratching sound came from the area of the peephole. The door opened but she remained behind it, just sticking half her head round. She smiled.

'Yes? Can I help you?'

Adam held out his left hand, waving a bottle in a thin transparent plastic bag. 'Monty Poocharno. Wine delivery for a lady!'

She laughed and shook her head in disbelief at his appalling accent. 'Well, thank you, I suppose you'd better come in.'

He stepped forward into the small hall as she gently closed the door behind him. It clicked as the lock engaged. He turned around to face her. She just stood there for a second, back against the door, hands at her sides. What he saw took his breath away. She was wearing make-up: lipstick, eyeshadow, mascara, the works. She tilted her head coyly.

'You look shocked. Everything all right?'

'It's you, it's the make-up. I wasn't expecting—'

Her hands came up very fast as her right elbow brushed his arm holding the wine bottle to one side. There was a frightening urgency in her as she pulled him to her, tilting her face into his to ensure the maximum contact of their lips. She tasted of toothpaste, her lips were initially a little sticky, but not for long. She smelt of jasmine. Adam nearly cried. It was such a beautiful moment. All that suppressed emotion of the last few days flooded into that embrace, and they both knew it and savoured every second. They lost all sense of time. The kiss never ended; it simply intensified, paused and then resumed with even more urgency. He pulled her into him with his right arm. There was no cushion between them this time so he felt all the curves of her femininity soft against him. He still had the wine bottle in his hand, so he just kept hold of it and pulled her to him even harder. After a few minutes, he was conscious that he was beginning to stir against her. She sensed it too and gently pushed her abdomen back away from him. She slowed down on the kissing and relaxed her grip on his neck and face, signalling that it was time to pause for breath and just look into each other's eyes.

'Whoa!' she muttered, her lipstick all smudged. 'Whoa, Adam, wasn't expecting that.'

'What? Wasn't expecting what, lovely lady? A kiss that really just said everything that we haven't been able to say…?'

'Was it worth the wait?' She smiled, turning to her left and looking into the small circular gilded hall mirror to check the state of her lipstick. It was virtually all gone.

Adam shifted his weight, placing the wine bottle on the little hall table. He never took his eyes off of her.

'No, not really. I was expecting a warm greeting, some little clue that you might actually like me, not just a little peck.'

She laughed. 'Your little friend didn't seem to think it was a little peck; he was getting quite excited. Is he always like that?'

Adam smiled apologetically but said nothing.

She pulled a small paper hanky from the left cuff of her pale blue, high-necked blouse and gently rubbed her lips to remove the final traces of lipstick. Checking in the mirror and nodding to herself, she fluffed her hair and turned to him, coquettishly tilting her face up.

'Lipstick suits you, Adam, but not rose pink. May I clean you up?'

Without waiting for a response, she gently rubbed around his mouth, finishing her little task with a delicate puckered kiss on his now clean lips.

'We're both more than a bit hot-blooded, aren't we? We need to talk about that, come to an agreement. A code of conduct, maybe?'

Adam didn't know what to say. He just handed her the wine bottle, noticing as he did that she was wearing figure-hugging, tailored, slim, dark blue leather trousers fastened down the left hip. Very different to the drabbish shapeless clothes that she always wore on set. She had an hourglass figure. She obviously kept herself in good physical shape.

'Lovely trousers, Grace, very sexy!'

'I like them, Adam. They're my chastity belt. They're virtually impossible to get off!' she said, smiling reproachfully, rather like a mother reprimanding a much-adored child. 'You're impossible, Adam. Would you like a drink? Tea, Coke, Monty Pooochano?'

The smell of fresh air had great appeal for young Franco Cialente, as he overbreathed his first lungful, finally free and out in the street outside the Viminale police headquarters. It's funny how you like even the smell of traffic after you've been locked in a police cell deep in the vaults, woken every fifteen minutes during the night by an overweight, sadistic, man-hating policewoman who was determined to make sure he got absolutely no rest. He knew that she was man-hating because she dismissed all of his efforts to be pleasant and conversational, charms with which he earned his living as a journalist specialising in interviewing vulnerable women. She'd spitefully knocked his ego. Every few hours, they pulled him upstairs, interrogated him and then took him down again. He was absolutely drained. They had taken away his notebook, his belt, his shoelaces and his watch, searched his flat, taken away half of his clothes from his wardrobe and laundry basket and confiscated his passport.

The Ispettore had left him in no doubt that he was more than just a person of interest, more than likely someone guilty of murder, and all they needed to convict him were a few more pieces of the jigsaw. His newspaper had eventually posted a substantial bail, and he was now free to move around but not leave the city. He also had to phone the Sovrintendente every evening, giving his exact whereabouts and details of where he would spend the night.

He surveyed his surroundings. The sun was starting to go down, behind the buildings. Someone waved at him – a middle-aged, balding man with an engaging smile. Franco knew who he was before he even opened his mouth: a fellow journalist looking for a story. Now he was the centre of attention, not the other way round. The thought that flashed through his mind before the clammy handshake took place was how the hell did Smiley Features know that he was coming out of that particular building through that specific door at that particular time?

Grace gently put her half-empty wine glass back on the table. Empty plates and breadcrumbs on the cream tablecloth bore witness to the fact that they had both eaten well.

Adam's wine glass was nearly empty. He looked completely relaxed, his face giving away the fact that he had been totally spoilt. She tilted her head slightly.

'So what went on between you and Pia then?'

‘Nothing. Seriously, nothing, nothing at all.’

A blink of the eye told Grace that the question perturbed him.

‘I find that hard to believe. One minute she is watching your every move, getting quite damp about you and the next minute, she can’t look you in the eye and keeps as far away from you as possible. Something has gone on.’

‘Nothing has gone on, Grace, nothing!’

‘I’m sorry, Adam, but it’s been worrying me. She’s a lovely woman.’

‘You’ve nothing to worry about, honestly. Nothing at all.’

‘Adam, if I am going to embark on this train crash of an affair with you, there has to be an openness, an honesty. I want these few short months to be a time to look back on, to regard as good times, happy times, do you follow?’

‘We all have secrets, Grace, we all have a basement that we let no one into, and you are no exception.’

‘What do you mean?’

Adam nodded towards the dresser in the lounge behind her.

‘This house, the dresser, Grace, not a single photo, no mementos, nothing. Faded dust marks on the shelves tell me that picture frames once stood there. When, I have no idea, they’ve all been taken down, but by the look of them, I think that it may have been just before I arrived. So, we all have secrets, you more than me. You never talk about your earlier life. You seem to live in the present. There is not a single memento of your life on show anywhere in this house, no clues, no past.'

She shifted a little uncomfortably, smiled. 'My life is nothing special, Adam. I said that you reminded me of my dad, always joking, teasing, always understating, always making me laugh.'

Adam gently waved his right index finger. 'You're sidestepping!'

'Yes, I know I am. We need to come to some sort of agreement, don't we? I need to get to know you, Adam, need to learn to trust you. My life has secrets, and you will never know half of them; I will take them to my grave. It's probably the same for you, but we can still have a relationship that makes both of us happy, and that will be a good lifetime experience, the summer of sixty-nine for the memories of old age in the old people's home.'

Adam slid his glass gently around on the breadcrumbs, making a subtle dry grinding noise.

'I don't have any secrets really, some very messed-up relationships, some very exploited girls, but nothing overly dark!'

'Is Pia one of those exploited women whose memory you will take to the grave?'

'No! Nice try, Grace, nice try.'

'I actually know what went on with you and Pia. I asked Jose.'

'What, you asked Jose about me?'

'Let me finish, let me finish. I asked Jose what he thought about you, because, oh…because I knew I was finding myself drawn to you and sensed that things were likely to develop, if I was lucky.'

'You kept that well hidden.'

Grace smiled, gently taking hold of his left hand in reassurance. 'We are friends, very close friends. Jose, Sophia, Duke and I all worked on a really nasty picture a few years ago, nasty being an understatement. Anyway, it brought us all together, and the friendships have endured and prospered. I can call any one of them at three o'clock in the morning, and they would be there for me, as fast as they could. They are true friends, Adam.'

Adam nodded, taking in the full implications of what she was saying. 'Okay,' he said, a little uncertainty in his voice.

'Jose gave you an excellent write-up. He said that you were a really good guy, an honourable person and if he wasn't already in a relationship, he'd court you!'

Adam arched his eyebrows in overacted disbelief. 'I thought he was already. The way he…'

She gently shook his hand in affirmation. 'He's playing, Adam, it's just his way. So I know all about Pia, but I had to ask, Adam, I had to ask. I'm entering into a relationship with you, and I need to avoid getting hurt by a serial philanderer. I haven't been with anyone since my husband died. You are the first.' She paused momentarily and looked him directly in the eye. 'That makes you very special and makes me especially careful! We are both very hot-blooded, too hot-blooded really, but can we say that we meet up here two or three times a week? I will cook for you, teach you to cook, teach you Italian, teach you about wine, and in return, you will treat me with respect, make me feel valued, shower me with loads of expensive gifts,' she said, finishing with a little cheeky grin. 'And one day when the time is right, make love to me, set your seed free to swim within me, but that day is a long way off, Adam, a long way off. You are going to have to earn a lot of trust and respect before then.'

Adam extended his left hand and took hold of hers, their fingers intertwined. He looked at her, absorbing the full significance of what she had just said. 'Wow! I'm lost for words, Grace, lost for words.'

She gently shook his hands up and down. 'Just don't spoil it. Don't spoil it by trying to seduce me all the time. I know it's second nature to you, but I'm a very strong woman. One day, when the time is right.'

Adam nodded, tilting his head down and looking up at her through his eyebrows. 'A very hot-blooded, strong woman.'

Grace leant forward. Picking up the nearly empty wine bottle, she topped up his glass. 'Concentrate on the strong, and less on the hot-blooded. Do we have an agreement, Adam? Do we have a deal?'

'Yes, Grace, we do. We have a deal.'

'To be discreet, tell no one and keep the secret.'

'Yes, Grace, I understand where you are coming from. Am I allowed to practise seducing you, though?'

'Yes! Please, yes, please, but within limits, Adam, always within limits.'

She slowly let go of his hands, signalling that the serious talking was over.

He sensed her mood change. 'Right, all this earning respect stuff, does that mean that I have to help wash up?'

'Absolutely. You wash, and I'll dry and put away.'

Sunday 20th April

The large, blown-up colour photos on the crime board in Donna Tavazzi's office were disturbing, to say the least. Paulo Gatti looked at them again before respectfully letting the cover sheet fall over them. He turned slowly, deep in thought as Christina the Agente di Polizia offered up a tray with three coffees. He took his usual one with the big red heart.

'Psychopath, sociopath or just a numbskull who does what he's told? Left-handed, we know, very tall, we know, very strong, we know. I am looking for a reason here, and all roads point to Dino Burgio. However, he has a cast-iron alibi, which, of course, a smart arse like him would have. Having coffee with his two American companions on the Via Veneto at the Hotel Imperiale. Loads of witnesses. You can hear the three of them five tables away.'

Christina held up her hand. Paulo nodded.

'What about Franco Cialente, the journalist?'

Paulo sipped his coffee. 'It's not him. He's too much of a people person.'

Mauro Sofri turned from looking reflectingly out of the dusty, smeared window onto the busy street below. 'Psychopaths can be charming, they usually are. Well, initially anyway.'

Christina put up her hand again. 'I think he's a creep. He tried his overtures on me, said he wanted to do an article on what it was like being a female police officer in Rome. Uggh!'

Paulo looked at her small-lipped face, very prim with her tightly pulled back hair, her black uniform bulging slightly in all the wrong places from the overindulgence of pasta and all things sugary.

'He doesn't have the strength, Christina, plus he's right-handed. What would his motive be? He only knew of her existence an hour before she died. His notes point us back to Burgio. Straight back.'

Mauro walked from the window to his paper-strewn desk interspersed with empty cigarette packets and folders of official paperwork. He sat down and stared absently for a moment at the small ball of chewing gum stuck to the base of his Anglepoise lamp.

'Why did we hold him then and stay up half the night questioning him?' Mauro asked.

Paulo sipped his coffee, then nodded. 'Because, my young Sovrintendente, he is a journalist, and he and his story will soon be all over the media, papers, television, magazines. And we have to be seen, in the public eye that we graciously serve, to be diligently carrying out our appointed duties as defenders of law and order. Here endeth the lesson, my son!'

Mauro smiled. He liked learning from his superiors, particularly Paulo. He had such a pleasant, patronising air about him. 'Is that why you got me to phone that journalist before we let him go?'

Paulo nodded. 'Precisely, precisely. Let him tell his story; it may bring someone out into the open, although I doubt it. A single hammer blow straight to the forehead, no defensive wounds on her arms. It was instantaneous, very quick. She would never have felt a thing. No one was seen leaving the building either from the front or the back, apart from the journalist.'

He walked over to his spotlessly clean desk. The two polished, black phones, one on either side, had straight untwisted cables, and both devices were precisely the same distance from the side and back of the red leather top. He deliberately kept hold of his cup so as not to risk causing a coffee stain. He looked up momentarily, disdainfully, at the ceiling and the dusty cobweb-strewn static fan blade as if trying to mentally clean it.

'The film's production stills man overhears the conversation between the secretary, Gill Consalvo, and the publicity woman, Veronique. He phones from the backlot at the *Insight News* news desk studio to get his bonus for putting up a potential storyline.' He paused for a second, gathering his thoughts.

'Giovanni, the editor, writes up the case for attention on the news board. For forty-five minutes, anyone could have seen that and sent someone round to kill her, but why? It's more likely that Dino Burgio had a minion carry it out. Someone not connected with him, more likely. He has the most to lose in all of this, his reputation, if he has one, from what I gather… Maybe I should rephrase that. His perceived reputation, as perceived by him and only him. We know that he was with her most of the night at the hotel, so we can presume that he did actually have sex with her.'

Christina shuddered an overacted grimace. 'Uggh!'

Mauro noted her revulsion, then tapped his desk as if remembering something. 'When we went inside his villa with his two American friends, I smelt gun oil.'

Paulo waved his right index finger to make a point. 'Firstly, they were not friends. They were subordinates, hired help. Their body language was submissive, they are definitely not friends or equals. As to the gun oil, we are not going to get a search warrant because you think that you smelt gun oil. I think that we need to find out about single American males who flew into Rome from Burgio's home town of Los Angeles in the last couple of weeks. I think that we need to look much deeper into the personal life of Donna Tavazzi and deeper still into the professional life of Donna Tavazzi. Has she pissed anyone off in her recent house dealings?'

Mauro scribbled intently, noting the instructions, then looked up from his notepad. 'Are we interested in Luigi Mussomelli or Gill Consalvo at the studio?'

Paulo pensively moved his head from right to left, pursed his lips and faked a shudder. 'Not Consalvo, definitely not, no motive, and Luigi, he also has no justification. True, he sent the solicitor to buy her off. I can't believe he'd send a hitman to the same office at the same time though. No one is that stupid. And he was in his office at the studio at the time, plus the fact he's right-handed and he does not have the physical strength or height. Also, everyone else was on set.

'Might be an idea to find out who wasn't on set when they should have been, and also where Peter Dublin was and whether he has any possible motive. I think this is going to be a hard one, ragazzi. As to you, my Christina, you should do your story. Tell our little journalist friend how wonderful it is to work with two of the greatest detective minds in Rome, and what an absolute pleasure it is to come to work, and every fifteen minutes go up and down sixty steps to stop some suspected lowlife from sleeping.'

Christina screwed up her face. 'I don't think so, boss!'

Paolo looked at her pouting, make-up-free, scowling face, her starched shirt collar, her clenched fist. She was not going to change her mind. He nodded.

‘Right. I am concerned that this is the work of a professional. Look up past cases in the city and environs that involved the use of a hammer or similar instrument. Look for someone exceptionally well-dressed, maybe carrying a small briefcase in their left hand. People always notice running, sweaty, breathless, young thugs, but never someone smartly dressed like a solicitor walking chin upright, casually down the pavement. Get to it. Get some help from the pool if you need to. Ensure that any officer that deals with Burgio or any of his cronies are aware that they may well be armed and therefore very dangerous.

‘I, in the meantime, am going to have another chat with the beloved Mr Burgio and try to find a reason to take his passport away. Be good to cause a diplomatic incident, haven’t done that for years!’

Monday 21st April

Toni arrived early to collect Adam that sunny Monday morning, six-thirty instead of seven. The run to Civitavecchia was about an hour and a quarter. First north out of the city, across the Tiber, then west to the coast road and northwards up to the ancient port. All was going very smoothly. The conversations were, as usual, light and trivial, and from Toni's perspective, usually about the weekend football, which held no interest for Adam.

A couple of miles up the coast road, a fruit and veg van decided to overtake a lorry carrying sheets of steel. Misjudging the whole enterprise resulted in fruit and veg and steel being spread all over both carriageways. The tailback was immediate. In true Italian style, a couple of cars tried to wiggle their way through the melange only to get stuck in the mass of iron and vegetation, thus compounding the problem. The screaming police sirens announced their swift arrival on the scene, and some form of ordered roadblock ensued. No one was going anywhere.

Toni started to get very agitated, noisy and gesticulative. Adam calmed him down. It was what it was. Switch the engine off, turn up the radio and relax. Adam surreptitiously looked at his watch. He was due on camera at eight-thirty. It was ten to eight.

Eventually, the police cleared half of the carriageway, and they were finally able to trickle through the slender gap and continue on their way. The moment they were free and the accident was in the rear-view mirror, every untrapped driver, including Toni, attempted to make up for lost time. It was a miracle there wasn't another accident. Toni drove like an absolute demon, teeth clenched, gripping the steering wheel. Adam closed his eyes more times than he could count. My God, he thought, these Italians know how to drive. It's in their genes.

Once through the barrier into the docks, Toni squealed to a stop right next to the huge, dark grey lorry that was the electrician's generator, parked on levelling blocks outside a huge, imposing turn-of-the-century ornate marble building. There was an air of absolute calm. On his canvas-backed chair, the genny driver was sitting reading his paper, listening to his charge, murmuring away. He could hear the muffled motor change note as more lights were switched on, and the electrical load increased. He didn't need to check the gauges. He was her constant companion. She sang to him, telling him her story, and he understood every nuance of her song.

There were two arc lights, burning bright, on zip-up towers pointing through two large, first-floor windows. The two-inch cables from the genny went up through an upstairs window. Adam followed the second set of wires into the building, knowing that they would lead him upstairs to the set. He ran, hardly seeing anyone he recognised from the crew. They were all on set, presumably. It was twenty-five past eight. Every twenty feet or so, there on the floor was an electrical junction box with two wooden flaps, each about the size of a couple of shoeboxes, where the electricians joined their cables together. Adam knew there would be one bang in the middle of the set doorway, there always was. It was a standing joke between the electricians and everyone else.

Adam, still seeing no one, was about to turn what he hoped was his final corner when he heard an English voice ring out.

'So what do you think, Donaldson? Do you think she's up to it? She's local for sure, but everyone in the village will know she's been to England. Her chances aren't good, she'll probably get shopped.'

Adam recognised the voice immediately. That upper-class Eton accent was unmistakable, delivered as always with enough gusto to reach from the back of a theatre stage up into the deep recesses of the back circle. He didn't know how to speak softly. Marcus Pomeroy, the third generation of the acting aristocracy. Adam had met him many times. He always played the same sort of character: old-school establishment, minister or politician. One of the elite ten per cent of actors who worked continuously. Adam turned the corner, and there he was, true to life.

Late fifties, short, brilliantined, black hair neatly parted on the left, bushy, dark eyebrows, sitting on his canvas-backed chair. Immaculate in a blue, pinstriped suit, with tissue paper tucked in around his collar to prevent his make-up from migrating. He was looking at his script marked with the orange highlighter that identified just his lines. As he turned to his similarly dressed, thinner, balding, acting companion, waiting for his response line, he saw Adam approaching. He raised his eyebrows in overacted surprise.

'My God, old boy! What are you doing here?'

Adam smiled at the larger-than-life character, not in the least surprised that Marcus hadn't any idea what his name was. He was renowned for always calling everybody 'old boy'. It saved him having to remember who anyone was.

'I work here, Marcus. I'm on the crew, from Cinepan. I'm running a bit late, got held up. Can we have a chat later?' he said, as he continued his brisk walk following the black cables.

Marcus nodded. 'Of course, naturally, old boy. Look forward to it.'

Adam never broke his stride. He saw the cables turning into a room on the left with the mandatory electrical junction box right in the doorway. He knew that he had arrived because he could smell it. A space being baked, being turned into an oven by the lights. Every light gave off the heat of a large electrical fire, and there were ten or fifteen lights here. The temperature in the room was about a hundred degrees. Welcome to working on location.

Luca, sitting on the Focus Puller seat on the Elemack camera dolly, noticed him first. He nodded to Jan and muttered something. Jan turned. Andrea handed the clapper board that he was holding to Luca, with a reluctant smile as if to say the temporary upgrade party is over, guys. Adam's here. Get off his seat!

Jan raised his eyebrows in welcome. 'You okay, Adam? We were worried about you.'

'I'm fine. A bad accident on the motorway, sorry.'

Jan nodded. 'Well, glad you're okay. You haven't missed anything. Sven is just finishing off his lighting, and Lasse has told us that we are shooting the scenes with the British intelligence officers in 1942, discussing sending Gina back to Sicily to gather intelligence before the Allied landings. She should be in the next scene, but we've not seen her. She probably got held up as well. Isn't this a great set?'

Adam had been concentrating on his crew and not the surroundings. He looked around the room. At roughly thirty metres by fifteen it was opulent, to say the least, typical of a London Whitehall ministerial office. Floor-to-ceiling, carved, oak panelling, a large, heavy, leather-covered mahogany desk with a high-backed, black, leather chair to the back by the bright sunlit windows. Two lower, less significant chairs were set to the front.

Grace was tucked away in the far right back wall corner beside a light stand and the portable sound trolley desk. She did not attempt to hide her smile of relief and welcome, as did many on set. Sven, Lasse, Duke, the sparks and the Macchinisti virtually all giving a nod in greeting or a thumbs up. Everyone knew that the Englishman would not be late unless there was a very good reason. Luca had lost out on being upgraded to Focus for the day, as Andrea had almost become a Clapper Boy, but not quite. Jose was standing beside Grace, looking very smart in his tailored blue suit. He pouted his lips in slight disapproval, lifted up his left wrist and tapped his wristwatch with his right index finger, then smiled to indicate that he had clocked the fact that he was late. Then he gave a very coy grin and blew him a kiss, a gesture that caused Adam to laugh.

'Cheeky bastard!'

Luigi had phoned his driver at home requesting him to call into the newsvendor and bring to the house any newspaper running a main story on the murder of Donna Tavazzi.

He phoned Veronique Press to ask her how she was getting on with regards to requests for more information. She informed him there had been little interest and she had just sent out three press releases. She had, though, had a visit from a very rude, young policeman, who had been extremely disrespectful, demanding information about her stills man, how long she had known him etcetera, etcetera, and generally treating her like some kind of criminal. She was not a happy lady. 'Very bruised by the whole experience,' was her closing remark.

Nella had cleared away Luigi's breakfast things and had been given the rest of the day off. The early morning sun found her wiping the windscreen of her ancient faded blue Fiat Cinquecento with an old damp sponge. She rubbed hard at the remains of a kamikaze fly that had splattered itself right in the screen centre the week before, when she had last gone shopping in the local supermarket. She had left a note for Rino on the kitchen table, instructing him as to what she had left in the fridge for his lunch. Luigi would be off to the office at the studio later in the day once his driver arrived. As usual, she was wearing cream jodhpurs and an old pair of brown boots. She placed her highly polished, black riding boots gently in the passenger footwell and her black hardhat on the seat beside her. A cream, plastic carryall contained a light packed lunch for two, the essential bottle of wine, a towel, a warm jacket and her make-up.

She always rode the same horse, a cross between a Murgese and a Bardigiano. Fourteen hands high, a natural black-coated gentleman named Giotto. They had a unique relationship. His big, kind, black eyes always recognised her. Always glad to see her, he would push forward for a nuzzle and the carrot that he knew she carried in her pocket. He had once been a plough horse, working the local hilly fields, his harness hanging on the tack room wall bearing testimony to his working history. He was a pleasure to ride, with his lovely rhythmic trot. Mucking him out would be first, then she and her friend Ariana who owned the stable would tack up and ride out, up into the hills along the ancient tracks, marked here and there by wind twisted pines. Giotto loved being back in the hills. You could sense his enthusiasm by the way he held his head, sniffing every scent in the air when first riding out.

Sovrintendente Mauro Sofri, his tie loose around his neck, did not sit at his desk. He preferred to stand and look out of the window down into the street below. Watching the world scuttle aimlessly by, he sipped his coffee, contemplatively holding it gently with both hands.

'How did your search go, Christina, regarding hammer attacks?'

She looked at the pile of papers and folders on her desk, lifting some of them up with her stubby-fingered right hand.

'I've had a look at some of them, but nothing leaps out. It seems to be a relatively popular way of doing away with anyone, male, female, domestic or business, smashing their brains out with something hard. It's quick, quiet, easy and very portable, readily available.

'I have, though, found out quite a lot about Mister Burgio. It seems he was born in Sicily, 1913, and during the war his father was killed, murdered in some kind of local vendetta. After a few unexplained deaths in and around the area, he up sticks to America, becomes an immigrant in Ellis Island and subsequently crops up here twenty years later as a Film Producer. The interesting thing is, though, that the area where he lived was very near to Mussomelli where our Film Producer, Luigi, is from.'

Mauro tilted his head, his nose twitching. 'Do you think they knew each other back then?'

'No idea, but it does seem a strange coincidence.'

'Can you get any more information?'

'No, not without going there and interviewing an awful lot of old people. Police records don't really exist, if they even bothered to keep any, and most of this information the team has dug up from old newspapers and immigration records.'

'I think that you should bring all of this to Paulo's attention, Christina. Well done. Are you going to have time to do my desk?' he added, looking down woefully at the chaos of cardboard and paper strewn across his workspace.

'Yes, but I'd appreciate a hand looking at these old case records, if you have time, of course.'

Mauro scowled. 'Arghh! Must I?'

Nodding her head firmly, she said, 'Yes, you must. We are a team, not a hierarchy!'

Mauro grimaced. 'Nothing wrong with a good old hierarchy, Christina!'

The temperature on set had reached almost crisis point at over a hundred and ten degrees. Sven asked for the two zip tower arc lights providing the window light to be panned off unless it was an actual take. The electricians had brought up a couple of small fans to help keep things cool, and the main lights were switched off for rehearsals, but the problem persisted. The room had literally been turned into an oven, and it was sweating, giving off its moisture, as were the whole crew.

This presented Sophia with the familiar challenge of keeping the actors sweat-free for the take. Which meant that she was right beside the camera, mopping and dusting down her two artists right up until the clapper board clacked and cleared shot.

Jan was happy to have her nearby. He enjoyed the intangible sense of her aura. Adam knew how he felt. Fancying someone and not being able to show it was bloody frustrating, to put it mildly.

After the first scene and close-up were in the can, Duke called a break.

'Take a break, ragazzi. Twenty minutes. Back at eleven, please. Props, vent the room, please. Enzo, if you can help with that, it would be appreciated. Thank you, all. It's been a very good morning so far.'

Enzo nodded. With a couple of quick paces to the window, he was already whistling to the genny driver down in the street to switch off the genny. Within seconds the lights all went out as one, and they were left with just a couple of fluorescents vainly attempting to light the room.

Adam, through choice, found himself walking down the corridor with Marcus Pomeroy. In lockstep down the corridor, he turned to the striding, dark-suited figure.

'You must be a bit of an expert on all of this espionage stuff, Marcus. Last time I met you, you were playing a special branch officer, frightening the life out of some villain up at Heathrow.'

Marcus smiled a perfect tooth smile. 'Expert, no, old boy, but historian, yes. Very interested in World War II. Read a lot about it.'

'So, Marcus, why send spies to Sicily?'

'Intelligence, old boy, pure and simple. The Allies were planning Operation Husky to invade Europe, commencing in Sicily in the middle of 1943. They needed people to tell them what military units were there, how well they were armed and supplied, and what their morale was like. You can't do that with aerial photo reconnaissance from a Spitfire. You need human intelligence actually on the ground.'

Adam raised his eyebrows. 'Dangerous work, eh?'

'Bloody dangerous, old boy, bloody dangerous, particularly in Sicily, with small, very close communities where everyone knows everyone else's business, stool pigeons, informers everywhere. The only thing that was a positive, a very tiny positive, was that many Italians, Sicilians, were fed up with the war and wanted to get back to normal and get rid of the Germans. But the intelligence officer I am playing today would have known bloody well that he was sending any spy to almost certain capture, torture and death, particularly when sending them to Sicily.'

Adam was curious. 'Then why did people go?'

'Oh, easy! We lied to them, gave them an inflated view of patriotism and of course, understated the risks, anything to get even the smallest piece of useful information back home to dear old Blighty and Allied command intelligence. We were masters of exploitation, still are, actually.'

'You telling me that the SOE still exists, Marcus? Come on, this is 1969.'

'Oh, it does, old boy, it certainly does. Maybe not under the same name, but there are secret squirrels all over the place, still polishing their nuts, hah! Fresh air!'

They both stopped on the top step and looked out into the large courtyard full of Production lorries, with the white catering van directly in front of them, decorated with a huge knife and spoon logo with two long, white, cloth-covered tables laid out with coffee and croissants. Adam gestured to Marcus towards the refreshments.

The actor shook his head. 'Not for me, old boy. Going to Wardrobe to change my shirt, got a bit too sweaty in there. Nice talking to you, though!'

Adam watched him go as he carefully placed each of his shiny, black brogues down the steps. A truly larger-than-life character, always totally typecast. It was impossible to imagine him ever playing anyone weak or insignificant.

Gill liked talking to Luigi. It was always a pleasant experience. Not because he had promoted her to Production Manager, but because she actually liked the man, respected him. He had a very gentlemanly way about him.

He sat down on the cheap, lightweight, wooden chair in front of her desk. 'So young lady, where are we? What's going on in your world?'

She smiled at the fact that he had just sat down in the cheap seats, rather than wandering over to Dublin's old desk and more comfortable, high-backed, leather chair.

'Well, firstly, the set is well on schedule, averaging about four minutes ten a day. I changed the catering package to silver, the bronze was unpopular right from day one.'

Luigi nodded in approval but said nothing as he tried to get his left leg comfortable, which caused him to twinge slightly.

'My inside sources with the police,' she said with a smile to indicate that was probably her husband, 'tell me that Dino has a bulletproof alibi and that they are looking at all other possibilities, which at present are endless and undefined. Veronique has had little interest but has put out the fact that Donna was a well-respected actress and was more than likely to get a part long before she met Dino, which I thought was a clever misappropriation of the facts, but it helps Donna's family.'

Luigi nodded. 'Good! Smart lady, our Veronique. Anything else?'

Gill glanced down at her daybook and nodded as she ran her finger down to a crossed line halfway down the page.

'The construction of the sub is going well. They are fitting underwater stabilisers to either side of the tank to keep it level in the water. The old sub engineer has taken total charge, and everyone is just doing what he tells them. I have sent one of the painters, Duke's son, to Dino's house to redecorate the upstairs bedroom and the toilet. He's only there till tomorrow. After that, he is going to have to go to the docks to help paint the submarine before it's launched on Thursday morning. The track down to Dino's house has been levelled, and he has taken delivery of the Cadillac. He viewed all rushes with Veniero up to date yesterday and seems happy with the way things are going.'

Luigi clapped his hands gently in applause. 'So we are on schedule then?'

Gill bowed her head in thanks. 'We are, Luigi, we are.'

'Well done, Gill. Have you thought any more about getting an assistant?'

She raised her eyebrows. 'I have, Luigi. I worked with a girl on my last little epic, and she is intelligent, smart as hell, and has a great sense of humour plus she never panics, so I was thinking of her, if that's okay. She's free and related to Ben, the Assistant Director, cousin or something, I think. Her name's Valeria Sforza.'

Luigi uncrossed his leg, grimacing as he did. 'This whole business is related to someone, Gill. It's what makes the industry tick. Yes, go ahead, with that. I've heard the name before. Anything else?'

'No, not really. I was thinking of putting the English Focus Puller into a rented apartment and suggesting to him that the electricians could fix him up with a little car, if he's prepared to drive himself to and fro. It means increasing his allowance slightly but we save on the hotel and free up a driver every morning and evening.'

Luigi smirked. 'What, an Englishman driving in Rome? He won't last five minutes!'

'Well, he's fitted in very well so far. I understand that back home he's a rally driver, plus the Norwegians all love him, and he's very precise in his work. We haven't had any soft shots, and he's not a drama queen on set, he just gets on with it. So you happy for me to arrange that?'

Luigi, sensing that the conversation was over, stood up, pulling himself awkwardly to his feet. 'Yes, go ahead, Gill, go ahead. It'll give him some independence. Just don't give Veronique his address. She wants his shoes under her bed. Why, I have no idea!'

Gill smiled. 'Don't know about lasting even five minutes with her. Great way to go, though!'

Nella and Ariana had found a smoothish, flat rock to spread out their lunch while the horses nibbled at anything green that they could find, more for amusement than nourishment. A slight smell of baked pine resin carried on the anabatic breeze that got stronger as the day got hotter, bringing up to the buzzing cicadas sheltering in the shade of yellow rocks the smell and complex hum of the greatest capital city in Europe splayed out far below them.

They talked small talk, gossiped. It was the one time in the week when they were both able to be themselves. A time when there was no pressure to cater to other people's agendas. They were just like the grazing horses, where they wanted to be, doing just what they wanted and enjoying every second of it. The only thing that slightly spoilt the ambience was someone firing a gun some distance away. Nella knew it was not a shotgun because the report was much crisper, cleaner, more penetrating. It was a high-power rifle, and every twenty seconds or so for about ten minutes single bangs filled the air. Obviously someone was doing a bit of target practice. But eventually, the noise stopped, and as the background noise of the cicadas resumed they were able to chat and take in the gentle natural sense of their special place.

The wording of the dialogue scenes, after the break with Isabella and the two security officers in the oven office, Adam found more than a little disturbing, bearing in mind what Marcus had told him about conning susceptible young people to train as spies, to then be dropped off on some hostile foreign shore to fend for themselves. Everyone on set was a fan of Isabella, and it was apparent by the way that she played the scene that she was naïve and gullible. The power of the cinema to involve not just the viewers of the finished article in the dark of the cinema but the actual crew on set making the film in the first place was testament to it being a very powerful multi-sensorial artform.

Luciano Scordia smiled across the table at his daughter, Sylvania, dressed as usual in her dark blue business suit, ready for the office in town. She took a final sip of her orange juice before placing her lipstick-smeared glass back down on the table next to all of his newspapers.

She knew only too well that she reminded her father of her mother, his late wife, that he had married back in the thirties after a very stormy courtship. The tall, slim, fiery, voluptuous actress and the earthy, rough, six-pack petty criminal who was going places. Initially, he was just attracted to her physically and her voracious sexual appetite. But as the years passed and a son arrived, followed by a captivatingly beautiful daughter, the relationship changed. Her sexual appetite never diminished, but she became more considerate, less self-centred, and true love eventually blossomed until she died in childbirth a year later while attempting to present him with another son. Neither mother nor son survived the bungled surgery. Nor did the two surgeons. They both died three days later in a hail of bullets on the steps of their small hospital. No one was ever prosecuted.

Now everything that Sylvania did, the way she spoke, her earthy laugh, the way she flicked back her hair with long artistic fingers, reminded Luciano of his lovely Viola.

Sylvania was her mother's daughter in every way, and she knew it and took advantage of it. She never knew her mother, but yet she did, because of how her father used to speak about her, particularly after supper and wine. That was when all of the reminiscences flowed, and the small nuances and details came out. Sylvania took all of them on board and used them to her own advantage to manipulate the old man and twist his reasoning to suit hers. Most of the time, she was successful.

The square had a peaceful, calm air about it. The sun was lighting the tops of the buildings, throwing a gentle warm, soft light back down to where the head of the family, Luciano, sat in his usual high-backed leather chair at the head of the long table.

She deliberately, gently pushed her hair back behind her ear, watching his reaction. He smiled a gold tooth grin. It pleased him. Good!

'Anything in the papers, Papa?'

Luciano looked down at the pile of assorted newsprint that he ploughed through religiously every morning. He gestured aimlessly, his stubby, short fingers lightly covered in black newsprint ink.

'No, not really. Dino Burgio seems to be sidestepping the estate agent murder, which is a great pity because it would be much better for us if he felt the heat, buggered off back to America and gave us then a more straightforward run at increasing our interest.'

'Did you hear from Duke? Did he—'

Luciano nodded. 'Yes, he called. He's up to his neck in it, to be fair. He has three hours' planning work to do every day outside of his running the set.'

Sylvania pouted. 'I think we should teach him a lesson, Papa, just remind him—'

'No! No, my love, it's not about that. He'll never be on our side, and if he walks off the film, he walks off the film, and we are no further forward. We know what's going on from the Macchinisti and the Sound man. The exciting thing is that Luigi fired Peter Dublin. Now a very angry young man feels that he has been abused and is popping in to see me later this morning. I invited him here for lunch. Would you like to join us?'

'Can't today, Papa. Got a big meeting with our friends from the south. We are looking to review our distribution networks, particularly in some of the more rural areas, a bit of an untapped market, interesting possibilities.'

Luciano nodded, grinning. 'Good, good, keep on top of that. We have one of our own most likely going into the film office, Valeria Sforza. She will keep us informed of everything that is going on. Meanwhile our Mister Dublin has a very spoilt, indulgent, demanding wife, lots of bills to pay, could be handy, if directed in the right direction. Very useful, not that bright, spiteful, angry, what more could we ask for?'

Sylvania smiled. 'Could we ask for Luigi to have a heart attack?'

Luciano smirked. 'Ha! That'd be nice, wouldn't it? Wouldn't it just? One other thing: Gill Consalvo, the Production Secretary, has taken over as Production Manager. She's married to the policeman who came after us last year for the brothel fire.

Don't want to rattle that cage. The man's a bloody nuisance, but very smart.'

'Papa, we could always—'

'No, Sylvania! No! There you go again. Just leave him be. We're not a subject of his interest at present. You are always so keen to reduce the world population by ones and twos if you think that we will benefit. Sometimes, I agree, it's necessary. But if it's not, then don't make waves. We have enough enemies as it is without creating more, and if you get rid of someone, you never know who will replace them, step into their shoes. We could end up worse off.'

Sylvania did not like being lectured. She decided to change the subject. 'Papa, I need to talk to you about our Vinincio.'

Luciano's nostrils flared. 'What about him?' His eyes flashed. It was not a topic he liked discussing. The antipathy between his effeminate son and fiery daughter was a constant source of sadness to him. It was a subject that he tried, like an ostrich with its head in the sand, to avoid if at all possible.

Sylvania almost spat the words, 'He's in love with one of the film people.'

'So! So…?' Luciano was agitated now. A raw nerve was being tweaked. He didn't like being reminded of probably his greatest failing, that of the upbringing of his son.

'Papa, he spends a lot of time, and some nights with the Wardrobe man from *The Script Girl*.'

Luciano was starting to get defensive. 'And? He's forty-two, not a child.'

'Papa, he is here in the square for nearly all of the meetings in the evening. He hears everything that is going on…everything!'

'What's your point, Sylvania?'

'I'm worried, Papa. He never agrees with any of our decisions, never contributes, never contributes anything to the family business!'

Luciano smashed his open palm down onto the table and locked eyes with his daughter. 'He's my son, Sylvania, my firstborn son. Your mother very nearly died giving birth to him. He's family, my son.'

'Papa, I'm just worried that he may have his head turned and that he may be letting family secrets out. I'm worried!'

'Sylvania, just leave him be. He's my son, your elder brother, he's family. He'd no more betray us than fly to the moon.'

Sylvania continued, unfazed by her father's reasoning. 'I still have concerns, Papa. He's here less and less, and I've seen him talking on the phone. He's in love, very deeply in love, and we're losing him! I think that the Wardrobe man should meet with an accident.'

'And then what, Sylvania? Then what? You turn Vinincio against us, we lose him altogether, and he then has nowhere to go. Leave him be, Sylvania! Leave him be. I will speak to him, man to man.'

Her lip curled with incredulity. 'Man to man? Man to wimp, more like!'

Luciano forced a smile. 'Sylvania, I think it's time you went to the office. You are beginning to really irritate me, as only you can. It's always those you love, eh?'

'Sorry, Papa, sorry, but you need to talk to him because I am not prepared to lose everything I've worked so hard for over the years. One day I will take over the business, and I want it to be vibrant and expanding, not locked down and squashed flat by an outdated morality!'

Luciano waved his arms at her as if shooing a cat off a sofa. 'Go to the office, Sylvania, my darling! Go to the office. Have a good day.'

Nella and Adriana slowly and deliberately rolled up the small floral red tablecloth, then cleared away all of their lunch things and gently packed them into the beautifully carved, glossy, leather saddle bag on Adriana's horse. It was time to go back down.

Nella could sense in Giotto his reluctance to leave the hills, to take the winding downhill track back to the stables, steep at times, to be trodden with great care. She allowed the noble gentleman to choose his own path, use his experience to step his way surefootedly through the stones and boulders left behind by the winter torrents.

Back at the stables, he was treated to a sponge-down to remove any mud, followed by a vigorous rub-down, which always made him dance with pleasure, followed by a scoop of chaff, as a thank you for a perfect day. Then a light blanket, just to keep him warm, before hanging a full hay net on his door to see him content throughout the night.

Back in the house, Nella and Ariana would often share a hot bath together, and often the best part of a second bottle of wine, before Nella had to reluctantly leave and return to her duties at the villa. These days off were rare and precious. Each one would be engraved affectionately in both their memories.

After lunch, the crew moved downstairs out of the oak-panelled Whitehall office set, down to the ground floor, to a huge open space that had once presumably been a huge dockside warehouse. The Art department had dressed it as a customs arrival hall with multiple desks and dark-uniformed immigration officers.

Two buses had arrived from Studio Lazio containing about ninety or so extras, dressed as passengers coming off a boat with their humble belongings. They were all now sprawled around the outside of the building in little groups, having first checked the catering van tables to see if the crew had left any scraps behind. They hadn't; they never did.

Lasse, as was his habit first time on a new set, to gain height stepped awkwardly up onto one of the baggage trolleys. Anatra saw him climbing up and immediately rushed forward to grab the long-looped handle to ensure that it didn't move and cause the most important person in the Production team to fall or lose his balance – a gesture that did not go unnoticed by the grey, flappy-shirted, slightly built Norwegian. He smiled in thanks.

'Ragazzi! Ragazzi! Welcome to the arrivals hall at the docks in Sicily. It is 1920, and Eduardo has brought back from England his new fiancée, Margaret, back to his home where they will soon be married. Belinda and Fulvio will be with us for the rest of the day and the dockside arrival scenes tomorrow. Thank you!'

Adam had not worked with that many extras before. It was a new experience for him. ATV and London Weekend did not have the budget or the source of cheap labour to dress as many extras that the Italians had, which was why Italy was the European capital of film.

Lasse had put the camera up on a six-foot, zip-up tower so that Belinda and Fulvio would be seen from a high, wide-angle view being thrust along by the vast crowd up to the immigration desks. The smell of cracked oil smoke filled the air to enhance the beams of Sven's artificial sunlight pouring in through the dusty, high windows. The whole scene was incredibly atmospheric. Everyone on set was impressed and more than a little smug to be part of something so realistic.

Adam sensed Grace's eyes boring into him every time he went near Belinda or ran out a tape to her. Belinda, for her part, was also aware that this film was 'real big time' and that a large amount of Production money was being spent on the scenes in which she was the principal character. Very different from the usual 'mini-cast, country house dramas' back home. Fulvio was just overawed, very excited. The old electricians up on the light towers looked down and smiled. They had seen it all before, but it was pleasing to see that many extras and the real detailed quality of the set dressing. The dream makers had certainly weaved their magic.

After the scenes with the immigration officer involving Belinda and Fulvio both getting their passports stamped, the crew moved into a huge side room that had been dressed as the small immigration photo studio. Everything had been squeezed into one of the small corners on the far side away from the door. They were just filming two walls: the one on the left and a small part of the back wall. The rest of the room was completely empty, undressed. Adam smiled. An old camera operator had once said to him, 'You can always make a big room small, but never make a small room big', and that was the case here.

Just before the rehearsal, Duke put his hand up. 'Ragazzi, ragazzi, we are going to use flash powder, blitz pulver, magnesium. It is very dangerous. It can blind. I want everyone off the set except Camera and Sound, and, Adam, I suggest that you protect your lens. Thank you!'

Adam had heard of flash powder. His father, as a photographer in the thirties and forties, had used it for years, and his godfather had actually been blinded in his left eye by it, so he knew that it was dangerous stuff.

Sven asked for a demonstration. The special effects man with a missing right index finger shook some of the greyish-white powder into the foot-long, V-shaped tray, and everyone was told to look away as Duke gave the word to fire. To say the stuff exploded was an understatement. The blinding flash, though short-lived, was of incredible intensity, literally like a lightning bolt striking the room. The air was full of small pieces of falling dust, and there was a smell like burned salt that certainly cleared the tubes.

Sven frowned. 'Too much, too much! Just half of that will be enough, half, thank you.'

The special effects man smiled. He had deliberately overcharged the tray to show off a bit, but also to make everyone aware before the actors were brought on set that this 'blitz powder' was hazardous stuff, and that respect had to be shown and care taken.

After a final tweak to the lighting and Sven taking his meter reading, Belinda was brought in and positioned with her back to the wall, with graduated height measurement marked off in dusty peeling paint. She was given a small wooden chalkboard with a long seven-figure number, and the name Margaret Finch and the date written on it. She was ready for her immigration photo scene. She did not need to act being uncertain; apprehension was written all over her face. She physically tensed as the clapper board cleared shot. The immigration photographer hid under the black cloth of his ancient wooden plate camera, and on the command 'ACTION' from Lasse, pulled the string to the trigger unit that set off the flash.

Everyone looked away except Sven, Grace, Duke, Lasse, and Jan, who dutifully pushed his right eye into the camera eyepiece. Adam deliberately shielded Jan's exposed left eye with his cupped right hand, pushing it hard up against the Norwegian's cheek and eyebrow. He looked away down at the floor with his eyes more than half-closed.

As the flash went off, Belinda, like everyone else in the room, jumped. It took five takes before Lasse was satisfied and they were able to finally wrap, pack away the gear and prepare for the long drive home back to Rome.

The Production team had pulled a bit of a stroke that particular week, scheduling in a night shoot for the Wednesday night for the sub sequence. They gave everyone the Wednesday morning off but called the crew back for the late afternoon to work through the night until dawn on Thursday morning. Plus, the fact that Thursday night was a night shoot, the crew then had Friday, Saturday and Sunday off.

Adam didn't mind. He really enjoyed night shoots, apart from the fact that he and Grace weren't intending to meet up until Saturday because of the schedule. So a whole week without kisses, cuddles, cooking and Italian lessons. He looked around for an eponymous bike shed for them both to sneak off behind, but they both knew that was just too risky.

Outside the marble building at the head of a line of five unit cars, Ben offered Adam transport back with Belinda and Fulvio. He respectfully declined, opting instead to go back to the studio in the new, white, three-seater camera car with Anatra and Luca. He didn't want to upset Grace. He caught sight of her out of the corner of his eye, watching the whole little drama play out from just a few paces away. He was acutely aware that she didn't like her man anywhere near the doe-eyed Belinda. Grace exuded self-esteem, but when it came to him, he knew for all her bluff and bluster that she lacked confidence in their relationship, and that was something that he was going to have to work on.

The trip back in the Camera car was at least going to be an opportunity to learn some more colloquial Italian from Luca and Anatra.

Tuesday 22nd April

Rino, the gardener, was in many ways like a Labrador retriever. He could hear a fridge door being opened from the end of the garden and smell food being prepared even over the smell of his garden compost. This explained why he suddenly appeared in Nella's kitchen, with his usual lopsided grin and large beseeching eyes. As she gently placed the last hot oven dish down onto the iron trivet on the worktop, she glanced at his appealing face framed in the open doorway. He just needed to be wearing a large, black dog collar with a name tag to complete the scene.

'It's all right, Rino, I haven't forgotten you. It's chocolate cake with honey, but they're not all for you. I know it's your favourite, but they're for the kids at the Casa Annunciata. It's Tuesday today so Luigi is off for his usual visit. The small one at the back is yours though. You can have it as soon as it's cooled down.'

'Nella! Amore mia, a million thanks!' said Rino, with a big smile as he walked towards her, arms outstretched as if to hug her.

She quickly lifted up her long, wooden rolling pin and waved it at him. 'Enough!'

He stopped and froze, grossly overplaying the sadness at the abrupt rejection. It was a standing joke between them: she had never let him physically touch her, and he always played hurt when she rejected him. It was a relationship that had worked well over the years. They both really liked and respected each other, and although there was a lot of teasing involved, both of them, through choice, always kept their physical distance.

When the camera car drew up on the dockside, a very strange sight greeted Adam: an old, single-funnelled passenger steamer boat, half of the hull painted white and the other half dark blue. The colour change was right down the middle; the ship to the right of the centre was blue, to the left was white. They looked like two totally different ships. Adam sensed that the white ship to the left up to the bow was the original and the blue ship down to the stern had been built up and enhanced by the Art department to give it more height and a more luxurious feel with a large, white, gleaming deckhouse and an abundance of brass portholes.

Lasse had brought in a Chapman Titan crane which enabled the camera in a single movement to go from ground eye level up to a height of seventeen feet in a single smooth motion. Essential if you want to follow actors in close up, down the gangplank, from the deck of a ship to the concrete quayside. The crane, like a giant, grey, steel seesaw, took the camera and a seat for Lasse to the right, Adam to the left and Jan back behind the camera. They were all strapped into their seats and not allowed to get off without permission from the specialist crane Grip, Nick, who was in charge of the complex beast for the day. He was also in total command of Anatra and his Macchinisti. Crane work was very specialised, and weighting the counterbalance to compensate for the camera and Lasse and the two technicians was a fine art. Serious injury could result if Lasse, Adam or Jan suddenly got off, as the weight imbalance would allow the heavier end to dominate and flick the camera uncontrollably skywards, resulting in personal injury and almost certain equipment damage. So, all three of them had made sure they had been to the bathroom before being strapped into their seats. They knew that they were going to be whizzing around in the sky for most of the morning.

Adam had been on a large crane a couple of times before, back home at good old Elstree but never one this big. It was his turn to think, like Belinda the day before, that this was real 'big time'.

Grace sat and watched the whole performance as her man went smoothly and silently from ground level up to deck level in a couple of seconds. Under her breath, she was heard to mutter quietly, 'Boys and their toys!'

Duke, as ever the master of scheduling, had planned for actual filming to be delayed that morning, not only because of the use of the crane, which always devoured shooting time because of the complexity of operating it, but also because of the time-consuming make-up demands on Belinda and Isabella, the former being aged to forty and Isabella being reduced to look like a teenage girl to fit in with the 1938 time period of the sequence.

From the crane, Lasse announced, 'Good morning, everyone. It is 1938 in Sicily. Everyone knows the war is coming, and times are so hard for Margaret and her family that she is sending her daughter Gina off to England to live with her sister in London. I must congratulate the Make-up department for their outstanding work and thank Isabella for putting up with having her figure flattened to almost nothing. Thank you, Isabella. You are a real trouper.'

There was a lot of line-up work with the crane and stand-ins until Belinda and Isabella eventually appeared from the Make-up caravan, followed by Sophia. Everyone on set gasped in surprise. Belinda looked at least forty, strained, pale and overworked. Isabella looked similar to Pia from Wardrobe, virtually flat-chested, clear-skinned, bright-eyed youthful and fresh: a young fifteen-year-old.

Jan turned to Adam. 'Bloody hell, mate, that is amazing. She's gone from a no-beer girl to jail bait. Belinda looks absolutely knackered, she even walked differently. Clever people, all of them.'

Adam smiled. 'You never know, Jan, if Sophia got hold of you there is no end to the possibilities as to what she could do with you.'

Jan smiled a tight-lipped smile, and Adam suddenly got the distinct impression that he had touched a nerve. Maybe he should avoid that subject.

Gill looked down at the neatly typed curriculum vitae, then up to the oval-faced, short-haired, prim, thirty-year-old in a plain, brown dress sitting tensely on the high-backed seat in front of her.

'Valeria, we have worked together before, but I have many applicants for this job and would like to know why you think I should choose you over anyone else?'

'Well, my bribe would be bigger, a lot more substantial than anyone else's,' she answered, finishing with a smile, a pause and then a smothered laugh.

Gill looked at her in wide-eyed disbelief.

'Sorry, Signora Consalvo, sorry! I have a weird sense of humour that gets worse when I'm nervous. And the reason I'm nervous is that I really want the job. It would mean a lot to me. This is the biggest picture that has come into Studio Lazio this year, and to be part of it would be absolutely amazing…amazing! You will see from my CV that I've worked on other productions, usually as the assistant accountant, so I can be trusted with money. I'm good with figures and know about budgets, and I'm also a good typist.'

Gill looked down at her visitor's hands. Were the nails bitten? No. Were they painted? Yes, and carefully at that. Were there any rings? No. She continued her scrutiny. Was there an abundance of cleavage, or high-necked modesty? The latter – good. How was the make-up? How was the hair? Was it clean, groomed? Yes. So far so good. Gill had clocked Valeria's prim, lace-tied, brown shoes on the way in, and they were well polished.

Valeria shifted uncomfortably, wanting to fill the brief silence.

Gill sensed her discomfort. 'Do you drive, Valeria? Do you own a car?'

'Yes, I have a small Fiat and have been driving for about ten years.'

'Ever killed anybody?'

'Not yet! Wanted to a few times though.'

Gill smiled. 'Rome traffic would do that to anyone. Would you be happy to use your car if we paid a mileage allowance?'

Valeria smiled inwardly. This interview was going well. It was moving from the hypothetical to the practical. 'Yes, of course, if it was required, yes, of course.'

'You mentioned bribes earlier. I know you meant it as a joke, but how do you feel about bribes? What would your reaction be if you were approached, say, to get someone signed up as an extra, for instance?' Gill's eyes locked into every detail of Valeria's face, looking for any sign of discomfort or unease. She saw a momentary flicker in her eyes but nothing more, which could just be regret for the inappropriate joke at the start of the interview.

Valeria brought her hands together almost in a praying motion and then opened out her fingers as if to convey that she was opening up her innermost thoughts. 'I disagree with bribery. I believe that people should rise or fall on their own merits. If you haven't got the skills, then learn them. If you're lucky enough to have them, learn even more, self-improve, and enhance them. If you try to buy your way into any situation, it will always backfire eventually, and then you are back to square one, probably with a tarnished reputation.'

Gill watched her closely. The eye contact was there. This lady was, as far as she could tell, sincere. She leant back. 'Well, thank you, Valeria, thank you. Good to chat. I've got other people to see, and I may check your references, so we'll be in touch, as they say. Thank you for your time.'

Valeria pulled her hands back off the desktop and slowly stood up, looking down momentarily to gather her thoughts, a little disappointed not to be given the job outright. She picked up her bag and strolled to the door. Turning back, over her shoulder she looked at Gill sitting quietly at her desk, thoughtfully thumbing through her CV.

'I'm a hard worker and a fast learner. I'm not afraid of the hours, and you can trust me, plus I don't mind getting the coffee and cakes in on a Friday.'

Gill looked up. 'Well, that's good to know. Coffee and cakes are a must in this office. I'll let you know, Valeria.'

At that moment, the phone on Gill's desk shrilled. She reached forward for it and nodded a businesslike farewell as she watched Valeria slowly open the door and close it gently behind her with a click.

The earpiece on the way up to Gill's ear was already speaking at her. 'Gill! Gill, you alone?'

Gill frowned in concern. It was her husband Alberto. He was never usually excited! 'Yes. Totally alone!'

His toned changed, soothed by the fact that he could get to speak to her. He spoke quickly, a note of urgency in his voice.

'Are you sitting down? I have some very disturbing news, very disturbing. Luigi has been shot, well, executed more like.'

A chill went through Gill and her pulse rate shot up. 'What? What do you mean, executed?'

'He was coming out of the Casa Annunciata, and when he got to the main gate, he was shot. A single bullet to the head.

His bodyguard, Bruno, took the same bullet in his shoulder. He's in hospital being patched up. He'll live.'

Gill gulped and started to cry. 'What, what, what are you saying? Luigi's dead? Dead?'

'I'm afraid so, my love. He died instantly. Look, we are sort of busy here. I've got a team briefing in a couple of minutes. But I don't want you to drive yourself backwards and forwards, so I will collect you after work and I will drive you to work until such time as we find out what's going on here.'

'Alberto, I'm fine, fine. There's no need.'

His tone changed, a little louder, more commanding now. 'Gill! I do not want you to drive yourself. I will collect you after work. You just tell me when. If I can't make it, then I will send one of the Sovrintendenti. You are not to drive yourself. Is that understood?'

Gill frowned, tears rolling down her cheeks. He very rarely spoke to her like that. It was out of character. She could tell that he had suddenly gone into 'policeman mode'.

'Am I in danger?'

His tone softened as he sensed her fear. 'I don't know, my love. I honestly don't know. But first Donna Tavazzi, and now this. There are a lot of questions that we don't know the answer to, so we will take precautions. Sorry, hang on. YES! YES! COMING…COMING, ONE MINUTE. Sorry, my love, I've got to go. Sorry to be the bearer of such bad news, but I have work to do, and it's made more manageable if I know that you are safe. Okay?'

Gill was sobbing now. The words came out in ones and twos. 'I understand, understand. See you…later, hope to get away…six-thirty, seven.'

'Fine, okay, my love. I will be there, or one of the lads, and he or she will be carrying. From now on I want you to have armed police protection, whether you like it or not.'

Gill tried to get a grip on her emotions, sound less emotional, but she failed. The words still came out as a splutter. 'Okay, my love, okay. You take care too, please, please!'

'Must go, must go! Love you! Love you!'

The line clicked, and he was gone. Her hand was shaking as she wobbled the handset back into its plastic cradle.

Valeria Sforza gently lifted her foot off the corridor chair outside the Production Office, where she had been pretending to retie her shoelace. She clearly heard the phone being placed down onto the receiver and an uncontrollable sob: her cue to walk silently away, down the corridor and out of the building to the nearest phone.

Joe from Art looked uneasily at Dario and his three carpenters as the strange-looking, dark grey tank with a dark grey plywood, rusty on one side, painted conning tower was slowly lowered towards the water at the side of the dock. Como Trani pulled urgently at the heavy-duty hoses running back from the slowly swinging load across the quayside to two petrol-driven, two-stroke pumps. He wanted them straight and unkinked, a final little tug, then he waved to the crane operator to stop by holding his hand up. There was a sign language between them that they both understood. Como signalled, by making a pinching motion with his right hand, slower, slower, as the tank gently touched the water for the first time.

Everyone was holding their breath. Joe, always nervous, behind his blue sunglasses was biting his lip, his thin face drawn in apprehension, waiting for disaster to strike. The tank settled onto the water. The crane straps went a little slack, and Como signalled the crane operator to cease lowering by making a sideways movement with his hand.

He turned to Joe. 'Do you want it lower?'

Joe came out of his trance. 'Yes, Como, we just need about a metre above the water, no more…'

'Okay! Easy!' Como walked over to the nearest pump and flicked the start switch. The fire hose to the tank swelled and gargled momentarily as the water was pumped in under high pressure. The further hose to the other pump swelled, as the air being driven out of the tank in the opposite direction filled it.

Dario was open-mouthed in awe, as over the next couple of minutes he watched the tank with the wooden conning tower slowly sink deeper into the dock as it partially filled with water.

Como looked at Joe. ‘You look worried, Joe. Why? It won’t turn turtle or twist; it’s got a keel and side stabilisers. We can submerge it by filling it with water.’ He tapped the nearest gargling pump gently with his steel toecap boot. ‘We can make it rise by forcing air in and pumping the water out. It is, in effect, a submarine. That’s how they work.’

Joe looked at Dario for confirmation. ‘We are all in awe of you, Como. You have led us reluctant doubters over the last thirty-six hours to turning an old petrol tanker into a submarine. It looks bloody fantastic. You say that you can make it go up and down in the water?’

Como nodded. ‘Yes, but only slowly. If you want it to go up and down quicker like a submarine coming up from periscope depth, then we need much more powerful pumps, or more pumps, which will draw more power and require a small generator. It’s up to you. Just let me know.’

Joe smiled for the first time in two days. ‘I’ll speak to the Director, Como, see what he wants.’

Como grinned beneath his unkept beard. ‘Great! Any chance of a beer?’

Tomassino, the accountant, knew something was wrong by the tone of Gill’s voice when she phoned, requesting his presence in her office. He hung up his ‘Closed for lunch’ sign, and after double-locking the steel door, strode as fast as he could up the corridor to the Production suite. What he saw caused him great concern.

Gill was at her desk, her mascara virtually all gone, red, puffy-eyed and trying very hard to get a grip on herself. Paper tissues were scattered all over her desk. She looked up at him, her mouth open as she tried to get as much air into her lungs as she could. Tomassino had a diverse menu of smiles and charm, but he felt that now was not the time. She nodded to him to sit down.

'Tomassino, Luigi has been shot! He's dead!'

'What? You're joking!'

She gave him a look that told him in no uncertain terms that she was not messing about. 'Tomassino, I am the Production Manager of a film that has just lost its primary Producer. I need to know whether to stop production. I don't know what to do! I've only been in the job a few days.'

Tomassino smiled. He tried to exude an air of confidence, as he brought his hands together in a praying motion as a respectful tribute. 'I think I know what you are asking, Gill, and I will do my best to answer and reassure you. May I?'

'Yes, go ahead, go ahead.'

'As far as the actual film is concerned, nothing has changed. The money to make it, to continue production, is all safely lodged in the bank, the Banca d'Italia. They help finance films both here and in Hollywood. I sign the cheques. You should also be added as a signatory now Dublin has gone. The film's solicitor is also a signatory. There is more than enough money in the account because Luigi was such a rich man, he always overbudgeted; hard lessons he picked up over many years. The American distributors, represented here by Dino Burgio, have only put in eighteen per cent, which is fixed, but they are required for the final worldwide distribution. Luciano Scordia, the local entrepreneur, also has eighteen per cent because Luigi wanted to spread the risk a little advisedly. But Scordia does have first refusal to increase his holding if the production should go over budget. Both he and the Americans are unaware that there is a separate emergency account of over a million dollars that only I, the solicitor, and one other have access to. Luigi left nothing to chance.'

She looked at him, mollified by his answer, as she gathered the tissues up off her desktop, squeezing them hard not only to reduce their size but to take back control of her desk and her turbulent emotions.

'Okay, okay. So you are saying the film continues and the money is safe, bills can be paid, and there are emergency funds hidden away if push comes to shove?'

'Precisely, Gill, in a nutshell. You have nothing to worry about. The money is all there. The production continues as Luigi would have wanted.'

She looked him in the eye. 'Am I out of a job now Luigi has gone?'

'That, Gill, is another matter, although I don't see why you would be. Loretta, the solicitor, may be of more help on that. I just sign the cheques, keep the wheels turning.'

Gill grimaced. 'Thank you, Tomassino, thank you. I'd better pull myself together, hadn't I?'

'Gill, you are very liked and respected here. We have all experienced a very traumatic loss. Everyone will get right behind you and do all they can to help, you know that.'

Gill pulled out another tissue and blew her nose hard as if trying to finally shut down her emotions and get a better grip on herself.

Tomassino smiled his most sincere smile and held out his right hand to shake her hand. Her limp tentative response was shaky, hesitant. She was in turmoil.

Alberto Consalvo and Ispettore Paulo Gatti stood alongside each other, looking out of a deserted, first-floor factory glassless window down across the road onto the main gate and little pathway up to the Casa Annunciata. The whole area was a scene of businesslike police activity. Luigi's body had been removed, and the injured driver was in the hospital with an armed guard of two police officers. Four black-uniformed policemen stood in front of the gate, blocking all access to and from the property.

More police were searching the gardens using long, wooden broom handles.

Paulo half turned to his Sovrintendente Mauro standing back in the doorway behind him. 'No shell casings?'

Mauro looked at his notepad. 'No, sir. No shell casings, no cigarette butts, no chewing gum, sweet wrappers, nothing! We believe that the weapon was discharged from back here and that those boxes were used to support it.' He pointed to two dusty, substantially timbered wine case-sized boxes stood one on top of the other two metres back from the window. The dust on the box top had been disturbed. Alberto pointed to it.

'What's this mark here?'

Maura stepped forward a little and to his right to look around his two superiors for a clearer view of the boxes and the rotting window frame.

'We believe that it was caused by a sandbag. Probably used to support the weapon. The shooter knelt on the floor.'

Paulo grimaced. 'Sandbag! Any sign of it?'

'No, sir. No sign, no fingerprints here or on the way upstairs. The outside lock into the building was cut with bolt cutters. And there's no sign of the cutters or the padlock either, though we are still searching the whole site. Enquiries are also being made to see if anyone was seen coming or going, but we have no results so far.'

Paulo nodded a couple of times as if digesting the information before turning to the bulky figure of Alberto.

'What do you think, old friend?'

Alberto pursed his lips. 'I'm only an observer here, Paulo. But my initial thoughts are probably the same as yours…it's a hit! Professional shooter, one bullet, sandbag, fired from way back in the darkness of the room, no one would have seen anything, the building would absorb most of the sound of the shot. Before anyone would have realised what had occurred, the shooter is quietly down the back stairs and strolling, unobtrusively, away. I will say though, that the shooter is almost certainly ex-military. A military-trained sniper. The use of shadow in the room, the sandbag, no shell casing, no fingerprints, and just one shot! All points to military training. You've got to be on top of your game to achieve that, and you've also got to know your weapon really well. You have to spend time setting up your sights, it's not a two-minute job, and you can't do that unless you have access to a gun range or empty wide-open spaces. That single headshot is over one hundred and twenty metres. I couldn't pull that off.'

Paulo looked at him. 'Oh, that's a shame. I was hoping that you'd confess, and then we could all go home early!'

Alberto snorted. Police humour was never very subtle or heart-warming. 'It'd make your day if he'd left a visiting card,

Assassins Incorporated, all problems solved, no mess, no fuss! Call this number.'

Paulo nodded. 'Be nice!'

Once the Isabella-Belinda gangplank farewell sequence had been completed. Duke broke for coffee and to give Make-up time to de-age Belinda and get the crane moved down the dock to shoot the front, the white half, of the boat for her arrival in Sicily and the disembarkation sequence with Fulvio.

Lasse was cautious with his use of his period-dressed extras. Duke was instructing all of them to look enthusiastic, excited to be back in their home country and to show the same energy and momentum as they had the day before when they had surged en masse through the immigration arrival hall. The use of the crane enabled Lasse to keep the shot tight and not reveal anything of the modern-day backgrounds. Both Jan and Adam noticed a modern, plane vapour trail appear in the sky, which resulted in a slight change of shot, but apart from that, the whole sequence went well.

Because Adam was strapped in and unable to get off the crane, Grace had to come over at the end of each take to take the shot details, still somewhat amused by the great enjoyment that the three 'boys and their toys' crane riders seemed to be having.

Lunch was a very segregated affair with the crew being fed first, and then the extras, which was the same on most film sets worldwide. If it were the other way round, the crew would probably go short or, worse, get nothing. Extras are a voracious locust-like bunch, but when you consider how little they are paid, who can blame them?

Gill had checked her make-up, daubed on a bit of extra rouge and did her best to hide the fact that her eyes were red and puffy. As instructed, the unit car driver had pulled up right next to the entrance to the office block into the space where Peter Dublin used to park his Porsche. Gill stepped out into the sunshine, through habit slipping on her dark sunglasses as the warmth of the sun hit her face. She looked around, more than a little wary, but there was no bullet, no bang. She turned to the driver.

'The set, please, Civitavecchia. Thank you!'

Luciano Scordia looked up as his greasy, black-haired gatekeeper approached. He walked quickly for a small man, more of a shiny back beetle scuttle than a walk. He paused for a second, a metre away and nodded for permission to speak. A slight puff of breeze carried the smell of the overuse of chain store aftershave.

'Yes, Paulo. What is it?'

'Signore, I have just taken a phone call. It would seem that Luigi Mussomelli has been shot.'

'What? What!' Luciano was open-mouthed in astonishment. 'Tell me more, tell me more, nothing trivial, I trust?'

'No, sir, not trivial at all. He's dead.'

'Dead! Excellent! Excellent! Where was this?'

The gatekeeper moved a little closer and leant forward, lowering his voice as a young gardener appeared from the building in front of them, hose in hand as he began to water the terracotta plant tubs.

'At the children's home, sir.'

'Well, that'll teach him never to keep to a routine. Bring me a phone, bring me a phone, Sylvania will want to know. It'll make her day.'

A couple of weeks ago, the long drive down to Luigi's house had seen police cars for the pre-production welcoming party. But this one was real, not fake and bore no markings. A tearful Nella opened the door to admit Ispettore Gatti and his Sovrintendente Mauro Sofri. They asked all the usual questions: Can you account for your movements earlier in the day? Who else was here with you? Where is this gardener Rino?

They eventually found him out the back in the garden, working the very prolific vegetable patch. He confirmed that he had not left the grounds during the morning and to his knowledge, neither had Nella, though he had gone for an hour's run the previous evening. Mauro noted down all of his particulars, specifically those concerning his military service in World War II as a member of the elite alpine troop, the Black Feathers. When he showed them his German rifle hanging up in his room, they became very excited until closer examination revealed a couple of years of undisturbed dust that theoretically immediately eliminated it from their enquiries. But not so Rino, because having mentioned his previous military service, in Paulo Gatti's eyes, this made him the number-one suspect, and the policeman's more aggressive attitude reflected that.

Eventually, after about twenty minutes of further questioning, they left, taking the rifle with them. They requested that nothing in the house be touched until a search team had been all the way through the property to collect any information that may be relevant to their enquiries. They said that they were awaiting legal search warrants that should be presented later the following day. In the meantime, neither Rino nor Nella were to leave the immediate area. Both were asked if they had a passport, but the answer on both counts was in the negative.

Gill stood at the back, behind the line of lights, watching patiently for the last shot of the day to be announced as a print. Duke had seen her raised hand signalling that she wanted to speak to him before he called a wrap. He eventually nodded at her to confirm that shooting was over. She walked quickly towards him, right up into his personal space, before speaking softly into his ear.

Adam didn't know what was said, but Duke's reaction was sudden, open-mouthed shock followed by, 'WHAT? WHAT?', causing Gill to momentarily step back. Lasse, sensing that something was wrong, walked quickly towards them, and a huddle ensued. The whole set was quiet. Something was wrong, very wrong.

A couple of minutes of whispered, agitated conversation passed before Duke nodded to Lasse and Gill to confirm that they were all in agreement as to what he was going to say. He didn't need to clap his hands for quiet; the only sound was the lap of the sea against the dock and the odd cry of a seagull.

'Ragazzi, ragazzi, I have some bad news for all of you. Our Producer, Luigi Mussomelli, passed away this morning in sinister circumstances.' He paused, looking anxiously around, trying to take on board what he had just said. Taking a deep breath, he continued. 'Many of you regard him as a friend and may wish to have some time to mourn. Tomorrow is the night shoot with the submarine. Anyone not wishing to come to work should let Gill here know so that replacements can be organised. Thank you.'

Adam was stunned. He turned to Jan. 'Shit, that doesn't sound good.'

Jan said nothing, just shook his head slowly in bewilderment. Luca looked at Anatra; both were in a state of shock. Adam looked over towards Grace. She was sobbing profusely, tears rolling down her cheeks as she stuffed her typed papers and polaroids into her briefcase as quickly as she could. She flipped the lid of her typewriter closed and nodded to the old electrician Alberto who looked after her. He nodded in understanding and waved his hands in a shooing motion, signalling for her to leave everything and go.

She flashed a look of total bewilderment at Adam, shaking her head as to convey, *I can't believe what I just heard*, and almost ran towards the Make-up caravan and her friend Sophia, who was standing on the open doorway on the top step. She, too, was in tears.

Adam turned to Nick, the crane Grip, and Anatra.

'We've got gear to pack. Is it okay to take the camera off?'

Nick nodded.

They began the careful process of derigging and boxing up the equipment. By the time they had finished and loaded it all into the camera car, they were, apart from a couple of Art department guys fiddling with a gangplank, the last to leave the deserted dock.

By the time Duke pulled up outside his house it was nearly eight p.m. As he put down his briefcase to lock the car, his front door opened to reveal his twenty-two-year-old son, Franco, and his wife, Angelina, a couple of paces behind him in the hallway.

'Dad, glad you're back!' was the agitated welcome.

Duke paused for a second. This was not normal behaviour. Franco never opened the door. He was usually up in his room studying or playing that damn record player.

He smiled. 'Everything okay? Everything—'

Franco cut him short, as he looked anxiously up and down the street. 'Dad, something's happened. Need to talk…'

Duke stepped towards him. 'Okay, okay. What's—?'

'Dad, I know Luigi's been shot. I know who did it!'

Duke, though taken aback, continued walking through the door that Franco quickly closed behind him. He looked at Angelina, who looked absolutely terrified, close to tears, wringing her hands, not really knowing what to do.

'Dad, I was at Dino's house today painting. I heard who killed Luigi.'

Duke gripped Franco by the shoulder, wide and muscular from swimming, similar to him in so many ways, short curly hair, small ears.

'Slow down, slow down! Let's sit down and hear what happened.'

Angelina motioned them into the lounge, off to the right, while signalling a wine glass drinking motion to her mouth to Duke, who smiled a tight smile and just shook his head. 'No, thanks.'

Franco, in a loose denim shirt and blue jeans, silver identity bracelet, typical student attire, walked quickly over to the window and pulled the long, dark green curtains closed as if trying to blot out the outside world.

Duke decided that the best way to calm the situation was to sit down himself. So he indicated with a firm nod and a gentle wave of his hand for Angelina to do the same. She sat on the edge of her high-backed, green-winged armchair, hands tightly clenched in her lap.

Franco walked back behind the sofa. 'I shouldn't have gone back, shouldn't have gone back, but you know what I'm like, like you, never leave a job half done. I parked the scooter round the back and went in through the back door. I've still got the key.' He held up the key as if it was hot, not really knowing what to do with it. He looked around and dropped it unceremoniously on the small coffee table.

'The upstairs bedroom was red, Dino wanted it white, and you know what red's like. It's a bugger to cover in a couple of coats. So as I had nothing to do, I thought that I'd go back, give it another final coat and finish it off nicely. I was upstairs, and they came back—'

Duke held up his hand. 'Who came back?'

'Dino, the guy who was arrested at the party by the singing policemen, plus his two Yanky friends. They'd been out to lunch and come back.'

'Whoa, slow down, Franco, slow down! Did they know that you were in the house?'

'I don't know. I suppose they didn't. I was upstairs painting, nearly finished. In twenty minutes I'd be gone! Dino was talking about a very tasty alibi at the Hotel Manfredi. He said he'd go there again, and then this third guy turns up, called Max. He's the guy who shot Luigi. He drove up. I heard a car!'

'Whoa! Slow down, Franco, slow down! I'm going to stop you for a second, and we are going to write down everything while it's still fresh in your mind, like a police witness statement.'

'Oh, no, Dad, I'm not going anywhere near the police. If I was a witness, they'd kill me long before I got—'

Duke held up his hand and gave a reassuring smile. 'Franco, stop! Let's go back to the beginning. Just wait a second while I get some paper out of my bag here.' He reached down into his bulging briefcase and pulled out a well-worn, black, A4 notepad with a cheap biro clipped to it. He nodded to indicate he was ready.

'Right. You arrive at the house, park your scooter round the back. No one is about. There are no cars. You let yourself in through the back door with the key and go upstairs to the bedroom to paint a final coat of white emulsion onto a patchy wall – okay so far?'

'Yes! Yes! This guy that arrived, Max, they called him, he—'

'Slow down, Franco. You are upstairs painting. Who then came back and when? I need details! Details! What did you hear?'

Adam felt at a loss. He wasn't hungry. It was apparent that the news on set had upset a lot of people, none more so than Grace. She looked as if she had been totally mortified by it all, and he felt helpless at not being able to help in any way. They were in a relationship, after all, a strange but quite intense relationship, in his opinion. He didn't have her phone number, didn't even know if she had one as he'd never seen one in the little house. So he decided to call on her. It was only a few thousand lire in a taxi. She would probably appreciate a shoulder to cry on.

The taxi dropped him off in the narrow lane as usual, pulling over to the right to let him out. Within a few paces he was at the little red front door. He tentatively rang the bell. There was a scratching sound from the area of the peephole. A voice, a female voice, not Grace's, drifted through the door, its tone one of surprise.

'It's…it's Adam. Adam the Focus Puller!'

Then there was silence.

Adam was slightly taken aback. The door did not open. He could hear nothing from the inside. He was uncertain what to do. He thought about ringing the doorbell again but decided against it. He sniffed the air. The smell of the little lane was the same. It reminded him of happier times when he had stood in the same place a few days ago with a partial erection and a bottle of wine in his hand. After what seemed an eternity, he heard the long top bolt being withdrawn, and the door eased half-open to reveal Sophia.

'Hullo, Adam! Not a good time, but you'd better come in.' She pulled the door fully open and stepped back to allow him in.

The smell of her, as he walked past, was a light summery fragrance, very female, apple blossom or the like. She was wearing exactly what he had last seen her in on the top step of her Make-up caravan: loose-fitting, red and blue cotton trousers and a silk, copper-coloured blouse, her hair in a bun held in place by an orange pencil.

Adam walked into the little lounge. Grace was sitting on the sofa. She looked up.

'Adam, nice of you to come.'

Adam could hear Sophia locking the two front door bolts behind him.

'Sorry, Grace, I wasn't expecting Sophia to be here. I thought you'd be here on your own, thought you might need a friend…'

'It's all right, Adam, it's all right. I was going to tell Sophia anyway. She knows…knows I have someone.'

Sophia walked in. She had been crying too, but not as much as Grace who looked utterly ravaged, her eyes red and puffy. Grace stood up, and Adam walked into her outstretched arms. The embrace was different this time; there was no kiss, just a damp cheek on his shoulder and a short shudder. Her clutch didn't last long before she gently eased him away.

'Why did you come, Adam, why?'

'At the docks, I saw your hurt, Grace. Friend or whatever I am, I couldn't not do anything. I had to come, offer a hug, a shoulder. I think you'd do the same if the positions were reversed.'

She gave a wan smile. 'That's kind, Adam, that's kind. You've caught us unawares. Sophia and I have both lost someone very important in our lives, and the future is very uncertain now, very uncertain.'

'Is there anything I can do, Grace?'

'No, nothing. It was kind of you to come.'

Adam looked at Sophia. She was looking him straight in the eye, expressionless, completely neutral. He turned to Grace.

'It's not about just the good times, is it, Grace? It's about the bad times as well. Being there for someone…'

'Stop, Adam, please stop.' She sat back down on the sofa, grabbing a cushion that she pulled hard into her chest.

Sophia leant forward and put her hand on Grace's left shoulder. 'Grace, this guy is telling you in so many words that he really cares about you. That's what he's trying to say…'

Grace squeezed the cushion to her even harder. 'Oh, shit! This is dreadful. Adam, I think it's best that you leave, and we'll pick this up another day. I cannot think right now. Soph, let him out, please, and we'll chat later.'

Adam felt uneasy, felt that he had intruded. 'Do you have a phone number, Grace, so that I can call you?' He looked around the room, no phone, but he noticed that the dresser top was covered in picture frames of different colours and sizes, all placed downwards, thus obscuring the memories.

Grace noticed him clocking the dresser. Her voice unexpectantly had an edge to it. 'Another time, Adam, another time. Thanks.'

Sophia moved quickly towards the front door, pausing at the little hall table to pick up a biro to jot down some numbers on the small shopping list notepad. She said nothing, just handed him the torn page, followed by a meaningful stare. She then moved quickly to slide back the bolts on the front door. As she gently pulled the door open, she leant in towards him. Her eyes were slightly puffy and red, her cheeks and nose shiny from constant tissue-dabbing. Her soft breast touched his chest, her perfume filled his nostrils as she whispered, 'Thank you for coming, Adam, thank you! Call her tomorrow. She is going to need you more than she realises. Be there for her, be there. The reward is the most amazing woman.'

Adam was more than a little moved by the passion of Sophia's feelings for Grace. It took him by surprise, but there was something else that bothered him. He was almost sure that there was someone else in the house. He had heard a slight movement or shuffle coming from upstairs, and he wondered who on earth it could be. But by the time he had really digested what had just taken place, he was standing at the end of the little lane, and it was starting to drizzle.

Wednesday 23rd April

Nella and Rino were appalled at the intrusive energy of the very early morning police investigation, which seemed more like a raid than an investigation. Two white vans, two unmarked police cars and a police dog. They waved their search warrants and marched straight in as if they owned the place. Neither Nella nor Rino had a fondness for dogs, and this one was particularly obnoxious, not only because of its intimidating behaviour but also because it smelt. How a search dog that relies totally on scent was able to detect anything past its own body odour was a complete mystery. But after about two hours of looking in every cupboard, under every bed and even in the loft, all they seemed to take away was a load of folders and papers from Luigi's little den up on the first-floor landing. At one point during the proceedings, Rino asked the dog handler what he was searching for, and the grunted reply came back, 'Explosives, drugs, firearms, anything.' This caused Rino no alarm because dogs can't climb trees to search bird nest boxes twenty-five feet off the ground. If they could, they might have found something interesting,

Jose looked affectionately across the small pine kitchen table to Vinincio, who was just forking away the last piece of scrambled egg. 'More coffee?'

Vinincio, with his blue serviette tucked into the neck of his white satin pyjamas, smiled. 'No, thanks, no, thanks.'

His shoulder-length brown hair was all ruffled, and he needed a shave. He was tall and slim, like his mother and sister. He had also inherited his mother's sexual appetite, which was probably why he was spending more and more nights in the luxurious flat above Jose's shop rather than back at the Vaticano Nero, something that his sister Sylvania vehemently disapproved of.

He looked at Jose resplendent in a silk red and gold Chinese-style dressing gown as he gently poured himself a second cup. 'They don't approve, you know, they don't approve.'

Jose smiled a slight grimace. 'I know they don't, but that's because they don't understand. There's not much we can do other than just be discreet.'

'I've kept a diary, Jose.'

Jose smiled broadly. 'Oh, that's so sweet!'

Vinincio shook his head. 'No, not about us, them! I've kept a diary about them. Everything that they have been up to over the last few years. Sylvania worries me. She's a loose cannon. Dad is mostly a reasonable man, a businessman, but

Sylvania does things behind his back, has one of the men do things, without Dad knowing. I worry that she may try to hurt you.'

'Oh, don't be so silly, Vinincio! This is 1969 Rome, not 1930s Chicago. It's a totally different world nowadays.'

Vinincio was not convinced. He shook his head. 'Even so, even so! You don't know them. They have done some terrible things, really awful.'

'Vinincio, we have had this conversation before. If they were going to do something they would have done it eighteen months ago when we first began. I think that they accept us now, maybe reluctantly, but they do! I'm sure of it.'

'I am not so sure. She's getting more aggressive, day by day, trying to take over from Dad. That's why I'm telling you about the diary. It's in my weekend bag under the bed. If anything happens to either of us…'

Jose raised his voice. 'Vinincio, stop it! You're becoming paranoid. Nothing is going to happen, nothing.'

The little alley and little red door were seeing more than their fair share of visitors as the broad-shouldered Duke was ushered in just after 11 a.m.

Grace paused by the kitchen door. 'Coffee? Espresso?'

Duke looked down into her face, slightly puffy-eyed from crying. She looked wounded, like she had been physically mauled, but there was a fire in her eyes that he had never seen before. She was giving off a strangely conflicting combination of emotions.

'No, thanks. Thanks for the opportunity to chat, much appreciated.' He walked into the lounge and motioned if it was okay to sit down on the sofa.

She nodded. 'Course! Have a seat.' She decided to sit on the nearest high-backed dining table chair, turning it round to face him before sitting down and crossing her legs, then deliberately folding her brown dress over her knees to protect her modesty. He tilted his head down and looked up at her almost through his eyebrows.

'This conversation, Grace, must never leave this room. Is there anyone else here?'

Grace tilted her head to one side and arched her eyebrows, frowning slightly in surprise. 'No, there's no one else here. We are alone.'

Duke nodded a couple of times as if thinking how best to begin. 'I think I know who killed Luigi, Grace.'

She opened her mouth in wide-eyed disbelief. 'What? How on—'

He cut across her, speaking a little quicker, 'It was Dino, Grace. Dino, or rather one of his men who shot him on Dino's orders.'

Grace was open-mouthed in astonishment. 'How do you know that? How on earth do…' She shook her head, unable to fully take in what he was saying.

'Let me tell the story, Grace. Let me tell you what I know.'

Grace nodded and clenched her hands together, trying very hard to give off an air of composure, but her whole body was too tense.

Duke took a deep breath. 'My son, Franco, back from university in London, for a bit of pin money has been filling in as a painter on set and elsewhere. He spent the last few days decorating at Dino's house. Yesterday he went back to finish off an upstairs wall, parked his scooter around the back and let himself in and through the back door, the same way he's done all week.'

Grace, spellbound, started to frown in concentration and gently licked the inside of her top lip.

Duke noted her rapt attention and gave a short nod before continuing. 'While he was upstairs, he heard Dino and two Americans come into the house and start talking about the lunch that they had just had at the Hotel Manfredi. They referred to the meal as the alibi lunch. Franco didn't have to eavesdrop. Dino talks so loud that Franco could have heard him up in the attic.'

Grace nervously refolded her dress over her knees. Her expression told Duke that she was listening to every word but not really liking what she was hearing.

'After a couple of minutes, a third Yank turned up, Franco heard his car. His name was Max, and he began bragging how in true Ranger style, he had taken out the old man and the bodyguard with a single shot.'

Grace stared. 'Shit! Duke, is this for real?'

'Sorry, Grace, it is, it all is. Dino asked him if he still had the gun, and Max said that it was in the car. Dino got agitated at that point and said that they needed to bury the gun and torch the car, finishing with the fact that they still had the Stens if needed.'

Grace just shook her head in disbelief. 'What happened to Franco, Duke? Is he okay…safe?'

Duke nodded, his face betraying a sadness. 'He's fine, Grace. I put him on a plane to Schiphol late last night. For obvious reasons, we have a large "run-for-the-hills fund" that I keep in the safe at home. He may go back to uni in London and sofa-surf, but knowing him, he will probably go to Thailand and lie in the sun.'

'My God, Duke, how much money did you give him?'

'Enough, Grace, enough. He's my son. Cash in dollars and sterling, plus traveller's cheques. He has effectively disappeared.'

Grace chewed her lip for a second. ‘Did they know he was there?’

‘I don’t believe so, Grace. I think that any one of us would have kept quiet in that situation. We will know soon enough if Dino starts asking Gill who the painter was. Franco also said that Dino was shouting about teaching Luigi a lesson. He reckoned he totally humiliated him at the party.’

Grace was sceptical. ‘I heard about the party from Sophia. But you don’t kill someone for a prank, a bit of fun.’

‘Dino didn’t see it that way, Grace. Franco said he was shouting, explosive, really riled up about the way Luigi humiliated him, making him “look a f**king c***” was what he said. Really nasty.’

Grace looked at the floor, quietly pursing her lips as she mulled things over. ‘Are we going to the police?’

Duke shook his head. ‘Don’t see how we can, Grace. The only witness is my son, and once Scordia, through his network, finds out what he knows, he won’t last five minutes. Come to think of it, none of us would. Even if they managed to arrest the American Army Ranger, Max, Dino would deny everything. With his training, Max, at the slightest sniff of cops, could disappear instantly and never be seen again, only to be replaced by someone just as deadly. I don’t know what to do!’

Grace arched her eyebrows. ‘We could make anonymous tips to the police.’

Duke shook his head. 'I don't think so, Grace. That would make Dino aware that they were overheard at the house, and then that moves my family, my whole family, right into the gunsights.'

Grace stood up, suddenly angry. 'We can't let him get away with it, we can't, we just can't'

Duke looked up at her as she paced backwards and forwards.

'I know, Grace, I know, but there's more: before they left, Dino was going on about the man who killed his father and how killing Luigi would finally flush out their family. He seemed to think that Luigi was protecting them and that his will would reveal who they were.'

Grace was stunned. 'What? What? This is madness. What are you talking about?'

'I don't know, Grace, I have no idea. I don't know anything about Dino or his dead father, but it sounds to me like vendetta. The national sport of Sicily, good old-fashioned vendetta, like he had a lifelong grudge against Luigi, and his coming to Rome and seeing him again, plus the party prank, rekindled all of it! You're originally from Sicily; you should know all about vendetta!'

Grace paused and looked down at him. She shook her head. 'This is all hyperbole, Duke!'

Duke decided to stand up and hopefully calm the situation.

'I don't know, Grace, I don't know, but there is going to be a reading of his will at some point. Then we will see if it's hyperbole or vendetta.'

Grace leant forward and walked into his space. Her eyes hardened. 'We could always take matters into our own hands, Duke, and blow the bastards away.'

It was Duke's turn to be open-mouthed. 'You don't have that kind of money, Grace.'

She tilted her head in fake curiosity. 'What do you mean, don't have that kind of money? What's money got to do with it?'

Duke looked bewildered at her logic. 'Hit men! Good hit men that can never be traced cost a great deal of money, Grace.'

She smiled, tight-lipped. 'We need to talk more, a lot more, but I was not even for a second considering hiring anyone.'

Adam tried phoning Grace three or four times during the day, but each time it just rang and rang. She never picked up, so in the end he just gave up. As compensation, he took himself across the piazza to his favourite little trattoria and treated himself to a big sit-down, late steak lunch. The staff welcomed him with genuine open arms, not just because they realised he was a regular returning customer and not simply a one-meal tourist, but because he was their very own VIP who worked on the big films at Studio Lazio. They treated him like a megastar.

The unit car was early and dropped Adam off right on the dock next to the catering caravan, which had laid out coffee, Italian bread and platefuls of cold meat and prawns. Much to his surprise, the first person he saw that he recognised was Captain Steve.

His suntanned, white-toothed smile was genuine. 'Afternoon, Adam, afternoon. Looking forward to a bit of bobbin' on the oggin?'

Adam did not have to feign surprise. 'Steve, what are you doing here?'

'I'm your assistant. My old mate, Duke, has put me with the camera crew.'

Adam was surprised. 'Why? Why?'

Steve smiled. 'Boats, Adam, boats, seawater, risk of drowning. I'm here to help you.'

Adam shook his head. 'What do you know about boats, Steve? I thought you were army.'

Steve smiled. 'Wrong, Adam. You should have looked at my cap badge; the motto is *Per Mare et Terram*, by sea and by land. I'm not army, mate; I'm a sea soldier, a naval officer. My job tonight is to make sure that your camera is safe, adequately tied off, lashed down, that your kit stays dry, and that none of you airy-fairy blighters fall into the oggin. We've been lining up all day. Do you want to see the chart?'

Without waiting for Adam's reply, he quickly reached round to the table and indicated for Adam to step beside him to look at the greeny-blue sea map in its transparent waterproof plastic folder on the white tablecloth.

Steve pointed at the chart. 'Look at it like a clock face, Adam. The sub, here, is the centre of the clock face, in the middle. Out of shot, at eleven o'clock, is a boat with a generator and a very big light, lovely old Sven's moonlight. At the nine o'clock position, also well out of the left of the frame, is the support boat for the sub with pumps and stuff on board, and here you are at six o'clock in the camera boat.'

Adam was impressed. 'Is that what we're doing tonight then?'

Steve beamed a huge grin. 'Yup! We take you and the camera boat out to the mooring buoys, and you film the sub sequence bobbing up and down, tied up to a couple of old van engines that we dropped as anchors very early this morning.'

Adam patted him on the back in congratulations. 'I'm amazed, Steve, bloody amazed.'

Steve tapped his nose. 'Oh, it's not all wine and roses, mate. The camera boat is an old fishing boat. It stinks like a Grimsby trawler. You are definitely going to need a bath afterwards, maybeee two!'

Gill had not had any requests from the crew to be replaced so they could have time off to mourn Luigi, so the call sheet was effectively unaltered. She had tried phoning Veronique to let her know about Luigi, but there was no response. Everyone was called to Civitavecchia for four-thirty to be on the water and ready to shoot from six. Sven had made it clear that he wanted to shoot during 'magic hour', which was the forty or so minutes between daylight and true photographic darkness. She had no intention of going back to set, and there was no need anyway, so as instructed, she had called her husband to let him know that she was ready to leave.

As they left her office, she forgot to tell him that she had taken a unit car to set. It just didn't seem worth the row.

He paused for a second in the weakening sunshine outside the doorway. Standing in front of her, he looked carefully around, before moving forward to open the car door and usher her in. Then he walked round to the driver's side.

She was glad that he had turned up in his own car because the unmarked undercover police pool cars all stank of cigarette smoke. The ashtrays were always brimming with fag ends and chewing gum, with the unforgettable additional optional extra aroma of empty food packaging and drinks cups floating up from the littered floors, a truly sensorial experience.

He never took his eyes off the road when he drove, he never did, never had. He spoke to the windscreen, it was his way, advanced police driving techniques did that to someone. She was used to it.

'You'll be glad to know that Paulo does not regard you as a suspect.'

Gill mirrored the way he spoke at the windscreen. After years of travelling together, there was no point in turning to look at someone if they were just going to avoid eye contact and only look forward.

'I'm glad about that. What convinced him?'

He smirked. 'Fear! I told him I'd kill him if he gave you a hard time. All part of our new initiative of unbiased policing!'

She turned to look at him momentarily. 'I don't believe you. How are you all getting on?'

He tapped the steering wheel with his wedding ring, making a slight clicking sound. 'Pillow talk now. Pillow talk.' He nodded as if just to confirm the contract of confidentiality that they both shared. Gill nodded in assent. He caught the movement out of the corner of his eye.

'With regards to Luigi, we don't have a clue. It was a hit man, most probably ex-military, a very confident shooter, could have been sent by anyone. Certainly not cheap to hire. We are looking at motives, but Luigi had been a mainly philanthropic figure as far as we can tell. Never married, no children, worth an absolute fortune. Maybe the beneficiaries of his will have been trying to cash in early; we are seeking court orders to look at that— Bloody hell!'

He jammed on his brakes to avoid crashing into a scooter that had suddenly pulled out in front of the car, nearly taking off the front bumper before turning right down a small sideroad.

'Little idiots, why are they all such idiots? He was nearly in a wheelchair! Idiots!'

Gill smiled. 'What about Dino?'

'We have been quite busy with all of that. He has a cast-iron alibi for the time of the murder, obviously. But we found out that he was born in 1922 in Sicily near to Mussomelli, where Luigi comes from, which makes him forty-seven now.'

Gill was wide-eyed. 'Forty-seven! Forty-seven? He looks sixty! Must have had a hard life.'

'Don't know about hard, but he lost his dad in the war and a couple of years later his elder brother. Police records from that time are non-existent, so we have been looking at old newspapers, and it seems that during the war, throughout Sicily, there was a lot of killing going on, family vendettas and the like. Probably due to the conflicts of being a fascist or a patriot. Don't know and never will.

'Very soon after his brother is killed in suspicious circumstances in 1948, he up sticks and emigrates to America, Hollywood. Gets a job with Banca d'Italia, in their film loans department. He has had one paternity suit thrown at him and numerous charges of indecent assault, all unproven.'

Gill crossed her legs in revulsion, and grimaced. 'Sounds like a real charmer. Now I have some pillow talk for you.'

'Great! Gimmee, gimmee!'

'Only if you slow down. You're driving as if you have your blue lights on.'

'Sorry, just want to get home.' He looked up in his mirror, before easing over to his right and slowing down, checking again in his rear-view mirror.

Gill smiled, please by the reduction in speed. 'The film is fully financed and all of the money to make it is in the bank. Dino's American backers own eighteen per cent, and the businessman Luciano Scordia also—'

He let out an explosive snort. 'LUCIANO SCORDIA, BUSINESSMAN! BUSINESSMAN? He's the biggest crook in Italy. He runs drugs, protection, gambling, people trafficking for prostitution. You remember that brothel fire last year, all those British and Eastern European girls? That was one of his little enterprises. Thirty-five kids died in that. His only business, my love, is with the devil. He is one person in Rome who, if he came to a sticky end, we at Central and the carabinieri wouldn't lift a notebook; we'd party for a week. He is the constant cancer corroding Italian society, and his filthy tentacles affect everyone.'

Gill pushed her head back against her headrest, blowing her breath out through pursed lips, taken aback by the passion of his words. She shook her head slowly. 'Whew! Well, like him or not, he's on eighteen per cent of the film with an option to increase that if Luigi goes over budget, which is unlikely because of Duke.'

He shook his head. 'That's not good news, love, not good news at all. We didn't know about that. But why…why would Luigi go into business with him? Maybe better to have him on the inside than on the outside causing mischief? Dunno.'

She smiled, raising her eyebrows for a second in silent agreement, then turned to look at him, proud of what she saw: a strong-jawed, greying at the temples conscientious, honest policeman. He momentarily flashed a look at her out of the corner of his eye and smiled, confirming the bond between them.

She leant to her left and also looked at the rear-view mirror. 'Do you think we're being followed?'

He flicked another quick look at her. 'No, love, no, clear as a bell. Another thing about Scordia, he has a daughter, who runs an apparently legitimate legal business in the centre of town, house sales and wills and the like. She would most likely have had contact with Donna Tavazzi. There's also a son, but we don't know a lot about him. We don't think he's connected with his dad's business. We know he's gay though as we gave him a verbal warning for inappropriate behaviour in the toilets at the

Venus club a couple of years ago. His dad's lawyers were all over us on that one. Thinking about his daughter though, her business must be a front, because she doesn't need to work; the family is awash with money, dirty money, but money nevertheless, and loads of it.'

Gill looked at him. 'I don't need to work, but I do.'

He smiled at the windscreen. 'That's because you are very intelligent and require constant stimulation.'

She smiled as she gently moved her left hand to his inner right thigh. 'That'd be nice. After supper?'

'What?' He frowned, pretending not to understand.

She smiled. 'A bit of constant stimulation. After we've eaten.'

Alessandro Mosena was a northerner from the motor city of Turin, an ex-FIAT research engineer and now Studio Lazio's resident vehicle mechanic for the last fifteen years.

His workshop was immaculate and spotless, you could eat off the worktops. Every spanner had its own wall space, with a minimum of two clips each to hold them onto the glossy white painted surface. The smooth concrete floor was painted a spotless gloss grey.

He was just about to lock up after finishing the fitting of a sump shield to a police car action vehicle that next week was going to be driven down a flight of steps in a chase sequence for a TV commercial. The phone rang: Dino Burgio wanted to know how to stop his car from being stolen from his driveway. It would seem the vintage Cadillac had attracted a lot of attention over the past few days.

Alessandro had little time for the man. When Burgio had first collected the car, he had treated him like a lowlife, showing absolutely no interest in him or the boot full of spares that the old, previous French owner had, as a gesture of goodwill, passed on. He just told him with a dismissive wave to clear out the boot, and then just drove away. So Alessandro never got the opportunity to say that he would hold a spare set of keys, which was something that he always did as a matter of course because film people were wired differently to everyone else. None of them knew where the bonnet catch was or how to top up the oil. And losing vehicle keys was just an everyday occurrence. It was just the way these artistic filmy people were. This was why he had over the years accumulated over three hundred key sets all neatly clipped up in his office, all ringed and neatly labelled.

His curt, tight-lipped answer to Burgio was to lift the bonnet, remove the distributor cap and take the thumb-sized rotor arm into the house overnight, thus effectively immobilising the vehicle.

Burgio just grunted and rang off.

Alessandro pursed his lips. 'Cazzo!'

Captain Steve had been dead right about the camera boat; it was truly blessed. Every atom of weather-beaten wood, rusty part-painted metal or weed-laced rope stank of fish and the sea. No eau de cologne could compete. The olfactory battle had only one victor. Adam knew that tonight would be engraved indelibly on his memory. What other profession would get you onto an old Mediterranean fishing trawler, motor you out to sea, past half a submarine bobbing gently on the light swell, and then tie up bow and stern to a couple of buoys and wait for the sun to go down? On the way past the sub, Adam had noticed that the conning tower was just meant to be filmed from one side. It had no back to it, just wooden stairs going up to a narrow standing shelf, and three chairs that looked to be roped to the hull.

Duke controlled everything through a bullhorn which could probably be heard five kilometres away.

Ben, his Second Assistant Director, had a non-speaking part, and was dressed as the second British naval submarine officer. Duke wanted him on the sub to herd the actors and the stunt double.

Sven was rubbing his monocle pan glass more than usual, his worry bead. That told Adam that he was nervous. He had a boat with a large arc light way back off to the left behind the sub. Its light was not lighting the sub, but the sea behind it, which Adam found a little surprising. The camera boat had no arc lights, just a small one to illuminate the clapper board.

They did a couple of rehearsals with the sub captain coming up onto the conning tower, scanning around with his binoculars, followed by the uniformed Ben. Then the stunt double for Isabella appeared over the top of the conning tower, climbed down the step rungs onto the deck and into the inflatable dingy that was being held by two darkly dressed sailors with black camo paint on their faces.

Duke turned to Sven. 'How long, Sven?'

Sven looked at the sub, turned to his right and looked at the setting sun just above the horizon. 'Ten, fifteen minutes.'

There was silence. The only sound was the *slap slap slap* of wavelets against the side of the boat. Sven turned to Adam. 'One day you will have to do this, Adam, shoot day for night!'

Adam snorted. 'Yeah! One day, one day!' he said with a smile.

Sven smiled back, in his grandfatherly way. 'My advice is don't let them rush you, choose your time, know when it's right and plan to do three takes, one which will be too light, one which will hopefully be in the middle and the last one which will probably be too dark. Don't let them rush you! This is nearly all in silhouette, no light on the foreground, only on the sea behind, and using a bit of light from the setting sun just to fill in a tiny bit of detail.'

Adam looked at the sub and squinted through half-closed eyes, trying to get an impression of what it would look like on film. He knew where Sven was coming from. He, like everyone else, was really looking forward to seeing the rushes on the following Monday.

Grace was sitting further back on the deck on a couple of the Macchinisti's boxes, next to Captain Steve. They were murmuring to each other out of the corner of their mouths, just looking forward, which suggested to Adam that they knew each other well. Adam caught her eye, and she nodded. Her expression said to him: don't get jealous, Adam, I will talk to who I want to.

Adam nodded again, a momentary pang of jealousy rippling through him. God, this woman had got under his skin. His thoughts were interrupted by Sven saying to Duke, 'Okay, Duke, time to make smoke, please.'

Duke smiled, pleased to be getting on with the business of the day. Lifting his bullhorn and pointing at two small cabin cruisers far off to the right, which Adam had presumed were tourist onlooker boats, he instructed, 'FATE FUMO, RAGAZZI, FATE FUMO, MAKE SMOKE!'

Within half a minute, a light white smoke began to drift from the nearest cruiser gently across the sea towards the sub, like a soft sea mist. Sven nodded in satisfaction as the light sea breeze spread it out. Its effects were very subtle, very atmospheric.

Sven nodded to Duke. 'Take, please, first of three.'

Duke merely nodded. Captain Steve leapt up and came to the boat rail on the far side of the camera to watch the scene play out.

The bullhorn boomed, 'GOING FOR A TAKE, RAGAZZI, GOING FOR A TAKE.'

Grace moved into camera left, right next to Adam, to have a clear view of the action. Smiling a *Good evening* at him, Jan and Sven, the latter leant over between them and tapped Adam on the shoulder as he said, 'Wide open, wide open, please.'

Adam didn't need to open up the camera blimp and check the lens aperture setting; he had already set it, he wasn't anticipating anything else. He did, though, Selvyt cloth in hand, quickly check his front glass for any drip of water or passing insect, but it was clear.

Como Trani, with the three construction crew, sat on a hatch cover on the sub support boat way off to the left, a cold bottle of Nastro Azzurro in his hand. Two long hoses stretched invisibly beneath the small waves to the sub tank. He didn't anticipate having to pump air or water; the whole structure was just sitting on the gently bobbing swell like it was born to it. The light rolling sea mist surprised him. It was a nice touch.

Luca clonked the clapper board and whisked it out of frame. Lasse watched Jan's eye at the eyepiece. Jan nodded that he was framed. Duke held the bullhorn in front of Lasse's mouth to transmit his instruction.

'ACTION!'

At the lip of the conning tower, the silhouette of the British naval officer came up from below and began to scan the sea with his binoculars.

Alex Dublin was annoyed with whoever was at her front door. They were continuously ringing the bell and knocking very loudly and insistently. Clearly irritated, she yanked the door open and was confronted by two police badges being held in a somewhat threatening manner at her eye level. There were no smiles. The older, thin one spoke first.

'Mrs Dublin, I am Ispettore Paulo Gatti, and this is Sovrintendente Sofri. We'd like to come in and talk to your husband, Peter, if we may.'

Alex was not pleased to see them. Her over made-up face deliberately gave them the impression that they were both most unwelcome. Her look of supercilious distaste only confirmed it. Mauro paused for a second before following his superior into the oak-panelled hallway, looking up and down her pale green, tightly belted figure, dwelling a little too long on her cleavage and her three rows of pearls for her liking. He eventually locked eyes with her.

'Thank you, Mrs Dublin.'

Gatti turned, pausing to give a tight smile as she closed the door.

Alex just waved them forward in a businesslike way. 'He's in here on the right.'

Gatti turned and walked into the room. It stank like an old wine bar after closing time. What he saw surprised him. A figure sprawled out full-length on a shiny, long, black, leather sofa. One leg drooped to the floor. He was wearing a white T-shirt blotched with red wine stains and pale grey running bottoms with a lot of dark staining around the crutch and down the inside of both thighs. He was either asleep or unconscious and in need of a shave. His shoulder-length permed hair was a greasy, tangled mess.

He did not respond in the slightest when Alex shouted, 'PETER, IT'S THE POLICE!' She moved forward and shook his shoulder roughly. There was little response, maybe a muffled grunt, nothing more.

Gatti looked at her for an explanation, an enquiring look on his face. She stood up, waved her hands in desperation, shuffled back, sniffed disparagingly and turned to face him.

'He lost his job last Friday. He's been drinking ever since. Countless bottles of wine…whisky. He's been virtually out of it for days. We're going to have to move back to England. He's lost his job. There's nothing for us here…'

Gatti held up his hand to stop her protestation. 'Where was he Tuesday around lunch time, do you know?'

Her eyes blazed. She flicked her long permed hair back behind her ear. 'Of course I bloody know! He was here, there on that sofa…drinking. He hasn't moved. He's had nothing to eat for three days.'

Mauro casually turned away from the sofa, taking in the luxury of the light sage green décor as he walked back across the deep pile red carpet to the large oak window, framed by full-length gold and red embroidered curtains. He looked out into the street, showing no sign of recognising the unmarked pool car with two officers who in rotating shifts had been watching the house for the last few days. He knew that if he went to the back of the house, he'd see a similar vehicle.

Gatti paused for a moment. 'Can anyone else verify that?'

'Yes, of course. I held a house party, invited all our friends round to watch Peter demolish our wine cellar.' She turned to look at Mauro, now standing with his back to the window, notebook in hand.

He gave a sarcastic smile. 'I'll take that as a no then. How did he feel about Luigi Mussomelli, the man that fired him?'

Alex raised both her fists as if lifting barbells in frustration. 'Betrayed him, more like. He betrayed him. After all of the work and hours he put in, he just betrayed him. The man's a user.'

Gatti looked at her. She was in a state of high anxiety. 'You know Mussomelli is dead, don't you?'

Alex nodded her head from side to side. 'Yes! Yeah. Saw something about it on the TV. So what's that got to do with us?'

Mauro smiled and nodded. 'Well, someone killed him, and your Mr Dublin here has more than a good motive,' he said, gesturing at the prone, lightly breathing, somewhat odiferous figure draped like an old stained blanket across the sofa.

Alex looked from one to the other of her unwelcome house guests, shaking her head with disbelief at the sheer insanity of the statement. 'Look at him! Look at him! Do you honestly think that he's in a fit state to kill anyone except himself? Look at him.'

The night shoot had gone well. All the organising that Duke and Captain Steve had done was clear for everyone to see. It had been planned with military precision. Everyone knew their various roles, and there were no unforeseen delays.

After the main sub shot, they motored slowly back to the dock to break for a midnight meal. Duke stood down the sub actors and the stunt double and brought in Isabella from the second cabin cruiser that was hovering off on the right, next to the smoke maker boat, to get a few close atmospheric shots of her being rowed by the British sailor in her inflatable dingy, clutching her little suitcase radio.

Back on terra firma, Ben, the Second Assistant Director, dressed in his Royal Naval officer's uniform, had a wicked time with all of the Macchinisti saluting him at every available opportunity. They all shared a tremendous sense of fun, and if there were awards for piss-taking, they would all have won an Oscar. Ben took it all in good humour, not that he had any choice in the matter.

Grace, probably in order to warm up, had gone to the Make-up caravan with Isabella and Sophia. The Third Assistant Director, Beatrice, brought their food to them on a tray with silver cover lids over the plates to keep the food warm.

Adam sat down at the far end of the catering bus with Captain Steve. The two ex-pats had bonded well and now shared a healthy respect for each other's skills. Adam put down his Coke after a hearty swig.

'Thanks for your help, Steve, the tripod tie off and all, much appreciated.'

'Sokay, mate, you have to make anything like that actually part of the boat, you can't have it floating about, won't shoot straight if you do. Want to know what's happening for the rest of the night?'

Adam raised his eyebrows in an exaggerated enquiring manner as he forked down a spoonful of hot chicken and rice.

Steve smiled. It was apparent why they had made him an officer. He just had that military decision-making air about him.

'Well, as we speak, the sub is right now being pulled alongside the dock and tied off. From there, we will do the close-ups of the sub captain, and Isabella. With their "Good luck, take care" dialogue or whatever a sub captains say to a young spy who is probably going to be betrayed, tortured and dead within a few days. Then if we have time, we are going to try to fit in Isabella coming ashore in her dingy at the little beach down the road. That's a big ask though, as dawn will probably be upon us by then. We'll probably have to leave that for tomorrow.'

Adam smiled. 'Well, that's a lot more than is written on the call sheet.' He paused. Smiling, he said, 'Saw you chatting to Grace, Steve. Looked like you know each other well?'

Steve leant forward and lowered his voice to a confidential whisper. 'No, mate, just met her a time or two, was asking if she fancied a quick bunk up down in the engine room while all you airy-fairy types were waiting for the sun to go down.'

Adam bristled, his nostrils flared momentarily, and his lips tightened. Steve totally avoided any eye contact, spending more time looking down at his food and then forking in another mouthful, all the time showing much more interest in eating than watching Adam. He leant forward again, whispering quietly, confidentially.

'She turned me down, mate, turned me down, can you actually believe that? Said she now finally had someone in her life and was very happy. This Luigi business has really upset her, though, really upset her.'

Adam forced a smile and pretended to make light of the conversation, but his vice-like grip on his bottle of Coke said the opposite. He looked around to see if anyone nearby was listening to their conversation. He whispered as casually as he could, 'Did she say who her new someone in her life was? Any gossip on that?'

'No, mate, she didn't.' He lifted his fork up to his mouth, and suddenly looked Adam straight in the eye, holding him in his grey flint-like gaze. 'God, you're so easy to wind up, Adam! What we were actually talking about, apart from Luigi, was what a nutty business this filming lark is and what a diverse, talented bunch they all are. The thing that gave you away, old son, was the filthy, dirty look that you gave both of us when you saw us talking together.' Steve smiled and gave a little chuckle at Adam's now obvious discomfort. 'I am a very happily married man, Adam. I have a great deal of respect for Grace. I'd never proposition her, certainly not in the engine room of a stinking old trawler. We both deserve better than that. But you've given yourself away, mate. I have no idea what she actually thinks of you, never asked, none of my business, although I have more than a fair idea. However, you needn't worry, your secret adoration is safe with me. I'm very, very good at keeping secrets. Very good!'

Mauro stopped opposite the unmarked police car and lit a cigarette, nodding surreptitiously to the courting couple sat in the front seats. They really looked the part, and so they should; they'd worked undercover together as a male-female team for over three years, with a long list of arrests to their credit.

Paulo came up beside him, and they strolled together down the long street to where they'd parked the car.

'What did you make of that?'

Mauro smiled. 'Well, he was pissed or drugged for sure, but I get like that every Friday night. It doesn't take that long if your heart's really in it!'

Paulo smiled at his Sovrintendente's sense of humour, nodding. 'She's lost all respect for him, that's obvious. But he's our only real suspect. We deliberately left him alone so as not to tip him off. Put in a wiretap on his phone right from the outset, plus the surveillance, and there's been nothing. No phone calls to speak of, no callers to the house out of the ordinary.' He smirked. 'Apart from the wine delivery. No hit man turning up on the doorstep demanding payment.'

Mauro drew on his cigarette, puffing upwards so as to keep the distasteful smoke away from his superior. 'What do you want to do, sir?'

They both stepped to one side to let a young couple holding hands go past. Paulo waited until they were out of earshot and collected his thoughts for a couple of paces.

'Keep the phone tap in place, tell surveillance to immediately arrest them if they see any sign of them trying to leave with suitcases.' Mauro nodded. Paulo looked behind them to make sure that no one was following. 'And if she goes out alone, follow her, see where she goes, who she meets, and if she makes any phone calls. Apart from that, there's bugger all we can do until he sobers up – if he ever does. Check his financials both here and back in Britain if you can to see if he's made any large payments recently. Worries me though, two murders both connected to this bloody film.'

Dino Burgio sipped the last drop of red wine from his crystal glass, putting it gently down on the polished wooden table. He sniffed at the light smell of woodsmoke still lingering in the air and looked around his surroundings.

'I'm off to bed now. You all all right? All sorted?'

Lou lounged in a chair at the front window overlooking the drive and the silhouette of the Cadillac parked in the moonlight. He looked back. 'No, we're good here, boss.'

Dino nodded, more than a little worse for drink, his white shirt half undone. 'You okay, Max? Got your grab bag, case they come lookin'?' he said, addressing the grey-suited figure in the high-backed armchair, in front of the now flameless, charcoal, fire.

'Don't you worry, boss, first sign of blue light I'm out the back door, up the hill and gone.'

Dino nodded. 'I'll pay you all the way home, you know that. How long?'

Max smiled. 'Freight trains up to the north, Switzerland, flight to Ireland, max ten days, boss, about ten days.'

Dino nodded in satisfaction, looking at his house guest. Until he had signed him up three or four years ago, Max had been used by American intelligence to gather information and photograph sensitive documents. By breaking into small, inadequately protected embassies in South America, there was absolutely nothing remarkable about the man, not his height, not his voice, hair, or facial feature, even the way he dressed. He was the sort of person who just melted into a crowd – becoming a nobody virtually immediately. Part of that success was down to the fact that he kept his head down and never held eye contact, walking like someone with no self-confidence or esteem. Plus, he was also fluent in four languages, with a Swiss mother and a Hispanic father being the prominent influencers in that talent.

Dino nodded. 'Night, guys.' He wandered a little unsteadily out of the room and up the stairs.

Nobody spoke until they heard his final footfall on the last creaking step. Lou gave a casual look out of the window as the moon drifted behind a cloud and everything outside went black. He rose from his chair and came over to the sofa, sitting down next to Lank, a tall slim bear of a man who needed a shave.

Lank acknowledged his arrival by swinging his long, blue-jeaned legs to the right before looking over to Max.

'Why freight trains, Max?'

Max looked up, smiled and nodded, speaking quietly. 'It's the fastest way to travel around off the grid, no stations, no ticket barriers, no police, just get down to the sidings, none of 'em are fenced and just get on a train. They spend a deal of time travelling empty, and they go all around the country at forty-fifty miles an hour. It's the fastest way to get out of any city unchecked and unseen. Once you get to a main line wait near some signals, preferably at night, and just get on one heading in the direction that you want to go. Simple!'

Lou smiled. 'Back home in ten days?'

Max shook his head. 'Five, more like! But the extra dollars come in handy. Dino can afford it.'

Thursday 24th April

Gill looked down at the neatly typed sheet of white paper entitled 'Luigi Mussomelli Film Producer, PRESS RELEASE', reading every word, checking for mistakes. Veronique, over perfumed and over made-up, as usual, dressed in a pocketed pink suede jacket, sat opposite, clutching her shoulder bag. She checked the sideboard and grimaced slightly at the sight of only coffee cups.

'It wasn't easy, Gill. He never talked. I've created most of it through rumours that I heard and artistic licence. It's not very good actually.'

Gill looked up. 'There's one person who knows him better than anyone, and that's Duke. I think the bit about being a fishmonger in the early days in Sicily is accurate. And then setting up an extensive distribution network in the south before he came to Rome and got involved in the movie business, I'd heard that as well. I think that I'd rather send out a short press release that's affectionate and accurate than anything elaborate and concocted.'

Veronique nodded. 'D'accord, ma chérie, I agree, but where is Duke? Is he around?'

Gill looked across her desk as she leant forward and fingered the top of the unit call sheet beside her phone. 'He's on nights, back on the clock at five-thirty tonight in Civitavecchia. I am happy to give you his home phone number, but don't call him before four because he had a very long day yesterday with the sub pre-rig and needs a break.'

Veronique smiled. 'Okay, chérie, okay! I will keep my 'ands off 'im till four.'

Gill smiled. 'Thanks, Vee. I'll warn him you're after him.'

Veronique smiled a naughty girl grin. 'Oh, he knows that, chérie, has done for years.'

Gill smiled reproachfully and waved her right index finger.

Veronique smiled lecherously, sensually licking her top lip. 'Work in progress, chérie, work in progress.'

Joe from Art looked down the little internal phone list beside the phone and, lifting the receiver, dialled two numbers. After about forty seconds, just before he was about to give up and hang up, he realised that he had finally got through.

'Hi, is that Veniero, the editor?' Joe nodded as he received the confirmation. 'Veniero, how are you this morning? Good, good. It's Joe from Art here. The guy with the blue sunglasses…yeah.'

There was a slight pause as he waited for an acknowledgement.

'Veniero, just to tip you the wink, the sub sequence we shot last night, after rushes this afternoon, when Lasse has chosen the take that he wants to use, we are going to ask you to get the neg copied and sent to Lumaxfilm in London. We'll get them to create a graded print and send it to AP films in Slough. They will then be able to match all of the sub model work they've got to do with the live-action that we shot last night. I, for my part, will send them all the copies of my construction drawings, and all of the stills that were taken as well. Is that okay with you?' There was a pause. He nodded as he heard the confirmation reply and finished with, 'Thanks, Veniero, Thanks!'

Gently putting the receiver down, he looked at his daybook and put a fine blue biro line across the first of many things on his to-do list.

Adam tried to have a lie-in, but his body clock pushed him out of bed at around ten-fifteen, so he decided to do some laundry and get rid of the smell of fish that was coming from the pile of clothes on the chair by the window.

He made his way down to reception and without even being asked, the concierge, Nello, on seeing him approach with his bursting pillowcase, reached under the counter and with a smile presented him with two small boxes of washing powder. He then, from the keyboard, gave him a key with a long piece of greyish ribbon attached, in order to let himself into the little basement laundry room.

Eleven o'clock saw Adam sitting on his little chair in the corridor, just watching his clothes clunking round behind the scratched circular window. Two working girls, one of them dressed as a schoolgirl in a white shirt and tie together with a brown leather satchel, came down the corridor giggling and laughing. But they virtually ignored him as they clacked by in their high heels, leaving him with the smell of cheap perfume and a view of their curvy retreating backsides wrapped in micro short skirts. He smiled to himself. Stereo! Someone had an enjoyable party!

Adam returned to his room just after twelve and decided to give Grace a call. She picked up reasonably quickly, saying, 'Pronto', which took Adam a little by surprise because he always thought of her as English and had not really got his head around her being half English and half Italian. The conversation was a little laboured. She was still very upset about Luigi. However, she did freely admit that she missed him and apologised for being so abrupt the previous evening.

As the conversation wore on, it became very apparent that Adam did not do small talk. Though he was like his father, who could kick-start from zero a conversation with absolutely anyone, he found it awkward chatting on the phone just for the sake of it. There were things that he wanted to say, but he was definitely a face-to-face sort of person so after about fifteen minutes once they'd arranged to meet up on the Saturday, they blew each other kisses and ended the call. Adam grimaced as he put the phone down, realising that he had shortcomings and that Grace was now aware of one of them.

Virtually every available police and and carabinieri asset on duty that night had converged in a mass of screaming sirens and blue lights to the little street just off the Piazza San Calisto. The three red fire engines of the Vigili del Fuoco had beaten them all to it. Black-clad fire crews were already starting to put up plastic barrier tape and run out a hose to extinguish a small fire burning in the blown-in window display of a small haberdashery.

A little further down the road, the still form of an Indian-dressed mannequin lay inert and twisted on the pavement together with her fibre-glass companion, a lightly tanned, North African version of Twiggy, both now unceremoniously partially clothed and covered in small pieces of grey dust, masonry and broken glass.

The remains of what had once been a car were now just a few pieces of blackened metal that all pointed skywards, sitting on a two-feet-deep crater, blasted into the cobbles. The front door frame of the haberdashery shop had filmy red blood like smears running down it. The two cars on either side of the crater car were little more than scrap, charred, burned and windowless.

They were now layered in a light pinkish red mist. A white van lay on its side in the middle of the road, looking like it had been side-swiped by a flaming demolition breaking ball, its black oily underside seeing direct sunlight for the first time. There appeared to be a pool of fluid leaking onto the roadway from its distended fuel tank. The whole area was covered in tiny shapeless shards of thin blackened metal and small pieces of reddy brown material that could have been body parts or car upholstery.

Onlookers, though very curious, kept their distance. Little groups started to gather in ones and twos as people dribbled nervously out of the nearby shops and apartments. A photographer with a heavy equipment shoulder bag labelled PRESS pushed his way through them and started taking pictures as frantically as he could. A tall carabinieri, erect black boots gleaming, walked quickly up to him and grabbed hold of the end of the lens, pulling it forcibly and unceremoniously downwards.

Looking him hard in the eyes from beneath his glossy peaked hat, he hissed through clenched teeth, 'Show some respect! People have died here. Show respect!'

Sylvania was very flushed, as she always was after her sessions with Toro. That was the whole idea. The cascading shower water streamed over them as they lathered each other all over with Badedas. Toro had been in good form that morning. The elfin-like Nichola, though being instructed to watch for an hour, was not asked to join in and after a while was sent back to the front office and told to change out of her white overall and continue with her secretarial duties. That secretly pleased her because things could get a bit rough in the studio sometimes when Sylvania and Toro were in full flow.

Sylvania turned off the shower and walked back into the small dressing room, taking a towel off the warm radiator and energetically towel-drying her hair. Toro, as usual, was left to pick up his own towel. Mentally these sessions always ended for her when she turned the shower off. After that, the quicker Toro could dress and leave, the better. He was by this time surplus to her requirements.

He looked at her back, the light, long fingernail scratches running randomly all over now starting to fade.

'I did you a favour early this morning.'

She turned both hands aggressively, rubbing her hair. If it was intended as some sort of sexual innuendo, she did not pick up on it, probably because she did not possess a sense of humour and was not renowned for her witty repartee.

'Oh! Really? What did you do?'

Toro leered as he dried his chest and armpits. 'I took out the Wardrobe man Villabianco at his shop.'

Sylvania stared at him in astonishment. 'WHAT? YOU DID WHAT?'

Toro smirked. 'In true Bratina style, just like Dad, you were always going on about how you wish someone would get rid of him, so I did it. Just like the house girl Tavazzi, never felt a thing.'

She stopped rubbing her hair and faced squarely up to him. 'What? What have you done?'

'Just a bit of C4 under his car, clean as a whistle.'

'What! You used plastic explosives under a car in Rome? Are you mad? Did anyone see you do it?'

'Naw! The old stopped to do the shoelace trick very early in the morning, pushed the stuff under the car and used Dad's old invention of the plasticine dog pooh switch under the back tyre. Job done. Twenty seconds, no crawling around messing with starter motors or ignition switches.'

Sylvania's nostrils flared and her lips thinned. 'I didn't ask you to do that!'

Toro smiled, his cocky smirk. 'Well, be careful what you wish for. You've been going on about how you wanted him out of the way for months, and the bonus for Tavazzi came in useful.'

Sylvania pursed her lips thoughtfully for a second or two, then smiled. 'Well, if you have been successful, well done. Well done! But this is going to cause waves, lots of waves. You may have created a bigger problem than you've solved.' She half closed her eyes and tilted her head to one side. Through a tight mouth, she softly articulated, very slowly and very deliberately, 'But never ever do anything unless my father or I specifically ask. Your dad, Renzo, has been the family enforcer for years. He may not be happy to know that his little boy is starting to encroach on his empire. He never goes off-piste.'

Toro smiled, his chauvinistic ego now in full swing. He failed to take in the tone or significance of what she was saying. 'He doesn't know. I just went down to his store in the catacomb and took what I wanted. He hasn't a clue what's down there anyway. He doesn't exactly do a stocktake every month.'

In the front office, Nichola, still slightly flushed and aroused after having watched the acrobatic sexual antics of her boss, listened open-mouthed, realising the implications of what she was hearing, and came up with the only solution she could think of at the time. She slowly turned up the office radio in the hope that its noise would be perceived to dominate the room.

Jose had witnessed lots of explosions on film sets over the years, a few gallons of petrol, a huge whoof of bright yellow flame and a few bits of painted polystyrene and fullers earth flying toward the camera. Very visually believable, and cheap and easy to repeat for multiple takes, but this was different. It had more force than a lightning bolt. The whole building shook momentarily. The noise was a frighteningly crisp, tight, energetic, deafening boom followed by the sound of falling debris and metal sliding on the roadway. Then total silence. Both windows to the shop were suddenly cracked and covered in dust but remained intact. The two mannequins were nowhere to be seen.

Jose stood transfixed for about thirty seconds, waiting to see if there was going to be a second explosion. He edged tentatively towards the window beside the door and looked down the road. What he saw made him retch uncontrollably. The roadway just down the street to the left where he had parked his car the previous evening was now a twisted mass of black seared steaming metal. He was beside himself. He had not even three minutes ago lovingly handed Vinincio his car keys so that he could drive across town to pick up some wine for the long weekend. He rushed towards the door, grabbing frantically at the handle. But something stopped him. No one could live through that, no one, and it was no accident. That was his car, in his usual parking space. He was the target, not Vinincio.

He backed away into the depth of the shop, totally oblivious to the fact he was treading on broken glass ornaments that had fallen from the display shelves, and sat down in a cloth-draped chair. He sobbed uncontrollably, head in hands for about three or four minutes until the sound of screaming sirens started to fill the air and the flicker of blue strobe lights flashed in through the windows and across the ceiling, giving the room the appearance of some bizarre daytime discotheque, which caused the various mannequins to flicker and pulse, giving them an almost animated appearance.

Jose looked down at his shirt, which stank of the vomit of his breakfast. He had to run, disappear. He was to all intents and purposes now a dead man walking. The attempt on his life had failed, and he knew that they would try again and again if necessary until they succeeded. He carefully eased his odiferous shirt out of his trousers only to discover that he had stained them as well. He slowly stood up and, with both hands held out to the front, created a cotton-like scoop to prevent even more spillage. He walked tremulously upstairs. Outside even more arriving sirens were echoing off the narrow street walls.

A few minutes later saw him anxiously locking the front doors from the inside, before unobtrusively leaving through the small back door. Beneath a black French beret, he wore the biggest pair of sunglasses that he had snatched from a display in the shop to go with his brown Balmain jacket. Unmatching leather holdalls, one in each hand, completed the image of a French tourist.

A couple of minutes later, the Vigili del Fuoco knocked urgently and repeatedly on his front door. Getting no response, they chalk-marked a large blue X on the pavement to signify that the property was unoccupied.

Jose walked north towards the Piazza di San Egidio for about three minutes, at every opportunity turning to look behind him before eventually a free taxi appeared. He instructed the driver to take him to the main railway station, Termini in the Pizza di Cinquecento. There he went into the toilets and changed his jacket, hat and sunglasses to something darker, more Germanic. He made a phone call and left by the north exit, and took a taxi to a residential street in the north of the city just down from Parioli. As he paid the taxi and walked up to the front door, it opened in front of him and the familiar figure of Duke appeared.

'You sounded upset, Jose. What's up? Come in! Come in!'

Jose looked nervously around up and down the street, saying nothing until the taxi had turned the corner and disappeared. 'Oh, Duke, I'm in a right old state. They tried to kill me, blew up my car. I need somewhere to hide for a couple of days so I can sort myself out.'

Duke frowned in disbelief. 'You mean that explosion that I just heard 'bout on the radio was your car being blown up?'

Jose started to retch again, but this time he pulled a large handkerchief from his pocket and held it up to his mouth.

The main incident room on the third floor of the police headquarters was about the size of a tennis court, with mature, polished oak floors and large windows all down the side that overlooked the street. About fourteen or so desks of various style and qualities were dotted around, together with corresponding pairs of chairs. Nearly all had telephones, some were littered with folders. Grey and brown steel filing cabinets covered the left wall up to eye level. The whole room smelt of cigarette smoke, fresh sweat and old cardboard files mixed with a faint tinge of wax polish. About fifteen people had gathered, most of them covered in silver braid, which meant they all had to be saluted.

Christina's, the Agente di Polizia, elbow was slightly aching from having to show so much respect in such a short time. Now, as instructed, she was sitting in front of the two departmental telex machines. The room occupants were half-listening to the public relations 'suit' from the top floor who was sounding off about how important it was to be seen by the public to have a firm grip on the situation.

Christina's boss, the Primo Dirigente, dignified by his immaculate uniform, was a tall man, with short, black hair, greying at the temples, a large hooked nose and rosy cheeks. He looked at Christina and made an espresso drinking motion with his right hand, up to his lips, then nodded affirmatively. She stood up, and Mauro Sofri, without being asked, walked forward and sat down to continue watching the telex machines.

As the pontificating public relations expert momentarily paused his droning, the Dirigente, sensing his opportunity, coughed. 'Refreshments, gentlemen, refreshments! Christina here will take your orders. Just tell her what you want.'

Christina smiled and walked up to the Colonnello of Carabinieri who ordered an orange juice, the head of the Bomb Squad, a hot chocolate, the counter-terrorism chief, an espresso, the Dirigente himself, an espresso, Alberto Consalvo a latte, Ispettore Paulo Gatti an espresso, the public relations suit and his assistant, a mocha and an espresso. She continued around the room, ending with Mauro, another espresso. As she left the room, the Dirigente made a mental note that she had taken around fifteen orders for drinks and made no notes, written nothing down.

The telex machine started to chatter. Everyone's attention now turned to Mauro, who, once the machine beeped to denote the fact that it was finished, tore off the paper sheet and quickly walked over with it to his superior, the Dirigente. The Colonnello of Carabinieri, putting his glasses on, moved somewhat purposefully to stand behind him and read over his shoulder.

There was silence for a second, just the odd beep of traffic horns from the street below.

The Dirigente looked around to ensure that everyone was listening. 'It's the preliminary report from the Vigili del Fuoco. Three dead, the vehicle driver obviously, plus two passers-by, a six-year-old girl and her mother who were out shopping. The explosive used, believed to be C4, was triggered by a switch under the rear tyre covered in brown plasticine. The owner of the car is a Jose Villabianco, his monogrammed keys were in the ignition. He owned the shop down the road and used to park in the same spot all the time. His premises are locked up, and there's no sign of him. The vehicle driver was completely vapourised, and authentic identity will take some time to establish. So my thoughts are that until we have more information, we assume that the driver is Villabianco. We make enquiries into his personal life, his business life, conduct house-to-house to get every available piece of information. We get court orders to enter his home if he has one, his shop and anywhere that he worked, leave no stone unturned. Within forty-eight hours, we need to know everything that we can. We need to find out who hated him enough or who he had upset enough to want to blow him to smithereens along with a mother and her child. With regards to the press, I think that my learned friend here will agree that it is in our best interest to say that we have no idea who the principal victim is at this moment in time.'

The 'suit' nodded obsequiously, then nodded again to his assistant to make notes.

The Dirigente turned to the Colonnello of Carabinieri, still gently breathing garlic at him over his left shoulder. 'You happy with that?'

The blue-uniformed, short-haired, bespectacled Colonnello nodded. 'This is business. We all know that. Something tells me to clear the morgues and prepare for a lot more trade. There's something going on here, and I don't like the smell of it, not one bit.'

Gill did not often have difficult conversations, phone or otherwise, with her husband, for it was very unusual for him not to be totally forthcoming.

'What are you trying to say, Alberto? What are you trying to say? I feel confused. You're saying that Jose's car has been blown up and that there's a possibility that he may not be coming in to work, but you can't tell me anything. Is that right? Okay, okay! I think I understand you now. This is another one of those conversations that never took place. And if Jose doesn't turn up for work this evening, I should maybe think about getting someone to stand in for him, but I never heard anything from you. I think I'm with it now. What's happened, Alberto? His car blown up? What's happened? Is he okay? Oh! Okay. You don't know, can't say anything, I get it. Shit, Alberto, what's going on here? I'm starting to get frightened. No, I'm not going to leave the office, promise. I'll wait for you to pick me up. I'm staying on till eight tonight. It's the night shoot. Love you.'

Adam felt that the mood on set that evening was varied in the extreme. There was a sense of anticipation because parked up next to the catering caravan, painted in German military dark grey, was a World War II iron cross marked 'Kubel Wagen', which resembled a heavy-looking, military jeep, and a military motorbike with its side car also from the same period. Half a dozen grey-green German soldiers sat off to one side, waiting for their marching orders and a chance to get at the catering table once the crew had eaten.

Lasse, Sven and Jan were all on a high because of the rushes they had viewed earlier. The moment Jan saw Adam, he rushed up to him, coffee in hand.

'Adam, hi! You should have come to rushes this afternoon, bloody fantastic. That sub sequence last night was bloody amazing, bloody amazing! I tell you something, Adam, learn as much from Sven as you possibly can. The man is a genius. It was so realistic, unbelievably atmospheric, the sub dropping off a spy at night. The way he lit the water with dirty, greeny creamy moonlight, I don't know how he did it, but find out, Adam, find out as I'd like to know too.'

All of that contrasted with the fact that the whole crew to get to the location had all been funnelled through an armed police roadblock further back up the road, something that had certainly got all of the tongues wagging. The gossip was that the Production Office had paid for them, but it was never confirmed.

Pia was now sewing a regimental shoulder badge onto one of the German soldier extras, assisted by an old grey-haired Wardrobe man who had been involved with the dressing of all of the considerable number of extras for the immigration hall scenes earlier in the week. There was no friendly wave or blown kiss from Jose. He was nowhere to be seen.

Captain Steve drew up in his car and took six rifles out of the boot, which he handed to the six grey-green uniformed Waffen SS, Hermann Göring Division soldiers, all of whom were chattering away in high-speed Italian, which seemed quite bizarre. Steve, as usual, was meticulous. He had a clipboard and made sure that he got each of the extras to sign and print their name before they were allowed even to touch their allocated weapon. He was cheery, as always. 'Different hat tonight, Adam! Different hat, armourer!'

Isabella made a point of chatting to Adam by the catering table, which surprised Adam because usually, the la-de-das don't bother too much with the lower ranks. Though she had always been friendly and jokey, this evening she was a little more so, which surprised him slightly. However, being chatted to by such a beautiful woman is always good for one's ego.

The single thing that Adam felt was wrong on set was an underlying sense of unease. It was quieter than it usually was. It could have been the armed police security roadblock that was spooking everyone, but Duke was definitely not his usual self. He kept looking around, and as the late afternoon turned into night he became more uneasy, constantly looking around as if trying to look into the surrounding darkness. Something was worrying him. Adam sensed that he did not feel secure or safe, which was totally out of character for him. After all, it was his set.

Grace sensed the same atmosphere as Adam and did everything she could to crack a joke and lighten the mood. She even came over to Adam and gate-crashed his conversation. In a perfect cockney accent, she joked, ‘Watch him darlin’, watch ’im! These bloody English, you know wot they’re like! Only ever after one fing!’

Everyone within earshot who could understand English fell about laughing, leaving Adam a little red-faced and Isabella giggling like a schoolgirl.

The scene of Isabella coming ashore in the little rubber dingy was followed by skulking shots of her hiding behind trees and low walls to stay out of sight of the German military patrols chugging up and down the little beach side lanes in their Kubel Wagen and their motorbike and sidecar.

Adam now started to pay a lot more attention to how Sven did things and stored away where he positioned his lights and the kind of shadows that he wanted to create. As an old camera operator had once said to him years ago, ‘Any fool can light day interior, it’s night work that sorts the men from the boys’, a sentiment Adam was in total agreement with.

Night scenes don’t have bird song, and the feathered community had a job to do every single day to welcome the rising sun coming up from behind the trees. As they started to shoot the last scene, their joyous dawn chorus was not received well by the Sound department, who shouted and clapped to shut them up, to little avail. If anything, it made them sing louder. The departmental moaning and muttering really only stopped when Duke finally called 'WRAP' off in the distance. Adam could hear Captain Steve reading the riot act in very emphatic fluent Italian to one of the soldier extras, who had somehow managed to get mud jammed up the barrel of his loaned rifle.

Adam walked over to Grace's little table to give her the lens settings for the final scene. She looked up at him, and for the first time on set, she gave him an honest look of affection. But it was still quite gloomy, and there was no one else nearby.

'Five ish, tomorrow, montee pooch eee arno for two? Thanks, Adam, for being so understanding I'll try to be a little more welcoming than the last time. You enjoy your day off, get some rest and have a shave before you come. I don't like scratchy beardy men.'

Angelina, Duke's wife, had put Jose into her son Franco's room. She then tried watching TV, which did nothing for her disturbed state of mind. Picking up a book and trying to read didn't help either, and after a while, she decided that she was too wound up and took a sleeping tablet, something she very rarely did. The expiry date on the prescription box of three years ago reinforced the fact.

Jose didn't sleep at all. He just propped himself up on the bed with a couple of pillows and started reading Vinincio's ornate, leather-bound, handwritten diary, which went back over five years. Sometimes it was very detailed, sometimes not so, but its purpose was clear: it was a get-out-of-jail card for him if it all went pear-shaped and his father and sister were arrested. It was evident from the tone of the diary that he was not an enthusiastic participant, merely a witness, and that is what he had done, witnessed, then written down everything that he had seen and heard. The entries became more and more detailed over the last year or so since the start of his relationship with Jose. What he read made Jose's hands shake in sheer unadulterated fear.

Every word detailed how Vinincio's family and rent-free neighbours operated totally outside the rules of civilised society. They had no moral code at all. It made chilling reading. It must have been absolutely horrendous for Vinincio living under the same roof as people who could literally order a kill at the drop of a hat, almost on a whim, like crushing a fly. The recent murder of the house agent, Donna Tavazzi, was mentioned. It would seem that Sylvania had taken a phone call and seen an opportunity. Within a couple of minutes she had sent Toro round to her office to kill her. The fact that her death would possibly, just possibly, implicate Dino Burgio, or at least the ensuing police interest, would make him run back to Hollywood.

Sylvania wanted Burgio out of the way, out of Rome. He was far too smart. In her reasoning, it was worth sending Toro to kill her, a bit of a gamble, but heh, ho! nothing to lose!

Friday 25th April

Como Trani had been given the all-clear by the Production Office. The early morning found him with the two welders methodically removing all of the recently fitted brackets and lugs off the petrol tanker so that it could be dropped back onto the lorry chassis and repainted. He'd had a few beers the night before and his head ached a bit, but Production had certainly treated him well and made him feel like a bit of a hero. However, like many people who briefly encounter the magic of the film business, he now felt a powerful sense of anti-climax.

Working through the night, at sea, with massive lights on boats and a codded-up sub conning tower, launching an actor into a rubber dingy was not something that you forget quickly. But now the fun was over. A couple more days and then back home to the north to try fixing up the old sub and driving school kids around again.

Usually, if Jose were overnighting after a party, Duke would wake him up by rattling a wooden spoon around a saucepan or shouting 'FIRE!'. But this morning, he was not feeling that energetic, so having gone virtually twenty hours without sleep, he gently knocked on his door. There was no response, so he knocked again a bit louder. Eventually, there was a snorted response and the sound of someone moving about.

Duke stood back as the door opened, and a dishevelled Jose, still wearing the clothes he arrived in, appeared, looking like he had slept in the street somewhere. Creased would be a good description; his clothes and facial expression all totally out of kilter with the immaculately groomed image that usually paraded around on set and in the studio.

Duke nodded a welcome. 'Jose, I have not had a lot of sleep lately, but if it's okay with you, I'll crash for a few hours, and when I'm up, we'll talk. And then we'll see what can be done to help you. In the meantime, Angelina will fix you up with breakfast if you're up to it. That okay?'

Jose tried to straighten his crumpled top, to little effect. 'Yes, yeah! That's fine, thanks. I'll tidy myself up, and we'll talk later. Thanks, Duke. I'm not sure I'm going to survive this.'

Duke held up his hand and smiled reassuringly. 'Calm, Jose, calm! We'll talk later. There is always a solution.'

Beatrice Mosena had managed to grab a few hours' kip, but the two-night shoot had thrown her body clock entirely out of kilter, and so being unable to sleep, she decided to work through the list of tasks that Duke had given her to do over the long weekend.

One of the most pressing was to confirm that the fish gutting hand artist down at the market would be available the coming week to be filmed at the studio. She could simply have phoned. But she had been asked to check that the good lady's arms, hands and nails were still in good condition and not covered in cuts, bruises or blackened nails, or worse, in a cast.

As Beatrice weaved her way gently through the traffic, she reflected on the fact that her boss, the lovely Duke, was a planner and co-ordinator with an almost unparalleled skill set. He really did the detail and always did his 'what ifs', leaving nothing to chance. Sending her down to the market was a case in point. Take nothing for granted. She just hoped that one day she would be as good and respected as him.

Ah! Slower moving traffic and the smell of cheap plastic toys, hanging red meat and dead poultry. She must be nearly there.

The Primo Dirigente leant forward, looking up from his large, lined notepad. 'We don't seem to be getting very far with any of these cases. Donna Tavazzi, no one saw anything; Luigi Mussomelli, no one saw anything; and now the bloody bomb blast, no one saw anything. I am getting a great deal of crap from upstairs. The common denominator running through all of this is the bloody film. But no one ever sees anything. You need to help me here, gentlemen, or we will all be back directing traffic before very long.'

Alberto Consalvo nodded at Paulo Gatti, requesting permission to speak. Paulo nodded his assent. Alberto lifted his head.

'I'm not directly involved in this case, sir, due to a conflict of interest. As you are aware, I'm married to the film's Production Manager. I'm just an observer. But I have an opinion: film people generally are not violent. They are in the main artistically creative, and that is how their little minds work. But outside of the actual production, off the set, vast sums of money are involved, and where there is money there is mayhem. I would be looking to Luciano Scordia, Peter Dublin, Dino Burgio because they are all involved in the money side of the business. It's not going to be some Macchinista or extra who had a disagreement or row. It's got to be at a higher level where the real money is. Access to C4 explosive is usually connected to break-ins at quarries where they store the stuff, and we've checked there have been no recent reports within a hundred miles, so who holds a load of C4 for months on end, just in case?'

Paulo Gatti raised his index finger. 'Sir, I agree with Alberto. I think that we should re-interview Dino Burgio, bring in Peter Dublin and book a consultation with Luciano Scordia and his six lawyers and see where all of that takes us.'

The Dirigente snorted. 'Well, good luck with Luciano Scordia, but I agree, he's a person of interest and has got to be interviewed. How we actually achieve that, I leave up to you talented gentlemen, and, Alberto, conflicting personal interest aside, I want you to work more closely with Paulo on this. You know more about the film business than all of us put together. I'd also like Christina to be plain-clothed and on the team with Mauro from now on. I believe that the lady has a phenomenal mind, and that is what we need right now, a collection of exceptional minds if we are to get anywhere. By the way, what were the findings on the Wardrobe man's shop?'

Paulo grimaced. 'No sign of him. We found out that he owns a small stone house in the woods up above Lake Como, no phone, no running water. No car or van rented in his name. So we are left with buses, trains or a friend or taxi. It still looks, though, like it was him that was blown up, but as to why we have no idea. He had a male friend who stayed there occasionally, but no one knows who he is, and no one has come forward. He was a dichotomy, a very flamboyant but very private character. He always kept his personal life private. We'll re-examine the shop to see what else we can find. I'll get a sketch artist to chat to neighbours to attempt to draw up a picture of his elusive friend if we can.'

The Primo Dirigente nodded. 'Okay, gentlemen, thank you all. Just remember what it's like to be standing in the same place in five-hour shifts directing traffic six days a week! Good luck.'

Angelina had deliberately dressed for the outdoors, grabbed her gardening gloves and secateurs, and gone out into the garden to prune something. She was trying her best to keep out of the unpleasant business that was now going on around the kitchen table between her husband and the dishevelled, frightened Jose.

Duke looked up from the leather-bound diary on the breakfast table, tapped it and looked at his friend. 'If they knew that we had this, or even suspected, our life expectancy could be measured in minutes.'

Jose shuffled uncomfortably. 'Can we give it to the police, let them deal with it?'

Duke smiled a tight-lipped smile. 'No, Jose, first sign of trouble, a siren or blue light, and they all disappear down into the catacombs, and from there, whoever they are, they pop out and wreak havoc to create silence or revenge with complete impunity. The prosecution service and the police department are full of Scordia informers. Fear talks, money talks. It doesn't have to be a Chief of Police. It could be a cleaner or an Agente di Polizia. Anyone who is near the investigation could flip open a file, listen, overhear and simply phone through what they've heard, and actually, Jose, I'm not prepared to spend the rest of my life looking over my shoulder. I've already had to send my son away to the other side of the world to keep him alive, and I want him back. I'm going to need some time to think about all of this, and then I'm going to probably talk to a few people, take a drive or two, but first, if I may, I'd like to sit down and spend the rest of the morning reading this diary.'

Jose nodded, his face giving away the fact that he was more than a little ashamed that he was contributing so little to the situation. 'Of course, of course. What do you want me to do?'

Duke smiled, tilted his head down and looked at him affectionately through his eyebrows. 'The problem that we will have, old friend, is bringing you back from the dead, back into society. I've been thinking that the best rue is for you to suffer from memory loss. Are you happy with that?'

Jose looked up and gave a half-smile. 'Yeah! Memory loss, good idea, whatever you think is best.'

Duke smiled. 'In order for that to work, my friend, you are not to shave, wash, or change your clothes, clean under your nails or even cut your nails. You need to build up an aroma. Over the next few days, you need to build up a stink, and then you may well be believed.'

Jose shook his head in resignation. 'Okay, okay, got it. Even my underpants?'

Duke leant forward, putting his face half a metre from his friend's. 'Particularly your underpants, they need to become stiff! But like it or not, Angelina and I have you as a house guest. So it would be nice if you cook us one of your fabulous lunches with whatever we've got in the freezer and fridge. We intend to take full advantage of your culinary skills. Angelina will be only too happy to come in from the garden when the gong goes and sit down to a prepared meal.'

'You know, Duke, you really are a true friend. I really appreciate it. I'll happily cook. But what are you going to do?'

'Get you a pair of rubber gloves and pinafore and then I'm going somewhere quiet to sit down and read the diary from cover to cover. Then I'm going to make some plans to make sure that everyone involved has a watertight alibi.'

Adam had a lie-in for as long as he could until finally eleven o'clock saw him out in the sunshine. He got a friendly wave from the waiter at his favourite trattoria across the square before he decided to turn to the south, put the sun over his left shoulder and wander down to the Fontana di Trevi.

Rome never failed to amaze him with all of the histories all those beautiful buildings crammed into a tiny area. The Fontana di Trevi was a lovely place to sit, even for just a few minutes. To watch couples and families from all over the world throw coins over their shoulder and then giggle afterwards. It made Adam acutely aware that he was on his own for nearly all of the time when he was not working. The money more than compensated, but to do the job, you had to be a person who was very self-sufficient, very at ease with just their own company, that was for sure.

The thought of lunch down in Trastevere began to appeal, and feeling not for the first time a bit of a 'Billy No-Mates', he wandered slowly down towards the Tiber and across the Ponto Garibaldi.

It crossed his mind that Jose's little shop was just a few minutes away, and having not seen him for a couple of days, he thought that a bit of 'Ciao, bello' banter would not go amiss. So he gently strolled towards the now familiar Piazza San Calisto and turned the corner into Jose's street.

What he saw more than somewhat surprised him. Half of the street was like a war zone. Jose's shop was all shut up. His two partly clothed mannequins lay immodestly head to toe on the pavement in front of his door. All of the windows were cracked and covered in soot and dust. Further down the road outside a blown-in and badly burned shopfront was a large white tent. Across the street, from shopfront to shopfront, ran plastic police ribbons, backed up by about half a dozen police and carabinieri.

On the other side of the tent was yet another police line with three black-capped uniformed officers. Adam was stunned. Outside of the cordon lines, up the street and down the street in true Italian style, normal life was continuing. People were going about their daily business, walking about, shopping, café life blossomed. As the habitual patrons sat down to read their papers, drink espresso and gossip, Adam retraced his steps a dozen or so metres and sat down outside a small trattoria so that he could take in the whole scene.

Eventually, the short, round-faced, white-aproned waiter appeared, with a welcoming nod and a smile.

Adam looked up at him. 'What happened here?'

The waiter's expression turned to one of distaste. It was not a question he wanted to answer. 'Bomba!'

Adam shook his head in disbelief. 'A bomb? Bloody hell! And Jose? What about Jose, do you know?'

The waiter grimaced again, embarrassed, getting a little impatient, anxious to take his order. 'Jose? Si! E morto, dead, bomba!'

Ispettore Paulo Gatti should not have expected anything less from Signor Luciano Scordia. He was, of course, like any law-abiding citizen, only too glad to help the wonderful Rome police force with any enquiries. That very day, he would be dining in a private suite right in the centre of town at the St Regis Hotel.

'Does twelve-thirty suit?'

Across the other side of town. Alberto Consalvo, accompanied by Agente di Polizia Christina, rapped hard on Peter Dublin's front door.

Alex answered. She looked haggard, to say the least. A pained resigned expression came over her lined face when the callers identified themselves. She had just a trace of lipstick mixed in with the white saliva corners of her mouth. Her hair looked greasy and unwashed. Her green dress was creased and dishevelled as if she had slept in it.

'He's not here. You've just missed him. They've taken him to hospital.'

She was obviously very weary and appeared to be hanging on to the door for support. She turned and walked, shoulders hunched, back into the hall. They followed her for a few paces until she stopped and then turned back towards them.

'He's gone to hospital. I couldn't rouse him. He's pretty sick. Your people outside called an ambulance for me, and they've gone with him.'

Alberto slowly raised his right index finger. 'What people outside?'

Christina gently pushed the door closed.

'Oh! Don't patronise me! The two little rozzers in the black Fiat, they've been watching since Tuesday. I'm not bloody stupid. They stand out a mile. I thought that if they phoned, at least I'd get an ambulance here today instead of having to wait till the bloody weekend.'

Alberto sucked in his cheeks. 'That's very uncharitable. Response times here are excellent, very good in fact—'

‘Oh, yeah, right! Anyway, I’m not really in the mood to chat right now, so if you’ve got nothing more to say, I’d appreciate it if you’d shove off.’

Alberto nodded and paused for a moment before turning and nodding to Christina to open the door. ‘Mrs Dublin, I am sorry to hear that your husband is so unwell, but he remains a person of interest in our enquiries, and therefore we have to look into every aspect of the case. I bid you farewell but know that we will have to meet again soon. Thank you.’

Christina stepped through the door onto the front step, waiting for her superior to join her. The loud slam of the door behind them made them wince.

Alberto turned to Christina. ‘My wife never taught me “shove off” and “rozzers”. Might be an idea to look them up when we get back to the station.’

Adam was more than upset to hear that the vivacious Jose had died in a bomb blast. He was sure that no one on the film set was aware of this. The news sent a chill through him. Why? Why? He was harmless enough. It put a sour taste in his mouth, and for that reason, he didn’t spend long at the little café. He found the whole scene more than a bit depressing, with the police cordon and plastic tape right across the road, people walking by and averting their eyes from the scene, as if trying to pretend there was nothing there, a bit like seeing dog mess on the pavement.

He knew that Grace would prepare some kind of a meal for later, so he decided to change streets and wander about until he found a likely little trattoria that could provide a good place to people-watch and a light lunch.

Fifteen minutes later found him sitting down at a table that gave him a view of the Via Della Luce and an ice-cold Coke in his hand; exactly what the doctor ordered.

During his short stay, Adam had become addicted to Spaghetti alla Carbonara, allegedly a Roman dish eaten by charcoal burners, of long ago. Well, that's what the menu said, and Adam went for it because that's what he always did, but the vicious death of Jose churned his guts, and he was only able to eat half of it.

Gill ticked off the line in her day book to order for the Sunday morning Production meeting in the office next door coffee, biscuits and orange juice from the catering manager Fausto. She was now looking down at the five call sheets for the following week spread out on her desk. They were not yet typed, still in rough form, pencil and biro. The final details would be finalised on the Sunday.

Then like a genie in a puff of pantomime smoke, Veronique suddenly appeared in the room in a dark purple silk blouse which matched her hip-hugging, short leather skirt and a gold-plated string necklace of small sparkly buttons. As her shoulder bag donked onto the floor, she immediately started to sit down. No polite door knock, or 'Permesso'.

'Bonjour, chérie, 'ow are you?'

Gill looked across at the larger-than-life character and just smiled and shook her head. 'Don't you ever knock, Vee?'

'No, chérie, why?'

Gill shook her head again. 'Anyway, I'm glad you've popped in. I need your advice…'

Veronique placed her hands on her thighs and nodded. 'Go ahead, chérie, I am full of wisdom, you know that!'

Gill couldn't resist another smile. 'We have the English actors, Marcus Pomeroy, Belinda Sharp and chatterbox Anita, staying in the same hotel. And it would seem that Belinda, last night, was on her own in the bar having a night cap, and Marcus staggered in having had more than a few drinks and started mauling her.'

Veronique frowned for a second. 'Is he the one with the shiny hair?'

Gill grimaced. 'Yes, Brylcreem, lots of it!'

Veronique twisted her top lip in a curl, as only the French can do. 'Oh! Nasty, slippeee in all the wrong places. Je prefer my men straight off the rugby field.'

'Thank you for that, Vee! Anyway, it would seem that he got hold of her room number and began knocking on her door and generally giving her a very hard time. She wants us to change her hotel. She wants to get away from him because he won't leave her alone. But I seem to remember, Vee, that we had a similar situation last year with that German actor, and you stepped in. Suddenly apologies were flowing in every direction, and flowers were being delivered. How did you do that? Can you do it again?'

Veronique gave a little thumbs up. 'Certainement, chérie. All you do is say, do you know about syndication, and the answer is nearly always no! I say that syndication is a network of the world's news outlets, little printers chattering away twenty-four hours a day, all talking gossip. So a tittle-tattle article that is nothing more than unsubstantiated rubbish, something that I specialise in, goes into print here, only to turn up as a teleprinter, news feed in Paris, Munich, Madrid or London, anywhere in fact. So I just ask him about all his screen credits. What excellent acting parts he has done, and just before I leave, I ask him about the sexual harassment claims and rumours that are flowing around his precious reputation as a serious actor here in Rome. And voila! The apologies come, the flowers arrive and the case is closed. It works every time.'

Gill smiled. 'You really are a villain, Vee. Can I give you his hotel and room number?'

'Oui, chérie, oui, d'accord. Just so long as I don't have to sleep with him.'

Gill laughed. 'No, Vee, you don't. He's too slipeee in all the wrong places for you!'

Duke walked out into his high-walled garden. The air smelt fresh and clean. Angelina was kneeling on the lawn next to a flower bed on a small plastic green mat next to her large woven cane basket. You could see the colour and texture change in the soil where she had weeded and hoed.

He touched her lightly on the shoulder. 'Lunch is ready, my love. Jose has cooked up a storm, and it'll be ready in five minutes. After lunch, I'll need to go out for a couple of hours, but I'll be back for tea.'

Grace didn't disappoint. The kiss in the hall behind the hastily slammed door was even more intense than the very first time. One hand round his neck, one around his back, but it was different somehow. There was something else. Adam didn't quite know what it was, but it was obvious that she was delighted to see him. He blindly put the bottle of wine on the small hall table and pulled her into him, both his arms now totally encircling her. She was wearing her usual jeans and leather belt, but she didn't pull away this time. She could feel his enthusiasm hardening against her, but she held her ground, which made the kissing even more intense. Adam tried to bring his right hand round to her front, but she sensed that it would be his next move and gently grasped his forearm to stop it from roaming. The kissing continued, becoming more delicate, more sensual, more light, fleeting tongues across the lips until they both realised that they had made their affectionate peace with each other.

She eased away from him a little so that there was a small space between them. She brought both her hands up and cradled his face in her long cool fingers, and just stared into his eyes.

'This is madness, Adam, but it's lovely madness. You really are a wonderful snog!'

Adam laughed. 'You want to see it from where I'm standing, Grace, amazing! Any chance of…?'

She playfully smacked his face with her left hand. 'Adam, I think the excitement of that would probably cause a heart attack, the way we both are at the moment. Would you like a drink? Something to cool you down?'

Adam turned and looked down at the wine bottle on the hall table. He had blindly placed it right on the edge; it was a miracle it hadn't fallen off. He lifted it up.

'Montepulciano per Lei, cara,' he said, in faultless Italian.

Grace's mouth fell open. 'Italian! You spoke Italian. Your accent is perfect.'

Adam smiled. 'I bought a phrase book and a dictionary and practice with Jan, Luca and Anatra every day. Jan speaks good Italian.'

She smiled. 'Well, that will be two of you. Well done!'

Adam grinned. 'I even know the Italian for "any chance of a leg-over".'

'I bet you do!' She smiled at him reproachfully like a mother to a naughty child. 'That would be the first thing that you learn. Would you like your drink in a glass or hurled?'

Duke looked across the country-style oak cabinet kitchen at the draining board, by the sizeable glazed sink, with just a few pots left airing, everything else having been cleared away. He got up and gently closed the kitchen door. He could hear Angelina watching a rubbish TV quiz show with the sound turned up. She didn't usually watch things like that. She was clearly finding the current goings-on very disturbing, her inability to eat more than a third of her supper each night reinforcing the fact.

Jose looked up, a little ashamed of his inability to deal with the fact that he was, in his own eyes, now a hunted man. Duke smiled down at him reassuringly.

'The diary is a work of art. Your Vinincio was a bit of an enemy within. He really didn't approve of hardly anything that was going on. The level of detail is quite surprising. He's even got polaroid photos of paperwork that he's copied, not the best,

I'd never employ him as a photographer, but in the main, they are readable. You do realise that it could have been him that was the target and not you?'

Jose shook his head. 'No, no, it was me. It was his sister Sylvania. She never approved of our relationship. His dad just turned a blind eye, he adored him.'

Duke nodded in understanding. 'They've got a meeting scheduled for late Friday afternoon, evening, with all of their area managers, as they call them. Some fifteen or so individuals, plus their enforcers and bodyguards. Talk about a collection of the ungodly, all coming to Vaticano Nero, brought in through the catacombs, not through the front door…'

Jose looked away, down at the floor, lost for inspiration, a look of despair on his face.

Duke got up, walked over to Jose and stood behind him, placing his hand on his shoulder and giving it a short squeeze.

'Cheer up, my friend, we can work through this. I'll give it some thought, but I'm beginning to think that while they're having their little get-together, we should hold one too, at the same time. Different venue, naturally, different kinds of guests…but a party… Yeah, a party to commemorate Luigi's life.'

Adam was reluctant to mention Jose but just had to bring up the subject. They were both standing in the kitchen. She had given him the job of slicing up the melon. She handed him an old bone-handled knife with a pointed blade, about eight inches long.

'Be careful with that. It's so sharp you could shave with it. It was my mother's so you are very honoured. Family heirloom.'

Adam took it carefully and looked down at the unfortunate melon on the well-used rectangular, wooden chopping board, that was about to meet its demise.

'Grace, you know that Jose's dead, don't you?'

She looked up calmly, grimaced. 'Yes, Adam, I know, I know. A bomb—'

'How did you know, Grace? No one else knows, do they?'

She turned away from him towards the stove to check on the bubbling pasta. 'Jungle drums, Adam, jungle drums!' Turning back to him, she said, 'Adam, I don't want to talk about Jose, I don't want to talk about Luigi, I want to talk about us and enjoy us, because, dear man, you are one of the only really good things that is happening in my life right now, and I intend to enjoy every minute of it. You can stay till Sunday night if you want, but you will be sleeping down here on the sofa, and I will be upstairs alone in my room unless you want Mum's knife in your groin. You happy to play by that rule?'

Adam looked at her face devoid of lipstick and her confident body language defined by how she held her wooden stirry spoon upright, vertical, like a police baton.

He nodded. 'Got it, Grace, got it. But just for the record, do you sleep in the nude?'

She smiled, walked around and very gently brought her knee up into his groin. At the same time, she put her arms around his neck and pulled his head towards her. It was a very mixed message; the slight pain in his groin countered by the passion of her kiss.

She cradled his head, as she always did. There was a fire in her eyes as she searched his face. 'Adam, I am having a lot of trouble keeping my undies on with you. I have not been with anyone since my husband died ten years ago. You are the first person to come into my life and actually flick my switch. But I have to be sure that you are what you say you are, and only time will tell. So please do not make it any harder for me. There's a great deal of hurt around at the moment, and we don't need any more, do we?'

Adam shuffled a little awkwardly. Her bringing her knee up had taken him by surprise. He blinked and raised his eyebrows. 'Sorry, Grace, sorry. You really turn me on. It's in my genes. I can't help it!'

She slowly shook his head. 'Well, as long as it stays in your jeans, young fella me lad, we'll get on fine. Tomorrow morning you may want to go for a walk because I have to do my piano practice for about an hour, and you may not want to endure that. I presume that you don't play?'

Adam shook his head and leant forward. He put his arms around her neck, gently pulling her towards him. Though taken by surprise, she came easily, offered no resistance. The kiss went on for about a minute, and was as always, incredibly tender and gentle, finishing as usual with his fleeting tongue across her top lip. Eventually, she gently drew back and blinked in overacted surprise.

'Ooah!'

'No, Grace. I only play twin carburettors. My mum used to play the piano, but not me or Dad. I will stay and listen though if that's okay. A bit of culture never hurt anybody!'

'Well, that's a surprise. I'd thought you'd make a run for it! On Sunday, if you're still here and not in the American hospital recovering from a castration, we could go out down to Porta Portese market. Sophia has lent me a wig which makes me look a bit strange, but it hides who I am. If I see someone coming who knows me, I can simply walk away and meet you at a pre-planned place a bit later. It would get us out and save you from being cooped up here. Gives you a chance to be a tourist in one of the greatest markets of Europe. We are bound to see someone I know as Rome is such a big, small place if you get my meaning.'

As the evening wore on and supper was cleared away, Adam sat down on the far end of the sofa. Grace came and put the two cushions on the floor, then leant up against him, kicking off her shoes and then twisting her feet up. Adam rotated more anti-clockwise towards her to make her more comfortable. Her head nestled very naturally into his shoulder. To make himself a little less contorted, he twisted a little more and because he couldn't think of anything else to do with his right hand, he draped it over her right shoulder and gently cupped her right breast. She turned her head a little, just momentarily to acknowledge what he had done, but smiled to herself and gave a little snuggling movement with her shoulders, easing herself into him. She smelt of something fresh, a slight tang of citrus maybe, not her usual jasmine; it was gentle, very light. Nothing was said, and that was how they both fell asleep, the two-night shoots and the wine eventually catching up with them.

Adam was the first to wake, probably because of the two she was a lot more comfortable and was breathing lightly, entirely out for the count. He smiled as he looked at her. She really was a lioness, this one, afraid of nothing, yet appealingly vulnerable. He looked around her little room. It was already beginning to contain some memories. The old dark dresser opposite, with not a single photo in sight, unlike the other day when he had called uninvited. Her black shiny upright piano in the corner with the sheet music on the top and the heavy-looking, dark green, upholstered stool. To the right, just past the little table with the old, unloved, never-switched-on TV, were stairs leading up to the bathroom and the two bedrooms. She always kept both of those doors closed, so he never tried to get a sneaky peek, instead respecting her privacy. The little hallway with its little sticking out table opposite the kitchen door where Sophia had tearfully said to him, 'Be there for her, Adam, be there. The reward is the most amazing woman', or words to that effect. The warmth from her, the smell of her and her gentle, rhythmic breathing made Adam aware that this was no ordinary relationship. It had some profound secrets and some very high morals. But it made Adam aware that he really enjoyed every micro minute with her and that she had well and truly driven a coach and horses into his emotions. Throwing all of his usual way of behaving with women right out of the window, which really was no bad thing, but he got the impression that it was just as difficult for her.

Looking down at his hand still cupping her breast, it would certainly seem so. The rhythm of her breathing, her warmth against him, was almost hypnotic. Before long, he closed his eyes, and his breathing joined the rhythm of hers.

Saturday 26th April

If she had a choice, Belinda Sharp was not an early riser, but she was already dressed, although lacking any make-up, when there was a knock at her bedroom door.

'Room service,' came the call.

She cautiously opened the door to be greeted by the young, long-haired, dark blue-suited, bow-tied hotel receptionist, holding a massive bunch of fresh-cut flowers and a bottle of Asti Spumante.

'Ooohh!' was all she could manage before thanking her profusely and closing the door with one hand. The attached handwritten envelope containing a scrawly written note, though hardly written in copperplate, was at least legible.

Belinda,

Regarding my over-enthusiastic behaviour the other night, I hope that I did not cause you embarrassment. I trust that these flowers and bit of bubbly clearly convey my most genuine apologies. I sincerely hope that our excellent working relationship has not been affected.

Enjoy!

Very best wishes

Marcus Pomeroy

Belinda read it again and muttered under her breath, 'Excellent working relationship – what a load of crap! I've only worked with you once, and that was an exchange of two lines in a TV detective drama a couple of years back, creep. Thanks for the bubbly though, that will go down very nicely!'

Grace was full of surprises. It started with her waking him up on the sofa by waving a French baguette under his nose that was jammed full of hot crispy bacon: the standard Focus Puller breakfast. The previous evening she had thrown a light blanket over him before leaving him out for the count and creeping off to her own room. She woke early to go shopping locally for a fresh French breadstick. The salted bacon English-style was trickier, but you can buy anything gastronomic in Trastevere if you know where to go.

After two cups of tea, he was sent upstairs to shave because the lady did not want to snog a hedgehog. She confessed the reason that Sophia knew she had someone was because their recent kissing activities had roughed up her chin, and Sophia, of course, had noticed.

As to the mid-morning piano recital, to say that Adam was impressed was an understatement. He was not really into classical music – three guitars, drums and a vocalist with three pair of socks rammed down the front of his trousers all playing as if their lives depended on it, usually in small village halls around Surrey, was his usual fayre. But the lady once again totally surprised him. He was treated to Debussy, Rachmaninoff,

Schumann all played with a delicate, note-perfect touch, the little piano, though aged, giving off a lovely tone that the room respectfully reflected.

When she finished playing, Adam applauded and shouted 'ENCORE' before going over to her and gently massaging her shoulders. He jokingly whispered that he'd like to massage a lot more of her, but she just tapped both his hands in gentle reprimand before looking up at him and offering herself for yet another affectionate kiss.

Between films, when he was not working, Duke was a very keen photographer. He owned a matching pair of state-of-the-art, 35mm Asahi Pentax cameras and a full set of lenses, plus every filter that the photographic magazines insist that you absolutely must have in your kit bag.

He had a meeting at the studio at twelve-thirty with Sven, Lasse and the electricians to look at pre-lighting the set for Monday. But before then, he wanted to talk to a few people, take a few photographs around town, and gather his thoughts about the upcoming party in a week's time. He had a venue in mind, in precisely the area that he wanted, but he didn't know if it was available. So that would be his last port of call, because from experience, he knew that hospitality folk were not early risers, 2 a.m. finishes every working day being the main reasons.

The photographs he'd get developed right across the other side of the city, not in his usual shop. Not that they'd keep copies; they only did that with the sexually explicit, raunchy ones, but you can never be too careful. On his way into the sound stage at the studio, he'd pop his head into the Production Office and ask Gill, if she was working, if there was any slack in the budget for an early finish on Friday, plus the cost of a party. He planned to sell the concept to her on the grounds that it was only going to have a very select number of guests, mainly friends, people who Luigi himself would have wanted there had he been alive, no one else.

He was optimistic about the outcome. Gill and the accountant Tomassino were very understanding people. He didn't know about the legal eagle. Maybe if she were on the invite list, she'd back the idea.

There was a lot of activity in the principal case room at police headquarters. About eight male officers were all at their various desks. Paulo Gatti was sitting at his spotlessly clean, red-leather desktop opposite Sovrintendente Mauro Sofri, and the plain-clothed Christina who was now dressed in a more feminine, high-necked, dark brown, long flowing dress complemented by a splash of make-up. Alberto Consalvo sat ten feet away with his chair the wrong way round, clutching a large cup of coffee as he listened attentively.

Christina had two pages of handwritten notes and, as was her habit, constantly waved a biro in her right hand. The crucifix around her neck was very prominent because she wanted it to be. She looked at Paulo and smiled nervously.

'First, the bomb explosion. We found sick on clothes in Jose Villabianco's bedroom, which is unexplained. The sketch artist has created a picture of the shop stay-over visitor, but it is inconclusive. It could be anyone. It would seem he never shopped locally and did everything he could to keep a low profile. Marks on the bedsheets lead us to believe that Jose was in a physical relationship, presumably with this stay-the-night male visitor, which may explain the reason for the low profile. Whether the relationship was romantic or purely financial, we have no idea.

'Single American men aged twenty to forty-five who flew in from Los Angeles ten days prior to the Luigi murder number eighty-two. Two of them are companions of Dino Burgio and go literally everywhere with him. We have their names: Lou Sabatini, he's the one who dribbles a lot, and Vito Bovara, nicknamed Lank, 'cos he's so tall. You remember they both shared the alibi of dining with him at the hotel at the time of the shooting.

'As to the other eighty, seventeen of them have left the country since the Mussomelli murder. Sixty-three remain, but we have only been able to speak to ten who are still staying at the hotel addresses that they gave to immigration on entering the country. As far as we can determine, none of them have any history of recent military service, as it's not a very popular calling in the US at the moment with everything that's going on in Vietnam.'

She looked down at her paperwork. 'As for the remaining fifty-three, some of them could be draft dodgers and just be hiding out with friends or family, or have simply changed hotels or moved on. Needless to say, we haven't yet been able to track them. As of fifteen minutes ago, Peter Dublin is on life support at the American hospital and is not expected to live. He has potentially committed suicide by alcohol poisoning. I've asked the hospital to call me if they have any news. That's about it so far, sir.'

Paulo nodded. 'Thank you, Christina, good work. I don't know why we promoted you though. You haven't solved the case; all you've done is muddy the waters,' he joked, with a smirk and a nod.

Christina forced a smile and reached nervously for her crucifix. 'Sorry, sir! Promise to try harder.'

Paulo grimaced. 'Well, my little conversation with Luciano Scordia was tantamount to accusing the Pope of rape. I have seldom met anyone so indignant. If you'd asked him the bloody time of day, he'd check with three of his lawyers before he gave an answer. It achieved absolutely nothing. He knew nothing. He did not know anybody who could help, and all the time there was this totally valueless smear of greasy charm that oozed out of him like a pus. Ghastly individual, ghastly! If he is involved, which he most probably is, he now knows that we are investigating, which means that if he does know anything, he would be looking to kill any potential information coming our way, which, knowing how he works, means more bodies.

'As to the American Producer, our beloved Mr Burgio, it's the same: indignant denial of any knowledge of anything. Both he and Scordia went to the same school, in that regard, which begs the question did they actually go to the same school? Roughly the same age, Sicilian roots. No idea. Christina, look into that, would you, please.'

Christina nodded and leant forward to rest her paper on the gold leaf-bordered leather desktop to write a note. Paulo coughed loudly to stop her. A look of short horror came over her face.

'It's not a desk, you know!' he hissed.

Sunday 27th April

Spring mornings in Rome can be a little chilly until the sun gets a grip. So Adam was glad Grace had loaned him her blue woollen scarf as he loosely tied it around his neck and tucked into the top of his denim jacket. It smelt of her, clean and jasmine, but he got used to the smell within a few minutes and after that failed to notice it. Grace was wearing a full-flowing blue skirt and a puffy dark grey quilted jacket, together with a big pair of highly reflective sunglasses. Plus the frizzy dark brown wig that Sophia had donated. She was totally unrecognisable. The wig was natural permed hair, beautifully made, showing no trace of any wig line at the front. It was a real quality job. The only thing was that Adam wanted to see the real her, but he had her voice, humour and lovely mouth, so he was happy with that.

It was nice to be out like an average couple walking in the sun. He was tempted to casually hold her hand, but she preferred not to. So whenever they came to cross a road, or there was traffic about, he'd hold her back by the elbow or put his arm out in front to slow her down, which made her giggle almost uncontrollably.

Porta Portese market was a tourist's dream. You could buy anything there, from a set of triple Maserati air horns for your car to cheese from all over Europe and Parma ham or even a cheap screwdriver. It was a 'proper' flea market.

A quilted, pure white ski jacket on one of the stalls halfway down attracted Adam's attention.

'How much?' he asked.

'Fifteen,' came the reply with three rapid flashes of five fingers to reinforce the price.

Adam grimaced, shook his head and walked away with a nod and a smile.

Grace came right into his side. 'Adam, dear one, you haven't got a clue, have you? This is Rome, Porta Portese market. You ask the price, get told "fifteen", you snort and come back with "ten", flashing your hand twice. He will then snort, as if you have insulted his mother and all of his ancestors, and say "fourteen", almost certainly followed by another snort, the classic stallholder *take it or leave it* attitude. You then start to act, just show as little interest as you can, say, "No! Ten!" and give a similar *you have insulted my ancestors* sort of snort. Then you smile. Never ever be aggressive. Say for the last time "ten" and then turn and slowly walk away. And it's that turn that does it for you. He will allow only three paces of a potential sale to walk away before he calls you back. He's bought the bloomin' thing for four thousand lire in the first place. He's not losing money! Look, there's another stall up here with the same jacket. Want to try? Never be aggressive. Just master the snort.'

Adam looked at her. She was such fun to be with, frizzy wig or not. He decided to try to master the snort, the non-aggressive attitude, the faked disinterest and the three-pace walk away. Heart thumping, as casually as he could, he walked up to the hanging jacket, checking the size first on the label inside the neck, before asking, 'How much?'

They were both giggling as they walked away, Adam carrying a plastic bag containing his eleven-thousand-lire white ski jacket. She patted him gently on the back.

'Well done, Englishman, well done, we'll make a local of you yet!'

She stopped and bought some olives, something that she confessed was a vice of hers. A little further up, they came to a stall selling cheap bracelets, bangles and necklaces. Draped in the middle on a bed of loosely folded blue velvet were several oversized, heavy-chained, large chromium-plated crucifixes.

Adam stared at them. 'Jose sells these!' he said, immediately regretting the use of the present tense.

She took his arm for a second. 'He does. He did. It's okay, Adam, it's okay. We don't know for sure he's dead, do we?'

Adam looked at his reflection in her sunglasses. 'Well, someone died. And there's no sign of him, so what are we supposed to think?'

'We think positive, Adam, we think positive.'

Captain Steve had many friends and acquaintances in Rome, having lived in the city for over ten years. Some of them were ex-pats, most of them were locals, but a few of them had a military background. British military presence in Rome was very thin on the ground, apart from the dozen or so strong security detail at the British embassy. So an early lunch in Trastevere with an old military mate, Geoff Whittaker, was always a joy, an opportunity to just chew the cud, talk about old times and crack all of the same old jokes that had amused them over the years.

Being a Marine Lieutenant Colonel, Geoff outranked Steve by some measure. Steve was of peasant stock and Geoff was a product of Dartmouth Naval College, but they had just clicked as friends many years ago, and the question of rank had never entered the equation.

Unlike Geoff, Steve was no longer one of Her Majesty's employees, making for even easier banter between them. Steve, though, had suffered more than a few hangovers over time, mainly because of Geoff's bad influence, and today was probably going to be no exception. They were starting early, which was always a bad sign.

Monday 28th April

Alberto Consalvo did not like rainy Monday mornings. The traffic was always slower for reasons that no one had really quantified. He was now, as usual, driving Gill to and from Studio Lazio each day. The back seat concealed under a light grey jacket a fully loaded Beretta M12 submachine gun. On the advice of the police armourer, he had on the previous Thursday exchanged his underarm Beretta pistol for a brand-new weapon with fresh ammunition. His old gun was a bit long in the tooth and, like all aged automatics, could be prone to jamming. Since the Luigi incident, he also had tried to spend about forty minutes or so each day in the police shooting range, down in the basement, trying to improve his marksmanship, with mixed results. He was never going to be a sharpshooter.

They had the police radio on very softly, as regulation. The partially muted, perfectly enunciated female controllers kept up a constant stream of information regarding minor traffic accidents and violent domestic abuse incidents, which for some strange reason, always seemed to proliferate on Monday mornings.

Gill looked across at him and gently rubbed his right thigh with her left hand. 'You've got mud on your knees, love.'

He grimaced, never taking his eyes off the traffic. 'Yes, looking under the car for devices. Sorry!'

She squeezed him again affectionately. 'Next time pull out the footwell mat and kneel on that.'

Before he could respond, the radio blurted, 'Centro, centro, Ispettore Consalvo, one, three, five, seven, channel sixteen, please.'

Alberto nodded to her as he unclipped from the dashboard the coiled cable, push-button hand mike. As she had done many times before, Gill pushed the one, three, five and seven buttons on the front of the radio and twisted up the volume knob, something that he had taught her to do many years ago.

'Centro, centro, this is Consalvo, one, three, five, seven, go ahead.'

The voice was crackly, a little tinny. 'Message from your office: Peter Dublin died early this morning. Please contact Christina for more information. Message ends.'

Alberto grimaced. 'Thank you, centro, message received and understood. Going back to channel zero, five, thank you. Out.'

Gill leant forward and waited for his nod before pressing the zero button, followed by the five and gently twisting the volume back down. He handed her the mike, which she gently clipped back to the dashboard.

'Sorry you had to hear that, love. Not a nice way to…'

She raised her hand. 'It's okay, it's okay. He wasn't one of my favourite people, quite the opposite, in fact! But to drink yourself to death just because you lost your job is pretty bloody pitiful. Life always goes on, doesn't it?'

He nodded and paused for a moment. 'I blame his parents. Everyone should learn to live with failure. I mean, look at me, I had to marry a bloody foreigner, couldn't get a local girl.'

Her left hand moved quickly to his crotch and she gently smacked him.

'Owww!'

'Well, that's your sex life on hold for the next month, my little Italian sweety.'

He smiled. 'You couldn't last that long.'

Her hand went back to his thigh and rubbed him slowly, affectionately. 'True! Very sad, but very true.'

Lasse was in great form for a Monday morning, bouncing up onto one of the props trolleys as he usually did. Anatra was by now well used to his little leaps and, anticipating his step-up, grabbed hold of the handle to make sure that the most important person on set once again came to no harm.

'Buongiorno a tutti. Good morning, everybody. Today in the famous Pinewood Studios in England it is 1942, the middle of the war and we are filming Gina Isabella with her English auntie Dorothy Anita. This is where the British secret service first contact her. Important scenes today because this is where the title of the film, *The Script Girl*, comes from. Thank you!'

Adam turned to Jan. 'Bit of history over there,' he said, nodding towards the set at the bulky, black blimped American BNC Mitchell camera on a very substantial, but very ancient, tripod.

Jan stared for a moment. 'I've never actually ever seen one before. We always use Arriflex in Norway.'

Adam smiled. 'I hate the bloody things. They're very quiet, totally silent, but you can't see through when you're filming as it's all operated through that viewfinder on the side. So if I go out of focus, I don't find out till rushes the next day. Monstrous thing.'

Luca walked up, an empty cigarette holder jammed in his teeth, and presented Adam with his first loaded magazine of the day. 'Short end, Adam, three hundred feet okay?'

Adam nodded. 'Should be. We've got one take Marcus Pomeroy on set this morning. We'll all be finished by lunchtime if we're lucky.'

In fairness to Jose, he wasn't starting to smell yet, but he had taken to wearing Angelina's dressing gown over his old clothes simply because it smelled nice. He had been given his instructions for the day and was now copying on to writing paper the various pieces of information from the Vinincio diary. Duke had been precise. There were specific names and addresses that he needed to have recorded.

Angelina had gone shopping, allegedly to buy some food, but in times of crisis, death threats or not, a bit of retail therapy does wonders for a girl, and she let everyone know that she would not be back before three, at the earliest.

Jose had also been asked to create, in his perfect copperplate handwriting, all of the formal RSVP invitations. Plus, all of the small name placeholders to go on the tables for the Friday party guests. Duke wanted people in certain positions, not randomly spread about the room hence his instructions to Jose: 'Take your time. Make them as flowery as possible.'

Gill smiled as the ever-smiling Tomassino politely entered her office. He was purposefully carrying in front of him a clean white envelope.

'Here we are, Gill, the cheque for the ristorante, the deposit and half of the food costs, with the rest payable in cash on the day.'

Gill nodded and smiled at one of her favourite people. The true gentleman accountant, Mister Smiling White Teeth! As usual, dressed in a spotless, ironed white shirt, sleeves rolled up to each elbow, tie neatly tucked in at his third button.

'Thank you, Tomassino, thank you.'

He very respectfully placed the envelope onto her desk, and his long fingers gently eased it towards her. 'Gill, the extra security men on the front gate and on set, how long will they be on the payroll?'

She screwed up her face and frowned. 'I'm afraid that I don't know the answer to that. The police recommend it, and Duke, as usual, is playing better safe than sorry, so apologies but I can't answer that at present, but not for much longer, I hope.'

Tomassino nodded understandingly. He then leant forward, reminding Gill of a naughty schoolboy about to ask a question that he shouldn't.

'How are the police investigations getting on? Do you know?'

Gill grimaced. 'The official answer is,' she coughed and deepened her voice, '"We believe that enquiries are progressing at a lightning pace and that the few outstanding matters should all be resolved very shortly".' She reverted back to her normal voice. 'Which is Alberto speak for "enquiries are progressing at a lightning pace and the few outstanding matters should all be resolved very shortly".'

She finished with a non-believing nod, which made Tomassino laugh. He got the picture.

The morning had gone well. The scene was the Pinewood set filming a World War II propaganda film. Production had found a local ex-pat English actor who looked and sounded exactly like the man who fronted the Pathe News at the cinema back home in England. He played the entire scene with a condescending, clipped, perfectly enunciated Oxford accent from underneath a greasy 1940s central hair parting.

Anita played the part of the Pinewood script girl with young Isabella sitting beside her on a stool as her understudy. It was interesting to see Grace giving both of them tips on holding a stopwatch in the left hand and making written notes with the right. For realism, the ancient black Pinewood studio BNC film camera was crewed by three local film technicians, all of whom gave Adam slightly malevolent sideways glances as the foreign interloper taking over their jobs, be he a Cinepan expert or not.

A couple of the electricians had been dressed by Pia in baggy grey trousers and scruffy white shirts and turned into paid actors for the day. With great humour and no small degree of overacting, they moved the Pinewood prop studio lights around as instructed by Duke. The whole set, as usual, had a great sense of realism about it.

Marcus Pomeroy appeared at around eleven o'clock to run his scenes with Anita and Isabella, and as usual, he took over the whole set. His overloud voice and exaggerated mannerisms took everyone back to 1942 and a time when 'awareness films' shown at the Saturday morning cinema were one of the British government's most powerful propaganda tools. It was as if everything had gone full circle, because that was the main reason Mussolini had invested so heavily in Studio Lazio: solely to create film propaganda.

Adam, try as he may, could not get Grace out of his mind. She was there in front of him, just a few paces away. He was falling in love with her, and he knew it. Her every move, her every word was an experience that he savoured and enjoyed.

On Saturday afternoon, she had entertained him in the kitchen, where she showed him in great detail how to prepare slow roast Italian shoulder of lamb with all of the herbs, garlic and trimmings. Their formal sit-down supper later that evening was an absolute gastronomic delight. Adam had rarely tasted food like it. The trip out to the market on Sunday had been great fun. They had spent most of the day smiling and giggling like a couple of teenagers. She was determined not to let the passing of Luigi and Jose tarnish her time with him. It must have been hard for her, but she never referred to any of it.

Leaving her on Sunday evening was incredibly difficult for both of them, Adam detecting that she was near to tears when she eventually came to close the front door on what had been a very emotional weekend. The photos from the dresser never appeared. So the deep secrets remained. Adam wondered if they would ever be revealed, but only time would tell.

Nella had the hand-turned Singer sewing machine out and was busy sewing two-metre-long ribbons onto each corner of a large piece of stiff, old, heavy, dark grey patternless curtaining material that had been residing in one of the linen cupboards upstairs for longer than she could remember. Rino was up a tree right at the back of the large vegetable garden, fiddling with one of the bird nesting boxes.

Nella was pleased as things were going well. When she had asked Adriana if she could borrow the majestic Giotto in the middle of the night along with his ploughing harness tack, she had been momentarily in two minds. Then when Nella mentioned that she wanted to paint his beautiful glossy black hindquarters white, she really did have her doubts. But she agreed, not because she was given a lot of information, she wasn't given any, but Nella just said that it was something that she needed to do, and it was very, very important to her. Adriana knew that Nella had just experienced losing her employer to an assassin, which had cut her to the quick. Plus the fact she was most likely, once everything was finally settled, going to be turfed out of her home in the next few months.

Over the last few years, Adriana had been begging her to stop housekeeping, and come and live with her at the stables. But Nella was stubborn, to say the least, and possessed a very strong sense of duty to look after the maturing Luigi. But now, all of that was in the past, and lives were about change. So Adriana agreed, no questions asked, none answered, to loan Nella the beautiful Giotto on the condition that by dawn the following morning there would not be a single trace of white paint anywhere on the horse, the tack or the stable. But the main reason that she agreed was not the fact that she trusted Nella. It wasn't just that; it was because she was head over heels in love with the woman.

A few minutes before Duke called wrap, as Grace was taking her polaroids, Adam was surprised to see Captain Steve half in the shadows just outside of the ring of light. He gave a casual wave as a greeting, but the look on his face gave Adam the impression that he wanted to talk to him. Adam took the magazine off the camera and gave it to Luca so that he could get on with canning up his rushes and writing his reports.

Twenty minutes later, Adam was being driven towards the centre of town in Steve's light tan-coloured Alfa Romeo.

Steve stared fixedly ahead, rarely flicking a look at his passenger. 'The thing I like about you, Adam, is you don't do panic, and you're careful and methodical. You'd make a good Marine.'

Adam snorted slightly. 'Don't know about that, Steve, not teararse fit, not that keen on authority.'

Steve smiled, acknowledging his modesty. 'Well, don't short-change yourself. You seem to have a great sense of what is right and wrong. I want to show you some places, and after that, I'm going to ask for your help with a little matter. Then it's up to you to let me know how you feel about that, okay?'

Adam was not at all sure where this was going but he decided to play along. All his previous dealings with Steve had been very amicable, so he had no reason to be concerned. After a couple of turns, Steve drove past the main railway station, pulled into an old industrial area and stopped outside a prominent pair of wrought-iron gates. He turned off the engine, removed his sunglasses and turned to look Adam straight in the eye.

'At those gates last Tuesday, Luigi Mussomelli was shot through the head and killed, killed outright. His driver Bruno is now unemployed because he can't work. He has the same bullet that killed Luigi lodged in his shoulder. He has a wife and three young kids at home, and there's not a lot of food on the table. Behind the gates is the Casa Annunciata, a children's centre that provides care for very sick young children. Luigi was one of the leading financial supporters of that charity. And from now on, they will be cash-strapped.'

Adam frowned, taken by surprise at the tone of the conversation. This was undoubtedly not the Forum or the Colosseum or a tour of the sights of Rome. This was something entirely different. He was lost for words.

Steve sensed his discomfort. 'I don't need you to say anything, Adam. I am aware this is all a bit strange for you, but

I'm going to take you to three other places, and all I ask is that you bear with me and just listen to what I have to say. The next place is just a couple of streets away, so sit tight.'

A few minutes later, Steve eased his car to a gentle halt outside a large, old-fashioned, three-storey, yellow-grey, stoned apartment block. The windows on the block looked new and it had a clean-scrubbed look about it, compared to the properties on either side. Once again, Steve took off his sunglasses and turned to Adam.

'Last year, this was a brothel run by a local villain. Because he wasn't prepared to spend any money on maintenance there was an electrical fire in the basement which resulted in the whole place going up in flames. Twenty-six young girls died either in the fire or from smoke inhalation in their locked rooms. They were daughters and sisters who had been trafficked from Poland and Britain. Five of them were from my part of the world, South Wales.'

Adam looked up at the building, trying hard to take in the information. 'Did you know any of the girls, Steve?'

'No, mate, I didn't, but I know the valley they were from. I grew up there. There are two more places. Please bear with me. I'll buy you supper afterwards.'

Ten minutes of virtual conversational silence found them on the edges of Trastevere. Steve eased the car to a halt. Once again, he turned, took off his sunglasses and held Adam in his grey-eyed, flint-like gaze.

'This little office here is where a beautiful young house agent named Donna Tavazzi worked. She had her head beaten in with a hammer, died for no good reason. Her parents thought that she was going to be a movie star.'

Adam bit his lip. 'This is all a bit heavy. Why are you showing me all these places, Steve?'

Steve grimaced, nodded in understanding. 'Because I'm going to buy you a meal and ask for your help, mate. I think that you can help me. Just one more place.'

The streets got smaller, similar to those that he and Grace had run down when they had fled the gutter muggers. Eventually, much to Adam's surprise, they suddenly turned into Jose's road. The tent was still there, and the police ribbons on either side of it still stretched across the street, just like when Adam had last seen it. The only difference was that Steve had brought him in from the other end of the street. The police presence was reduced to two, one for each lightly flapping ribbon. Adam turned to Steve before they had come to a stop.

'This is Jose's street. Jose died here in a bomb blast.'

Steve waited for a large white delivery van to pull out in front of him before he eased the car into the ample space. This time he kept his sunglasses on. He continued looking ahead, out through the windscreen.

'Yeah, a bomb on the streets of Rome, the eighth wonder of the world, in my opinion, killing Jose but also killing a mother and her young daughter just because they happened to be walking along the pavement at the wrong time. But what else do you see, Adam?'

Adam shook his head. 'I don't know what you mean.'

Steve nodded at him but continued to look straight ahead. 'I'll tell you what I see, Adam. I see people walking in fear. I see people ashamed of the society that they live in. I see people angry that this happened in the place that they live and work. But I also sense a feeling of total impotence to fix it or do anything about it. They deserve better, Adam, they all deserve better. That shop owner has lost virtually everything. They deserve better. So now I'm going to buy you supper and ask for your help, if that's okay.'

Impatient, Adam said, 'Sod sitting down for a meal, Steve, tell me now. We can eat later.'

Steve looked at him and nodded, giving a tight smile. 'Okay, mate, okay. The police are never going to solve any of these crimes. They never have, and they never bloody will. I believe that if something is not done, it's just going to get worse. More people will get their heads smashed in, shot, blown up, set fire to—'

Adam cut across, 'So what are you going to do, Steve? What's on…?'

'I'm not prepared to tell you, Adam, because I don't want anyone to know. It's all on a need-to-know basis, and that way it protects everyone that's involved. I was hoping you could do a series of actions for me that will not include any form of violence and will not put you in any danger. What happens in the lead-up to your actions by other parties and after your actions you will have no knowledge of, and that is how I operate. The main objective for me is to make sure that everyone has an alibi, and your help would ensure that.'

Adam shook his head. 'Everyone? Who is everyone?'

'Adam, I can't tell you. No one will ever know of your participation, and you will not know of theirs. Apart from me, you will not have to interact with anyone else.'

'What about my alibi, Steve?'

Steve snorted and gave a tight smile. 'Well, mate, if I were a copper, you would be the last person I would question. You are utterly unconnected with everyone, an English tourist almost and a short-term working visitor, but I'm not going twist your arm. I just sense that you have a great sense of right and wrong, a sense of social justice, if you like, and a desire to do the right thing. Am I wrong?'

Adam smiled to himself. This was emotional blackmail, the kind that the security spy masters used to convince young people to spy for the SOE way back. But he had to admit he was falling for it.

'What do I have to do, Steve? If you tell me and I decide not to come to play, to back out, where does that leave me?'

'You've signed the official secrets act, Adam. Say nothing, keep schtum, and nothing more will ever be said, and that's the truth. You have my word. But on Thursday evening, I can run you through what I want you to do. The actual event will only be about forty-five minutes on Friday evening. You okay with that?'

Adam frowned. 'Okay, Thursday evening, what happens then?'

'I'll pick you up at your hotel and take you somewhere and run through in absolute fine detail what needs to be done on Friday. You okay with that?'

Adam nodded. 'And if I don't want to come to play, I can just walk away, nothing said, no bullet in the back of the head.'

Steve lowered his voice, changed his tone to one of reassurance. 'No, Adam, no! You can just walk away, and there will never be any bullet in the back of your head. There's been too much of that already. Oh, just before we end this little chat, you do ride a bike, don't you?'

Tuesday 29th April

Fishmongers don't usually have chauffeur-driven cars except for weddings and funerals, but today was an exception. True, it was very early in the morning, but most of Viola Ballesi's family were watching out of the window, waving her off as a smiling, black-suited unit car driver opened the rear door for her and respectfully ushered her into his highly polished, black Mercedes.

She was in awe of the smoothness of the ride and the smell of leather upholstery and polish. She felt a little uncomfortable though as this was way out of her comfort zone. However, her family had said to her, 'Enjoy it, Mum, enjoy it! Every minute of it!'

As they approached the studio gatehouse, the driver deliberately slowed down more than he usually would so that she could fully take in being driven into one of the largest, most prolific film studios in Europe. He didn't take her to the workman's café, but instead, straight to Make-up, where Sophia's senior hair stylist was waiting for her. She was asked with great courtesy if she would like a totally free makeover, hair and make-up, before being called to the set. Viola couldn't get into the leather Make-up seat quick enough.

Her long hair was fluffed and primped, and she was asked if she would like it dyed back to her original dark brown before the invasion of the thready greys. Then would she prefer a temporary rinse or permanent dye that would last for about a month. She was asked to tell them what style she wanted the cut to be. An hour and a half later, the principal Make-up supervisor, a lady called Sophia, came in and engaged her in conversation as she spent about fifteen minutes carefully putting the finishing touches to her make-up.

Two girls on either side of twin boys, twenty or so years ago, had not been that kind to her figure and when a Wardrobe lady named Pia was introduced and asked her if she would be happy to wear a new padded uplift bra to match the lady that she was doubling for, Viola's answer was 'Yes, thank you very much!' She only found out later that the new bra she found so comfy was a gift from Production.

At nine o'clock, the Third Assistant Director, Beatrice, came and walked with her to the set. She sat down next to a funny owl-like man who introduced himself as Petros, the unit interpreter. One of the Props men came over and told her that the fish she had sent over the previous day was in the fridge behind the set ready for her.

Viola looked at the set. Even though it was inside, it was very bright, like a sunshiny morning. Twelve totally different market stalls, each about three or four metres across, stretched down the little one-sided street setting. Behind the stalls were a line of small sandstone-coloured houses. The stall near the middle was obviously a fish stall, with all of the ice trays ready to house their stock of fish.

Sylvania was holding a meeting at her plush, dark blue carpeted apartment at the Vaticano Nero. The room was half the size of a tennis court with large-pane windows all down the right side that looked down onto the courtyard where her father Luciano, as usual, was sitting in his red housecoat reading all of the early morning newspapers from cover to cover.

She stood as she always did, at the end of the four-metre-long, French dark oak conference table with her back to the wall. Always with her back to the wall. She insisted that the four men and the female housekeeper were all seated. She preferred to look down on them; it kept them in their rightful place. She was dressed in a tight-fitting, two-piece, pale blue suit with a large, gold-monogrammed SS brooch. It wasn't easy to judge what had cost more, the brooch or the suit. Her make-up was, as usual, very detailed, her dark hair curled naturally onto her shoulders. Her eyes though portrayed little warmth.

She tapped the table with her unadorned ringless left knuckle as she managed momentarily to force a tight smile. She looked across the room to the far side, where a large picture of her mother and father painted while they were on their honeymoon was hanging in its heavy gold frame. She seemed to draw energy from it. For a moment, it seemed to have an almost hypnotic quality.

'Right. I expect you all to take notes. I have no intention of going through any of this again. This is to be no different to any of our previous meetings with our area managers. As usual, our guests and escorts I want brought in through the catacombs, not a single one through the street doors. If the police are watching, which they are often are, I want them to have no idea what is going on here. Marino, you and your team are to liaise with all of the out-of-towners as to where to meet up so that you can unobtrusively escort them in. Got that? The meeting starts at seven-thirty sharp. It goes without saying that every one of them will be disarmed and their weapons locked in the master safe until their time comes for them to leave. Plus, all of your men will be discreetly wearing underarm, and none of them will drink, not a bloody drop!'

The black leather jacket figure seated nearest to her on her right nodded in affirmation, overacting writing down the instruction so that she was more than aware that he was following her instructions to the letter.

She turned her head slightly to the left and looked at the middle-aged female seated figure.

'Aurelia, I want a first-class cold buffet for around forty-five of them plus around ten of us, so fifty-five, sixty. No outside catering staff on-site, at any time. This must be staffed entirely by the people we have here in the complex. We will collect everything from suppliers, so no deliveries.'

The thin-lipped, hawk-faced, greying-haired woman looked up momentarily. She made a half-hearted attempt at a pleasing smile and eye contact, but it was not reciprocated, so she bent her head and busily scribbled on her notepad.

Sylvania raised her chin and stretched her neck slightly, attempting to assert herself even more. 'I will announce the toast of loyalty and prosperity as usual at precisely nine o'clock. I will be wearing my white dress, and I will step up onto the main table and call for the toast. Marino, you are to assist me. I expect you to be on hand, Aurelia. You are to make sure that everyone's glasses are topped up by eight-fifty.'

Sylvania turned her head and slowly looked at the solitary, silent, grey-templed, bulky figure sitting at the far end of the table dressed in a blue denim jacket. A flash of red bandana adorned his muscular neck. His face was cold, expressionless.

'Mister Bratina, your role is, of course, unchanged. You and your son Toro are also to remain teetotal, and neither of you are ever to leave my father's side for the entire evening. If you need to go to the toilet, piss in your pants. If anyone causes my father even the slightest alarm, you are to deal with them, and, Marino, you and your armed men will, of course, back them up should the need arise. There is potentially always some little arsehole that wants to take over things, and an extra body or two for the dogs down in the catacomb makes no difference to me.'

Adam had worked many times in the past with hand artists, coming as he did from a background in the making of television commercials. Hand artists always had beautiful hands, nails and arms, but their faces were more often than not plain, not ugly, just unremarkable, and it didn't matter, because all you ever saw of them was their hands, sometimes their arms. That was where their talent lay.

So when the fishmonger lady from the local market came to do her very high-speed fish gutting takes, doubling for Belinda and Isabella, Adam was surprised to see that she had been put through make-up, and that Sophia was touching up her face between takes. Her arms, yes, her hands, of course, her nails, naturally. But why her face? Halfway through the morning, Sophia drifted near to the camera, and Adam beckoned her over.

'Sophia, explain to me why you are doing the make-up on her? We never see her face, only her hands.'

Sophia smiled. 'Oh, the ever-practical, unromantic English.' She gave him a gentle punch in the left shoulder. 'I'll tell you why, Adam. It's because we are Italian, we here at Studio Lazio are the dream makers, the creators of fantasy! And today, we have given a normal working mum the day of her life that she will remember until the day she dies. She will not stop talking about it for the next six months. It cost us nothing but a bit of time and a bit of hair dye and make-up. But look at her, Adam, she is positively glowing!'

Adam looked towards the shadows, and the ever-present semi-circle of canvas-backed chairs and the seated figure in deep conversation with the person she was doubling for, the international film star Isabella Marco. Sophia was right. Viola Ballesi was buzzing. Her whole noisy, arm-waving body language just said it all. She was on a real high!

Adam turned back to Sophia, who had half turned, about to walk away. 'Sophia, whose idea was it to treat her?'

She smiled. 'Me, Lasse, Duke, we all think the same. It's minuted that we would do it in a Production meeting. Someone helps us, we help them.'

Adam nodded, taking on board the ethos that some of his co-workers chose to live by. He lowered his voice. 'Sophia, why did Grace lend her her kitchen knife? She said it was her mother's.'

Sophia respected the air of confidentiality that he had suddenly introduced and dropped her voice to almost a whisper. 'I don't know, you'll have to ask her, but it's exactly the correct period for these early twenties and forties scenes, and people do tend to hang on to things that they like. Don't know. You'll have to ask her if there's any time for talk in your relationship,' she said, finishing with a very affectionate smile and a gentle right-handed rubbing motion across the point of his bristly chin.

Jan, watching from five metres away on the far side of the camera, sipped his coffee and frowned. He did not like to see the good-looking Adam chatting to Sophia.

The previous evening, Captain Steve had arranged to meet up with someone from his past at the Parco Trentani, a forested area about forty minutes or so to the northeast of the city. Steve was carrying his old fawn-coloured army issue commando rucksack. After locking his car, he walked casually into the woods, checking down at his marching compass every now and then to make sure that he was on the right path. He looked, to all intents and purposes, like a hiking tourist. Not that there was anyone around, the whole place was totally deserted.

After about fifteen minutes, he reached the agreed rendezvous point, took off his rucksack and sat down at the base of a large chestnut tree that was just starting to come into leaf. He picked up a finger pinch of leaf mould and gently smelt it before gently tossing it back to the ground. It was good to be outside in the woods again.

After a few minutes, the birdsong that had ceased when he walked in now slowly began to start up again. The wood was mainly pine, but here and there, chestnut and beech flourished, which made it a very tranquil place to be at one with nature. The smell of pine resin and the damp leaf mould was all-enveloping. Every now and then, Steve's left hand clicked a small metal clicker, a World War II cricket, which had been issued to the D-Day troops to avoid shooting by friendly fire. A responding click from behind a tree or hedgerow told you that the unseen soldiers were friendly.

Steve never heard his old friend approach until there was a metallic cricket click virtually in his left ear. Steve leapt up and turned to see a short, grey-green cotton jacketed man with lined, thin features caused by fifty years of living and working in the outdoors. A huge genuine smile that started in his small black eyes appeared all over his face.

'Steve, how are you?' came from behind a thick, bushy moustache. The energy of their man hug emphasised the fact that there was a powerful bond between them.

Moustache man eased his heavy bulging rucksack to the ground and sat down, his back to the tree, mimicking Steve. He gently squeezed his rucksack with his knees.

'I'm sorry, Steve, I couldn't bring everything you asked for. There's one missing. The old store's nearly empty now. The American stuff's all gone, still got a bit of Nazi German, but hardly any British. That's almost the last of it. Gets used up year on year. 'Spose we should be grateful it lasted this long, twenty-five years, 1944 to 1969.'

Steve smiled. 'Yeah, you're right. A long time, but it had to be British, had to be. One less, I can live with that, my friend, absolutely fine. That will do very nicely, thank you.'

Moustache man smiled again and twisted his head round enquiringly. 'Am I going to read about this one in the papers?'

Steve smiled, then chuckled. 'Oh, yes, my old mate, you are definitely going to read about this one in the papers.'

God had been kind. It was a cloudy overcast night, with a light breeze and no sign of the waning moon.

Rino was sitting on the tree stump outside the house. Dawn was not that far away, and he wanted her back. He looked down at his watch. It was over an hour and a half since he had last seen her at the top of the ridge. After, as instructed, he had coasted the Caddi down the hill and into the shadows, he had given her a thumbs up before watching her slowly turn and trot off into the darkness. He locked all the car doors and placed the keys on top of the front left tyre. The few kilometres' run back to the house took him no time at all. The worst thing was his holster banging against him all of the time. So he stopped for a moment and twisted his belt around to put the weapon on his left hip, which seemed to help slightly.

It was refreshingly cool, a slight aromatic breeze starting to rustle through the leaves. The birds' dawn chorus was just beginning when car headlights appeared on the main road above the house, materialising quite quickly into Nella's little blue Fiat Cinquecento bumping down the drive towards him. He was on his feet and opening her door at the exact moment that she pulled on the handbrake and switched off the lights.

He looked down. 'You okay? You okay? Was worried about you.'

She stepped out of the car, and for the first time they embraced each other. Not a sensual embrace, the top half of the body only, head into the shoulder and a warm hug. But it said that they had recently bonded, and they both wanted to acknowledge the other.

'I had to clean up Giotto and his tack. That paint got everywhere. Mixing it with washing-up liquid helped, but it was still a bugger of a job. I found all of that quite exciting, didn't—'

Rino interrupted her. 'Yes! Yes! But did you bring back the paint, the brush, the manure bag, my rope?'

She shook her head in irritation. 'Yes, of course I did. They're all in the footwell!' Nella was buzzing. 'When Giotto whinnied when he started to pull the car up the track, I thought they'd wake up and come rushing out.'

'Well, they'd be like the rabbits in the garden if they had, ten metres, bullet between the eyes.'

'Would you really have shot them?'

'Yes, without any hesitation, would have enjoyed it! But that's not the master plan, is it? That's all about making sure that everyone has an alibi.'

Nella went round to the far door of the car, opened it and handed Rino his long hank of thick tow rope, followed by four large square pieces of thick lorry inner tube rubber about a quarter of a metre square that looked a bit dusty and full of holes.

Rino looked down at them. 'My question to you is: what kind of a mind insists that the horse wears rubber boots, gives you a colour photo of a foreigner's black-and-white horse in a field three kilometres from here, then tells you to paint Giotto to match it and insists that we leave no manure behind. I find all of that a bit over the top.'

Nella reached into the footwell and grasped a large piece of thick grey cotton curtaining with long ribbons attached to each corner. She sniffed at the light brown stains in the middle. Rino was revolted. He hated the smell of horse poo. She smiled patronisingly at him.

'Hoof prints are unique. They can quickly identify a horse. Poo can identify a livery yard because they all feed something different, and as to making Giotto a piebald, there's always some old nonno with a bladder problem, going to the loo at three in the morning looking out of his window.'

Rino smiled. 'I hope you don't include me in that?'

She smiled back. 'No, I don't. I think we should be bloody proud of what we've done, Rino, bloody proud. As we have been repeatedly told, you now need to put your pistol back in the birdbox and stick all of this lot in the incinerator, including the paint and brush, and smoke out the world before everyone wakes up. When you've done that, I'll cook you breakfast.'

Rino looked at her and smiled affectionately. 'Yes, boss.'

Engineers are like bank managers. They like their routines: nine-to-five, coffee at ten-thirty and three o'clock on the dot, lunch at twelve forty-five on the dot. Creatures of self-inflicted habit, all of them. But the engineer Alessandro Mosena didn't baulk at having to get up at three in the morning and take two bikes in the back of his small Fiat van fitted with a tuned oversize Abarth engine across the city. That was the crazy film business for you. He knew the vehicle he was going to, and he knew that it would need a couple of spare parts. He had asked lots of questions and got few answers, but he totally trusted the person who asked him. They had been more than helpful and loyal, not only to him but to his close relatives, over the years. And in his eyes, those of a devoted family man, that counted for a lot.

He turned the corner, and there she was, the red Cadillac. Parked in the shadows, on the right of the sloping, badly lit, cobbled street, just down from Parioli. Alessandro pulled up behind it and swiftly walked to the front nearside wheel arch. His searching hands immediately found the duplicate ignition keys that he had handed over the previous day. He walked to the driver's door to check that they worked in the lock and the ignition lights came on. He quickly lifted the bonnet and flipped off the top of the distributor cap, and inserted the rotor arm that he had in his pocket; one of the many spare parts that the old French restoration enthusiast had left in the boot for the ungrateful Dino.

Bonnet gently closed, and a quick flip on the ignition switch brought the Detroit monster to murmuring bubbling life. Satisfied, he quickly switched it off so as not to wake a slumbering street. He quietly went to his van and eased out the two bikes, and opened up the Caddi's rear doors. He had an adjustable spanner in his pocket in case he needed to take off the front wheels, but they both fitted in the back, with a bit of fiddling and chain oil smearing onto the leather upholstery. Fifteen minutes later found him free wheeling one of the bikes back down the hill to his van. Having, as instructed, carefully parked the Caddi into a sizeable lock-up garage two kilometres away up to the north, he then meticulously checked that the second bike was in perfect working order and that both its tyres were rock hard.

He was back home by twenty past four, cleaned up and back in bed by a quarter to five and within five minutes asleep and snoring like his wife, the mother of his children, beside him.

Wednesday 30th April

Lank was on the move, his blue and white striped pyjama bottoms flapping loosely around the calves of his skinny hairless legs as he sleepily ambled. He gently scratched his right armpit with his left hand. He bent down and peered out of the front window onto the drive. The early morning sun was casting a long shadow from the pine tree in the distance. At the top of the rise, the distant clouds to the west were grey with incoming rain.

He turned to his companion, Lou, who was gently easing his barefoot way down the carpeted oak stairway, dressed in a stolen, white, gold-logoed hotel towel dressing gown.

'Boss is out early.'

Lou stopped in his tracks, a look of perplexion on his unshaven face. 'What do you mean, boss is out? He's upstairs. I just heard him in the toilet!'

Lank frowned, perplexed. 'Well, it's just…just the Caddi's gone.'

Lou scuttled to the window. 'What! It can't be!' Spittle sprayed from his thin lips.

Lank turned round and looked at the small wall table next to the door.

'It can't be, can't be, the keys are still here and that distributor thingy that you take off every night… It can't be!'

Lou wiped the spittle from around his face with the back of his hand. Then looked out of the window again, just to reaffirm his statement. He looked back, a wild look on his face.

'It's gone, Lank, bloody gone! The boss is going to go mad. You'd better go tell him.'

Lou shook his head. 'No 'effin way! No way! You tell him!'

Ispettore Paulo Gatti laughed. 'Hah! There is a God! You say his car's been nicked?'

Christina nodded a little uncertainly. 'Yes, sir. In the middle of the night, just vanished into thin air. He is absolutely crazy about it. I won't tell you what he called me.'

'Well, it's hardly your fault! Have uniform been out and had a look around?'

She shuffled uncertainly. 'Yes, sir, but they found nothing, nothing at all. As you know, it's pouring with rain, so they didn't stay that long. Burgio had even removed the Rotar arm to immobilise it, and yet it's still gone.'

Gatti thought for a minute, tapping his desk with his right index finger. 'Send out an all-points to all officers, particularly plain clothes. A heavy car like that is only ever going to be used to ram something, all that power, all that weight. I'd be worried that it could be used to ram any vehicle carrying gold bullion, large amounts of cash, or take out the front wall of a bank. It'll never be used for social, domestic or pleasure, that's for sure, because it's probably the only one in Italy. Stands out a bit. Fake number plates are going to be a total waste of time. Even our beloved car thieves of Rome aren't that stupid. So if it's sighted, follow and call for a heavily armed response team. Also, my dear, post to our good friends in the carabinieri and all sea ports, just in case. I think, though, that this has been stolen to carry out a particular task, one involving pure brute force.'

Thursday 1st May

May Day, Labour Day in Italy, is a national holiday, and for most businesses a day of rest. But film productions often have to run to a different set of rules.

There were lots of mutterings, particularly among the Macchinisti, electricians and the standby Construction crews that it should be observed. But reasons given by Production was that there was a day and a half shooting left to finish all of the street stall scenes. If 'we' could get all of that completed by Friday lunchtime, Art and Construction would then have two whole days over the weekend on overtime pay to revamp the set, 'a total rebuild', for the following week. The concept did not go down well.

Adam was caught up in the mutterings. Neither Anatra nor Luca were happy, and the pace of the set seemed to slow a little. Duke noticed too, but there was little he could do about it. He couldn't tell people how quickly to walk. He'd been around long enough to know that by the following Monday, after a good weekend break, fresh onto a new set, they'd all be back up to speed.

It's not often that days on a film set drag, but this was undoubtedly one of them because it was a significant street scene, involving lots of extras. Even though the main focal point was Isabella, the extras were needed in the background and crossing in the foreground to give the whole scene a busy realism.

Adam became aware of what an art it was to organise fifty or so people to walk, talk and act naturally in a pretend street. Going for a second or third take meant everyone going back to their original start positions, which they all did very quickly and with great humour, although never quietly. Organising it all, Duke and Ben seemed just to have a sixth sense about how it should all play out. To say that they were on each other's wavelength was an understatement. Adam was in awe of how organised they both were. Having so many extras wandering about made the maintenance of continuity even more difficult for Grace. She was shooting polaroids virtually non-stop between every take, leaving Adam to decide that he'd got the easy job on that particular day. But despite all of the bustling activity, Adam was more than pleased when 'wrap' was finally called, and all of the kit was back in its boxes in the camera room.

Back at the Spanish Steps, Adam had his usual Coke and Spaghetti alla Carbonara at his regular trattoria before he drifted into his hotel bar at around eight-thirty to meet Steve.

They had a quick drink together before Adam took him up to the first floor and then back down the fire escape stairs to the Porta di Potana corridor. He wanted to show Steve where he would be popping out on the Friday night. They then retraced their steps to the hotel's front, got into Steve's car, and drove off into the traffic to begin Steve's demonstration and recce for the Friday night activity.

Friday 2nd May

It was pretty true to say that Adam was in a bit of a state that Friday morning. Multiple emotions were running through him. Fearful anticipation of what he had agreed to do that evening. Would he be able to carry out all of the instructions? Would it go well? Would he mess it up? If he did, what would be the outcome?

Back on the film set, the street scene, there was the no small matter of some very challenging focus pulls involving small German Army badges worn by extras who were crap at hitting their marks.

The scenes concerned Isabella, the spy, noting which soldiers were walking up and down the street by her fish stall. Shooting her face shots were a walk in the park. Bless her, she kept her head in one place and just moved her eyes. Only one focus setting. Thank you, Isabella, you're a pro! It was shooting what she was looking at that was the problem. The extreme close-ups that Lasse wanted were of the small regimental badges on the shoulders and collars of the German soldier extras as they shopped at the stall and walked up and down the street.

By lunchtime, Adam had been the cause of more than a few feet of wasted film and was definitely feeling the pressure. Fortunately, much to his relief, by lunchtime it was all in the can.

After lunch, the workload got easier, with fewer close-ups and more wide shots, plus the fact it was a pre-planned early finish. Adam was more than pleased to be getting out of Toni's unit car at the Spanish Steps at around five-thirty. He went straight up to his room and crashed out on the bed. The amount of concentration required that morning had drained him. He was shattered. He also knew that he would have to be on top form that evening and so he set his alarm for seven-thirty, which would give him time to nip out and get a bite to eat over the road first.

Steve was exactly where he and Adam had planned he would be, parked up, engine running in the little off-street service road that was behind Adam's hotel.

Adam was wearing dark black denim jeans and a matching jacket, courtesy of a little shopping trip the previous evening. His sand-coloured desert boots had made no sound as he had walked down the back stairs, along the ground floor corridor, past the laundry room and out through the Porta di Potana. He had seen no one, and no one had seen him.

The personalised handwritten invitation had said 7.30 p.m. Fancy dress, any dress, just come!

As is always the way with such events, some enter into the spirit, some go over the top, some make no effort at all, and some make no effort and turn up late.

Gill was one of the former, dressed in the dark grey, full-length, belted dress, short red shoulder cape and shoulder-length white headdress of the Australian nursing corps.

Her husband Alberto was dressed up, as he always was for any fancy-dress do. Tonight he was a black-suited Chicago gangster with overly padded shoulders and a large, bright white tie, all topped off with a big al Capone-style, pale grey, wide-brimmed Fedora hat.

Pia was taking coats at the front door. She looked utterly stunning, dressed in a bronze and gold flapper dress from the 1930s and draped with an abundance of metallic necklaces. The whole outfit looked like an honest take back in time to the period of the flapper.

When Gill walked into the room, the first person that she saw was Solveig Larsen. She was dressed in the traditional costume of the Norwegian fjords, a full, ankle-length, black embroidered dress, covered by a perfect white, full-length apron beneath a broad, ornate, gold-embroidered belt. Her top was a split red bodice over an elaborate embroidered white blouse.

Sven, wearing a horned Viking helmet and rust-coloured, modern, two-piece suit, was standing off to one side, a bemused grin on his face as he bathed in the reflected glow of interest that his beautiful wife's costume was causing.

Duke, wearing a green and gold olive branch headdress, was shaking hands with Alberto within a few seconds of them entering the room. His white toga, hanging neatly off his wide shoulders, gave him an effortless air of authority as he extended his hand in welcome.

'Gill, Alberto, welcome, welcome. We have a little seating plan. I've put you up the top here with myself and Angelina and Loretta and husband Principio. Thank you so much for making an effort, Gill. I love the outfit, Australian nurse, I'm guessing.'

Gill smiled. 'Yes, my mother's. I had to let the seams out a bit. She was a bit slimmer than me.'

Duke smiled. 'Great! It suits you. Well, now that most of us are here, I'll make a little announcement if that's okay.'

Leaning forward to the table, he picked up a knife and gently tapped his empty wine glass.

'Good evening, good evening, everybody, and welcome to this little party to remember Luigi. As you can see, there is a bar to the left, here in the middle of the room a warm buffet will be laid out which we have planned to start around eight-thirty, if that's okay with everyone. While we are eating, Grace has volunteered to play a little light piano music for us from up on the balcony. Stand up, Grace, give us a wave.'

Down the far back right of the room, a figure in a bright dark blue, loose-fitting, below-the-knee, flapper dress stood up and gave a high-handed wave. Gill hardly recognised her take on the fancy dress. She was wearing a dark brown, curly wig and a pale blue, felt cloche hat with a dark blue feather that matched the rest of her outfit. The three waist-length metal necklaces, which, as she stood up, she flicked burlesque style in a circular motion, making a slight clacking sound. Still, the smile was unmistakable. It was definitely Grace.

Duke beamed and raised his eyebrows. 'But that's not all. Before we eat, we have a magician in our midst, young Fulvio, who will be coming round the tables, doing a few card tricks, to keep you amused.'

At the far end of the room, on the left side opposite Grace, the slim figure of Fulvio stood up and held up his left hand, in which a playing card suddenly appeared. He looked at it with an expression of complete surprise. He smiled and sat back down.

Duke nodded and chuckled in approval. 'And finally, after we have eaten, around nine-thirty we will have the pleasure of listening to the voice of one of Luigi's oldest friends, the tenor Llanfranco Lucarelli. Stand up, Llanfranco.'

To Gill's right, the bulky figure sitting at the next table, adjacent to Isabella, stood up and gave an exaggerated bow of fake humility.

Duke smiled again and acknowledged his bow with his right hand. 'He will be accompanied on the accordion by one of our own, our very own chief electrician Enzo.'

The familiar lantern-jawed, tan cotton jacketed, bulky figure scraped his chair as he stood up at the middle table down the far end of the room. He just gave a gentle, open-handed, waving gesture and sat down.

'So that's it from me, my friends. Stay seated, stand up, walk around, talk to each other, go to the bar, do whatever you fancy doing, but please make sure that you all enjoy yourselves. That's why we are all here. Thank you.'

As he sat down, Alberto turned to Gill and without saying anything, made a drinking motion with his right hand up to his mouth. Gill smiled and nodded.

'Please! The usual. Thanks.'

Alberto nodded and made his way over to the queue forming at the bar.

Gill stood and took in the scene. It was obviously a restaurant and a big one at that. Very high, wood-beamed ceilings denoted that it must have been an old barn or agricultural building earlier in its history. To her left, above the now seething nine-metre or so, well-stocked, wooden bar was a line of small windows letting in the last of the daylight. The centre of the room was taken up by a huge table about five metres long and a metre and a half wide, covered in lines of small pure, clean white sheets, presumably the buffet for later. The soft, subtle, though not that bright, lighting came only from yellow and grey shell-shaped art deco style uplighters dotted at two-metre intervals around the walls. To say the room was themed was an understatement.

To the right, hiding the doors to the kitchen, was a three-metre long, two-metre high, painted panel depicting in some colourful detail the waterfront at Portofino. Two other coastal scene-painted panels of a similar size were sited at the far end of the room to conceal the two toilet doors. In front of them were three circular tables, each set for four diners, which were the place settings for, among others, Fulvio, Pia, Enzo and Grace.

Even the bar was theme-painted beneath the countertop with a long-familiar scene of the old Venice waterfront, protected from kicking punters by Perspex or glass sheeting. But the most striking artwork was a four-metre by two-metre painting of Tuscany at sunset, with rolling hills and the shadows cast by the traditional tall, slim Lombardy poplars. That was bracketed, and chain-hung to the front of the very substantial dark oak balcony. The artwork seemed familiar to Gill in some way, but she could not precisely place it.

She knew most people in the room, but not the woman on the table to her left, with her back to her. A companion of Nella, the housekeeper. She found out later that she was called Adriana. An utterly charming woman. In all, Gill thought that there were about twenty-six or so guests, nearly all whom she knew from Production. It should be a very enjoyable event.

As Steve eased his car to a halt, he turned to Adam and smiled.

'Good luck, me old mate. You've got all the keys, so can we synchronise our watches now, at seven forty-two.'

Adam peered down in the failing light and twiddled his watch, setting it to seven forty-two, making sure that the button was well and truly pushed home.

Steve reached into his pocket. 'Here's another watch, old son, just to make sure. Keep it in your pocket. You need to leave here at around eight thirty-five, drive slowly and quietly so as not to draw attention to yourself. Sorry to give you time to kill, but I didn't want you getting a taxi, and I need to be somewhere else fairly soon, so if you want something to do, you can rub down every part of the car for fingerprints, that will keep you busy. You've got the newspaper in your back pocket, haven't you?'

Adam opened the door and turned back and smiled. 'Yes, of course! You really are a fastidious bugger, Steve, aren't you.'

Steve laughed. 'Got to be, mate, lives at stake. Anyway, break a leg, as they say in your business. Don't forget to put on and keep on your black leather gloves before you go anywhere near that building.'

Veronique Press was totally predictable, dressed in a long, full-length, white skirt and a pale blue, high-necked satin blouse with a white and gold scarf. She swanned in half an hour after everyone else and headed straight for the bar. She eventually gravitated to her place and sat down between Rino, the gardener, and Tomassino, the accountant. It didn't take her long to establish that Rino was a man of the soil, who ran every day for exercise and had very rough hands. After that, he really stood no chance at all as the seductive onslaught of many years of experience of French sex appeal came his way.

Someone else who also had a promising night ahead of them was Pia, down at the far left table with the actor Fulvio. It was evident by their frequent kissing that they were now an item, and the sooner they got a room, the better.

The carabinieri officer strode purposefully up to the front door of the little tenantless shop. The three-metre-wide windows were covered in multiple layers of pasted pamphlets and posters, many advertising the Russian Circus visit six months ago. He didn't look furtive; he confidently opened the door and lifted his heavy, black bag across the threshold, and closed the door. He ignored the dozens of letters and pamphlets that had come optimistically through the letterbox to now lie spread out, unwanted and unloved all over the front mat.

The open-plan, dusty ground floor of the shop had a musty, damp unventilated smell. As he strode up the narrow squeaking stairs to the first-floor landing, the accommodation part of the property, the aroma changed to mature dried cat pee. Flies flew and buzzed around him as he quietly eased open the squeaky, metal, bolted top door out onto the roof. The smell of fresh air was more than welcome, but it didn't make the olfactory experience of the building any more appealing.

Duke looked at his watch and gently tapped his wine glass with his dessert spoon. He scanned the room. Many of those there were more than used to being told by him to be quiet on set. So after a few seconds and a couple more taps, silence ensued.

'Friends, the time has come for a little food. I hope that you enjoyed Fulvio's card tricks. Luigi would have, I'm sure, so thank you, Fulvio. A little round of applause for Fulvio.'

Duke clapped loudly, and was enthusiastically mimicked by the rest of the room as Fulvio bowed. After about a minute, the noise naturally died down, and Duke resumed his master of ceremonies role.

'Now, my friends, our Grace is going to pop upstairs to the balcony and gently tickle the ivories while we eat.'

Duke extended his right arm towards Grace at the far end of the room, a gesture totally befitting the role of the ancient Roman Senator that he was playing. Grace smiled and bowed slightly, then picked up from the table in front of her a large, white feather boa that she flicked over her right shoulder. Waving her sheet music in her other hand, she smiled, turned and walked up the steep twelve or so wooden steps behind her to the dark wooden balcony.

To the right of the suspended Tuscany landscape was a very comprehensive drum kit covered in grey dust sheets and three head-height microphone stands without their mikes. To the left of the Tuscany artwork was a small, glossy, black grand piano. How they had got it up there was a mystery.

Gill watched Grace go. The stairs didn't look that safe. Fortunately, there was a bannister rail on the right wall that she was able to grab a couple of times. When Grace started her journey up the stairs, the three white-aproned catering staff were ceremoniously lifting the white sheet covers off the buffet food on the central table. There was a loud crash from the kitchen that made everyone jump. But it was just the trolley with all of the hot food dishes hitting the two-way kitchen doors on its way into the room from behind the Portofino painted panel. Supper was served!

Adam reached his destination a little earlier than planned, so he knew that he had a bit of time to waste. He turned off the headlights and switched off the engine. He took his time to take out the bike from the rear seats and gently lean it up against the low, ancient, moss-covered verge-side stone wall. He then went around the car and meticulously wound down all of the front and rear windows.

He looked again at his watch. Too early still, have to wait quietly for a few minutes. He pulled out the white-faced watch that Steve had given him as a spare. It lined up with his exactly, which was a relief.

The carabinieri officer walked silently across the flat rooftops. The sound of people talking below and the early evening TV programmes wafted up to mix with the various eclectic smells of food being prepared. It did not take him long to reach his destination: a lead, flat-roofed area about nine metres square overlooking a small, brightly lit courtyard.

A very large, lightly carved, North African-style, circular, wooden tray leant against the little lead-clad gully wall, and next to it were five identical white and pink cardboard boxes, each about the size of a small car battery. He was relieved to see that they were all exactly as he had left them the previous night.

Gill looked up from her food. It was obvious that Duke had not skimped on any aspect of the catering. It was turning out to be a very enjoyable evening. Loretta Alonzo, the production's lawyer, and her husband were great company. Almost all of them, with the exception of the diabetic Loretta, had consumed nearly a bottle of wine each. The tone of their conversations changed the more alcohol was consumed to less superficial and idealistic topics, all of which resulted in a lot of laughter and a jovial mood.

From where Gill was sitting, Grace's piano playing from the balcony was having a hard time competing with the room's background noise. But every now and then, there was a lull, and it was evident that the lady way back up there in her cloche hat and white feather boa was a very talented musician.

The light smell of woodsmoke filled the room. The fire was dying, and there was no energy left to rush upwards, so its smell was spreading out and hanging around, very much like the room occupants, all of whom were a little the worse for drink. The two armchairs and the sofa were arranged in a horseshoe shape facing the fire.

Dino took up the whole sofa. Half seated, half sprawled across its opulent shiny, buttoned, red-leather surface. His shirt was half undone, revealing the mass of chest hair which was greyer up towards his fat neck. There were red marks of spilt wine down his front, and on the small low occasional table to his right were two nearly empty red wine bottles and a half-full wine glass.

Lou, on the far side of the room, away from the fire, was sitting over by the smeary front window, nodding, half asleep in his high-backed chair, a dribble of saliva sliding from the left corner of his mouth.

The black Mercedes hire car on loan from the Production Office was parked tidily off to the right, out of the way to the side of the house, making it less visible from the road. The keys were on the table next to the door; should they be needed, everyone knew where they were.

Lank was asleep in the far armchair to the right of the fire emitting slight nasal snoring noises every minute or so, which annoyed everyone in the room. But they lived with it. He was not a person to upset. The reputation of his violent temper preceded him.

Sitting with his back to the front of the house in a matching armchair was Max, clasping in his lap a half-empty bottle of beer. He had leant his Sten, stock to the floor, barrel up between his legs, squeezing it with his knees now and then in pure boredom. Of all of them, he was the one that was most alert. Occasionally, he stared down to his left at the flickering dying embers of the fire that had over warmed the room for most of the evening.

In front of him, Lank was half asleep, subconsciously fingering the trigger guard of his Sten gun. He hated the weapon. He kept telling everyone that it was not as reliable as the Tommy gun that he had left back home. And in his loud opinion, it was 'a mass-produced piece of crap that was prone to jamming'.

There was no passing traffic on the quiet little country lanes, which helped make the waiting less stressful. Adam looked at his watch. It was time to move. The car started straightaway so without turning on the lights, he slowly drove the murmuring monster the final fifty or so yards to the driveway leading down to the villa, braking gently before switching off the engine. Before doing so, he made absolutely sure that the steering wheel was dead straight so that the car was pointing directly at the house front door, a hundred or so metres below him. He firmly pulled on the handbrake then slowly got out so as not to draw attention to himself. Sudden motion gives you away, he'd been told. He placed a brick under the back wheel to act as a chock. Phase one complete.

Once again, he leant slowly back into the car to gently ease the handbrake off, making sure that the brick chock was holding. His pulse was racing like crazy, probably the fastest it ever had been in his twenty-nine years. He walked round the back, up to the front passenger door, which he gently opened, then leant in again to double-check the steering wheel was absolutely centred. There was a damp, wet rope firmly knotted to the top centre spoke of the steering wheel. As instructed and rehearsed in great detail, he pulled the rope gently out of the passenger door, making sure not to over tension it and pull the steering wheel out of alignment. Then, as quietly as he could, he closed the door, firmly trapping the end of the rope between the door and the car body. On the front passenger seat and the long rear back seat were piles of rags that a quarter of an hour ago he had drenched with what smelt like paraffin. About forty or so firecracker squibs were spread randomly on the dashboard, the seats and floor.

Adam looked down at his watch. A couple of minutes too early!

In the darkness, a black-gloved hand silently pushed a metal rod firmly into the soft earth of the lawn. There was a thin, matte, black, metal wire attached to it. The wire was tight, set about three inches parallel to the ground.

The carabinieri officer sat down and carefully placed the large wooden tray on the flat, grey, lead roof. He looked at his watch. Plenty of time! Plenty of time to be meticulous and careful. He gently leant forward and pulled open the first white and pink cardboard box.

Adam had a good look around to make sure that there was no passing traffic. Nothing. Perfect. He pulled out a brand-new, small, plastic cigarette lighter from his jeans pocket. He had been given a second as backup, but it lit first click. Producing a piece of newspaper from his back pocket, he touched its corner to the lighter flame. As it started to burn, he half placed, half tossed it onto the paraffin-soaked cloths. There was a faint *whoof*, and the flames began to take hold. Adam looked around again to make sure that there was no one about. Satisfied, he firmly closed the back door. He repeated the torching with the cloths on the front passenger seat. He had been briefed to make as little urgent movement as possible, to take his time, but his body was producing so much adrenaline it was proving impossible.

He still had two more things to do. He pulled the damp, left-hand steering wheel rope out through the driver's front side door jamb while keeping it tight, then closed the door, like the passenger side trapping its braided thread in place, like a bowstring, to stop the steering wheel from turning.

Finally, he had to kick the brick out from under the rear tyre, which was more challenging than expected because of the weight of the vehicle. Beginning to panic slightly, he pushed the car back with his left shoulder against the rear window frame. The vehicle only moved a couple of centimetres, but it was enough to take the pressure off the brick, which succumbed to his third rather frantic kick. The car, now free, needed no encouragement to roll down the slope towards the villa. The flames from the rags were starting to get quite enthusiastic by now. He could see them quite clearly flickering away through the rear window. After a few yards, the two-and-a-half-ton Detroit monster was already at a fast walking pace and starting to pick up speed. Adam quickly strode the few yards back to the bike.

Lou, half asleep, still dribbling, looked back up the drive. A movement up at the end of the drive by the road had caught his partially open eye. He couldn't make out what it was, but knew something had moved.

'MAX! MAX! GET OVER HERE!' he shouted over his shoulder. He turned back to the window and stood up to get a better view.

Suddenly up by the road, he saw flames which were lighting up a vehicle of some kind. A car appeared to be on fire. The flames slowly started to increase and move down the drive towards the house. He could make out a car, a big car, which was gathering speed. The whole thing had turned into a fireball.

He screamed hysterically, covering the window glass in spittle, 'MAX! MAX! LANK! LANK!'

Max leapt up from his armchair, turned and rushed the six or so paces to the window, pushing Lou unceremoniously to one side to stare up the drive. A look of sheer horror came over his face.

The faint sound of multiple bangs, one after the other that sounded like pistol shots, could be heard. He couldn't see who or what was shooting. The burning car was fast approaching, heading straight for him at the window.

Max turned. 'FUCKING HELL! IT'S THE CADDI. FOR GOD'S SAKE, WE'RE BEING HIT. IT'S A HIT.'

Dino was half-heartedly pulling himself up, as was Lank, looking very confused. They stood, riveted to the spot.

Max grabbed the off-balance Lou by the shoulder and pulled him back. 'OUT! OUT! OUT THE BACK NOW. SAFETY'S OFF.'

The fireball car was moving inexorably down the drive, and there was no doubt it would hit the house head-on. Lank took one last look out of the window. It was plain now: it was Dino's Cadillac, bouncing gently up and down towards them. There didn't seem to be anyone in the driver's seat, but it was by now about seventy-five metres from the window, and the sound of small arms fire was becoming more frequent.

Max rushed past the frozen Lank towards the back door, punching him on the shoulder as hard as he could to jolt him out of his reverie. 'DON'T JUST STAND THERE. GET THE BOSS.'

Dino was by now on his feet, not knowing which way to turn. Lank grabbed him by the shoulder and propelled him unceremoniously towards Lou and Max, who by now was frantically pulling back the stubborn bolts on the back door, making his fingers bleed in the process.

The sound of gunfire could be heard, and the flickering flames of the oncoming car were becoming apparent, reflected on the walls of the room. Eventually, the back door submitted to Max's frantic efforts and banged open. He led the way out into the night, jerking himself evasively to the right in a crouching position, his Sten gun pointing into the darkness in an effort to offer as small a target as possible. He swung his short black barrel left and right to cover every likely eventuality. Behind him followed the scuttling figure of Lou, crouching, a sweaty finger on his Sten trigger ready to fire. Much to Max's surprise, no bullets came his way. Dino followed, having been unceremoniously grabbed by the shoulder and propelled along by the agitated Lank.

'COME ON, BOSS, COME ON, NEED TO GET OUT OF HERE.'

There was a loud bang, followed by the sound of a wall caving in, as the flaming Caddi crashed into the front of the building and began to infect the interior with its flames. Intermittent bangs like pistol shots could still be heard.

Max reacted to the sounds behind him, but he was more concerned, like any good soldier, about what lay ahead of them in the blackness. They were all standing on the patio, their weapons waving and pointing uncertainly in every direction. A few seconds passed. There was no burst of gunfire from the darkness. All four of them breathed a small sigh of relief. They looked around. There didn't appear to be an ambush. They relaxed a little, turning to each other grimacing, making sure that they were all unharmed.

The dark figure behind the large pine tree was unrecognisable. A right gloved hand was hiding the top of the face, firmly covering the eyes. A left gloved hand clicked a World War II metal cricket clicker. It clicked twice. The metallic sound carried. It was out of keeping with the surroundings.

Max stepped forward, pointing his Sten purposefully towards the sound, as he moved slowly towards the tree where he thought the noise had come from. Each step was measured, very deliberate. As he stepped down off the patio onto the lawn, his right shoe snagged a thin, matte, black, tensioned wire.

The carabinieri officer looked at his watch. It was nearly nine o'clock. Time to get ready. He had perched the large wooden tray on three of the pink and white cardboard boxes. It was essential that he would be able to pick it up evenly and cleanly. It now weighed about fifteen kilos, but everything on it looked exactly as it should. He tentatively looked over the half-metre-high parapet down into the small piazza courtyard below. He knew that he couldn't be seen because downlighters lit the courtyard from all around the building walls, and up higher beyond them was nothing but blackness.

He watched Sylvania in her white dress climb up onto the long, old, oak table and raise her glass up towards him. Forty-nine of the most anti-social villains in Italy followed her lead, raising their glasses heavenwards to greet a large spinning, lightly carved, North African wooden tray, nineteen metal rings with long pins all flying loose, accompanying their nineteen British Mills hand grenades, each carefully encased in its own individual wine glass.

The carabinieri officer had just six seconds to stuff the three remaining cardboard boxes containing the new wine glasses into his bag along with the other two and put as much distance between himself and the parapet as possible before night turned momentarily into day and the whole world shook like an earthquake. The ensuing noise was deafening.

The bike ride to the top of the ridge was about two hundred yards away. Behind him, Adam could hear the sound of the firecrackers going off like pistol shots, followed by a loud crump as the car crashed into the front of the building. By now, he had reached the ridge and was ready for the long freewheel down towards the city.

Behind the tree, the gloved hand pushed harder into the face, protecting the eyes. Suddenly the whole garden was lit up by the most blinding light. A pure white flash of unbelievable brightness. The four figures were totally traumatised, instantly blinded, their retinas scorched, stunned by the incredible intensity of the light. They were completely and utterly disorientated. The air was full of falling white dust, and darkness had returned. The house was silhouetted by the pale yellow fire burning and crackling at the front of the building. There was a loud *whoof* as the contents of the Cadillac's petrol tank exploded. A bright orange-red fireball tore momentarily into the sky, adding to the atmosphere of confusion.

The Enfield service revolver in the right gloved black hand spoke four times. Max was the first to die. He was the most dangerous. A 38 bullet between the eyes, as a second later Lou took a similar headshot, this one slightly higher, hitting him in the forehead and removing half the back of his skull. Lank, hearing two shots, lurched defensively to his right, but not being able to see, had no idea where the threat was coming from. Bullet three tore into his chest, knocking him to the ground. The final fourth blew his brains out.

Dino was now the only one left upright, hunched, frightened, blind, pathetic. He sensed a figure near him. 'What the fuck's going on?' he said, almost as a whimper.

The leather hand slowly put the service revolver back in its hip holster.

Dino screamed again, his voice cracking in terror. 'WHAT THE FUCK'S GOING ON?'

The same black-gloved hand was now holding a knife that moved with frightening speed from waist level to up under

Dino's rib cage, straight into his heart, where it paused for a second before it was given an energetic twist, and then jerked out.

The ensuing scream that echoed off the building walls was shrill, positively primaeval. Dino fell to the ground, twitching, convulsively now, in the final minute or so of his life. There was blood pumping everywhere, all over his white shirt and down the front of his recently urine-saturated trousers. The three bodyguards were totally lifeless. The only standing figure now moved forward and kicked at the wired metal post to loosen it, bending down briefly to pull it out of the ground by the matte black trip wire. The shadowy form then walked the three metres to a photographic flash tray, which had until two minutes ago been overcharged with five times the usually recommended amount of magnesium 'Blitz' powder. The tray was still hot, so the pistol barrel was used to lift it up and carry it away into the darkness.

There was hardly any traffic on the road as Adam freewheeled down off the ridge, back towards the city, the cool breeze blowing through his hair.

After five minutes, as planned, he turned into a narrow dark alley that was a small deserted cobbled service road. He undid the top of his black denim jacket and took it off. He pulled out the black beret tucked into his belt before tying the jacket sleeves tightly around his waist. His newly revealed pale blue, faded denim shirt housed his sunglasses in the top pocket, but the lenses had been removed, leaving just the flimsy frames. He then firmly pulled on the black beret, settled the lensless frames on the bridge of his nose and continued his freewheeling back towards the city, his appearance to any observer completely changed.

He had quite enjoyed the last half hour, particularly the adrenaline rush. He wondered how things had gone back at the house. He thought he'd heard a few shots, but couldn't be sure.

He left the bike leaning up against a wall two streets away from the Porta di Potana back door of his hotel. It would have a new owner in less than twenty minutes. Anything not actually manacled to railings was more than fair game for most of the local inhabitants.

Duke looked down at his watch. It was nine-thirty. The caterers had done well. Most of plates had been cleared away and the guests were now enjoying their coffee. He looked over to the tenor, Llanfranco, with a quizzical nod. Llanfranco picked up his serviette from the table, rubbed enthusiastically around his mouth and nodded an 'I am ready' nod, followed by a smile. Duke looked down to the far end of the room to Enzo, offering him a thumbs up or thumbs down gesture in keeping with his Roman Emperor costume. Enzo got the joke and grinned, giving him an affirmative nod and thumbs up.

Satisfied, Duke gave a waving attention-seeking thumbs up 'okay to finish' signal to Grace who was still happily tinkling away at the piano up on the balcony. Nodding, she completed the last few notes with an exaggerated flourish. As she closed the piano lid, Duke tapped his glass and, using his 'on set' high volume voice, addressed the room.

'Friends, guests, I hope that you enjoyed your food as much as I did. Now we are in for another treat. Llanfranco and Enzo are going to entertain us with some traditional Italian music, which I know that you are really going to enjoy. But before that, I think that we all owe the lovely Grace a big round of applause.'

He looked over to the far right corner of the room where the slim figure dressed in blue was just coming down the last of the rickety steps from the balcony, gripping the handrail tightly. As she reached floor level, she dropped her sheet music onto the table and theatrically pulled her white boa down from around her shoulders, and bowed repeatedly to great applause.

Alberto turned to Gill. 'She's outstanding! Outstanding! We could maybe ask her to play at our silver wedding anniversary next year.'

Gill looked at him and gently placed her hand on his thigh under the table. 'What makes you think that either of us are going to live that long, my dear? We film people seem to be becoming an endangered species. This party for Luigi, no, Jose, it all sort of proves it.'

The Vigili del Fuoco were the first on the scene. Apparently, a car had crashed into one of the remote country villas and caught fire. By the time the two local volunteer-based appliances arrived, the fire had taken a tight grip on the front of the building.

The first thing they had to do was drag the parked Mercedes with its tank full of petrol away from the side of the building. Once that was done, they did all they could to bring the energetic fire under control, but even though they were working on low ground there was no nearby lake, pond or well from which to draw more water. Therefore, the fire was left to burn out, thus conserving what water they had left in the appliances to stop the spread to local vegetation.

That was when the four bodies were discovered, lying on the back patio. Water overspray and flying hot embers had contaminated the scene, which caused lots of tutting from the police and carabinieri when they finally arrived at well past three in the morning. Most of them had been otherwise engaged in attending a massive explosion in central Rome, and each and every one of them was physically exhausted and in need of a break. 'Irritable' accurately described their mood.

Saturday 3rd May

The main incident room on the third floor of the police headquarters was a scene of great activity. Twenty to thirty people, coming and going, some in uniform, some not. There was the slight odour of nervous sweat in the air. The hubbub of animated discussion intermingled with the chatter of the two teleprinters in the far right corner.

There were now three vertical picture board stands, each about three metres by two metres. The one on the left displayed about nine large photos of a burned-out car crashed into the front of a roofless smoking country house. The other ten photos from a variety of angles showed four male bodies lying on the patio, all soaked in water, overspray and burned wood ash. The other two display boards, the ones generating the most interest, were of the blown-out Vaticano Nero. The 1950s houses had fallen in at the centre like a breached dam. All of the windows and doors along the front were blown out. The pictures of the interior of the small courtyard did not lend themselves to easy viewing. Even in black and white, the reality of what had gone on was plain to see. The colour prints, which were not due till mid-morning, would definitely upset the squeamish.

The Primo Dirigente, his silver braided hat on the desk in front of him, stood tall and erect in his starched, white uniform shirt. His short black hair was meant to make him look younger, but the greying temples supported the fact that retirement was not that far away. He stood supportively beside the slightly shorter squat figure of the Colonnello of Carabinieri. Both of them looked tired and strained, both had been summoned from their beds early in the night, and like nearly everyone else in the busy room, they had barely taken a break or eaten anything for hours.

The Colonnello's uniform jacket was draped loosely on his shoulders, but did not detract from his tall, upright, imposing figure. He clapped his hands to get everybody's attention. His glasses were perched on the end of his thin shiny nose. He looked around the room at the many expectant, weary faces. He spoke quietly and calmly; there was no need to raise his voice. His rank gave him the unwavering attention of the whole room.

'We're going to call a break for six hours or so while teams at the sites gather more information. There's little more we can do at present. Because of the exact similar timing, we believe that both events are linked. It's too much of a coincidence. Our safebreakers are working flat out on the multiple safes that are at both locations. The anticipated harvest from that comes when it comes, it's just a question of time.

'There were no survivors, and the body count is impossible to assess at present because the whole scene has to be cleared up with scoops and buckets. There is nothing on the ground larger than a joint of beef, so identifying actual individuals will be almost impossible. We must all keep an open mind. One of the early morning papers has come up with the theory that it was a mass suicide. Where they got their information from is completely beyond me. It is evident that there was some kind of party going on. But at this moment in time, we can rule nothing out. It's most likely a hit from a competing criminal organisation that wants to take over Scordia's empire. Still, at the moment we don't know how the explosion occurred and who caused it. It's certainly opened up, literally opened up, in every possible way, the criminal world of Luciano Scordia. Whether he is one of the victims, we may never know.

'So, go home, get some rest, and we'll get the day shift to prepare information packs for you when you come back on. Oh, I said that there were no survivors, but two large, very aggressive Alsatian dogs were found alive in a basement at the Vee Nero. They only eat raw meat, free to a good home if anyone wants them, might make a nice gift for the mother-in-law.' He looked up and smiled a tight smile.

The teleprinters in the corner momentarily paused their chatter for the first time in eight hours. A few people snorted a snigger, but mainly the joke fell on deaf ears. The teleprinters' information pause over, recommenced their clacking, chattering information rollout.

Ispettore Paulo Gatti nodded and turned to Ispettore Alberto Consalvo standing beside him. His gaunt features smiled a thin smile, as he half turned and in a whisper without moving his lips said, 'Best thing that's happened round here for decades, Alberto. Fancy a celebratory late breakfast beer?'

The kitchen smelled of fresh coffee and croissants. The circular wooden table was covered in a sprinkling of flaky brown crumbs.

Duke smiled enquiringly across the table. 'Jose, how are you now, old friend?'

Jose, by now shaved and groomed, wearing a pale blue pullover, smiled. 'I'm fine. I'm okay. The hospital treated me like a king. The two policemen yesterday were very understanding when the doctors explained to them that I was suffering memory loss due to the traumatic event at my home, the explosion. The doctors all told them that partial or complete memory loss after a traumatic event was not at all uncommon, and that it could last for days, months, years or even a lifetime.'

Captain Steve cut across, 'You could always go to Lourdes, get a miracle cure.'

Jose smiled. 'No, I'm fine, bit shaken about emotionally, but fine. Very fortunate to have such good friends, can remember everything back to my childhood. How did Operation Sheepdog go?'

Duke smiled an exaggerated smile. 'Very well. Incredibly well, in fact. The party was a huge success and everyone had a good time.'

Grace leant forward. 'Talking about the party, who was Sheepdog? I expected it to be Alessandro Mosena, the mechanic, or the gardener, Rino, but they were both there all evening. Rino looked like he got lucky. Veronique Press was all over him. So was it your mate, Steve? The storekeeper from the Trentani Forest?'

Steve shook his head. 'No, it was someone else.'

Grace frowned. 'What? Who? What do you mean, someone else?'

'It was just someone else. Someone else.'

Grace looked at him, suddenly concerned, her knuckles starting to clench tight. 'WHO, STEVE? BLOODY WHO? I HAVE A RIGHT TO KNOW!'

Steve sat back as far as he could in his chair, momentarily putting his hands up in an overacted defensive position in front of his face. 'Whoa, Grace, Whoa! You know the way that these things work. Need-to-know basis, need-to-know.'

Grace stood up and leant forward, staring unwaveringly straight into his face. 'Need-to-know, bullshit. We are all involved in this, Steve. For the last time, who was Sheepdog? Who was—'

Steve held up his hand again in an attempt to calm her down. Duke and Jose stared open-mouthed at the highly charged scene like a train crash that was now playing out before their eyes.

Very quietly, Steve said, 'Adam. It was Adam.'

Grace exploded. 'ADAM? ADAM? ENGLISH FOCUS PULLER ADAM?'

Steve nodded, then looked uncertainly from a perplexed Duke to Jose, the latter now showing a look of slight panic at the negative energy around the table.

Steve grimaced. 'Yes, Adam. It was Adam.'

Grace stood up violently, tears welling up in her eyes. 'Adam! The bloody sheepdog. You made Adam the bloody sheepdog. Shit! Shit! Shit! Can't be! How could you do that?'

Steve looked away, avoiding eye contact. Speaking slowly and calmly in an effort to soothe the volatile atmosphere, he repeated, 'It was Adam. I thought that he would be the last to come under suspi—'

Grace cut him off. 'You should 'ave asked me. You should 'ave bloody asked me.'

Steve held up the palms of his hands in an appeasing gesture. 'He was ideal, ideal, the last person you'd think of, panic-proof, does the detail. Ideal. Knows how to keep a secret, has signed the official secrets act.'

Grace looked wildly from side to side, her lips drawn thin with anger. 'I'll say he knows how to keep a secret. He keeps secrets bloody well, and so do I. My secret is…I'm in love with the bloody man! Shit! Shit! Shit!'

She gave Steve a final venomous look, then stooped down quickly to pick up her shoulder bag from the floor, before running as fast as she could out of the room.

Duke looked from Steve to Jose, both of whom were stunned. Steve looked down at the centre of the table, slowly letting out a breath through pursed lips.

'Well, that went well! I think that's my cue to take back the carabinieri uniform to young Jose's Wardrobe department, collect the van from Mosena and meet you two at the ristorante to collect the artwork sign. You both happy with that?' he said, with a forced smile.

By ten o'clock Adam had finished his laundry at the hotel. As he handed back the laundry room keys, Nello on reception commented on the fact that he had seen him come back early the previous day and then not seen him go out or come in until this morning. As one of their long-term 'star' residents, he genuinely wanted to make sure he was okay. Adam brushed off his concerns saying that he had worked a long hard week and felt a bit headachy and the best cure for that was an early night. Nello was very sympathetic, as was the slim, tall, large-eyelashed assistant receptionist, Renata from Switzerland. A very warm-blooded, multilingual young lady who rather wanted to get to know Adam a little better. She wanted to hand him another set of keys for a change; those to her small staff accommodation room on the top floor. But Nello, the all-seeing prude, missed nothing, and for conduct unbecoming like that, she would most likely lose her job. So all Adam ever got from her were just very warm, friendly smiles.

By ten-fifteen, he was on the streets looking to buy a new pair of sunglasses. Had he been a little later leaving, he would have heard the phone in his room ringing, and ringing every few minutes for the next half hour.

He and Grace had decided to meet up at her place at around one-thirty, and so as usual, as he had time to kill, he decided to walk and continue his sightseeing. Experience had told him that sunglasses-wise, the best-priced were sold on the little news stands dotted randomly around the city. The early morning papers seemed to be selling like hotcakes, causing people to stop like frozen statues in the street and virtually read the headlines on the spot. Multiple pictures of a building that seemed to have had the front blown out of it. Adam judged from the headlines that it was called the Vaticano Nero. Even Adam knew that Nero was the Italian for black…black Vatican? Must be some kind of Italian joke. He didn't buy any papers because although he was able to get by in simple conversational Italian, he couldn't read it that well. Vocabulary issues, as Grace kept telling him.

As he walked, he reflected on the previous evening. A shuddering chill of damp sweat ran down his back. What could be have been thinking to have got talked into that? He must be crazy. He grimaced. It was done now, part of his history. But the nagging perfect wisdom of hindsight told him that he should have just said no. He just prayed that he did not live to regret it. Every time he thought of it, though, he shuddered in apprehension, even if he had enjoyed the adrenaline rush at the time.

After consuming with no great enthusiasm a breakfast orange juice and a small mushroom omelette at a streetside bar, he brushed his teeth with his serviette, popped a strip of chewing gum in his mouth and hailed a taxi to the Via Cigno.

His knuckles had barely touched the red door when it flew open, and Grace was standing framed in the doorway, her eyes full of tears, a look of great apprehension on her face.

'OHHH, ADAM!' was all she could manage before she pulled him inside, pushed her head into his left shoulder and started to sob uncontrollably. He plopped the bottle of wine, once again unsighted, onto the hall table.

As she sobbed between breaths, she managed to blurt out, 'Oh, Adam…what have you done…you silly, silly boy…'

Adam didn't understand. He was expecting her long cool fingers to cradle his face and her breasts to push tight into him along with a kiss that never ended, not a sobbing competition. He put his hand on her shoulders and gently pushed her away.

She brought her chin up and looked at him. Tears poured down her cheeks. She fought for breath between sobs. 'Oh, Adam, what have you done? What the hell have you done?' Her high-necked, mid-blue, cotton blouse above her bust was sprinkled with dark circles of damp caused by her tears.

Adam could hear the sound of an approaching scooter echoing off the far street walls and nodding to her that the front door was still open, he let go of her and turned to his right to push it firmly closed and slide the central bolt. By the time he had finished and turned back, she had moved quickly and was already starting to sit down on the lounge sofa, grabbing her bloated fawn-coloured huggy cushion as she did. She watched him as he sat down beside her.

'Oh, Adam, I so wanted to keep you out of my grubby little world. I tried so hard.'

Adam put his hands on his lap and stared blankly at the piano. He was savvy enough to know that this was going to be a fairly heavy-duty encounter. Out of the corner of his eye, he saw her squeeze hard on her pillow, followed by a huge sigh as if she had come to a major decision.

She arched her neck and looked upwards. ‘I think that it’s time to tell you what’s going on. To tell you all of the secrets, and then you can decide whether to stay or walk away.’

Adam turned to look at her. The tears had stopped, and a look of determined resolve was slowly coming over her face.

She stared fixedly ahead. ‘I never dreamed that when I jumped into this affair with you without a parachute that it would come to this.’

He just nodded like a college student settling down for a long lecture. He had the feeling that it was going to be a long lunch hour.

She got up and walked over to the dresser, opening each of the three drawers one after the other. She slowly reached into the middle one and pulled out a small bordered photo. The silver frame was battered. The palm-sized black-and-white image was of two kids standing next to each other. One had a walking stick. The poor quality made recognition impossible. She smiled, almost apologetically.

‘This is my dad and his friend, Luigi Mussomelli, around 1905 just after Luigi damaged his knee. It was taken by the only guy in the village to own a camera.’

Adam took the picture and looked at it. It so lacked definition that it could have been anyone. He put it down respectfully on the sofa beside him. The next picture she gently handed him with both hands, like a gift offering, was one of two young people covered in pigeons in a square.

'This was taken in 1920. That's Mum with Dad in Leicester Square. Dad left Sicily to go to London to make his fortune, but instead he came back just as poor a couple of years later with an English fiancée.'

Adam looked at the faded print and turned it to see the date and the misspelt 'Lester Square' in faded blue ink. Grace handed him another similar wooden frame.

'This is their wedding back in Sicily, 11th of June 1921.' She pointed to one of the assembled guest figures in the background. 'That's Dino Burgio's father. Later, during the war, he became a fascist, a follower of Il Duce and Hitler, a very dangerous man.'

Adam had no idea where any of this was going, but he respectfully placed the picture down beside the slowly growing pile of memorabilia beside him. She seemed to be relaxing a little now. A little less tense, almost as if she was getting a lot off her chest.

'This is my wedding back in 1956. You can see Mum and Luigi, but no Dad. He's dead by now, killed in an altercation back in the war.'

The way she said the word 'altercation' prompted Adam to inquire further. 'What sort of altercation, Grace?'

She looked at him momentarily then broke off eye contact. 'The worst kind, Adam. Vendetta, family rivalries. My father was killed by the young Dino Burgio in revenge for my father killing his father. Soon after that, Dino Burgio fled to America to flee prosecution.'

Adam was having trouble following her explanation. 'Grace, why did your dad kill Dino Burgio's dad?'

She had a lump in her throat, and the words did not come easily. She was close to tears. 'This is the part I wanted to shield you from, Adam. During the war Dad killed him to stop him betraying me to the Gestapo. I was an SOE agent. This film we are working on is a vanity, Adam, a huge vanity.'

Adam looked at her incredulously. 'AGENT? VANITY? What's a vanity? I'm not with you.'

Grace attempted an apologetic smile. 'A vanity. A product of the very vain. This film, which we have been making for the last few weeks, is a vanity for my grandchildren, for Isabella's children to tell the—'

Adam exploded. 'WHAT GRANDCHILDREN? ISABELLA? You told me your daughter died a babe in arms, and what the hell's this about being an agent?'

She smiled and looked away as if ashamed of what she was about to say. 'Hear me out, Adam, just hear me out. I fled to England, to Mum's sister just before the war. We were so poor, we were starving. We've filmed those scenes at Civitavecchia already. You know how I left, how I came back, and how I was recruited when I was there.'

Adam simply stared at Grace, open-mouthed. She collected a few more photos from the drawers, then gently sat down beside him. She tentatively put her hand on his knee and turned and looked at him.

'This is what I wanted to keep you away from, my nightmare of a life. Isabella is my lovely daughter. The part that she plays in the film is my life story, my family's story.'

Adam was dumbfounded. All he could do was watch her as she avoided eye contact and looked away. Adam slowly shook his head in total disbelief. She sensed the tension in him.

'As I said, the whole film is a huge vanity. After Dino fled to America, for our safety, Luigi, my godfather, brought Isabella and me to Rome. Changed our names and hid us both in plain sight.'

He looked at her. She couldn't look him in the eye.

'I'm sorry, Adam, you needed to know.'

Adam shook his head. 'I didn't need to know any of that, Grace. You could have…'

Her voice hardened. 'Oh, you did, my love, you did. Because last night you herded like a sheepdog Dino Burgio onto his back patio, where I killed him and his three bodyguards—'

'WHAT?'

She put her right index finger up to his mouth to silence him. As she did so, her whole expression changed to one of affection. 'You are part of my complex story now. Like it or not, you have unwittingly helped me and Isabella come out of the shadows, finally end the vendetta and maybe even given us back a normal life.'

Numb, Adam gently brushed her hand away from his face and slowly stood up and looked back down at her clutching a small black-and-white photo of a babe in arms. There was no doubt that the young mother was her. The proud smile was unmistakable.

'Why, Grace? Why kill Dino? And Isabella's your daughter?'

She looked at him, a hard glint in her eye. 'Well, for starters, he killed Luigi, or rather one of his men did. When Dino turned up here in Rome, Luigi knew that he represented a danger to me and Isabella, so he humiliated him at the party with the fake police and the planted pretend drugs in the hope that he'd be so embarrassed he'd bugger off back to America. But unfortunately, he didn't. Instead, he did the other thing and flew in an ex-army Ranger and a couple of other hoods and shot Luigi dead.'

Adam shook his head. 'You don't know that for sure.'

She smiled. 'Oh, but we do, Adam, we do. We also think, but are not sure, that he killed a young estate agent after having sex with her. Plus the fact that early on at that same party, he mauled and tried to have sex with Isabella. I don't tolerate that kind of behaviour.'

Adam's head was spinning as he stood up and walked over to the dresser, trying very hard to rationalise everything he'd just heard. Adam didn't do panic, but his pulse rate was dangerously high. It's not every day you discover that you're an accessory to multiple murders. And that you're working on a multimillion-dollar film that's your girlfriend's life story and that the star is her daughter. He clenched his hands, trying to get a grip on the new information. He looked down at the drawers full of various-sized framed photos, most of them in black and white. One of them stood out more than the others. It was a pin-sharp professional pose. He picked it up, turning it towards her.

She smiled. 'It's Isabella's first day at stage school. Luigi paid for her to go. She lived here with me until a few years ago when she became a starlet and earned enough money to buy her own place.' Grace gestured the room with her right hand. 'Luigi paid for all of this. We were his family in many ways. This is our hiding place.'

Adam looked directly at her. 'Where does Steve fit into all of this. Tell me about Steve.'

Grace looked up at him. 'Come and sit back down, Adam.'

Adam realised that standing up was winding him up, so he decided to do as he was asked and rejoin her on the sofa. He noticed that she was still holding tightly onto the picture of her and the babe in arms. She smiled coyly as he made himself comfortable. He sensed that she was calmer now, almost as if the worst was over and she was on the home run. She waited for him to settle before continuing.

'Just like all of the scenes we have filmed, Steve, Sergeant Steve as he was then, back in the war, was my personal training officer back at SOE spy school in Scotland. He taught me all the spy stuff, how to kill, maim, shoot, defend myself, make bombs, blow up stuff and use a radio.'

Adam was still finding it hard to join together all of the pieces. He decided to ask a question that had always troubled him 'When we were mugged, Grace, our first night, you did something to that mugger. Was that part of your training? What did you do?'

She unsmilingly looked him in the eye. 'Did what I was taught to do: fight dirty, dislocate his kneecap so that he couldn't stand up and chase us. I'm not proud of it. I could have killed him. It would actually have been a lot easier, taken a lot less effort!'

Adam paused for a second, taking in the full implication of what she had said. He was starting to sweat with anxiety. But his curiosity was piqued. 'You said that the film was a vanity about you. I didn't really follow that.'

Grace smiled momentarily. 'Luigi is, was, probably one of the richest people in Rome. He had no children, never married. I've always suspected that he was secretly in love with Mum. She was a beautiful lady, died far too young. We'll never know, but the result was that my family was close to his family. He was my father's best friend, my godfather, my protector, and as the years passed, we became his family. He is a very successful film producer. He knew a good story when he saw one and decided to make all of it into a film. He also joked it would also serve as the ultimate family history picture book for Isabella's children, my grandchildren, as yet unborn. He never intended to have the caption at the end "Based on a true life story". That is why it is a vanity. So what do you want to do, Adam? What are you going to do? Now you know my story and all of the lies that I have told you. Not exactly a relationship based on trust, is it?'

Adam stood up and walked back to the hall table to pick up the bottle of wine that he had been forced to plomp there when he walked in. He walked into the kitchen and collected the corkscrew and two wine glasses. He took his time opening the bottle and pouring two very generous servings. He handed her a glass.

'Who else knows, Grace? Who else knows?'

Grace took a large gulp of wine. 'Need-to-know basis, Adam, need-to-know.'

Adam smiled. He had heard those exact same words before. 'You sound like Steve.'

She smiled. 'It's not unique to Steve, Adam; it's a code that we have to live by. Say nothing, tell no one, keep a secret.'

Adam nodded. It was all starting to come together now.

Grace looked at him straight in the face. 'You don't have to worry, Adam. You won't come to any harm. We'll look after you.'

Adam was puzzled. 'Who exactly is "we"?'

She smiled. '"We" is the collection, the group, the family, the band, whatever you want to call us, the elite cadre of ex-serving intelligence operatives who have never really retired. They are now in their maturity in every walk of life and by now every age, shape and size. Spread all over Europe and Scandinavia, and every now and then, they sneak out of retirement, do a little job and disappear back into the shadows.'

Adam frowned. 'Sounds like a private army.'

Grace put her hand on his thigh. 'It is, Adam it is. A little, exceptional private army, one that is more often than not directed from London, or sometimes more locally by senior people like Steve. You may have unwittingly become one of us. But we don't know the answer to that yet, do we?'

Jose was certainly no handyman, he did not really do DIY around the house. Give him a sewing machine, and he was as good a tailor if not better than any seamstress. But screw eyes into beams, bits of rope and large, heavy plywood picture signs waving about were not his forte. He half-heartedly clung to the two-metre wooden step ladder as Duke, perched virtually on the top rung, used a screwdriver to finally twist out the last screw eye out of the ancient beam. He looked down at the rolling landscape scene of the Tuscan sunset now lying beside him on the floor.

'Why did you get this painted, Duke? It's a copy of the picture in Luigi's lounge. I sit opposite it at Production meetings.'

Duke stepped slowly down the steps and stuffed the screw eye and screwdriver into his jeans pocket. 'I could lie to you and say that it was Luigi's favourite painting and that it would have brought him great joy to have seen it here at his farewell party. But the real reason, because you weren't here at the party last night, was firstly, to hide the door to the fire escape door back there, and secondly, to mask the changeover from Grace to Sophia.'

Duke half turned and pointed to his right. 'Grace came up the stairs over there, walked across behind this painting to Sophia, waiting exactly where you're standing. They're both dressed the same. Sophia is literally her stunt double. A bit of make-up latex on her forehead and chin to exactly match Grace's profile. No one was nearer than twenty metres, so nobody noticed. Sophia waited here and seamlessly continued Grace's walk over to the piano. It was Sophia who tinkled away for half the evening until Grace came back up the back fire escape over there. She then gave the ivories a final ripple, got up and walked over to the painting. The girls swapped back around, and Sophia left via the fire escape as Grace took the applause at the bottom of the stairs. At the exact time of the changeovers I distracted the room to look at the caterers or me. Enzo was deliberately stationed at the bottom of the stairs to stop any drunk who wanted to go up and ask for a request or do a karaoke, but as it turned out, only half the room could hear her playing anyway, and he had a quiet night.'

Jose looked down at the painting. 'Can I buy this? It'd look lovely on the end wall of my shop.'

Duke smiled at him. 'Yes, you can, of course you can. I was just going to dump it in the scene dock, but you can have it at cost, Art department mate's rates. You can pay for the piano as well if you like.'

Jose looked puzzled and turned to his right to look at the small black upright in the corner. Duke gripped him lightly on the shoulder.

'I'm joking, mate, joking. The piano tuner arrived yesterday morning to find that the bloody thing hadn't been played for a decade, and he spent most of the day freeing off foot pedals and partially restringing and completely retuning the bloody thing. Cost an absolute fortune. But I'm paying for that as a gift to the restaurant for letting us move all the band stuff over to the far corner and hang up the sign. They did us proud. You missed a great night.'

There was a clunking followed by a scraping noise from the back of the balcony as Steve appeared, framed in the old barn loading door at the top of the fire escape. Duke smiled in welcome.

'Change of plan, Steve. It's going to Jose's shop. If you've got a few extra minutes, maybe we can help him put it up.'

Jose smiled a wicked grin. 'Oh! I'd like Steve to help me—'

Steve cut across him, 'Don't even go there, Jose, don't even go there. You're obviously feeling better.'

Adam looked at Grace's retreating figure as she walked to the kitchen to flash up a couple of steaks and some salad. She said that she was hungry even if he wasn't.

The wine was slowly seeping into his logic circuits and calming him down. Many things were starting to make sense now. The person that he'd heard moving upstairs in the little house when he'd called unannounced the day Luigi died must have been Isabella. The fact that Steve was never more than three metres away from her when she did all of her assault course scenes, often stopping the whole scene during a take if 'Her Majesty', as he called her, was likely to be hurt. The fact that Luigi's large bodyguard driver Bruno was always in her shadow, everywhere she went. The fact that Grace was always magically there if ever her precious daughter got into a one-to-one with him.

He wondered if Steve saw the fearless total commitment in Isabella that he must have seen when he trained her mother way back.

A voice floated from the kitchen. 'Do you want some more wine, Adam?'

Adam looked down at his empty glass. 'No. No, thanks. Not just yet.' Common sense continuing to tell him that the day still had unpredictable outcomes. Wine most likely wouldn't help. 'A Coke, if you have it, would be nice.'

An 'Okey dokey' floated down the hallway. He thought about getting up and looking at more photos from the drawers but decided against it. Did he really want to see pictures of her dead husband? Not really.

Adam thought about the fishmonger hand artist that had been brought in to do the gutting scene for Isabella with a knife that you could shave with, the family heirloom once owned by her grandmother. Isabella must know. She must. Adam got up and walked into the kitchen.

'Grace, does Isabella know about any of this? The spy thing, Dino's murder?'

She turned from the sizzling frying pan with a look of surprise on her face. 'No, of course she doesn't, Adam, and I don't want her to know either. At least not till I'm long gone. She thinks that Luigi's script is part fiction and part truth, like most film scripts, and that's the way I'd like to keep it. She doesn't need to know. It'll be best if she doesn't. But you know, Adam. You now know everything, and you have decisions to make: either to leave because I am a compulsive conspiratorial liar or to stay. It's your choice. But you will have to keep your silence. You've signed the official secrets act. A lifetime in prison for betraying that, and if you talk about the cadre and you were found out then your life expectancy would be measured in hours, not days.'

She handed him a Coke, flipped the cap with an opener, then gently from the frying pan levered two steaks onto two dinner plates of neatly arranged green salad.

Adam looked at her. The hard glint had gone. There was something in her eyes that was silently pleading with him.

'There's something else you need to know, Adam. This conspiratorial, compulsive lying spy is in love with you and has been for some considerable time.'

Adam paused and looked down at the two plates of food on the worktop, next to the hob, and then back to her face. She was near to tears; the hard-eyed spy had gone, and standing there was a woman in a state of emotional turmoil that suddenly looked incredibly vulnerable.

Adam put down his Coke next to the plates and walked towards her, holding out his arms to encircle her. She did the same, but there was no haste. It was all in ultra slow motion. Their arms slowly went around each other, and they stared into each other's eyes until their lips gently met. To say that the kiss that followed was emotional was an understatement. It was one of those events that one remembers for a lifetime.

Eventually, Adam eased away. 'I've made my decision, Grace.' Her eyes were damp with emotion because she knew the answer before he said the words; the kiss had told her.

'I'd like to stay, Grace. I'd like to stay with you, keep the secrets, share your values, share your life, feel that one can do a bit of good in this mad world, plus the fact I'm a bit of an adrenaline junkie, so actually almost enjoyed the rush, if you know what I mean.'

She cradled his face in her long fingers. 'Well, Adam, you now have another decision to make.' She smiled. 'The decision to eat your steak or to take me upstairs and make love to me every half hour for the rest of the weekend. It's your call.'

Monday 5th May

Adam did not exactly bound out of his hotel like a gazelle early that Monday morning. He was absolutely knackered. Grace had not been exaggerating when she talked of making love every half hour for the rest of the weekend.

Initially, Adam was able to keep to her schedule. The first three or four were quite frantic, rough, noisy affairs that Grace the lioness said were the inevitable result of releasing the pressure of many years of pent-up frustration. But after that, everything changed, and the gentlest light touch, sensual encounters ensued that seemed just to go on forever. By the time he eventually reluctantly left her, less than eight hours ago, he had been made love to in so many different ways that it was like she was a different person every time. She had done to him what she accused Belinda of planning to do, wrap him in her spider's web and gorge on him. It reaffirmed that he had been right when their fingers touched for the first time at the little café after the mugger incident way back in their history. There was something exceptional and unique about their relationship.

Captain Steve was waiting outside the Production block when Toni dropped Adam off. His smile was genuine, his handshake warm.

‘Morning, Adam. Not going to hold you up, left you alone over the weekend as I guessed you were busy. Just wanted to say well done for Friday, very well done. If you’ve got some time later this week, I’ll take you to the embassy, they’ve got a NAAFI there, and you can buy McVitie’s chocolate biscuits and cheddar cheese, if you want. If you’re up for it, I can give you a bit of pistol practice down in their firing range too. Up to you. The offer’s there.’

Adam smiled and nodded. ‘Yeah, that would be nice.’

‘Good, good. We’ll be in touch. There’s one more thing, Adam. We’ve taken a look at Luigi’s will, which will probably be read late this week, or early next. Say nothing to no one. Grace doesn’t know it yet, but she inherits a very large part of his estate, the house and most of his money. She is about to become one of the richest women in Rome, just thought you ought to know.’

Adam was surprised, a bit taken aback. ‘Thanks, Steve, thanks. But how do you know this?’

Steve smiled. ‘Oh, old solicitors, old buildings, old locks, old safes, never much of a challenge. We needed to know, in order keep her safe. Even someone like her, when they are that wealthy, is going to need someone watching their back. Job for you, maybe? Anyway, keep sharp. Have a good day.’

Over a hundred and forty hours after the big explosion at the Vaticano Nero, the media was already starting to move on. Immediately after the event, it was all they could talk about. But story after unsubstantiated rumour began to drip out: that the dead were allegedly criminal ganglords from all over the county, that the big bang was the best thing to happen to the justice system in years. Every day there were more arrests, all to do with the treasure trove of information found at the scene.

Veronique's syndicated stories of a religious criminal order and a mass suicide plot just seemed to confuse the picture. But Ispettore Alberto Consalvo wanted to speak to Duke and had asked his wife Gill to tip him off as to when he would be leaving the studio after his daily evening planning meeting.

Nine p.m. found them both sitting in Alberto's car, parked in Peter Dublin's old parking space at the studio.

Alberto had not flashed his badge. He had dined out a few times with Duke and Angelina over the years and was keen, if possible, to keep that friendship. He clicked the off switch on his police radio and looked across to his right at the bulky figure seated beside him.

'Duke, I have a carefully rehearsed monologue that I'd like to bore you with, if I may.'

Duke smiled giving off an air of complete relaxed ease. 'Go ahead, Alberto, go ahead. I'm all ears.' He relaxed his arms and slowly lay his hands palm down on his thighs.

Alberto thought for a second and decided to look half out of the car window, using the right-hand wing mirror as his focal point.

'My grandfather was a policeman, and my father was a policeman. I was brought up with the values that society, in inverted commas, needs a non-political, incorruptible, non-malevolent force to keep it straight and narrow. That is why I, too, followed Papà and Nonno and twenty-eight years ago became a police officer. But sometimes society goes off-balance, out of kilter, and the forces of law and order occasionally fail to keep that required, acceptable balance, simply because of how they're managed and the rules that they have to be seen to work by.'

He smiled, lost in thought for a second, then continued.

'Once in a generation, society is forced into a situation when it has to seize the reins to redress that balance, self-heal, cure itself, if you like. And that is what I think has happened here with Scordia and Burgio. You have no idea how much shit we got from the American embassy regarding the killing of four American nationals on Italian soil, until we very politely pointed out that three of them were carrying illegal automatic weapons, covered only in their fingerprints, and all with the safety catches off. Plus the fact we also found buried in the garden a rifle all greased up and buried in plastic that ballistics identified as the one that killed Luigi, a very prominent Italian national. But we still had four very dead bodies, executed bodies. We looked hard for the single perpetrator of that event, little men with size six boots. Even interviewed the diminutive stunt man who fell out of the tree for you last week. He incidentally had a cast-iron alibi. Every other single person who could even remotely be a person of interest was right in my sight all evening at the party on Friday except one, Captain Steve Lewis. His alibi though, Duke, was right up there with an audience with the Pope. Believe it or not, he was taking drinks followed by supper with the British ambassador and his family at the British embassy. The ambassador's son, a Lieutenant Colonel Geoffrey Whittaker OBE, actually personally confirmed it. He arrived at 6.30 p.m. and left at ten the following morning looking a little the worse for wear.'

Duke smiled. A curious smile. 'Very interesting philosophising, Alberto. I heard that the incident at the Vaticano Nero was a mass suicide. That's what the papers are saying.'

Alberto snorted. 'Mass suicide! Mass suicide! A collection of fifty of Italy's biggest villains coming all the way to the centre of Rome to commit suicide. They were drug dealers, sex traffickers, not a bloody religious cult faithfully following the demi-god Luciano Scordia. I don't buy it. I really don't buy it. But do you know what, Duke? Do you know what? I believe that it is fundamentally wrong for anyone, let alone a police officer, to have to check under his car on his hands and knees every day for explosives. It is also wrong to have to bodyguard drive your wife to and from her workplace with a loaded submachine on the back seat.'

Duke slowly nodded. 'I agree, totally agree.'

Alberto nodded. Out of the corner of his eye he had been watching Duke like a hawk. But there was not even a flicker of emotion or change of body position. He just sat there and listened. Alberto looked back to the wing mirror.

'A safe at Dino Burgio's gave us details of his links to organised crime in America, his penchant being a so-called acting school for young aspiring actors and actresses that was used as a front for sex trafficking and underage prostitution. At the Vaticano Nero were a number of safes dotted around the complex, plus three hidden away beneath it, down in the catacombs. Thirty-two firearms were recovered from one. Over half of those weapons, when we checked them for ballistics, had been used during the last five years to kill three judges in the south of the country, plus nine police officers as well as literally dozens of other unsolved cases from all over the place. Other safes gave us very detailed information regarding very organised crime, drugs, sex trafficking, prostitution and the names and payments to corrupt government officials and law enforcement officers, a real treasure trove. As we speak, multiple arrests are taking place.'

Alberto was expecting some kind of reaction, but there was nothing. Just a silent, passive, listening figure. He paused for a second as a noisy group of half a dozen people came out of the office block door and wandered down the car park to their cars. As they dissipated, he looked back to his wing mirror.

'But the forces of law and order cannot really take any credit, can they? Because everything was handed to them on a plate the moment those walls were blown out and we were able to march in.'

Duke nodded gently in agreement, then smiled to encourage him to continue.

'So, Duke, do you know what I think? I think that the society I love and serve healed itself on Friday night, and as far as my core beliefs go, that is fine by me. But I have to ask myself, who do I know who could have organised such a series of events, put them into effect in such a short time frame, and on top of that provide everyone who could possibly be even loosely connected with the case with a cast-iron alibi, that party?'

Duke nodded, speaking for the first time. 'Do you know what, Alberto? I'm thinking that what you have just told me, and all of the plot and reasoning behind it, could be worked up into a great film script. What do you think?'

Alberto smiled and slowly turned his head to look at him. 'You also know my thoughts, Duke. You know very well where I am coming from with all of this, but it's now all in the past. So I'm saying to you to leave it there, my friend, leave it there. We and the silver braid brigade, the proper custodians of law and order in this city, will over the coming weeks make a considerable amount of huff and puff on the TV and in the papers. But between you and me, those two events are already dead and buried and gathering dust in boxes down in our basement. But, please, my friend, our society has now healed itself. Please just leave it there.'

Duke turned and smiled, an expressionless sort of smile.

Alberto watched his every move and thought to himself, God, I'd hate to play this guy at poker. I'd lose a bloody fortune!'

THE END

Notes

One

Operation Sheepdog seemed to have surprisingly long legs when Rhodri Jenkins answered his front door in Crickhowell, in the very well-to-do residential area just across the hills from his happy hunting ground, the Welsh valleys.

His five-foot-tall, cherubic-faced, red-cheeked, fifty-ish female visitor was all smiles. Her blue bobble hat pulled down around her ears had a large red CYMRU enamel badge on the front.

'Hello, sorry to trouble you, I'm from Premium Bonds tracing. We're looking for a Rhodri Jenkins. We think he is one of our lucky winners.'

Rhodri smiled a wolfish grin, the dollar signs already starting to flash in his eyes. 'I'm Rhodri Jenkins.'

She smiled and giggled. 'Oh, goody good! So glad we've established that. Can I just check your profession, luvvy? We've got you down as a people smuggler and sex trafficker. Would that be right?'

The look of sheer horror on his face told her that she was at the correct address, talking to the right person. There was a brief movement and the double *tap tap* of a silenced 45 automatic. And the valleys suddenly became a much safer place for young Welsh girls to book exchange trips to Europe.

Rhodri's brother, also in the same line of work, together with his so-called business partner, met a very similar fate at precisely the same time that Friday night, all around 9 p.m., Rome time. And all because someone just kept a diary.

TWO

Three days before the film was due to finish shooting and everyone was to scatter to the four winds, Sophia Mandini, the senior Make-up supervisor, was walking through the Studio Lazio canteen attempting to find a space to sit down during her lunch break when, unexpectedly, Jan Mattias, the Norwegian camera operator, appeared in front of her. He knelt down on one knee and at the same time outstretched his right arm towards her to offer up a small red box containing a gold wedding ring. The whole room went silent. You could have heard a pin drop.

Sophia looked down in utter amazement, turned bright red and in front of one hundred and eighty-two people, put her tray down on the table next to her, and then just simply nodded in acceptance before bursting into tears. The whole room went wild. The noise was unbelievable.

No one else in the canteen had known about their romance. It had begun when Sophia was left alone in her Make-up caravan at the assault course set, way back in time. It would seem that the Norwegian had simply walked up to her and told her exactly how he felt about her, and in no uncertain terms asked for permission to court her. It would seem that he had been successful, as they now operate a wedding planning business in Sorrento, for mainly Scandinavian clients. He takes the photos, she does the make-overs, and together with their baby daughter, named Grace, after her godmother, they all prosper.

ABOUT THE AUTHOR

ANTHONY NEWBER

The author began his career in the 1960s as a floor sweeper/trainee Clapper boy for a London-based film company making TV commercials. Within a decade he had learned three languages and worked as a Focus Puller in virtually every country in Europe and Scandinavia on every genre of film from documentary to long-running TV drama series through to big-budget feature films.

Later years saw him graduate to become a Lighting Cameraman/Director of Photography and set up his own facility company that worked at one time or another for virtually every major broadcaster in the UK.

If you have enjoyed reading this book then please leave a complimentary revue on Amazon. Thank you!